CITYFALL

LORNA HOPKINS KEITH

To my husband Greg,
my true partner in life.

ACKNOWLEDGEMENTS

My appreciation goes to my critique group, the Wordsmiths of Avon Park, including Suzanna, Dottie, Sue, Paul, my husband, Greg, and many others, for helping me pull a garbled mess into a professional book form.

ACKNOWLEDGMENTS

1

DEEP IN THE HEART OF CITY, Sam expected it to be just another day in her inquiry agent office ... until she logged on to her screen and saw the message.

> This is to inform Samanda Lar that if she wishes to reproduce, she must do so in the next six months. At that time, her birth control will become permanent.

"What?" Sam exclaimed. She couldn't be that old, could she? All women's birth control became permanent at thirty — a form of population control.

Something inside her awoke. *What had she done so far in her life? Not much, just solving other people's problem and puzzles.* After her disaster of a marriage, a husband was no longer an option, and she'd never even considered children.

I don't want to end up like old Mrs. Jones who couldn't find her comm hanging around her neck.

Sam glanced around her tiny gray office. Her gray worktable with the screen on the beige wall behind it; two gray chairs, with shelves behind the padded one; and the toilet room and storage cubicle, filled the room.

Was this going to be my life for however long I survived?

NO.

But how do I get out of this rut? What can I do?

Sam shook her head, unease roiling up inside her. It came to her that something was missing in her life — something necessary to her survival. *But what? How could I get out of this rut?*

A request popped up on her screen. A schoolchild wanted answers to a math puzzle. Sam chose to respond. Children should do their own research, she thought, but she needed something to do. With her eidetic memory, she found it simpler to pull up the answer in her head than to key through several menus to reach the information on her screen.

After signing off, Sam stared at the picture of trees on the beige wall above her screen. Everything in City was gray or beige, except for the pictures on the screen or the walls. Outside the vast gray block of City there were trees, she knew. Was this what she needed? Trees and other plants and grass, waiting for her? If she could just get out.

Around her, City, a pile of two-level gray cubes made of the indestructible Volen material, hummed its own song. Layers upon layers of cubes of apartments and shops along dim gray streets, City was her life. A life that no longer satisfied her.

Her screen comm beeped. Sam answered, hoping it was her twin, Brad. He was supposed to be coming home on leave soon. Her heart sank when she found it was a young man who wanted answers to a list of questions. She pulled them out of her head as fast as he asked.

Another three credits. Whoopee.

Sam wanted to scream but didn't dare. She didn't want to upset Max, her alien brother.

Another call.

"Samanda Lar, Inquiry Agent. How can I help you?" she said automatically.

"This is James Fleetwood from Spaceport Management. A female of the Ambaak species who has just arrived on the Jarry liner is in distress and requires an investigator."

"I'm not an investigator, I'm an inquiry agent. Why an investigator, anyway? What kind of distress?"

"The female has had a loss she refuses to specify. She wants a female investigator. You are the only one we could locate. Are you able to come to Spaceport?"

Spaceport, Sam thought, tingling with excitement. *Finally, a chance to go to Spaceport.* The space station hung in a fixed orbit above the planet. Brad had told her about the shops. Not that she had any credits to shop with. It didn't matter what the job was; just to go there was enough. Someplace new, someplace other than here.

"Yes, I can come up." She had to preserve her outward professionalism, despite the excitement roiling inside. She would figure out how to get there later.

"You are to go to room 666 at five hours tomorrow morning. The female will have finished her sleep period then. Turn right from shuttle exit, turn left into first main hall. Room will be on right. You will be reimbursed for cost of shuttle fare."

"Do you have any idea what this is about?" Sam's business side took over.

"No. Companion wouldn't say."

"Do you have any idea how long this will take?"

"No. Be prepared to stay overnight."

"Very well." Sam looked at the picture of trees. "I'll be there. I require fifty credits plus expenses."

"Agreed." Fleetwood clicked off.

"Whee!" Sam jumped up and did a two-step in place.

"Happy, Sam?" Max, her alien brother, poked his head out of his cubicle.

"Yes. I have a job at Spaceport tomorrow."

"Go, I?" Max, a grey-furred teddy bear about her size, had been brought to the xenolab as an infant of an unknown species. Del Lar had adopted Max and raised him as a little brother to Sam and Brad. Max had turned out to be a shapeshifter, with his own version of their language, Standard.

"Oh. I'll have to think about it."

His face sagged.

Sam smiled at him. "I have to talk to Todd first."

"Okee." Max disappeared back into his cubicle.

Sam jumped up, put her mug back into its little cupboard, paced a few times, and then told Max she was going out to run. She couldn't call Todd until he went to lunch at noon. She wasn't made to just sit and stare at the screen until then.

After a two-block run in the narrow, dim street, she felt more relaxed and called Todd as soon as she could. "Todd, guess what? I have a job at Spaceport tomorrow."

"Wow." Todd, Brad's and her legal expert, was also their best friend. "Are you sure it's legit?"

"Why wouldn't it be?" That it might not be had never occurred to her.

"What was the name of the caller?" Todd asked.

"James Fleetwood. He sounded very businesslike."

"I'll look him up." After a pause, Todd reported, "Okay, he is what he says he is, and a ship did arrive last night. I think it's safe, but I'm going with you."

"He said it might be overnight. Do you think it's all right to leave Max that long?'

"Do you have any food?" Todd sounded concerned.

"Not much."

"Bring him as Brad. I have a duplicate ID."

"Okay."

"At five hours there won't be any traffic, so we should be able to catch the four-and-a-half-hour's shuttle, so I'll pick you up at four hours."

Sam groaned.

∗   ∗   ∗

Sam set her loudest alarm to wake herself, but awoke before it went off. She had been dreaming about a house on a hill. As Spaceport sparked her mind, she fell into her clothes and ran downstairs to her office.

"Max, time to get up," Sam called.

"Mmm," came from the cubicle.

Sam crawled in and wrestled Max awake. She'd finally gotten him to sit up when Todd arrived. Between them, they got Max on his feet, dressed in a coverall as Brad, with his nutrients in his pouch. The human food didn't have one vital enzyme he needed.

They walked Brad-Max down the street to the up-tube and squeezed on. The platforms only held two large adults, and every corner had an up-tube and down-tube. At Level Fifty, they stepped off and took the stairs up to the shuttle port. By this time, Brad-Max was looking around at everything.

Todd had timed it well. The shuttle hatch opened; they embarked and found seats. Sam grabbed one by a window. She peered out and saw green below. *Were those real trees?* she wondered. *If I could only be down there with them.* She had to pinch herself to make sure this was real. If only Brad were here.

As they approached Spaceport, Sam caught glimpses of a round, gray structure. The three disembarked through a square blue room where a large man glanced at their IDs. She held Brad-Max's hand tightly to keep from floating away. She was actually on Spaceport.

Spaceport was City-world's one connection to other worlds. It had hung here forever. Most of the time when offworlders had business with citizens, the latter came up here to meet with them. The Space Service that Brad was a part of flew out of Spaceport. Knowing this and being here were two different things.

The checker waved them down a long blue hall. As they stepped out into a great open space, Sam and Brad-Max gaped. The area curved away to the side in each direction farther than she could see, wider across than half a street block.

Shops and booths decorated in blues and greens lined either side, selling a variety of goods and food. People, mostly clad in brightly-colored clothing, moved in both directions.

"They have a lot of things we can't get in City," Todd said. "Many people from the upper levels come up here to shop. Come on."

They turned the corner and Sam stopped at a shop with colorful scarves. "I want one of those," she said.

"After your job." Todd tugged at her arm. "When you have the credits."

"Pretty," Brad-Max said.

They moved on. Sam stopped at each shop, and Todd moved her along. She had never seen anything like this; her home, her job, even Brad had completely left her mind. She wanted to go into every store, look at everything, soak in the colors.

Sam planned that, someday, when she had plenty of credits, she'd come back here and explore these stores. The colors fascinated her and drew a sense of longing.

They came to a place with narrow doors on the outer side of the port with the familiar female and male silhouettes, and several more oddly shaped ones. Opposite them, a hallway led inward.

"This is it," Todd said.

As they turned into the hall, an announcement blared.

A SHIP FROM BARDAK IS ARRIVING AT DOCK TWENTY-THREE. REPEAT, A SHIP FROM BARDAK IS ARRIVING AT DOCK TWENTY-THREE.

Sam wondered if Brad was on it. Although she wanted to see him, it would be awkward, to say the least, if they ran into each other, with Brad-Max.

At the room, she knocked.

A tall, gray-haired man opened the door. "You are Samanda Lar?"

"Yes. This is my brother, Brad, who won't let me go anywhere alone, and this is Todd, a friend who showed me how to get here."

They all moved into a square brown room with another door at the back. A long seat, small table and chair, and a screen on the wall graced the place.

"You men do not need to stay."

Sam felt Brad-Max stiffen beside her.

"I stay." Brad-Max said.

"I believe I will, too." Todd stood with crossed arms, that suspicious expression on his face.

The rear door opened, and a dark man with beady little eyes close together stuck his head out.

"Is she here yet? Oh, there you are, Miss Samantha."

"Samanda," she said, stressing the '*d*'.

"Get rid of the men. Biida only wants to see the woman."

6

Brad-Max pulled Sam toward the hall door, and Todd moved to her other side.

The dark man stepped out, leaving the door ajar. Sam peeked into the small dim room and saw nothing but a large container.

Where was Biida? Sam sensed something wrong and eased back. *What the eff?*

Another, larger man charged out from behind the inner door and grabbed Brad-Max. Sam was too startled to react as the dark man yelled "No", grabbed her and pulled her into the back room with the other two.

"Hey," Todd yelled as the door closed in his face.

"Todd!" Sam screamed.

A hand covered her mouth, the room went dark, and she couldn't breathe.

✳   ✳   ✳

World slept.

2

SAM BECAME AWARE OF MOVEMENT and Max, as he curled against her. She opened her eyes. Darkness surrounded her. Stretching, she hit a wall. She felt around and discovered that they were in a container. It was moving, bouncing along as if someone were carrying it. She rocked back and forth inside it.

"Max?" Sam whispered.

"Iss."

"Okay?"

"Iss."

After several turns, a section that slanted upward, causing her to slide down to one end, and another pair of turns jostling her side to side, the container dropped to a stop. Sam heard a few creaks, snaps, and a voice.

"You can go." Someone yanked the top open.

Sam sat up and blinked in the light. "What is this?" she demanded. "Who are you and what do you want?"

The dark man from the brown room stood there, staring down at her. "I am Jerg. You have this suite. This cabin, the head," he pointed to a side door, "and another cabin beyond the head, with a connecting door. I will come for you when he is ready."

He left, and Sam heard the click of the lock.

He who? Sam thought, climbing out of the container into a small, brown room with no windows.

Where am I? What's going on?"

She felt ready to spit.

Where is Biida? What kind of job was this?

She shivered.

Max. She turned to him. His legs moved back and forth, and his arms twitched.

"Max, you okay?" she asked him.

His eyes opened. "What is?"

"We've been kidnapped. We're on a ship, I think."

Sam had been on Todd's ship, and this room made her think of that one. She helped Max out. He sat on the bed, keeping his Brad shape.

"Food?"

"I don't see any here."

Sam gave him a food bar from her bag. He needed a lot of food to keep his unnatural shape.

This room was like the first one they'd been in, except there was a bed instead of a seat. Sam opened the side door and found a bathroom with a counter and sink on one side, and a toilet and shower stall on the other.

Sam slid the far door open, saw pink, and slammed the door. She hated pink. Pink reminded her of her mother, who had left City when Sam and Brad were five.

She returned to Brad-Max and sat beside him on the bed.

Max looked around. "Safe, is?"

"No." Sam clenched her teeth.

Who was this Jerg and what did he want? Why were they brought here? Wherever here was.

Thoughts rattled through her mind.

"Other room, like."

Sam nodded. Her primary task was to take care of Max. Before she could do anything, the cabin door slid open and Jerg reappeared.

"What's going on?" Sam demanded, as she jumped up. "And why are we here?"

"Come," Jerg said, and led them toward the front of the ship.

"Answer me," Sam demanded. She stopped and stomped her foot.

"Want to know, we do," Brad-Max added.

Sam sucked in her breath, hoping the man wouldn't notice the awkward phrasing.

He said nothing, and they arrived at a larger, pale blue room. There were no windows here, either, but a large screen hung on the pale blue wall opposite the door. Shelves of artifacts lined the walls.

Then Sam saw him. Her ex-husband. The wall between her current life and her hidden past crashed down. She clenched her fists and took a step back. Her ex-husband, Eugene Waller, lounged on a complicated structure of dark blue pillows. Jerg pushed her forward.

"No," she moaned under her breath. *This couldn't be happening.* He had given her nightmares for years after he left.

Waller's pale gray eyes glittered in his puffy face as he waved languidly. "Welcome, my dear Samanda. Welcome to my ship."

Too stunned to speak, Sam shook her head. Brad-Max held her arm, and she leaned on him.

Why was he here? What does he want? How can I get out of here?

Memories of her past life raced through her mind and let loose the pain.

"You have grown even more beautiful than I remembered," he continued, stretching his arms toward her. "I have always kept you in my mind. There were times when thinking of you kept me sane."

"What?" Sam managed. "What are you doing here?" *How could she ever have been attracted by this creature?*

"I came for you, my dear."

"No. Go away." Sam made a shoveling motion with her hand. *How could a job on Spaceport gotten her into this?*

"Come sit down." He patted the pillow beside him.

"No." She clenched her teeth.

Sam stepped back, but Jerg was right behind her and pushed her forward. She closed her eyes. Brad-Max croaked protestingly.

"What's the matter with him?" The man on the pillows frowned.

"Something he brought home from out there," Sam managed to say, her eyes open.

"Jerg, take him back to his cabin."

Brad-Max looked at Sam, and she nodded. He went without protest.

At least, it got him away from Waller.

"Ah. Alone at last." Waller stared at Sam.

Sam felt like a child before her teacher.

"My dearest Samanda, I wish to offer you a life of luxury, comfort and unlimited travel. My ship is my home and she can be your home, too."

"Why?" Sam stuttered. *How did he get here?*

"Because you are my wife, and the only woman I have ever loved."

"No. Not wife. Marriage dissolved."

He had loved me, and I had loved him, back then, until he broke my heart and stomped on the pieces.

Sam wanted to run, but there was no place to run to. At Waller's trial of Dad's murder, she had been told he was being sent to Purgatory — the world of no laws and no escape.

"Also, you don't belong in that shabby little shop. Let your brother take care of it; it's more suitable for him. You belong here with me."

Over your dead body, Sam thought viciously.

He sat up. "See that black box on the shelf?" He pointed. "Bring it here."

Sam was halfway to the shelf before she realized what she was doing. Finally, her brain came back to life. She hesitated, looked around. Jerg still stood between her and the door. She moved over to the box.

Inlaid with a delicate pattern of reds and blues, the box was large enough to hold two good-sized loaves of bread.

Sam knew she couldn't get out of this room until Jerg left, and he wouldn't leave until Waller told him to. She thought about the tools of her trade in her bag. Nothing she could use here, but maybe later.

"Pretty, isn't it?" Waller came up behind Sam, took her arm, and breathed mint in her ear.

The mint was so strong she could almost taste it, as well as smell it. She pulled away as he reached around her to lift the lid. That masculine aroma that had so attracted her years ago was gone, replaced by unwashed fat-man odor.

The biggest stash of jewels Sam had ever seen glittered at her. Most of them were fake, glass or paste, but a few were real. Like that red ball of ruby threads in the corner that tinted to purple in the center. Sam had to tear her eyes away from it. That jewel was the most gorgeous thing she'd ever seen.

"Wow," she said. *Get me out of here.*

"All for you," He increased his grip. "Let me show you my ship, my home ... our home." He led her away.

This ship will never be my home.

The pain of the past continued to pound at her. At that moment, Sam decided that she would do everything she could to get off his ship and get rid of him permanently. Anger battled the pain and won.

He moved slowly. It occurred to her that the box had been a diversion, so she wouldn't see how difficult it was for him to get to his feet. His weight leaned on her.

Sam remembered stories of violence on Purgatory — the world without laws — but was unable to feel pity for this thing beside her.

At the bridge, he let her look in, but held her back at the doorway. She stored every control and screen she saw in her mind.

"Someday I will tell you what all these gadgets do." He waved a fat arm around and lost his balance for a moment.

Sam already knew what most of them did. Todd had taught her the controls of his ship, *Sam's Star.*

They turned and headed back down the central corridor. Waller indicated a door across from the lounge.

"My cabin." At the open door of the next cabin, he said, "This is your room, my dear."

13

Pink ruffles dominated the place, along with a shelf-rack of exquisitely costumed dolls. A fat teddy bear sat on the narrow bed, looking uncannily like Max in his native form.

"No," Sam snapped, turning away.

Her mother had always dressed her in pink before she left to find a world with nature, a connection with the planet. Because the twins had been born in City, her mother was not allowed to take her children, not even her daughter.

Max, Sam thought, *how is he? Where is he?*

She submerged her feelings as her ex-husband touched a button at the base of a large mirror surrounded by pink ribbon. An image sprung into view, of a grassy place surrounded by trees, with patches of red and yellow flowers. Sam could almost smell them, as she tried to absorb the picture into her bones.

"There are other views available." He squeezed her arm. "Come."

This must be a screen. Sam tried to pull her arm away, but his grip was too strong. *So he still has muscles under that fat.*

Waller led her through the connecting bathroom to Brad-Max's room. He sat curled on the bed, staring at a blank screen.

"Sam?" Brad-Max croaked.

The fat man barely glanced at him and pulled Sam out the door and across to the galley. He showed Sam how to access food and gave her a loaf of bread. They returned to Brad-Max's cabin and marched in without knocking.

Brad-Max, still curled up on his bed, looked up as they entered. "Sam?"

His cabin was all browns and greens.

"Ready to go?" Sam said cheerily.

Brad-Max sat up as the ship shuddered gently.

"Topping off supplies. Don't worry, my dear, we're not leaving just yet." Her ex-husband grinned, showing yellow teeth with gaps.

"We are leaving now," Sam said. "Come on, Brad."

He heaved himself off the bunk.

"I think not." Waller stood in the doorway. "You are mine now." He tottered away, sliding the door closed.

Sam tried the door. Just as she suspected, it was locked.

"Go we," Max whispered.

"No. We're locked in and we need to find a way out." Sam tried to marshal her thoughts. "Here's some bread." She wandered around the small room. "Todd," she said.

She pulled out her comm and called Todd. Only faint hisses responded, so she hit the alarm key. It would send her location, via chip, to his comm and anyone else's in range.

"More," Max said, having devoured the bread.

"That's all I have."

Please, Todd, Brad, anyone, hear me and get me off this ship.

Sam was beginning to accept the situation. She would treat it as a puzzle she had to solve.

Max wandered around, stopped at the screen and touched buttons at its bottom. The screen turned on, and he jumped back. Sam glanced at it. The screen showed the same image as the one in the pink cabin.

Sam turned to the door. She recalled seeing a hand pad by each door. Could she disable it from this side? At the other two doors on this side of the hall, the pads were on the right. She closed her eyes and pictured them. Right there. She tapped a spot on the wall, grabbed her bag, and pulled out a tool to mark it. *If only I had a laser …*

A wisp of air touched her cheek and she looked up. *The air vent.*

"Max, do you think you could get through that if I take the grill off?"

"Maybe. Looky."

White dots on a black background covered most of the screen, with a little box in the corner. The words were too tiny to read.

Sam pulled out her magnifier. Three lines listed: Ship layout, Registration, Inventory. She grinned and selected "Ship layout". It showed the two rows of cabins along the central corridor, the bridge forward, and the storage and engines aft. *Just what I need to know.*

She clicked on "Inventory" and sucked in her breath. Every item on the ship was listed, along with its location. *A great program. Why did those two leave it where I could find it? Did they think I was too dumb to notice it? My ex had never thought much of my brains.*

"Look here," Sam told Max. "I want you to go into the air vent, go back to storage, find these items, and bring them back." She indicated the items she wanted.

"Get out, help us?"

"Yes."

"Okee."

Max stripped off his coverall, devolved into his natural form, and Sam boosted him up into the vent. His head narrowed and elongated, his shoulders swung back, and his arms melted together with his body. She closed her eyes to avoid seeing the rest of his body melt into a long rope and slither into the vent. She still couldn't get used to seeing him change.

Sam sighed, took her bag of tools from her carry bag, and laid them out on the table. A few items went into pockets inside her coverall. The rest she swept back into the bag. Now all she could do was to wait for Max's return.

Time passed. She prowled the three-room suite, testing the doors again and again. She paged through the screens and tried to call Todd every few minutes. All she got was hissing.

Sam knew the comms worked from City to Spaceport and wondered whether they could reach from ship to Spaceport. Todd wouldn't have gone back to City. She worried about what Brad would do when he came home and found Max and herself gone. Max hardly ever left the apartment.

On one trip to the pink room, Sam found a large bowl of stew. It smelled heavenly. *Could there be anything nasty in it?* She'd heard of drugs that could make you do anything. Her food tester said there was nothing obviously bad in the stew. She tasted it. Better than she got in the caffs. She brought it through to Max's room and put it on the table. Max would need it when he returned.

*   *   *

World slept.

3

RESTLESS, SAM TOOK A FEW BITES, paced the small room, and headed for the pink room. She opened a drawer, saw more pink, and slammed it shut.

The ship's hum grew louder. *Was it moving?*

The hall door opened, revealing her ex-husband hanging onto the doorway, holding a round loaf of bread.

"What's going on?" Sam demanded. She no longer knew this man. "I want you to let us leave now." She stomped her foot.

"Everything I need is on board, so there's no point in hanging around any longer. We are on our way to wherever you wish to go. It took but a moment for the ship to make this." He handed her the loaf. She dropped it on the bed.

"I'm not going anywhere. I want to know what happened to the job I was promised. I want to do the job and go home. I don't belong here." She knew the job had been a ruse, but she wanted to make a point. Again, she stomped her foot.

Waller moved back and forth on his feet. "Yes, you do. You belong here with me. I fell in love with you the first time I saw you. I've never stopped loving you. Memories of you kept me going on Purgatory. I came back here to get you, so we could live the rest of our lives together."

His hands reached toward her, but dropped when she stepped back.

Sam tried to ignore the pleading in his voice. "I thought I loved you at first, but your actions destroyed that love. And Dad ... I could never live with my father's killer."

"I did not kill him." He made fists.

"You arranged it. Now let us go."

"I had hoped you would have changed." His shoulders slumped. "However. You have food, eat. You will stay in your suite tonight. I will see you ..." Suddenly the smell of human waste swept through the air. Waller's face turned red, and he yelled, "Jerg!" as he stumbled back.

Jerg appeared and led the stinking man away.

Sam heard him say, "I told you: I don't do diapers."

He really is a wreck, Sam thought, and tore off a hunk of the bread.

Chewing on it, she trotted back to Max's room with the bread in her hand. She sat and paged through the images on the screen.

Time crept by.

Sam was dozing in the chair when Jerg poked his head in. She kept still, eyes closed, and listened.

"Bitch," he muttered. "We never should have come back here."

Sam didn't even breathe until he closed and locked the door. *I'll have to watch out for him.*

More waiting.

She began to wonder who actually was in charge: Waller or Jerg.

Sam was ready to claw the door down by the time Max poured himself out of the air vent into a heap on the bed. He gathered himself together into his natural form and held out a handful of tools and a larger comm unit.

"You did good." Sam grabbed the new unit and called Todd.

"Todd, can you hear me?" She heard some garbled words. "Where are you?"

"Hear you. Brad here. Coming. Can you get off?"

"Locked in room, trying to get out. I'll let you know when we're out."

"Good. We'll be here."

Thank Oneness.

Sam relaxed, breathed, and thanked Oneness again. Brad was back. She didn't pray often, but this was one time she did. Now all she had to do was get them out.

"Hungry. Food, have we?" Max asked.

"On the table." Sam tore off another hunk of bread as Max attacked the stew.

While they ate, Sam looked through the tools Max had brought. She selected a small laser and a chip puller.

At the doorway, Sam pulled up her memory of the hand pad on the wall outside.

Where exactly was it? Ah, there.

She played with the laser and managed to cut out a piece of the wall. The back of the pad took more finesse. Finally, she was able to remove the chip and cut the wire of the lock. She stood in front of the door and slid it open just enough to tell that it worked.

So much for his fancy locks.

She tucked the laser and chip puller into an inner pocket.

Sam took her ninety-degree spyglass and poked it out the door. She saw Jerg helping Waller across the hall to the lounge and waited to see if Jerg would come out right away. When he didn't, Sam had a thought. She took everything out of her bag, except for her hardcopy ID, comb, the vials of perfume, and sleep drops Brad had given her last time he was home. She tucked those items, and the tools Max brought, under his blankets. If she got caught, she didn't want to have any incriminating evidence on her. But she wasn't planning on getting caught.

Her comm went into another secret pocket.

Good thing I'm slim, and the coverall loose.

Sam stepped out of the cabin, leaving the door almost closed, and tiptoed over to the galley. Keeping her ears perked, she gathered more food and took it back to their cabin. Max was sound asleep.

She yawned. They were both short of sleep, having gotten up so early. She passed through the head to the pink room and sprayed her perfume around liberally. Waller always had an allergic reaction to it.

Let's see how he likes that.

Sam returned to the galley and spritzed her scent all around. When she turned to leave, Jerg stood there. She aimed her sprayer at his face. He grabbed her arm as she pushed the plunger, but he still got some in one eye. He threw her into the doorway. She saw stars as he dragged her along and threw her into the cabin on the other side of the galley.

Jerg grabbed her bag, pawed through it, and threw it on the floor. "How did you get out, bitch?"

Sam had no breath left to answer. He tramped out and locked the door.

She lay on the floor, head throbbing, thinking, *oh, shit, oh shit.*

Slowly she picked herself up, grabbed her bag, and staggered to the door of the dull brown room.

I have to get out, I have to get Max out. Was he going after Max?

Panting, she reached into an inner pocket and drew out the laser. Within a few minutes she had the wall peeled back, the chip out, and the door open a crack.

Jerg slammed it open. "That's enough of that," he growled as he glanced at the damaged wall. He grabbed her and hauled her back to storage, shoved her in, and slammed that door.

Sam sat on the floor, gasping, and pounded it with her fists. Everything she did just got her further into this mess.

Oneness, help me.

She closed her eyes, breathed deeply. *Control,* she thought. She took another deep breath, opened her eyes, and looked around.

A mass of brown cabinets and boxes half-filled the place, with cables and conduits above. The air compressor stood nearby, and something massive hunched behind it. Up on her feet, she searched for the air intake.

"Here it is," she said. All the sleepy powder in the little green vial went into the air system.

They should sleep for a good, long time now.

After three tries, Sam finally found the chip. She unlocked the door, ran to Brad-Max's cabin, and breathed a sigh of relief. He was still there, asleep.

She called Todd. "We've got to get out of here now."

"We're closing in on you. We're on emergency life support. That ship you're on damaged us. Can you get to the bridge?"

"No." She didn't know when or where Jerg would pop up. "This comm is connected to their system, I think." Sam yawned, and began to shake Max. "I've got to get out of here before I fall asleep."

"Get Max and yourself into spacesuits right now. I'll match up my airlock with yours. Now move."

"Going." Sam gathered the items she'd hid in his bed and dumped them in her bag.

Max sat up. "What?"

Sam grabbed his arm. "Come on."

She took off for the airlock, dragging Max along. There was only one spacesuit: a Large. After she struggled into it, Max poured himself into the suit in front of her, his limbs laying along with hers. He felt warm and gooey, and she had to clench her teeth to keep from throwing up. Max stuck a narrow tube of a nose up into the helmet to the air intake. His exhaling tickled with a sweetish aroma.

Sam stabbed at the hatch release and pressed against the door. Jerg charged around the corner and grabbed her arm. Sam felt movement and looked down out of the corner of her eye. Another eye had appeared, winking, and the nasal tube sprouted a narrow tongue that waggled back and forth. Max also slithered his arm out from under her own.

Jerg yanked his hand back and yelped. "We will not forget this," he yelled, as Sam tumbled into the airlock and hit the "Close" button.

The outer door opened to reveal Todd's ship hovering a few meters away, its outer hatch open. A space-suited figure held a long, narrow object, touched it, and threw it toward her. A heavy rope with loop grips followed. The figure in the other ship made back and forth motions with its hands.

"What?" Sam said. She picked up the rope and looked at the other ship. *Am I supposed to use this to get over there?*

The figure repeated its motions.

"Okay."

Sam grabbed the nearest handhold and pushed off. As she proceeded hand over hand, the line reeled itself back into Todd's ship.

She tumbled into Todd's airlock, and scrambled to get upright so she wouldn't squash Max. The outer hatch closed behind her as the last of the line popped in.

As she turned toward the inner hatch, she saw Brad in a spacesuit, and her heart turned cartwheels.

"Stay in your suit," he said, punching the inner hatch release. "I'll just get Max out."

Inside, Brad helped Sam get her helmet off and the front of the suit unfastened. Max crawled out, and Brad helped the alien into a spare. Sam followed them to a cabin where Max could sleep, back in his natural form.

Brad led her to the bridge, holding her arm as she floated in null gravity. She heaved a great sigh of relief. She was finally out of that place, away from that awful man, back with her brothers.

Thank you, Oneness. Oneness, every being, thing and place that ever was, is and will be.

"Thanks, fellows," Sam said as she settled into a seat behind Todd, and the harness clicked shut.

"Welcome back," Todd said. "I need your new comm."

Sam handed it to him, her mind blank.

He plugged it into his screen and tapped keys. Suddenly the other ship took off, streaking away. Sam leaned back and closed her eyes. Right now, she didn't care if she didn't get paid for that so-called job.

"Look," Brad said, next to her, his hand holding hers.

Sam opened her eyes. Uncomfortable in the spacesuit, she watched as a red Space Patrol ship took off after the other ship. It would take a while for the authorities to catch up with her.

"They're gone," Todd said. "You're safe now."

Sam felt a strange emptiness where the pain and anger had been. Leaning back, she closed her eyes and saw the image of the green bushes and grass, and the blue sky.

Someday I will get there. I don't know how or when, but I'll be ready.

*　　　*　　　*

World continued to sleep.

4

Aᴏꜰᴛᴇʀ Tᴏᴅᴅ ᴛᴏᴏᴋ ᴄᴀʀᴇ ᴏꜰ ᴘᴀᴘᴇʀᴡᴏʀᴋ at Spaceport, Sam and the others went with him to his place. Larger than her own apartment, it had pale blue walls and a separate bedroom. She was still in shock from her experience, unable to take in details. She and Brad sat on the long seat, while Max curled up at the other end.

"Welcome to my place, friends." Todd collected food and water. "You must be starving. Brad and I are. It's hard to eat when you have to put your helmet on so fast you can't set up the nourishment equipment."

Everyone ate at the caffs, so there was no need for kitchens in apartments, but most people had some food available.

He handed out bread and protein packets. Max gobbled his down and slumped back into sleep.

"How are you doing, Sam?" Todd asked.

Sam shrugged. She was safe with her brothers, but something within her had changed. "I don't know." She just wanted to sit and stare at the screen, which showed a beach. "Trees."

Brad gave her a hug, and Todd changed the screen to a forest scene. "Can we stay here awhile? Sam needs it."

"Sure." Todd sat in a big chair at an angle to the seat.

Sam felt peace wrap around her and the others. She had no idea where she was going, what she was going to do — she just lived in this moment.

Sometime later, Todd rose. "Time to go eat. What I had here wasn't much."

"Okay, I could use some food, too." Brad helped Sam up. "Come on, Max, food."

Max uncurled himself and jumped up. Todd led them out.

At the caff, Sam discovered she was starving. They all ate two helpings. The peace continued to be with her

It must be the Oneness, she thought. *The Oneness, everything and every being that ever was, is and will be, in all the universes.*

✳   ✳   ✳

Sam, Brad and Max stayed over at Todd's: Sam on the bed, Max curled up in the closet, the other two on the long, padded seat. In the morning, they all went back down to Sam's place.

"When is your leave over, Brad?" Todd asked when they arrived.

"I've got two more days."

"Good. Stay with Sam. If you think she shouldn't be alone after that, let me know."

"Okay."

Sam listened to this exchange with amusement. It always tickled her how the two of them looked after her, how Todd always told her and Brad what to do. Just because he was two years older than the twins. Brad settled in his chair and Max in his cubicle.

"Sam, are you sure you're all right?" Todd asked. "If you don't want to stay here, you can always come back to my place."

"Thanks, Todd, I'll remember that. I'll be fine." Sam's heart ached for him, for his love for her that she could not return, except as for a brother. Todd was her legal adviser as well as her second brother. Sam, Brad, and Todd had grown up together; Todd's mother, whom Sam called Aunt Linda, had taken Sam and Brad in when their mother left.

He strode out of the office.

"I guess I better get back to work." Sam turned to her screen.

"Did you get paid for that job?" Brad asked.

"What job?" Sam snorted.

"They should at least reimburse you for going up there."

"They who?" Her screen came up and she logged into her accounts. "Whoa. They paid me that and half what I charged." Sam wondered why she wasn't very thrilled about that.

"Good." Brad jumped up. "I'm going upstairs." There was a second, small screen in the apartment up there.

*　　　*　　　*

Two days later, after late meal, when Brad prepared to return to his ship, he asked Sam, "Will you be okay here alone?"

"I'm not alone, I have Max. He seems to have recovered from his adventure."

We know so little about how Max and how his body functions, we don't really know how this affected him, what may show up later.

"Okay. You've got Todd's number if you need it. Gotta go." Brad gave Sam a big hug and trotted out the door.

As the outer door clanged shut, Sam sat back, fighting an emptiness that threatened to overwhelm her. She would have to find a new life. Slowly, she rebuilt her wall around the pain, this time just before the rescue.

*　　　*　　　*

The next morning, Sam focused on her job. Normally, she would have been delighted to find a half dozen clients' messages, but all she felt was, *'So what?'*. The peace had left in the night and she was right back where she'd been, pain and all, before she had gotten that call.

"Okay, get to work," she whispered. If Max heard her, he would come out. Sam didn't need his distraction now.

The first three clients were easy; all they wanted was information. Inquiry agents also served as librarians for people who didn't want to be bothered looking something up for themselves. Two others required deeper delving into the databases. The sixth one said he needed to see her in person.

Sam glowered at the screen while waiting for the client, who might or might not arrive. For all she knew, he took one look at the shop window and walked right by. One of these days she needed to set up a survcam from inside her shop, but not through the murky window. Shopkeepers weren't allowed to put anything on the outside of their shops.

She sold spy devices and fake product boxes for hiding things. People still wanted to know what other people were doing.

"Sad, Sam?" Max asked, concern on his furry face.

"Frustrated." She pounded on her table. "We got rid of Waller, but here we are, still in the nowhere life."

"Cave, food, warm have." He danced a little jig.

"That may be good enough for you, Max, but it's not enough for me." She sat back in her chair. "Even that is not enough." She pointed to the forest showing on the screen. "I know it's just an image, not real. And I don't know when I'll ever get to see the real thing."

"Sad, you are. Sad, most people."

Sam looked at him. They went for walks through the streets every once in a while, Max in the guise of an old man.

"You're right." She tried to remember the last time she saw a smile on someone besides Brad and Todd. Max had a perpetual smile.

Suddenly she wanted out of there — out somewhere where she could run through grass, see trees and sky. She closed her eyes and tried to picture it.

The comm buzzed, interrupting her reverie.

"Sam, it's me, Todd." She pictured his long, dark face and gray eyes.

"Hi. What's up?"

"We have been called to meet with a City Councilor at Level Forty-One tomorrow morning."

"Whoa. What for?" Sam shivered.

"They didn't say. I'll pick you up at nine hours. They wanted Brad, too, but I told them he's back on duty on his ship."

Sam sat back. A councilor meant either she and Todd had information they could use ... or they were in big trouble. Todd had already told Security everything they knew about the lab and her ex.

She tried to think. *What did we do to bring this on us?*

Prickles ran up and down her spine. The only thing she could think of was her ex.

Won't he ever leave me alone?

*   *   *

The next morning, when Todd arrived, Sam was ready, scarf around her neck and tools of her trade in her bag. Todd was her legal adviser as well as her second brother. Sam, Brad, and Todd had grown up together; Todd's mother, whom Sam called Aunt Linda, had taken Sam and Brad in when their mother left.

Sam was still shaky from the episode with her ex-husband, and apprehensive about this upcoming meeting. She could not image what the Councilors could possibly want from them. At least she wasn't going into this alone.

Thank Oneness for Todd.

Todd led Sam to the nearest tube and up to Level Forty-One, the lowest level of the government complex. On the wider and cleaner street up there, they passed buildings closer to white than the dull tan of their streets. They walked several blocks to the public entrance to Centrex, where a guard in a gaudy maroon uniform stopped them.

"Where are you going?" he demanded.

"We have an appointment with a Councilor." Todd pulled out his comm.

The guard grabbed at it, and Todd yanked the comm away. "No one takes another's comm unless the owner has been arrested for a crime."

"No appointments this day. Come."

The guard took them by the arms and marched them into the building, into a small, bare room next to the entrance.

"Wait."

"They used to be a lot nicer about it," Todd said. Sam looked around at the bland, brownish-gray walls, with little lights in the corners of the ceiling and rubbed her arm. That episode had done nothing to assuage her fears.

An official in dark green arrived and looked them up and down. "You say you have an appointment. With who?"

"Whom," Sam muttered under her breath.

Todd pulled out his comm, brought up the screen, and flashed it in the official's face.

He looked at it, glanced at his own comm, turned and left without a word.

"Well," Sam huffed.

Todd shrugged. "Now we wait."

"Wonderful," Sam snarled.

At least she was in a different drab room than her office. Sam still hadn't recovered from the shock of breaching her memory wall and had no idea how to deal with this upcoming meeting. She no longer felt safe, protected from the outer world. One thing, though: her curiosity had been awakened. Now she wanted to know what was going on out here.

Presently, a person dressed in an ugly shade of yellow-green opened the door. Sam couldn't tell whether e was a male, female, or other. "Come," e said.

"Who wants us?" Todd asked.

The person looked away. "I cannot say." E left.

"Uh oh," Sam remarked as they followed em. "Do you have any idea?" Her unease grew.

Todd shook his head.

The person led them to a meeting room larger than Sam's office, with a shiny brown table and chairs, and pale green walls. She wondered if she could get that color for her place.

As Sam and Todd sat in hard chairs, a man strode in. Something about the way he walked seemed odd to her. He looked like a man. Shorter than Todd, slim, with nondescript hair and clothing. Someone you would forget two seconds after you passed him on the street.

"Call me Dondo," he said in a deep voice, as he settled himself in the single chair across from them.

"Who are you? What is this?" Todd demanded.

"I am liaison between this world and the Volen, who oversee this world and many others. You are here for two reasons. First, you helped us solve the problem of Waller. He had a criminal organization on several other worlds and was beginning to set up one here. It, and he, no longer exist."

"What about Jerg?" Sam asked.

"Jerg?"

"His associate, who was also on the ship."

"Anyone on the ship is gone."

Sam desperately wanted to believe that, but a little knot of doubt remained in her mind.

Dondo continued. "The other reason is this. Once a year — I use your term for one revolution of your world around your star — I receive a report from your Council on the state of your sector, and reports from the other sectors. Normally, it is brief. This time, since I was here for this other matter, my Volen contact wanted me to do a deep audit. I found some very disturbing items."

Sam looked at Todd. Unanswered questions raced through her mind. She felt a need to know more about her people's background.

"Go on," Todd said.

"About two hundred years after your ancestors settled here, after leaving their home world, this world had been settled by other races, most brought by the Volen. The Volen did a survey of each sector, collecting baseline figures for the population, dimensions, growth, and so forth. Now, nine hundred years later, I was instructed to do similar surveys on all the sectors."

"Oh?" Sam still didn't get what this was all about. She knew there were nonhumans in the other sectors, but since her people didn't have anything to do with the aliens, she never thought of them.

Now, she wanted to know more about her background and these other people.

"In the first survey," Dondo continued, "the average height of a human male was five foot ten. In my current survey, it is five foot eight. I use your measurements for your convenience. For females, the previous was five foot four, and now it is five foot two."

Sam sucked in her breath. She was five six, and Brad and Todd were both six foot. Dad was tall.

There must be some really short people Down Below.

"Another item," Dondo added, "is that at the earlier time, your people were living for seventy to eighty of your years. Now, the average span is sixty."

"Wow," Todd said. "I've been doing some research for a client, and I came across a statement noting that we humans need to keep in touch with nature in order to thrive. Have you checked the stats for the upper levels versus the lower levels?"

"Good idea. I will. There are not many people who would think of that. Most of the lower level people just sleep, eat, go to their work, eat, and sleep. You people up here are more active." He paused. "In addition, people in other sectors are also regressing. They are having to import more foodstuffs and other necessary products. This world is becoming unhealthy for living beings."

"What can we do about it?" Sam asked, shaken.

How could this be happening?

She remembered Carol in the toy shop next door complaining about how her grandchildren weren't nearly as active as her children had been.

"I understand that structures in all the sectors are built of the Volen material, like City. Could something in that be affecting us?" Todd asked.

"The Volen say no. They have no problems on other worlds."

"Maybe something in it is reacting with something that's only in this world."

"Could it be something in the food?" Sam asked. Food wasn't as tasty as she remembered as a child.

Dondo cocked his head. "I will have that checked out. Now, Todd, you must do as much research as you can on the history of your people, relevant to environment and welfare. I cannot access the records you can. Samanda, I will have use for you later. We will meet here in nine days." He rose. "For your help with Waller, I have increased your credits account balance. Good day."

Sam and Todd followed him out, mouths open. Sam still couldn't totally comprehend the situation. Outside the building, well past the guard, she pulled out her comm and checked her credits balance. A good month's worth of earnings had been added to her account balance. Sam hadn't expected that and studied the numbers in disbelief.

"Look," Sam showed Todd. "At least we got something out of it. What do you know about this liaison fellow?"

"Not much. I knew there was one, and that he occasionally showed up to check things out to go tell the Volen."

They walked back to the lift tube.

"Can we go up?" Sam asked, hoping.

"I don't think so, but we can try."

Sam and Todd stepped into the up-tube, but nothing happened. A small screen on the wall said "Not Allowed" in blinking yellow letters.

"Oh, well," Sam said. *I'll get there some day.*

They hopped off, moved over to the down-tube, and grabbed the handholds on the central pole.

*   *   *

World slept.

5

W HEN THEY STEPPED OFF AT TODD'S LEVEL, several above Sam's, he said, "I think you should stay away from your place for a while. I've got one of those feelings."

Todd had always had a sense when something was wrong, even when they were kids. Sam and Brad soon learned to take him seriously.

"What about Max?"

"He'll be okay inside. Your place is locked, isn't it?"

"Of course." Sam glared at him. *My place is always locked when I am gone. Max knows how to get out if he has to.*

Todd led Sam toward his apartment. This street was wider and brighter than the one she lived on. The doors on the buildings — a very pale gray, almost white — and bright windows presented a feeling of cheerfulness. At the crossroad before his apartment, he stopped.

He closed his eyes, with that look of scoping out the area. Sam waited, wondering why he thought there might be danger.

"All clear." Todd opened his eyes. "Come on, Sam."

In his apartment, this time Sam noticed the shelves of books and curiosities clients had given him. She moved along them, observing each item. A little white four-legged creature with pointed ears and green eyes drew her attention.

"What's this?"

Todd set a tray with a bottle and mugs on the table in front of the long seat and went to her. "That's a cally. They live with the people on another world. A client gave it to me for service rendered. She got it at Spaceport."

"Oh." She didn't want to think about Spaceport.

Sam moved over to the long seat and curled into the curved corner. Too many things were happening at the same time. She stared at his screen, still on trees, without seeing it. Her once settled life had become totally unreal, and she didn't know how to handle it. She could only focus on tiny things, one at a time.

Todd sat beside her, picked up the red and white bottle, and poured the beverage into the mugs. "One of our clients gave me this, from off-world. It's been cleared and is safe." He handed her a mug.

Sam sniffed it. The drink smelled a little sour, but a sip tasted smooth with no hint of bitterness. The more she sipped, the more she liked it. She pushed the meeting into the back of her mind and decided to focus on her new surroundings. She'd be going back to her gray office soon enough.

Todd sat next to her and put an arm across the back of the seat behind her. His fingers drifted down to her shoulder, and she jerked at the touch.

"Sorry." He moved his hand away. "How is your business doing?"

"Not so hot. Just making enough to cover expenses. Today's deposit was a nice surprise."

Todd yanked out his comm. "My balance is up, too. I wonder if Brad's is. Let me check his account. Yes, his is up too. Does Max have an account?"

"No, we're trying to keep him incognito. That's why we're always bringing food home from the caff." Sam knew Todd handled Brad's finances while he was on duty.

"Probably for the best." He paused and looked at the wall screen. "I have to say this. The bed in the other room is big enough for two; there's room here for Max, and this place is much nicer than yours. What do you say?"

"Sorry, no." Sam looked down at her hands.

Todd had been asking her to marry him ever since her ex left for the first time, after he had made sure the marriage had been dissolved. Sam had been so chewed up by that man it was hard for her to even think of living with another one. Todd was like a second brother, and she loved him for that, but becoming man and wife was a whole different story.

"That's better than 'no'." He took a sip of his drink. "What do you think about what Dondo told us. Do you think it's true?"

"Why would anyone want to fake figures about height and life spans?"

"I agree. I've been noticing that fewer young people are anywhere near as tall as I am, but I don't see what we can do. We can't build much higher. We're hemmed in by the other sectors and the sea, so we can't expand outward. And I don't think we can dig much deeper."

"How did we get to this point, anyway?"

"Don't you remember your schooling?" Todd moved away a bit. "How humans from Old Earth came here to form a new colony?"

"Yes, but I mean where we are today."

"The colony just grew until the Volen found us and began growing our buildings. Whenever we outgrew one, the Volen just added on more and more levels. I heard talk that they were preparing to add another level."

"Oh." This was something Sam could focus on. At least hypothetically. "What if we could get the Volen to move some of our people to somewhere else and take out some of the upper levels, so people farther down could see the sky?"

"That's an idea. If the Volen agree, and they can figure out how to choose what people to take. But that's not nearly enough. And the people on top would object if the Volen took their homes." He put his mug down on the low table in front of them.

They talked for a while, then Todd stood up and gathered the empty mugs.

"I think it's time to take you home."

"I know how to get there. I can take care of myself." Sam snorted.

She rose and picked up her bag. The idea of living in Todd's place was tempting, but what would come with it, was not.

"Yes, I know, you have all sorts of gadgets in that bag of yours, but I think I'll go with you anyway." He put the mugs in the sink and led her out the door.

As they approached the corner nearest Sam's apartment, Todd put out a hand and stopped her. She glanced up at him.

"Somebody's lurking." He looked around.

"Where? There's no place to lurk around here." The streets were empty.

Suddenly a pair of scruffy men stormed around the corner and grabbed them. Sam kicked back and hit her attacker's leg. He yelled and put his other hand around her throat, over her scarf. She grabbed the end of it, pulled the string that let it inflate, and with her left hand reached back for his balls.

He screamed and let her go. She saw Todd give the other one a karate chop and let him fall. Todd grabbed her arm. They ran across the street, and down to her door. Inside, after setting all locks and alarms, they sat on her bed and caught their breaths.

"Are you all right?" Todd asked.

Sam shook her head, deflated her scarf, and took it off. She had reacted purely on instinct.

"Relax. We're safe here. Waller may be gone, but apparently he left some thugs behind."

Sam gulped.

Those two weren't much, but what else did he leave roaming around out there?

*   *   *

World slept on.

6

S AM TRIED TO COLLECT HERSELF. A thought struck her. "Max."
She ran down the stairs, Todd on her heels.

Max trotted out of his cubicle and caught her as she stumbled the last few steps.

"Max," Sam panted. "Thanks." She collapsed into her chair. "Bad news. No more walks for a while. The bad man may be gone, but he's left his helpers behind."

"Hurt Sam?" Max screwed up his face.

"No, but we did some damage to them. I don't want to take any chances of them hurting you."

"Another reason to leave this place." Todd dropped into Brad's chair. "If you move in with me, you'll have an escort whenever you go out." He smiled at Sam. "I'll sleep on the long seat and I won't touch you. What do you say?"

It was tempting, but ...

"You would need to escort me over here every morning and back to your place every evening. How safe would that be?"

"Oh." Todd blinked.

"Besides, I don't want to leave Max alone, either here at night or at your place during the day."

Todd sighed. "You're right. You two are much safer just staying right here. I'll call you in the mornings and come over in the evenings and bring you food." He glanced around. "But there's got to be a way to get you out of here. Is there any other occupation you'd be interested in?"

"Um." Sam looked at her father's photo at the top of the corkboard. "If I could get into some scientific endeavor, but not the xenolab. I could never go back there." Sam fought back the scene of her dad lying on the floor of the lab in a pool of blood.

"I'll see what I can find. That would probably help with our other problem."

Sam gulped. She'd been trying not to think about what Dondo had told them, it was too much for her to handle.

"How can two people like us possibly do anything?" She twiddled her stylus.

Todd shifted in his chair. "I don't know. I don't know what he thinks we can do or what he wants us to do. I'll keep researching, though I don't know for what. We need to find out more from him. You just keep doing what you usually do. There's a couple people I can talk to who might have some ideas."

"I don't really know anyone else except you and Brad. My customers are only interested in themselves. There's Carol next door in the toy shop and Wanda with her dolls down the street. I see them once a week at the caff, but they're mainly only interested in their kids and the toys. I wish Brad was here; he knows lots of people."

"Okay." Todd rose. "I need to get back to work. See you later."

Sam sat and thought about the xenolab. Originally set up to test native plants for nutrients the humans could use, it had evolved to handle anything brought to the colony — and later, City — that was not human-created. Including Max's mother and him. Max seemed to be healthy, but all they knew about him was what Dad had found out from studying Max's parent. Sam always had this little knot of worry in the back of her mind that something would happen to him and they wouldn't know how to fix it.

She checked her messages and turned to her accounts. Yes, the extra credits were still there.

"I can get you a new puzzle," she said to Max, sitting in the entrance to his cubicle.

"Nice." He grinned.

Sam went about her business the next couple of days, missing Brad, and with a feeling of unreality wrapped around her. Todd called and came as promised, but didn't stay long.

*   *   *

On the third day, Sam received a call from the chief of a Noreg tribe.

"Is this Samanda Lar, proprietor of Joe's Spyshop?" the deep voice asked.

"Yes, this is she." *Who in City? That was the old name of my place.*

"I be Mantz, leader of tribe Koo. A Dondo gave me your name to call."

"Dondo?"

"Yes. One you people stole child's Katta."

"Katta? Are you Noreg?"

It finally dawned on her. As the sector to the east of City, Dondo would have gone there next.

"Yes. Katta small creature, companion to child."

"How can I help?" Sam was back to her professional self again.

"One you people took and returned to you sector."

"Oh. Do you have any idea who? Or a description? And what does the Katta look like?"

"Katta small like new infant, green fur, two long pink ears, black pointed nose. Person who take be male; large face, hair on chin. Was trader. Know not name."

"Okay, was he a regular trader?" Sam looked up at the forest on the wall above her screen.

"Not. Two times only."

"Okay, let me see what I can do. How do I contact you when I find the Katta?"

A comm address appeared on her screen, along with a fuzzy image of a man with a beard. Sam saved the information.

"Thank you. I'll be in touch."

The Noreg lived in the sector next to the humans. The third people to colonize this world, they lived in treehouses. Sam had discovered that, on their home world, the Noreg had to avoid large, ferocious creatures who liked to eat the them. In their sector, the Noreg lived in giant, artificial trees made of the same Volen substance as City walls and floors.

Sam sat back.

So, was Dondo just trying to help me, or did he have an ulterior motive for sending me business from other sectors?

She looked up the Katta. Two large blue eyes peered at her out of a mass of green fur.

He hadn't mentioned the eyes.

She immediately wanted one. They ate most anything soft and were trained practically from birth to use a waste receptacle.

"Max, come here." Sam turned to his cubicle.

He popped out. "Is what?"

"Look at this. It's a Katta, and we have to find it."

"Baby."

Sam told him what the leader had told her. "I think this guy who stole the Katta probably wants to sell it. He could probably get a lot for it."

"Okee."

"I'm going to do some checking and see if I can locate him, maybe pretend to be a buyer. Then we go get it."

"Out, not go. Wants, Todd."

"I know, but we'll have you go as a little older man, not any taller than you are now."

"Good. Easier, no air sacs." He slipped back into his cubicle. Inflatable air sacs within his body could be inflated to increase his size.

After Sam checked the list of official traders, she accessed records of passage through the three nearest portals to Mantz' tribe.

Two traders were not on the main list. One was a very young man with no facial hair. The other name was not listed anywhere. She pulled up the image and stared at it. She knew that some portal managers were not as careful about checking IDs as others. *How could I find him?* All databases were listed by name, and she didn't have one.

Sam turned to the "Items Available" listing. This is where the Katta would be if he was trying to sell it.

What would it be under?

She tried several headings: Curios, Toys, Unique. No luck. She checked several other groups. No green balls. Finally. she started at "A" and began working her way through the alphabet. Finally, under "Comforts", she found an advert for a furzy. The picture showed a green ball, no eyes, ears or nose. The caption ran: Anxious, worried? Hold soothing furzy and relax.

"Aha," Sam said. "That has to be it." She ran upstairs and fished out her personal comm.

Comm units were tied to apartments. When Sam moved into this apartment and shop, she'd left her old comm in her other place and got two new comms, shop and personal.

Since she always used the shop comm, she'd tucked away the other. Now, since she thought the seller might trace her number to her shop, she used the personal comm to respond to the ad. She was told to come to a certain address the next day to see the item.

When Todd came by that evening, Sam told him about the job.

"I have to go. At least I have credits for a car." Electric cross-sector cars on tracks ran on every fourth level.

"Okay. Just be very careful when you leave."

"I will. What about food? We're hungry."

"Here." He opened the bag he'd brought and piled boxes of food on the little table by Brad's chair. "This is for tonight and tomorrow, so you don't have to go out to eat. If there's any more of Waller's toads around, they'll either be hanging around your doors or the caffs."

Sam sighed. "I suppose you're right. How long am I going to be trapped in here?" After seeing Todd's place, the last thing she wanted was to be stuck in her gray office.

Todd shrugged. "I've got a friend with connections who is trying to find out whether and how many toads Waller left behind. They're likely offworlders and staying with Waller's people, as they'd have no local IDs, and someone would have to get food for them."

"Don't they keep records of who comes in through Spaceport?"

"Yes, but there are ways to smuggle someone in."

They finished their meal, and Todd told her about several people he'd talked to — who were shocked at the state of the human decline. When he left, he warned her again about being prepared when she went out in the morning.

*   *   *

World slept.

7

T HE NEXT DAY, Sam wore one of her everyday coveralls and her
scarf. Max, as an older man her size, wore a long, dark shirt
that hung over his gray pants, hiding the slit that gave him access
to his tummy pouch. A special pocket inside Sam's outfit held her
comm; other pockets held other items, such as chips and trackers.

Sam opened the outside door cautiously. She held her
infrared scanner in her hand, waited for a couple of passersby, and
then stepped out and scanned. No one else was around. Sam and
Max walked briskly to the up-tube, took it up two levels, and over
two blocks to catch the east-west cross-sector car. Electric cross-
sector cars on tracks ran on every fourth level.

Sam breathed easier once they were inside the eight-seat
green vehicle. The couple seated toward the rear ignored them.

She didn't like skulking about and hiding from unknown
attackers. Her life had been turned upside down and she was still
trying to sort it out. She studied the picture of the Katta on her comm.

Since she knew very little about this seller, she'd decided to follow his lead. She would get the creature no matter what. She had pride in her professional work. Max played her Uncle Joe, who had chosen to accompany her, because it wasn't safe for a young woman to be out on her own.

They found the place easily and gave the fellow at the window the number the seller had sent her. The clerk ushered them to one of the cubicles that lined the place. A small brown table and three chairs nearly filled the gray-walled room. As soon as they were settled, a short, lean man with a bare face entered carrying a large box. He set it on the table and eased himself into his chair.

He could have been the man on the screen, and he could have shaved, Sam thought.

"I am Brosnet." He opened the box and pulled out a round green ball of fur, about a foot in diameter. "This is a furzy." He set it on the table between us. "I am asking one hundred credits."

I sure can't buy it.

Sam picked up the green ball. She'd palmed a minichip and eased it into the soft fur of the ball. She turned it in her hands, savoring the warmth that came from it. There were no obvious features, but she spotted barely visible slits where its eyes, nose, and ears should be. She held the Katta to her cheek.

Uncle Joe-Max reached out a hand and touched it gently. "Ooooh," he murmured.

"Very nice," Sam said.

Warmth and a wanting came from the creature. She was sure now this was the Katta. *But how was she going to get it?*

"I want it, but I don't have the hundred now. Would you settle for sixty?"

Brosnet snorted. "I'll go ninety, but that's it."

"I don't have that. Can I put sixty down and pay the rest next week?"

He closed his eyes briefly. "Yes, but I keep the furzy. And your credits if you don't show."

That was too much to risk, but how else could I get the Katta back? If I could get another green ball its size and swap them ...

"What if I put twenty down now and the rest later? I'm expecting a big input to my account in a few days. Can you hold it for me 'til then?" She held out her comm to transfer credits. She could spare twenty now.

"If I have not sold it, it's yours. But if anyone else wants it and has the credits, it's going to 'em." He shrugged. "I need the credits too."

"Where did you get it?"

"In a trade." He put the furzy back in the box and stood. "If you get the credits sooner, call me." He picked up the box, turned and left.

Sam and Uncle Joe-Max followed him out of the room and saw him head to the rear of the building. Out the front entrance, and a few doors down the street, she stopped. When no one was nearby, she turned on the tracer. Brosnet was moving down the street parallel to theirs.

"Come on," Sam told Max, and trotted down to the corner.

Brosnet had just turned the farther corner away from them. They followed, a block behind, and watched as he entered a building in the next block. Sam and Max walked to the corner and she pinpointed the building. All apartments in the midlevels were laid out the same. The front door opened right into the main room, so they couldn't sneak in.

"Go get we?" Max asked

"He'll eat soon. We'll go then."

They moved slowly along the building, watched the apartment, and waited. When the beep moved, Brosnet came out carrying a square case, a little larger than the box the Katta had been in.

"Oh shimmy," Sam said. "He's got it with him." There was no way they could get it away from him at a caff.

She looked at Max. He was sagging. She dug out a food bar and gave it to him.

"Come on, Max, let's go home."

On the way, Sam tried to figure out how to make the swap to get the Katta. She could just tell Mantz where it was. *But how could he do anything from his sector?*

At her office, Sam plopped into her chair and checked for messages. One, from Spacefleet, made her heart drop.

If anything had happened to Brad ...

The other message was from a client. Cautiously, she opened the first one and heaved a sigh of relief.

Bradford Lar has been released from Space Service and will arrive in five days.

Sam only briefly wondered why, she was so thankful he was coming home.

She turned to the other message. A young woman had just found out about an aunt she never knew and wanted Sam to find the aunt. With names and dates, that would be easy. It took less than two hours for her to find the aunt. Sam worked on a few more cases and measured how wide Max could open his pouch.

That evening, Sam explained her problem to Todd, along with the good news.

"If I could find a green fur ball like her, I could substitute it. Do you have any idea where I could get one?"

Todd knew where to get just about anything.

"I think so. How big is it?"

Sam imagined the Katta in her hands, spreading them apart.

"Okay. I got the message about Brad. I'm looking for a job for him here."

Sam didn't care what job he had, as long he was here. She had stopped thinking about the people problem.

*   *   *

Three days later, Todd brought Sam a green fur ball. She called Brosnet and arranged for a meeting the next day. When Brad arrived home that evening, she told him of her job.

"I'll go with you."

"No, you can't. Max has to go so he can hide the Katta in his pouch."

"Okay, I'll just wait for you outside."

The next morning, Brad paid for the car. On the way to the car, he kept Sam between him and Uncle Joe-Max.

At the meeting place, Sam asked to see the furzy again. Brosnet pulled it out. She picked up the Katta, turned the furball in her hands, and fumbled it into her lap.

"Sorry." Sam felt Max take her and shove the other green ball into her hands. She hastily picked it up and put it on the table. She sensed Max stashing the Katta in his pouch. Sam held out her comm to transfer credits, but there was not enough. "Oh, they messed up again. Please hold it for me."

"Not again." Brosnet picked up the ball, put it in his box, and stomped out.

Sam and Max went out and joined Brad.

∗   ∗   ∗

World slept.

8

S AM, MAX, AND BRAD MADE THEIR WAY to the nearest inter-
sector portal. Sam called Mantz and told him she had the
Katta and would wait for him at the portal. Max opened his pouch
so the Katta could breathe.

Inside, an attendant glanced at their IDs and waved them
through. Max used Uncle Joe's, which Todd had kept after her
uncle's death. The man pointed to a door at the back of the room.
Sam, Brad, and Max entered the pale green waiting area full of
variously sized green seats, pots of plants, and a large window
onto the Noreg sector.

Sam trotted over and gazed at the nearby towering trees.
Little wood-like houses sat in every nook and cranny. She knew
the trees weren't real, made of the same Volen material used to
build City, but they looked so real — pale trunk and green leaves
— that Sam wanted to run out and touch them.

Brad sat on a bench, and Sam could sense him watching her.

When Sam saw people on the walkway coming from the nearest tree to the portal, she went to Max, took the Katta, and held her up at the window. "Looks like your people are coming."

Her nose, ears, and eyes sprouted out. She made a mewing sound and wiggled in Sam's hands.

Mantz arrived, accompanied by a female and a little girl. Humanoid with dark skin and hair, he wasn't much taller than Sam, and the woman was several inches shorter. Their closefitting garments appeared to be fashioned from large green leaves.

When the three entered the room, the Katta pushed off from Sam's hands and sailed to the little girl, who caught her.

The parents smiled widely, and Mantz said, "Excellent. She is not harmed?"

"She doesn't appear to be."

The little girl cradled the Katta and sang to her. Her mother patted the child.

Mantz pulled out a gadget similar to City's comms and sent credits to Sam's. "Dondo see you?"

"Yes. Has he been here?" Sam glanced out the window.

Mantz nodded. "Our people used to be taller. Yours too?"

Sam nodded. "We need to find out why. We have a friend researching it. Are Kattas shrinking too?"

"Yea. They not grow as big as used to."

"I'll tell Todd and we'll keep in touch. We've got to figure this out."

*   *   *

Back home, Sam checked for messages. One from Dondo was marked a few minutes ago.

"How did he know?" she asked.

"He must have access to financial transactions," Brad said.

Sam called Dondo. "I received the request from the Noreg and have completed it. Is this what you wanted?"

"Yes. You come tomorrow," he said. "Bring Brad. Same place."

"It's not nine days yet."

"You come." He disconnected,

Sam sighed. "Dondo wants us. Including you, Brad. I hope we don't have to go running up there every few days,"

"Me, too. Probably be hard to get off work every time. When I start working. I'll call Todd."

*   *   *

The next day, Todd met Sam and Brad at Level Forty-One at the east corner of Centrex, and they went to the entrance together. This time, the guard let them in without question.

"What do you know about this world?" Dondo asked when they met in the pale green room.

"It's very similar to our ancestors' home world," Todd said. "That's why they settled here."

"Yes. And?"

"It has trees and flowers."

Sam knew that was not what he meant.

"There's a smaller continent in the southern hemisphere," Brad added. "Can we move down there?"

"Does it have trees?" Sam asked hopefully.

"It's mostly desert except along the coasts. Todd, what have you found out in your research?"

"Haven't had a chance to do much. Why now?"

"There have been reports of tremors at the west end of this continent."

"Tremors?" Brad looked up.

Now what? Sam thought.

"Small earthquakes. You won't feel them here. All City sectors are made up of modules. If pressure is strong enough, they can slide along each other, horizontally or vertically. There is a fault line along the west coast."

"Modules?" Todd asked.

"Usually a block; two levels."

"I see. If they slide too far, that could break power and water lines," Todd said. "So why did the Volen build here, then?"

"Your original colony was here," Dondo said. "When they needed more buildings, Volen built them here."

Todd nodded.

"We need you to go to other sectors, find out what they know, prepare them for possible upheaval."

"What? How?" Sam asked. "Why us?" She wanted no part of this.

"You have been selected."

"For what?" Todd asked.

"To lead the humans out of City."

"Why?" Todd sounded skeptical.

"No," Sam said, shaking her head.

The three of them looked at each other.

No, not me. She pushed the whole idea away.

"You, Samanda, will be called to Itz sector soon. You men go with her. That is all." He rose and left.

Sam and her brothers walked out of the building. She, at least, was in a daze.

"At least our ruts aren't so dull anymore," Brad said.

Todd returned to work, and Sam and Brad returned to her apartment.

At the door, Brad said, "Sam, I need to go see people. I'll be back later, with food."

"Okay." He was always going and seeing people.

"See you later." He strode off.

Inside, Sam collapsed into her chair. *Too much to think about.*

First, Waller and his ship. Now this Dondo and his talk about City falling apart, and she and her brothers being leaders. And Waller's thugs after her. At least they got home without incident today. She was no leader. Todd, two years older, had always been their leader. She'd wanted change, but not like this.

Sam turned to her screen and looked up Itza. The picture showed them as long and gray, with a stubby tail and four short legs. Their heads were round, like humans. Average adults were four feet long, including the tail. Their life span was about fifty years. They lived in desert, around oases.

Max's voice interrupted her. "For Sam, you."

Sam turned to see him behind her, a little gray pot in his hands. The pot held brown dirt, and a pair of tiny green leaves on a stem.

"Oh." Sam stared at it. "Is it real? Where did you get it?"

"From plant where Katta, others we wait for. Real, is."

Sam was stunned. *An actual, living plant.*

She took the pot and held it to her face. Barely visible veins marked the little leaves; a tiny nub showed where their stems met.

"Thank you, Max. This is wonderful." She carefully placed it on a shelf beside the screen.

"Every day, water." He grinned. "Look up, I." He had limited access to her screen.

She'd noticed the plants in the waiting area, but just assumed they were fake, like everything else.

After Max disappeared into his cubicle, Sam decided to look up the other peoples on City world. She found no more information on them than she had on the Noreg. The others lived in various environments — jungle, forest, a hive with hexagonal cells — but she could find no information on their cultures, how they thought.

Sam kept looking at the little plant.

How did he get it and the pot? Is this an omen of the future? Is my life truly changing?

*   *   *

Brad accompanied Todd when he arrived with dinner.

"I'm going to stay at Todd's," Brad said. "I've got a job in the mech lab."

She showed them her plant. "It'll need sunlight-type light," Todd said. "I'll see what I can find."

"Isn't that good for people? Would having that light be better for us?"

Todd stared at her. "Very good point, Sam. After all, sunlight is part of nature." Sam beamed.

"Yeah," Brad remarked. "Even on the ship, we were required to go to the garden every few days. It has sunlight light."

"With that light and a plant or two, wouldn't that help?"

"Sure, Sam. But will people take care of them?" Brad opened the dinner bag.

Sam's comm beeped. A message from Dondo:

The Itz need your help. One family is accusing another of taking their sunning stones. The Itz court cannot agree on a solution, so they asked for an outsider. I recommended you. The sunning stones are attached to the spiral walkway on either side. The ones on the inside, over the hot springs, are warmer than the ones on the outside. They all want the warmer ones. A flier will be waiting for you tomorrow at ten hours at Spaceport. Take one or both of the men with you. You must devise a satisfactory solution. Contact me at this address when you return.

The men read it from behind her.

"Holy stars." Brad patted her shoulder. "Too bad I can't go. This new job ..."

"I can take you to Spaceport, but I can't go with you," Todd said. "You can call me from Spaceport when you get back, and I'll come get you. You may have to wait, though."

"Okay." Sam wasn't sure she wanted to go back to Spaceport, or on this mission. "Flier?" she asked.

"Spaceport is over part of Itza."

"Oh."

As they ate, Sam pondered this new development. *Why did Dondo pick me to do this? Surely there were other, smarter people in the government.*

✳   ✳   ✳

World stirred.

9

T HE NEXT MORNING, Sam was ready when Todd arrived. She'd given Max all the food they had, and access to a few other areas on the screen.

"I don't know when I'll be back. Take care." He knew how to call her or Todd on the screen comm.

"Why not take him as Brad?" Todd asked.

"Because I don't know what it's like over there. In City, I know he'll be all right. But over there? I'm not taking a chance on anything happening to him."

At Spaceport, Sam found the flier and its pilot, one of the Itza. He wore a greenish brown tiled skin, and had great dark eyes, a tiny mouth and nostrils, and no ears that Sam could see. They didn't wear clothing the way humans did. In fact, they didn't look at all like humans.

The pilot chittered into a long comm. The City comms were square. Apparently, it included a translator, for "Sit," came out of the device in a high, tinny voice.

The silver flier was a four-seater, including the pilot, with not much room for her legs, and the seat Sam sat on was very uncomfortable and didn't fit her behind at all.

They flew down over brownish-green plains toward a huge sand-colored area. As they approached, Sam saw tall spiral structures around rough circles of green. Scattered here and there among them, clumps of tall green poles of plants reach for the hazy sky. Brown hills edged the west; shades of green showed in the far east. The craft drifted down to an open area near one of the spirals.

After they landed, the pilot led Sam through circles of sunning stones and cave-like homes to the spiral. The heat brought beads of sweat to Sam's forehead almost at once. On the round stone base stood a small stone building on one side, and the beginning of the spiral walkway on the other. About six feet up the spiral, a semicircular structure faced a large, flat stone hanging horizontally off the other side.

"Sunning stone," the pilot said. "Here." He led Sam to the building on the base.

A larger Itzan, almost as tall as Sam, standing on his back feet and draped in blue and orange ribbons, met her in a room with low benches around an oval table. He also had a translator comm.

"Greetings. I am Koz, head of court. Where is male?"

"He couldn't get away from his job."

"Hsst. You know two families fight over sunning stones. You know ones over springs are warmer than those outside. They must have heat. Need you to find solution."

"Why don't they just take turns?" Sam asked. It seemed obvious to her.

"Stone go with cave. Only move when oldest dies and all move down."

"Maybe you ought to consider changing that. I know it's no fun moving. What about if you choose pairs of families and let them switch off every few days. They would stay in their same homes, just switch from inside stones to outside ones."

Koz made a humming sound. Finally, he said, "I will talk to families. Wait here." He skittered out and up the spiral walkway.

"Water?" the pilot asked, holding out a gourd.

"Thanks."

He went back to his gadget, and Sam surreptitiously tested the liquid. The water tester pinged green for safe, and she drank it.

Sam walked over to the door and looked out. To the left, she saw tall, gray-green plants along the hot springs and a whiff of tart-smelling steam from above. The spiral circled above the springs to an enormous height. Lines dropped down from each cave. She noticed a basket on one moving upwards.

So that was how they got their food and things.

A walkway from the base circled the springs — at least she supposed it did, since both ends curved slightly in the same direction of the spiral. Farther along, the back end of an Itza stuck out of the plants.

Was it hunting or searching for something?

The plants drew her over. The nearest one sported gray, bristly leaves. These were nothing like what she had on her screen and pictures. The leaf appeared to be stretching toward her, but that must have been her imagination. She sniffed at it and gasped at its musty odor. But it was a real live leaf. Not what she wanted, but still, progress. And the air smelled fresher.

I am outside, Sam thought, grinning at the sky.

Someone called. Sam turned and saw the pilot point at the spiral. Koz was returning. Sam trotted back to the building.

"The families will consider it," Koz said. "Well done. Here is fee." He sent twenty credits to Sam's comm from his.

"Thank you," Sam said. "Glad I could help."

The pilot took her back up to Spaceport, where she called Todd.

"That was fast," he said. "I'll be up in a couple of hours."

"Okay. I'll be here." Sam found a comfortable seat.

One good thing, she thought. *At least I'm getting to see new places. And I got my twenty credits back.*

She called Dondo and reported.

"I want to see you in three days. Bring your ward."

"Max," Sam said. "Why?" She didn't like that at all.

"I need to see him."

"Can't you come to my office? I don't like for him to be out, to be seen."

"No, I am confined to the government levels."

"Okay." Sam still didn't like it, but if she didn't bring Max, Dondo could send Security to get them.

When Todd arrived to take her home, she told him about the meeting with Dondo and Max the next day.

"I'd like to go," he said, "but I can't get off work. However, Brad has a free day while they set things up for him, so he can go with you."

*   *   *

World became aware.

10

THE NEXT MORNING, Sam told Max they were taking him to see a man called Dondo. "This time you can talk. Answer his questions as long as it doesn't reveal too much about you. I don't want him to know any more than he needs to. And don't change unless I say so."

"Okee." Max made himself into a young man, about her height.

The comm pinged. It was Brad.

"Haven't you left yet?" he demanded.

"On our way out the door. Yes, I know how to get there."

Sam and Max headed for the up-tube. They met Brad at the entrance to Centrex and entered.

Dondo was waiting for them when they arrived at the meeting room. "Greetings. Who is this? Where is alien?"

"This is he," Sam said. "This is Max, in his man form. He uses it when we go out, so he'll blend in." She didn't know what Dondo expected, but it obviously wasn't this.

Dondo blinked and sat down. "I thought, small and furry."

"He was when we got him, but he grew up," Brad said. "He's still furry in his natural form. Show him a hand, Max."

Max looked at Sam. She nodded and glared at Brad. They had agreed that she'd do the talking.

Max let his hand go furry. "Hard, not," he said.

"I see. Is it intelligent?"

"He, I am, smart, I am," Max announced, sounding annoyed. It was the first time Sam had seen him this put out.

"He (Sam stressed the pronoun) is very smart, learns quickly, and accesses my screen in youth mode," she said. "He does all the puzzles, too."

"I see." Sam could tell by his expression Dondo was still confused. "Is he grown?"

Max looked at Sam.

"We're not sure. He's almost as big as his mother was, but we don't know whether the males were the same size as the females or not." She glanced at Max.

Dondo nodded. "I understand he was brought here as an infant."

"Yes," Brad said.

How did he know? Sam thought furiously. *He had no business knowing that. What else did he know?*

"Because they had his mother, even though she was dead, Dad was able to figure out what nutrients he needed. He was too little to be left at the xenolab, so Dad brought him home. He became like a little brother to Sam and me." Brad avoided my eye.

"I see. But surely, the authorities knew."

"They knew he existed, but thought he was in the xenozoo museum like all the others. He was always there in the daytime when they checked." Brad shrugged. "That's all they knew."

Sam kicked Brad's leg.

"By the time Dad died, Max was big enough that he didn't need to go back to the lab. A new employee, who didn't know what Max was, found him missing and marked him as having died. That was during the trial and all. We never knew about him being listed as dead until much later, so we let it be."

"Brad," Sam snarled.

"Hmm." Dondo stared at the ceiling. "Is it possible that this alien of yours could make himself look like your brother?"

"No," Sam practically shouted, as Brad said, "Yes."

Max looked back and forth at the two of them.

"No," Sam told him, sensing that he was about to demonstrate.

"Hmm," Dondo repeated, a smug look on his face. "I see. There was a Brad on Waller's ship and also a Brad on Todd's ship. Can you explain?"

"No," Sam snapped. *This shouldn't be happening.*

"Oh, the one on Waller's ship was Max."

"Brad," Sam growled.

Dondo looked at Brad, then Max, and shook his head.

Sam kicked Brad's leg again before he said anything more than 'ouch'. "I think it's time for us to leave." She stood.

"No, I do not agree. I need to understand this." Dondo motioned them to sit.

Sam sent daggers at Brad.

"Is this alien a true shape changer?"

Max stood up. "Max, I," he stated. "Alien not." He sat down.

"Very well, Max. Are all your people shape changers?" Dondo asked.

Max looked at Sam. She shook her head.

"Dad believed so." Brad looked away from her. "He was brought in with his mother. Her bottom half was a shell curled around him, and the spacer who brought them in said that others of Max's people were in ball shapes in death."

"Only us four, one gal at the lab, and now you know." Sam glared at Brad. "And I want to keep it that way. There are people in the science labs who would love to dissect him." Sam was ready to dissect Brad.

"Very well. Keep him safe. That is all for today. I must think about what I learned here."

Sam ran out of the building trying not to explode. "Brad, you idiot. Why did you tell him?" she screamed.

"Calm down." He took her arm. "I thought he needed to know."

"Why? Now everyone will know, and he'll never be safe. All those years of keeping Max hidden, all for nothing." She stomped her foot.

"Now, Sam."

"Don't you 'Now, Sam' me, Bradford Lar. I can't believe you did that." Sam jerked her arm away and stomped ahead.

"Quiet, you're making a scene." He grabbed her and pulled her along.

"Mad, Sam?" Max followed us.

"Shut up." Sam took a breath. *I wish we didn't have Max to deal with.* Immediately, she felt contrite and said, "Sorry, Max."

"Not here, Sam," Brad said in a low voice.

A group of people approached them. She kept her lips pinched tight. He returned one of the group's greeting.

After they passed, Brad pulled her to him and put a hand over her mouth. "Wait 'til we get home."

Sam yanked his hand away and kept her mouth shut.

He was right, of course. But he would get it later. How could he have exposed Max like that?

They took the tube down to their level. Brad led the way out, followed by Sam and Max. As they turned down the street, someone grabbed Sam around the breasts. She screamed, clawed, and kicked, and he let go.

"It's the girl," the man muttered, rubbing his leg.

Brad fought with a second man, and Max, hunched up, circled around to that man's back, drew his hand back into his body, and launched a huge fist into the fellow's kidney. The man screamed. Brad pushed him away and grabbed Sam. The three of them ran to the shop.

"So there are more."

Sam collapsed into her chair, and Brad into his.

"Good punch, Max," Brad said.

Sam's anger at Brad had diminished during the fight, but was not forgotten.

"Why on City did you tell Dondo about Max? Couldn't you tell he was fishing? What happened to our promise to never tell anyone else?"

Sam took a breath, and Brad broke in.

"Okay, okay. I know they did, but I think he already knew. He wants something from us, we need to let him know of all of our assets."

"Asset what?" Max demanded, patting her shoulder.

"All the good things and friends we have, like you."

"Okee."

"Are you quite through?" Brad mopped his face and stalked to the rear of the office. All five steps.

Sam closed her eyes, took a deep breath, and let it out through clenched teeth. It was done, over. No point in yelling at him anymore.

"Yes, for now."

He'd always had a way of getting under her skin. Innocently, of course.

He came back, took her hands, and kissed her forehead. "Sorry, Sammie, I thought you saw it too. I don't think he'll tell anyone, except maybe the Volen." He let go of her hands and sat down.

Sam leaned against what little bit of wall there was in her office.

After a pause, Brad spoke. "Why did the idiots only send two men against the three of us?"

"No more, maybe." Max settled in his doorway.

"Maybe," Sam said, "but they'll know better now."

"I think you should send in a report this time." Brad stretched. "I know it means more hassle, but Security has ways of finding people we can't access."

Sam sighed. The last thing she wanted was for this to get out beyond their family.

But if Security could get rid of them ...

"Okay."

She turned to her screen and opened an assault form. She replaced Max with Todd. No way was she going let them know about Max, and Todd was there the first time. She added that she thought they were Waller's men, trying to get her for what she did to him. At least they had good descriptions of the men.

A reply came with a long list of questions. Sam answered them the best she could. Some, she had no idea what they were talking about.

Sam checked messages, while Brad took the stairs to use the screen in the apartment.

*   *   *

A few days later, Sam received an amendment to her report. They had found the men, who claimed they didn't know anything about it, but found her DNA on one, and they were being sent to Purgatory.

"Two more gone, but how many are left?" she asked the air.

"I have no idea." Brad sighed.

Sam looked at Max, sitting cross-legged in his doorway, playing with a puzzle. Her little brother was growing up.

What would he become when he matured? From the size of his mother, he must be getting close.

*   *   *

World waited.

11

THE NEXT DAY, SAM RECEIVED A MESSAGE from Dondo to go immediately to the Ambaak sector, on the west side of the human sector. They were humanoid — the first people that came to this world after the humans. A youngster was trapped in a duct, and the Ambaaks couldn't do anything about it. She was to take Max and one of the men, take the Level Thirty-Two car to the west portal, where someone would meet her.

Sam checked them out on her screen. The Ambaak lived in clans and grew most of their own food. She called Brad. She knew his job had a lot of waiting time.

"I just got a call from Dondo to go to the Ambaak sector west of us, as soon as possible. Is there any way you can get off and meet us there?"

"I'll check. You go ahead and I'll call you. Where is 'there'?"

"Thirty-Two portal west."

"I'll be in touch."

Sam told Max and gathered up tools of her trade. She told Max to make himself a man face, and they took off for the cross-sector car. She had them sit in the front; two boys sat in the back row. Brad called when they were halfway across.

"Lucked out," he said. "In between projects, so I've got two days off. Meet you there."

Sam sighed with relief. At the last stop, she and Max disembarked and waited for Brad,

When Brad arrived at last, they all went through the 'airlock' door to the portal. This opened into a long gray tube connected to a square gray room with several seats and a controller's station. The female attendant wore a drab tunic and pants like City people. After she marked them as going through, she handed them breathing masks. Ambaak sector," she informed them, "has more oxygen than you humans can handle."

Sam stuck the box in a pocket and the tubes in her nose. Brad helped Max with his, but, by the time they arrived at the clan home, Max took his off.

"Need not."

Sam made a mental note to look into that later. Most of his senses were stronger than human senses.

They passed through into another room. Sam gasped.

Red and green vines grew over everything. A young female in a dark green shirt and bright yellow skirt, her dark hair tied back, waited for them. Long, narrow eyes and a tiny snub nose graced her face.

"Greeting. I am Liia." She smiled.

"Greetings. I am Samanda, this is my brother, Brad, and this is Max."

"Good. Come."

Sam, Brad, and Max followed Liia to a small yellow room that took them up a long way. There, they stepped out into a car corridor, piled into an orange car similar to City's, and Liia touched a button. They travelled for almost as long as they had in the car in City. When the car stopped, Liia led them through a door into the end of a corridor lined with doors of different pale colors.

She stopped at the first one, opened it, and they passed through a short, green hall to a great open space full of colors.

Sam soaked in the colors. She hadn't realized how much she'd missed them in her gray office and beige apartment. Suddenly Sam recalled that her family home, where they had lived before her mother had left, had a yellow door.

She could not tell the size of the place, but Brad told her later it was as big as one of their City blocks. Brightly lit masses of color were so bright that she had to squint.

"Here," Liia said, pulled a band of dark material out of a box by the door that she put around Sam's head and over her eyes. Sam could still see, but the brightness was gone. Brad now wore his own dark band.

"Natural light," Liia said, pointing up.

Windows in the ceiling revealed bright blue. As Sam stared, an uneven whiteness began to move across one.

"That is real sky," Liia said. "Sometimes there are clouds, and even rain."

Sam grabbed Brad's arm. "Look, it's the sky. Max, come here."

Max looked up and moaned.

"Can we go out?" Sam asked.

"Not yet. Over here."

She led them to a bench sheltered by a curved arch with flowers growing all over it. Benches with flower arches stood all around and, in their center, a dark green cylinder as big as a lift tube, with a door in its side, also covered with flowers, reached from floor to ceiling. People wearing bright colors sat on some of the benches; others bent over tables of plants.

"This is wonderful," Sam said. *I could stay here forever.* She noticed the second story, with balconies. *What a wonderful place. This could be my new life.*

"You do not have plants in your sector?" Liia asked.

"No, just gray walls."

"How do you live?"

"Not well. Our people are not living as long as they did when the ancestors first came here."

"This area is our clan courtyard. Some clans have gardens; some don't. Those clans are not healthy."

"That seems to be the case in all the sectors. I've been to two others."

"Ah. They must correct this. All our clans are separate from one another, and do not often communicate with each other. Ru, our youngster, was trying to reach the next one and became trapped."

"How? Where?" Sam remembered that she had gone there to do a job.

"Come." Liia led them across the courtyard, around benches and past tables of plants, to a corner with a ladder. "See the gap between room ceiling and clan ceiling?"

"Yes."

"Ru is in there. He tried to get to next clan through airway."

"I see."

Sam climbed the ladder and peered into the space. Using her lightstick, she saw the rim of an opening.

"Hello?" she called.

"Help," a faint voice came from the opening.

A hand smaller than hers poked out. Sam grasped it and pulled gently.

"Ow."

She let go, climbed down, and called Max, who was wandering around sniffing flowers. He trotted over.

"Job for you. Go up the ladder. A boy up there is stuck. See how we can get him out."

"Okee."

Max swarmed up the ladder and stuck his head into the space. He had much better night vision than the humans. His upper body stretched as he moved farther in. He spoke to the boy, but Sam couldn't hear what he said. Soon, he backed out and came down.

"Do I can, but clothes off need." Max tugged at his shirt.

At Liia's puzzled look, Sam said, "He needs to take his clothes off to get the boy out. It's all right, he's furry."

Max went up and disappeared into the space, except for his feet, which held onto the edge with long toes. Many of the clanspeople gathered. Brad stood by Sam, and she watched Max's toes wiggle. She heard grunts, a yelp, words from Max, and finally his feet began to back out.

He edged out with the boy, his red shorts and blue shirt torn and greasy. Scrapes covered his arms and legs. The boy's mother grabbed him, but, before she could take him away, Liia put out a hand and asked him if he saw the other clan.

"No." He shook his head. "There's a baffle in there."

Liia nodded, and the boy's mother took him away.

"Do you have the same language as them?" Sam asked.

"Yes. We all speak Standard, like you."

"Here's a suggestion. Write a note, put it on a stick and have a smaller boy push the stick through past the baffle so it will blow into the other clan's place."

"Oh." Liia's eyes widened. "I see. I will tell the group." She glanced at the far side of the place. "It is coming to end of day. We eat soon. Stay and eat with us, and we'll find you somewhere to sleep."

"Thank you," Sam said.

Since Max was here with her, she had no reason or desire to leave this beautiful place and return to her drab rooms. Except for the entrance hall, and a door on the far side that had three windows beside it instead of one, every vine-covered wall was lined with two levels of doors and windows.

"Our rooms," Liia said, as several women headed toward the door with three windows. "Look around. Chimes will announce when food ready. Follow others."

Sam and Max roamed around looking at all the plants. Brad wandered off by himself. The air in here smelled so fresh that Sam removed her nose tubes so she could breathe in all of the aromas. They watched a young woman in blue pick several small red fruits off a plant and lay them in her basket. After she moved away, Max touched a leaf and sniffed his fingers.

"Maa," he said. "Need, I."

"Oh, Max." Sam put an arm around him.

I need this, too. Everyone in City needs this. But how could we make City like this?

Tinkling chimes announced the meal. Sam and Max followed others, met up with Brad, and stepped inside.

She gasped. Large windows along the opposite wall looked out over the sea. A young man in green led them to a table by a window.

"Is this real?" Sam asked.

"Yes. Your meal will come." He left and soon brought their meal: a large bowl of green leaves, many vegetables, including the little red fruits, brown squares of protein, and yellow squares of something else that she had never seen before that tasted good. The server also placed a basket of long, narrow sticks of bread on their table. *Dondo said the Ambaak food was compatible with humans. I hope he was right.*

Sam spent most of the time staring out at the sea. She had seen pictures of beaches and water extending to a horizon. Here, large waves crashed onto rocks far below, then pulled back. Brad had to keep nudging her to eat.

Max gobbled his bowl of food and half the bread. "Good." He rubbed his tummy. When a server came to see how they were doing, he asked for more, and got it. "Food real."

"How do you know? You were too young to eat anything, only drink your mother's milk." Sam munched on a piece of bread.

"Milk, in." He looked at Sam. "We have, can we?"

"Not in our sector."

"Stay here, we?"

"Afraid not, Max." Brad burped. "If we don't go back, someone will come and get us."

Sam tore herself away from the sea, and Liia led them to a group of three benches with flower arches over them. A young man in yellow stood there.

"Wash in my room." He opened a door behind him. "At the back."

A long, narrow and light room, walls covered with painted vines and leaves, led to a bathroom at the rear. A colorful quilt covered a long seat. In the corner, a spiral staircase led upward. Many cabinets and shelves lined the walls. They took turns using the facilities and, when they went out, bright quilts lay on their benches.

Sam was thrilled to sleep amongst the flowers. It was the best day she could remember since she was little, when her mother took Brad and Sam to a park up top. Which she was sure was no longer there. Many of Liia's people sat in another part of the courtyard and sang soft songs. Sam curled up in the quilt and drifted off.

*　　*　　*

World stretched.

12

S AM AWOKE TO THE BENCH SHAKING. The skylights were still dark. One of the swinging vines caught in her hair. She sat up and yanked at it, fighting panic.

How could the place be shaking? Tremors, Dondo had said. Was this what a tremor was?

She would have to look that up when she got back home.

"Oh, no." Brad reached over and grabbed her hand.

The shaking soon stopped. No one came out of the rooms, although a few of the windows lit up. Max slept on, making his purring little snores.

Brad went back to sleep, but Sam lay and stared at the flowers hanging over her.

How on City are we going to deal with this? This area of plants was what we humans needed, but how could we do it, with all our walls and streets? There was no way to remove any walls. Unless the Volen could, and if they were willing to do it. Dondo wanted our world fixed, but did the Volen?

She sank into an uneasy doze.

Awakened by light streaming in through the skylights, Sam yawned and sat up. This place was real. The man in yellow invited them into his place again and, as they left, she heard the chimes. They made their way to the dining room. The waves still churned back and forth.

After the meal, Liia led them to a ladder in a corner opposite the one they went to the previous day. She ascended, fumbled with something, and a waft of cool air dropped down on them. Liia crawled up and disappeared. Sam followed and found herself outside.

A green hill rose in front of her, and she could hear the crashing of the breakers below. She grabbed the top of the corner of the low wall nearby and caught her breath. Still holding onto the knob, Sam turned and looked out over a vast expanse of green beyond a white wall. All she could do was breathe and soak it in. To her right, she looked out over the dark blue waves of the sea.

How wide it all was, how free.

It came to her that the area was the top of the building and the green was plants. Little towers dotted the plain, including one nearby, which was apparently the top of the green column she had seen inside.

Standing farther along a narrow path between the roof and the hill, Liia said, as if sensing Sam's curiosity, "Those are where other clans come up."

"Why don't you all come out and talk to each other." Sam took a deep breath.

"We do, if we can. No way to know when others are coming up."

"Put it in the note."

Sam moved over, still holding on to the wall, as Brad squeezed out, followed by Max. All sorts of plant aromas, the earthiness of real soil, even the saltiness of the sea, assaulted her nose. Sam was in heaven.

"Wow." Brad's jaw dropped.

"Have you ever seen anything like this?" Sam asked Brad, shivering in the cool breeze.

"No. One place had an area of plants, but it was under a dome."

Max began a little sing-song, bouncing up and down on his toes.

"This is the real world," Liia said. "We call it Amb One."

Sam slowly turned around, just looking. Green expanse on one side, as far as she could see, then green hills in a line along the green plain, and the sea below. She wanted to grab it all and hold it close, forever. She still couldn't believe what was happening to her was real.

"Come," Liia said, taking a trail lined with bushes that led up the side of the hill.

They followed her. Sam touched the leaves that reached out to her as she passed. Soft and slippery. Sam felt something she couldn't define, a feeling of connection with the leaf, the plant, the world.

Liia plucked a wide pink flower and handed it to her. The blossom smelled heavenly and the connection grew stronger.

At the top, they found a flat, grassy area with a small shelter over a seat.

"Sit," Liia said.

Sam and Brad sat, taking in every detail. Sam felt an ecstasy she'd never felt before. Max took his clothes off, dropped down into the grass and rolled around.

"I could stay here forever." Sam sniffed the pink flower again.

"Tempting, isn't it?" Brad rubbed her back.

Liia sat on a wooden seat at the side. "This is our escape."

"I wish we had one." Sam watched Max in the grass, pulling out a handful and sticking it in his mouth.

Liia smiled. "Maybe someday."

Someday, Sam thought, *I will live here, build a little house here, for me and Max.*

They sat and chatted and watched the ball of light too bright to look at move across the sky. When Sam closed her eyes, she felt a hint of a presence — not the others, but a sense of the world, of her mother.

"Take, can we?" Max sat up with a handful of grass and plants.

"If your sector allows." Liia stood.

"Does it?" Sam asked Brad as she opened her eyes.

Was that real, what I felt?

She pushed it away and let the feeling hide in her mind.

He shrugged. "I have no idea. Let's find out."

Max turned his back to them so Liia wouldn't see him stuffing his pouch. He only let Brad, Todd and Sam see him do it.

"Okay, let's go." Brad pulled Sam to her feet.

Sam wanted to record the area on her comm, but she knew, even on her big screen, it wouldn't be the same.

Liia led them back down. Max grabbed leaves and stuffed them into his pockets on the way.

Once they were back inside her clan area, Liia led her away from the others.

"We do not have many credits to spare, but perhaps two meals and the night would suffice."

"That's fine." *It was worth it to spend a day here.*

"I can give you this." She handed Sam a rough brown bag. "Seeds with instructions. Maybe they will grow in your sector."

"Thank you." It would be a project for Max.

They collected the men, and Liia took them on the car to the portal at her level, where they returned the breathers.

"Thanks for everything, especially letting us experience the outdoors," Sam said.

"Come any time," Liia replied.

Sam and her brothers passed through to their sector.

*   *   *

World trembled, moved the soil under the southwest corner of City, and shifted the particles of Volen material.

13

As soon as Sam stepped out of the portal into City at Level Forty-eight, her comm pinged. She had a message: call Todd as soon as they left the portal. After living in Liia's place for a day, her sector appeared even drabber than before.

Now what? Sam thought. She made the call as they waited for a car.

"What's up?"

"Meet me at Stop Twenty. If I'm not there, wait for me. Gotta go." He hung up.

"Well," Sam huffed. She didn't even have a chance to get a word in.

The car showed up, they piled in, and got off at Twenty. Todd popped out of the lift tube as Sam climbed out of the car.

"Hi," she said. "You should see the Ambaak sector. Vines and flowers all over the place."

"That's nice. Did you get your job done?"

"Of course. What's up?"

"There was an attack on a girl with red hair. I'm here to escort you home." Todd did not smile.

"Was she all right?" Sam pulled her own red hair back over her ear.

"She survived."

Todd led them to an up-tube, and they got off two levels above the one they were on.

"Why here?"

"Follow me."

They went two blocks to another tube, down fifteen, over to another and up one, and finally down to her level. They took a cross street to her corner.

"Hey, I'm starving," Brad said. "With four of us, we should be okay. Let's all go to the caff to eat."

"No," Todd said. "We'll go to Sam's place, and I'll go get food."

"Food, need," Max chanted. "Caff, go."

"No, Max. If Todd says it's not safe, we go home." Sam looked about, an uneasy feeling creeping into her bones.

"Here it is." Brad took her arm and led her inside, Max on their heels.

"No," Todd held Max back.

Max jerked away and followed them.

"Come on, you people, this is serious." Todd stood in the doorway. Someone pushed him in and, after a pause, he joined them at their table. "Don't you understand? There's danger if you stay here."

"Sit down, Todd." Brad picked up a menu. "I got us a corner. What can happen here?"

Sam's uneasiness grew. She believed Todd was right. Nothing could happen in here, but outside …

Suddenly she wasn't very hungry. The men ordered the stew; Max, the stew and the meatloaf, and Sam the veggie plate. She ate a few bites and pushed the rest around on her plate. She knew there was only one exit to this place that they could use. And Sam noticed one of the young men behind the counter watching them. He dropped his eyes when he saw her looking.

When the men were done, they rose. The young man had disappeared. At the counter, Sam and Brad slipped their ID cards through the slot, each pressed "2", for two people. A credit for each meal would be docked from their accounts.

Brad led the way out. Because they'd had their evening meal, they would not be allowed in again until morning.

As Brad stepped out the door, a pair of burly men grabbed him and Max, and two others slid large sacks over their heads and bound their arms. Brad kicked out and caught one of the men's legs.

"No," Sam cried, reaching for Max. The four men hustled Brad and Max away. She dug in her bag.

"I told you," Todd called as the other group headed for the down-pole.

He grabbed Sam tightly as she started after them. She went numb. Both Brad and Max gone; she couldn't believe it.

Oneness, protect them and help me get them back. The hell with aliens and City, my mission now is to rescue my brothers.

"I'm sorry, Sam. I told him, but you know how stubborn Brad can be." Todd pounded on the wall.

Sam had never seen him so upset.

"Especially when he's hungry." Sam hoped Brad had some food with him.

She pulled away from Todd and ran across to the tube, flicking her tracer on. When Sam lifted a foot to step on the down platform, Todd pulled her back.

"Can you tell what level they went to?" he asked. "Which way they went from there? What if they went down, over to another tube, up a few levels, then down again, like we did?"

"They aren't nearly as smart as you." Sam sagged against him. "What do we do now?"

"First, go to your place. While you pack up your stuff, I'll report this to Security."

"Pack up?"

"You're not staying there alone. You'll stay with me."

"My store, my business." Sam spoke the words automatically.

"I've got plenty of room on my comm; I'll transfer your business stuff to it. Just like if you get a new comm. You'll have to leave your business one there, but you can take your personal one. I can fix it so you can use that one at my place."

They reached her shop and entered. Sam picked a few items from her shop shelves and dropped them in her bag. Todd went on into her office and reported the abduction.

How are we going to find them? How are we going to get them back?

Thoughts whirled through her head. The pain enveloped her. She could only go through the motions.

Upstairs, Sam threw clothes and personals into her big bag and grabbed images off the walls. In a daze, she made sure the outer door was double-locked and lugged the bag down. She added food bars for Max for when they found him; took Dad's picture and a few other items. The little potted plant was drooping. She watered it and put the pot in a little box to take with her. The plant was so pathetic after Liia's place, but it was hers.

Todd handed her a paper. "Closed for duration", it said. "We'll put this in the door and lock the shop."

"Okay." Sam didn't want to stay there without Max and felt more lost than ever.

"Let's go." Todd picked up her big bag and carried it out through the shop.

Sam locked the office door, used her triple lock she'd never used before on the shop door, and stuck the keys in her bag. Todd and Sam tubed up to his level and over to his apartment. There were only apartments on this level, plus the ubiquitous caffs.

"You get the bedroom," Todd said, dumping her bag in there. Sam followed him. "I'll hook you up with this screen in here, and I'll use the one in the other room."

Sam sat down on the bed as it hit her: both pain and anger.
Who would have done that?

Serious crime was almost unknown in City. A narrow face with beady eyes popped into her mind.
Jerg.

She focused on the anger and pounded on the bed.

I'll get that Volen misfit if it's the last thing I do.

She ran out into the other room. "They need to find Jerg; I'm sure he's behind this. Can you find out if he's on a ship up at Spaceport?"

Todd looked at her. "I can't, but I know someone who can. Why there?"

"Because he came on Waller's ship, so he probably doesn't have a place here."

"Why him?"

"He was Waller's right-hand man and probably knew everything he knew." *Or more.*

A thought on the edge of her mind escaped her.

"Okay. Let me go to work on finding Brad and Max." He turned to his screen.

Sam curled up in the corner of the long seat and watched him. *Please find them,* she thought.

"I'll see if I can track their chips." Todd said.

Most people in the upper levels had identification chips. Sam and Brad had gotten theirs when they were little and living on an upper level, and Max had been chipped before they brought him home the first time.

Todd keyed menus and said, "Ah, here they are. I've set up the deep tracker, and they appear to be on Lower Level One, a few streets over from the seawall. That's mostly warehouse storage. That's a good place to stash someone or something you want to hide. You can see it on your screen, too."

Sam sat up. "Can we go get them?"

"Not right now. I'll tell Security where they are."

"No. I don't want them anywhere near Max. Tell them about Jerg."

"I did. Now, is there any way you can contact Brad other than by comm, like with your twinness?"

Sam stared at him. "I know he's alive, not hurt badly, but that's it." She'd tried to contact Brad by comm, but got no response.

"It looks like these guys probably dumped them somewhere and are waiting for instructions. Brad's not going to panic, he'll find a way out. We'll keep the tracker on and watch it. If they move, let me know." Todd went back to his screen. "Oh, and don't try to leave. The outer door is locked."

"Todd!" Sam wanted to throw something at him. Instead, she stomped into the bedroom and kicked her bag.

*   *   *

World paused.

14

B RAD STUMBLED AND SHOUTED as the man jerked him along. He could not move his arms; they were tied to his body.

One of the men with Max yelled, "Put your feet down and walk like a man."

Brad smiled when he heard that. Max was going into his hibernation mode. He'd be safe. Only he and Sam could wake Max.

Sammie, I'm sorry, he thought. *Screwed up again. Should have listened to Todd. He'll take care of her. Hope he moves her to his place.*

One of the men shoved Brad onto the tube platform. Brad concentrated. Twenty levels down, off and walk a block, twenty more, now down below ground level. Another block and down again.

Must be near or at the lowest level.

Off, along most of a block, into a building. Down a narrow hall, pushed into a room.

As Brad stumbled and fell, he heard the thump of Max being dropped. The door slid shut and the lock clicked. Brad rolled over and sat up, shaking his head. The breathing hole in the sack had moved around by his ear. As he moved it back over his nose, he smelled dust with a chemical taint.

"Max," he called.

No answer.

He tried to wiggle out of the strap around his arms, but it wouldn't budge. A dim light came from somewhere high on the wall with the door.

After trying box corners and the door handle, he found a large hook in the wall. Standing on tiptoe, he managed to get the strap over the hook and pulled down. He was able to duck clear out of the strap. Brad yanked the bag over his head and crawled over to Max. He used his multitool knife to cut Max's breathing hole wide open and pulled it down.

They'd taken his comm, but didn't find the tool in an inner pocket. He shook Max gently.

"Wake up, it's safe now," Brad said to the back of Max's head, all he could see of him. "Come on, Max."

Underneath Brad's anger at getting them into this mess, fear filled his gut.

Max stirred and tried to stretch.

"Make yourself skinny, and I'll pull the strap off."

Once freed, Max sat up and looked around. "Are we, where? Food, you have?"

Brad pulled a food bar out of his pocket. "Here. we're down on one of the lowest levels. We need to get out of here."

"Locked, door?"

"Yes, and I don't see any other way out. Do you? You can see better."

After wolfing down the food bar, Max rose and nosed around the piles of boxes along the back of the room. Brad could tell the air vent and window were too small even for Max.

"Here." Max beckoned, as the room shook.

Brad stumbled over and helped Max move boxes away from the side wall, revealing a door. Max pushed his way through, Brad right behind him, into another dim storage room. A fountain of water burst through the floor of the room they'd just left.

"This is the bottom level. Let's get out of here."

Brad ran over to the door to the street, found it locked, and Max began shoving boxes away to reveal another door to the next room. Twice more, they yanked stuff away and ran through doors from room to room. The third time, the door opened out on a street. Water and shrieking of City block capsules shifting followed them out.

"To the tubes," Brad yelled as they ran up the street.

They jumped on, and Brad yanked the start lever. As the up-tube moved, people streamed out of the warehouse across the side street, yelling, and one man tried to jump on.

Brad pushed him off. "It won't go with more than two," he called down.

At the next level, Max started to step off.

Brad grabbed him. "No, higher." They started up again, until the lift ground to a stop with the bottom of the doorway to the next level above just visible. Both the pole and the wall were too slick to climb. Brad fought the tendrils of panic.

"Up, me," Max lifted his arms. Brad leaned over, Max climbed on his back and up to Brad's shoulders as he straightened. Max stretched and grabbed the edge of the doorway, Brad pushed him up as high as he could reach, and Max scrambled out.

"Stay there." Brad put his foot in the lower grip strap on the pole and hoisted himself up.

Max reached a long arm down and, using the upper grip, Brad managed to get up to the doorway and out.

"Water, where from?" Max asked as Brad bent and caught his breath.

"The room we were in ruptured. This part is in an aquifer, and the pressure of the water is pushing it up into City. Capsules are separating. Let's take the stairs."

Brad and Max found the stairs in back of the tube and ran up to the next level, ignoring people milling and screaming in the narrow gray streets. Others saw them and followed.

"Two more," Brad said.

They trotted up two more flights before stopping. The shaking felt more pronounced up here. The streets were full of panicked people. One lone Security official tried to get the crowd's attention with no success. Brad went to his side and bellowed with him. Max collapsed, panting. The nearest people turned to them and, soon, quiet rippled through the crowd.

"Go to the safe rooms in your factories. We are assessing the situation. Go to the safe rooms in your factories."

A man larger than the others repeated the message.

Brad looked down at him and said, "Thanks." He looked around for Max. "Are you all right, buddy?"

"Tired. Run, not."

"We need to keep going. Can you get up?" Brad helped Max up, led him to the next stairway, and pushed into the line of people going up.

Men yelled, "Keep moving," and a couple of women were crying. They moved slowly, and Brad helped Max with each step.

More noisy people crowded into the next set of stairs, so Brad said, "Let's go north on this level."

∗   ∗   ∗

"Todd," Sam yelled. "They're moving up." She ran out to the other room, "Brad and Max went sideways, down a street, and now up. They're five levels up now."

"Good." He was looking at an image of water creeping up a stairwell. "They better keep going up. That area of the City is sinking."

"What?"

"Somehow water is getting in at the lowest levels." A message flashed on the screen. "Uh oh."

> Attention, attention. Due to unforeseen circumstances, the tubes in Districts Four, Five, Six, Seven, and Fourteen, Fifteen, and Sixteen are not working. Please stay on your level if at all possible. If you must go to another level, you must use the stairs.

"Unforeseen circumstances." Todd snorted.

Sam returned to the tracker. "They're going up. I know Brad's in great shape, but Max has never climbed stairs like that in his life. If Brad has to carry him, it'll really slow him down. Can we go down and help them?"

"You want to go down sixty flights of stairs? Can you pinpoint exactly which corner they are on? Much better to stay here and keep track of them."

"Well, not exactly. But I know within a block or two."

Her heart sank. She'd done three flights once when the three of them raced up and down ... when they were in school. But sixty flights now?

"Okay." Sam sighed.

Brad and Max had made it up two more levels.

*   *   *

World watched.

15

M AX SLUMPED TO THE GROUND. "Food, need."
Brad panted and leaned against the wall. "Can you make it over there to the caff?"

Max looked up. "Maybe."

Brad hoisted him to his feet, and they stumbled across the street to the caff. Max slumped onto the first seat inside.

"Out," the proprietress demanded. "No food."

Max had already grabbed a loaf of bread from the basket on the counter behind his seat and was gobbling it down.

"No food?" Brad echoed, staring at the woman with gray curls.

"No delivery. No reason given."

"Oh. The lift tubes aren't running in this area. City is sinking."
The old woman nodded. "Thought so."

A young couple walked in, took a loaf of bread from the basket on the counter and sat at a nearby table.

Brad told them, "Sorry, there's no food, just the bread."

"Is it because of the shaking?' the man asked.

Brad nodded. "The tubes aren't working." He turned to the proprietress. "Can you make more bread here?"

"Yes. I have flour for several more days."

"Make as much as you can. It'll be something to eat."

"You don't have to tell me," she snarled.

"Come on, Max. Let's use the facilities." He headed toward the rear of the caff.

The old woman followed them. Max went first. In a few minutes, when he opened the door to leave, the woman shoved Brad in and locked the door.

"Hey," Brad yelled, pounding on the door.

The old woman cackled. "At least I've got some meat, now." The place shook.

"Meat?" Max whispered.

"Us. Excuse me." Brad unbuttoned his trousers.

After Brad was done, he looked at the lock. "Cheap locks down here." He took out his multitool, selected a thin blade, and soon got the lock open. The old woman was nowhere in sight, and he heard a door close.

They ran to the front door, but that lock was much more complicated.

"There's got to be another door, for deliveries." Brad headed for the kitchen. At the end of the kitchen, the lock on the back door was the same as the one on the front door. "Well, let's see what we can find to eat."

Max stuffed himself and his pockets. Brad ate what he could, took a couple of large knives and Max back to the bathroom.

"They'll expect us to be in here." He arranged the door so that it appeared to be locked and sat down to wait. Max curled up in a corner next to Brad.

*   *   *

Sam and Todd watched the reports of the catastrophe. Only the area over the aquafer was sinking, but power and water conduits were being torn apart. Todd had the sound off, and it was eerie watching people running around and pushing each other up the stairways with their mouths moving. Sam kept looking for Brad, but didn't see him. He and Max were probably much farther up.

Even though Todd's place was well inland from the aquifer, it still shook.

"Look, Sam." Todd pointed. On the screen, two sections of a street at an intersection were at different levels. "About a foot difference, I'd say." The cross street was at the same level on both sides, but at a different level from each of the others.

Sam turned away; she couldn't watch anymore. According to the tracker, Brad and Max were not moving. Her uneasiness knotted up.

Sam's screen pinged. She jumped up to check the message. She'd never been able to ignore the ping of an incoming message.

It was Dondo. She hadn't heard from him since she called to report Max's disappearance.

Call me.

Not now.

Sam checked her other messages. Someone wanted to know why her shop was closed. She ignored that one. But Dondo kept nagging at her, so she finally broke down and called him.

"Have you found Max yet?" Dondo demanded.

"I know about where he is. They escaped the kidnappers, but are caught in the mess down below."

"Good. I have received a request for your services. The Ghind, in Sector Five, have a thief in their midst, and requested an outsider."

Sam closed her eyes. "No, I can't go now, not until we get Brad and Max back."

"You must. If they have indeed escaped and are on their own, Brad can handle it, with Todd on your end. Tomorrow morning, you will take a shuttle up to Spaceport and the local flier around to Sector Five."

"But that's on the other side of the world." Her heart dropped even further.

"Yes. You will be met at the local port by a guide who will take you down to their meeting place. The Ghind are not aware of any but basic technology, although they do understand Standard. There is a comm system set up there, which only The Elder knows how to work."

"The elder?" *This could not be happening now.*

"The oldest person is known as The Elder, the final arbitrator. The guide will take you to her. They do know there are other peoples on their world, they simply choose to keep their lifestyle the way it has always been. While their area is outdoors, they are surrounded by walls of other sectors or cliffs. They hunt small creatures and run the grain fields between them and the next sector. They also make intricate carvings out of the dead wood of their trees, which they trade with other sectors occasionally. Some of the carvings have disappeared. You must find them or discover what happened to them."

"Why me?" Sam felt she was being pushed into a position she knew little of and didn't want to be in.

"Because you and your brothers are the core group from the Terrans' Sector, which is the center of the worldwide association."

"What!" Sam almost shut the connection, that was so impossible.

She knew they were one of the top families, intelligence-wise, and the governor was a direct descendant from the captain of the second ship that brought the ancestors to this world, but this was too much.

"What's really going on?" Sam demanded.

A pause.

I guess he didn't expect that question.

"We will explain when you have visited all the other sectors and we gather you and representatives from each sector together."

"You mean I have to go to all the sectors?" *No.*

"Yes. In time."

"It looks to me like we've already run out of time," Sam said.

"Yes. That is why you must go tomorrow."

"By myself?" *Again, no. Not that I was scared. Much.*

"Yes. You may take any of your gadgets you can use without the Ghind seeing what they are." He paused. "It should not take you very long. Apparently there are two different opinions among the people as to what happened."

Sam sighed. He was right about Brad and Todd. They could handle Max.

"Okay."

"Call me when you return."

"Of course."

Sam went out and told Todd what she had to do. The tracker showed Max and Brad on the same level.

"How are you on food?" Sam asked. "Max will be ravenous when he gets here. And I'm hungry, come to think of it."

"So am I." He stood up. "We'll go to the caff, get two meals each, and bring them back here."

"Good."

When they returned, the blips had not moved. "Can you tell where that is?" Sam asked.

Todd pulled up a map and crosschecked it with the tracker map. "I think they're here. It's a safe area. They've probably stopped for the night."

"I'm sure they're exhausted. I hope Max got something to eat somewhere."

*   *   *

World stirred open a vent beneath the sea.

16

B RAD WOKE TO NOISE OUT IN THE CAFF. Someone was moving
around out there. He nudged Max. "Wake up, but don't move."

Max grunted but stayed curled up.

"They're in there," someone said, out in the caff.

"Max, sit up." His companion hunched up. "Here's a knife. Stab
like this." Brad demonstrated, holding it straight out on front of
himself.

Max stabbed a pile of towels on a shelf under the sink and
dropped the knife. "No."

Brad picked it up. "Run for the front door. Whoever's out
there may not have locked it."

"Okee."

Suddenly the room slanted, and the two of them slid along the
wall. Max curled up again. Somebody yelled out in the caff amid a
cacophony of crashing dishes and pots.

"Max, get up," Brad hissed, yanking the other to his feet. "We
gotta get out of here."

He opened the door a crack. Tables and chairs, part of the structure, had not moved, but dishes, utensils, and mugs lay all over the floor. From the sounds, the people were in the rear of the kitchen.

"Come on."

Brad opened the door wide and they ran uphill to the front door, Brad brandishing the knife. Someone screamed in the kitchen. Brad pulled Max out and shut the door. They ran across to the stairway and up. He stuck the knives in his belt. The north-south street across the next intersection was a foot higher than the east-west way, and slanting.

After the third stairway, they stopped to rest. Max pulled out a hunk of bread from a pocket.

"Don't eat it all now, we don't know when we'll find more food." The caff across the street had a big sign on the door: "Closed, no food." A pair of men stopped to read the sign, shrugged and went around the corner.

Brad and Max went up two more levels. Again, they stopped. Max slumped to the ground and Brad leaned against a building. A security officer came by and asked them for ID.

"Our comms were taken when we were kidnapped," Brad said. "We're trying to get home. Level Thirty-five Above."

"You expect me to believe that? Now, what are you really doing down here?"

"I told you. Are there any caffs open around here?"

The security officer snorted. Before he could speak, the place shook, and Brad grabbed Max to steady him.

"Since I have no place to put you, I'm going to let you go. What's the matter with him?"

Max had made himself shorter and wider, straining the seams on his shirt and pants.

"He needs medication, that's why we're in such a hurry. Say, do you have a comm I can borrow to call my sister? She'll be worried sick."

"Sorry, no."

Brad and Max trudged up another flight. The caff there did not have a sign on it. "Stay here." Brad trotted over. A young woman with black hair tied back opened the door with a sign in her hand.

"Sorry, mister, we're out of food." She hung up the sign.

"Not even bread? My friend over there," he pointed to Max huddled up by the wall, "desperately needs food."

The woman looked over at Max and smiled. "One bread." She darted in and came out with a long, narrow loaf.

"Thank you. Is there anything I can do for you?"

"Food cupboard is stuck. My helper left. Maybe you can open it?"

"I'll try." Brad broke the loaf in half, trotted across and gave Max one half, sticking the other in his pocket. He followed the woman inside to the kitchen. Using one of the knives, he forced the door open, breaking the knife. He saw where it stuck and honed it down with the other knife. "Should be all right now." He gave her the knife.

"Thank you. Food for me." She reached down a couple packets of dried protein product and gave them to him.

"Thanks. Take care." Brad ran back to Max.

"Good, bread." Max wiped his face on his sleeve. He was partway between fat and normal, his hands furry.

"Keep your hands in your pockets." Brad heaved Max to his feet. "Up we go."

Halfway up the next stairway, the shaking dropped them on their knees. Brad cussed at a loud crashing above them, and Max whimpered. When the world settled down, they pulled themselves to their feet and continued up.

The entrance was partially blocked. Max squeezed through, but Brad got stuck halfway. In his fight with panic, panic was winning. Max pushed at the opening, and Brad scraped through.

Max crumpled to the ground. "More, no," he gasped.

Brad gave him one of the packets of protein. With no idea what time of day or night it was; all he could think to do was to keep going. He had no idea how close they were to ground level, but hoped they could find a working up-tube there. The caff at this intersection was closed.

After a while, Max climbed to his feet and they walked north, dodging around a number of people wandering around: men cussing, a few women crying. Brad felt a brief desire to help, but getting Max home was more important than strangers.

Several blocks later, Brad found a rest area — a square building that sat in the center of a fake park. Inside, there was no food, but they found beds. Max collapsed onto one, and Brad lay on another.

Sammie, I'm coming home, he thought.

*   *   *

In the morning, the round-faced woman at the counter in the back served gruel and bread. Brad and Max feasted. Brad asked, but no one knew where they could find a comm.

"Are you able to climb stairs?" Brad asked Max, whose face was covered with fur down to his eyebrows and along his cheeks and chin.

"Must go up, we?"

"Yes, but also north, toward mountains, to find up-tube."

"One, maybe."

They slogged up one level to a residential area. There, several people, mostly women, approached from his right side.

"Hello," one said. "You came up?" Brad nodded. "How is it down there?"

"Bad. Going up?"

"Yes. We are going to find someone who can get us food. You have any?"

"No. We need some too," Brad told her.

"Come with us."

"No, too tired. We're going north to find a working up-tube."

"They're all dead," another, older, woman said.

"You know that for sure?"

She nodded, but Brad sensed she wasn't sure.

"Good luck. Come on, Max."

They trudged onward along the street.

*   *   *

World shifted under the aquafer.

17

S AM DEPARTED RIGHT AFTER BREAKFAST THE NEXT DAY. Todd gave her a pass and directions for the up-tube in Centrex and the shuttle to Spaceport.

Brad and Max were moving north. Sam wanted to wait for them, but didn't dare. She had checked on the Ghind, but Dondo had told her more than the web did.

At Spaceport, she called Todd.

"They are still heading north," he reported. "Go do your job and don't worry about them."

Ha, Sam thought. *How can I not worry?*

She found the silver flier and presented her ID. They sailed over the central mountains, through a pass between two high, black and jagged peaks that stabbed the blue sky. She barely noticed them, unable to enjoy the scenery; her mind on her two lost menfolk.

They came in over an area of cliffs and tree-filled valleys. Lower down, the valleys were larger, strewn with groups of trees and hills. The pilot landed the craft in a wide-open area near a tall hill. Sam didn't see people anywhere.

The pilot-guide led Sam up a winding trail to a large cave entrance on the other side of the hill. As they climbed, Sam felt the same connection to the world she'd felt above Ambaak.

What on City was this?

At the top, she found an ancient woman swathed in wrinkles and furs who sat in a contraption that rocked back forth on a wide area in front of the cave. A younger man sat cross-legged next to her on a pile of furs.

"Elder," the guide indicated the old woman. He uttered another word Sam didn't understand and motioned to her.

"Good," The Elder said in the voice of a much younger woman.

Sam thought she smiled, but it was hard to tell with all the wrinkles.

"Go." She made a shooing motion at the guide with a brown claw of a hand.

"Hello," Sam said, not knowing what else to do.

She nodded. "You are?"

"I'm Samanda Lar, known as Sam. Dondo sent me."

"Ah. You know some carvings are missing." Sam nodded.

She murmured, "Joba," to the dark-skinned man next to her.

He stood, a very tall, slim man with graying hair, a gray fur around his waist, and bowed his head to the old woman.

"Joba, my grandson." The Elder continued, "The carvings of two sisters have disappeared. They each say the other took them; possibly destroyed, possibly not. You must determine which, and location of the carvings."

To Joba, "This is she who will find the missing items. Show her the place where they were and answer her questions."

Joba ducked his head and turned to Sam. "Come."

Sam followed him down the trail and into the forest. Leaves and branches reached out to her, and she felt the hint of a presence.

What was this?

To put it out of her mind, she asked, "When did this happen?"

"Two days past, a young one saw them missing."

"When were they last seen before that?"

He shrugged. "Many days."

That didn't help. They arrived at a huge tree laying on its side, hollowed out. Inside, rows of shelves lined the sides, and rows of wooden carvings lined the shelves. Some looked like animals, some looked like people, but most were abstract curls and spirals.

Joba led her to an empty section at the end of a shelf. "Here is where they were."

"Were they special? More important than the others?"

"No. Like all." He waved an arm around.

"Why would anyone take them?"

Joba shrugged. "Can come look any time."

Could one of the sisters have been jealous of the other and taken them all? Sam decided not to ask that question yet.

Like he said: the place was wide open, and anyone could come in at any time. But why would anyone else want them?

"Do people keep any in their homes?"

Joba nodded. "Carvers give to partners, offspring."

"How many carvers are there?"

"Most people carve."

That doesn't help, Sam thought. "Can I meet the two people who carved the missing pieces?"

"I will bring them. Stay here." He left.

Sam sat on a bench to wait, studying the nearest items.

They must have very fine knives and files.

There was no reason she could see that someone would take those particular carvings, except they were at the far end and less noticeable if missing. But if everyone carved, they were only worth what their owner wanted. So that left revenge, so she'd see how the two reacted toward each other.

It was very quiet; the place was empty. They must be keeping the people away from her on purpose. Sam concentrated on a little carved creature with a long snout. Silky smooth, its tiny black eyes appeared to be looking at her.

Joba returned with two young women — girls, really. Both tall and dark, with long faces; one had a scar down her cheek. They eyed each other warily, and Sam even more warily.

"Hello," she said, standing. "I am Sam."

"This Jema and Jeul."

Jema and Jeul stood side by side, a person-width of space between them, and stared at Sam.

"You carved the pieces that are missing. These are all beautiful. Are you sisters?"

"All sisters," Jema sneered.

Sam stood there speechless. She had no idea what she could or should say, what words to say or not say. Like the others, what she could find out was no more than what Dondo had told her.

After a moment, she spoke. "Forgive me if I use an improper word. I was not given a chance to familiarize myself with your culture. Have you found partners yet?"

Ignoring each other, both girls said yes.

Sam glanced at Joba. His face was expressionless. "Ah. By any chance would it be the same man?"

"He's mine," Jema said.

Jeul, the one with the scar, shrugged. "He came to me first."

Sam recalled girls she knew from her teens. She looked at the man. "I suggest you look wherever Jeul keeps her private things." Sam didn't think she would have destroyed the carvings, it would not be easy to do.

Jeul lifted her hand to her face. "How did you know?"

"That." Sam nodded at her hand, which Jeul quickly dropped. "Males of every species seem to prefer attractive mates. I suspect you took them so Jema would not have one to present to him, and yours, too, so you wouldn't be suspected."

"Yes," Jeul whispered.

Sam ignored the smug look on Jema's face. "Joba, can you bring me the young man in question?"

He nodded and left.

"How do you people choose mates?"

Jeul looked up. "At coming of age time, twice a year, all select two, then Elder interviews and matches. Boba chose us, me first. Elder usually gives to first choice, but he said he wanted her."

"Oh, dear." Sam shook her head.

Joba arrived with a tall boy. "Here is Boba."

"So, Boba, why did you change your mind?" Sam gave him a stern look.

He stared at her red hair and shrugged. "Why you care?"

"All females are sisters, right?"

The girls nodded.

"I care about all my sisters. What you see on the outside is not important. Inside is the real beauty. I suggest you sit and talk about important things with both girls, then decide."

"Yes," Jeul breathed. Jema snorted.

Boba looked at both girls. "Who are you to tell me what to do?"

"The Elder brought Samanda to fix problem. This is part of her fix. Do you want Elder to know you did not cooperate?" Joba told the boy.

Boba shook his head. "I will do."

"Good. All go now. Jeul, bring carvings here."

The three ran off, Jeul with a smile.

Joba paid Sam and took her to a small cave. "You will stay tonight. Guide will return in the morning."

"No, I have to go home now."

"Cannot."

He walked away. The sun hung low in the west.

Sam looked around the cave, ready to cry, scream, or both. Dimly lit, from the entrance and an opening above, the cave contained a pile of blankets and a table with a bowl of some sort of stew.

Wonderful.

She didn't see anything to pee in, so she went behind a tree.

The knot in her insides turned over. She couldn't call Todd from here; the amplifier she needed was in her shop, where it did her no good at all.

Oneness, please keep Brad and Max safe.

Sam sniffed the stew, wrinkled her nose, and dug out her food tester. The button blinked red: Dangerous. She dumped it outside and ate one of her food bars to quiet her complaining stomach.

The blankets were no better, they barely padded the rock floor. She spent most of the night wrapped in them sitting up against the wall. She dreamed of words in her mind.

I am World. You are other. We may coexist.
She said, "Of course this is a world," and woke herself up.
What on City?
Sam shook her head and tried to sleep.

In the morning, the guide returned and took her back up to Spaceport. Sam slept most of the way. As soon as she stepped inside the building, she called Todd.

"I'll be there in a couple of hours."

*   *   *

World watched.

18

B ACK AT TODD'S, SAM CHECKED THE TRACKER. The blip moved a
little bit and stopped.

"At least they're still alive," she said. She still wanted to run
down and find them, but she knew that wasn't practical right now.

"We'll have to wait until everything settles down," Todd said.
"Or, I should say, when City finally settles down."

"Why? That could be much too late."

"I have a couple of assistants who will be going down."

"But, Todd ..." *Didn't he understand how important Brad and
Max were to me?*

Just then, her comm pinged. Dondo.

"Nothing new on your brothers," he began. "The Felce want
to see someone from another sector who can help them with a
problem, with access to higher authority."

"Who, me? Why?"

"I do not know, but the request was approved. Go to
Spaceport in the morning. A flier will take you to the Felce local

port. Tube down to the bottom. There will be two doors. Go out the smaller door and then forward out of the rear cave. Someone will meet you. They may appear threatening, but they will not harm you. Report when you return."

"Of course." Sam cut the connection and told Todd.

Not again, she thought. *Why can't he leave me alone? Why do I have to be the one to take care of these problems in other sectors? How much more of this am I going to have to handle?*

"Your pass from the other day is still good," Todd said. "Think of it this way. You're getting out of here and seeing new places."

"I wouldn't mind, later, after Brad and Max get back, but I can't enjoy it not knowing what's happening with them." Sam pushed her hair back.

"I know, but we have to do what we have to do."

"Thanks a lot." Sam snorted.

*   *   *

Brad and Max sat on a bench in the park area outside a rest stop. He had been able to get a small bowl of stew for Max and added the other packet of dried protein to it. All he had was a small hunk of bread, after giving half of it to Max.

Brad was running on automatic. They had to stop every block to rest, but the only way out was to keep going. A sign caught his eye: "North-south car two blocks" with an arrow pointing west.

"Look, Max." Brad pointed to the sign.

"Go, we?"

"If it's still running."

They rose and headed down the street. A car appeared as they arrived at the stop. They stumbled on and collapsed into seats. Down here, in Below, they could hop on any car without paying. Brad knew the cost was paid through workers' payroll deductions. When the car began to move, he sank into a doze on the uncomfortable wooden seat, with Max curled up beside him. He awoke when the car stopped and beeped at the end of the line.

"Come on, Max. Time to get off." He pulled Max to his feet, and they stumbled out of the car. Two children huddled on the nearby bench looked up eagerly, then slumped. The little girl began to cry. The boy, a few years older, sighed.

"Hello." Brad plodded over to them. "Waiting for someone?"

"Mom and Dad."

"I'm Brad and this is Max. We're trying to get back to our sister. How long have you been waiting?"

"Two days."

"How long since you've eaten?"

The boy shrugged.

"We're hungry too. Let's see if we can find a caff."

"That one's closed."

"There's a tube. Let's see if it works."

"Dad said to stay here until they come."

Brad thought, *What if they don't?*, but didn't say it aloud.

"We'll leave them a note." He took out a little notebook and a pencil.

The boy scribbled something, pulled the page out, and stuck it on the back of the bench with a piece of something sticky he dug out of his pocket.

At the tube, Brad discovered that it went up, but not down.

"No problem," he said. "We want to go up." They took the tube up to Level One Below, where it stopped. The nearby caff was closed, but there was an east-west car. Brad thought it would be safer to go west, so they took the westbound car. At the west end, the four of them stepped off and walked back a block to an open caff.

This one was small, and not as well-lit as the ones in Above. The food wasn't as good either, Brad thought. They found a table, ordered as much as they could on the boy's child-comm, and used the facilities. Large plates and bowls arrived, with three loaves of bread. The boy took a few bites, told his sister to eat, and started gulping.

"Take it easy," Brad said. "You too, Max."

The server brought large mugs of a pale, sweetish liquid.

Once they were sated, Brad burped and spoke. "There has to be a way to get from here to Ground. I'm going to look for stairs."

Max groaned.

"It'll only be one flight," Brad said as he left. "You stay here."

He crossed the street and found a door to what he thought was a stairway, but it wouldn't open. There was a slot in the door about four by six inches, and he could see enough to tell it was a stairway up. He returned to the caff.

"Come on. Max, I need your help."

Max jumped up. "Okee."

The boy paid, and they left. "What did you see in there?" the boy asked.

"Stairs."

At the stairway, Max extended an eye stalk into the opening. "Unlock, can, maybe."

He pulled back his eye, narrowed his hand and stuck it in the slot. After some fumbling, something clicked, and the door opened.

They climbed up a longer stairway than usual and found another locked door. Max repeated his lock opening maneuver, pushed the door open, and they came out into brighter light.

This street was wider, and the buildings a lighter gray.

"Aren't we going back to the car place?" the boy asked.

"Do you really think your parents are coming?"

The boy looked at him, then down at his feet. "No," he whispered. "But Momma said not to go with strangers."

"We're not strangers. We've had a meal together."

Now what? Brad thought.

They were off in a corner of the sector. They could tube up to Thirty-Five — Todd's level — but he wasn't sure where Todd's place was. He could get there from Sam's place. *Maybe we should go there first.*

*   *   *

World paused.

19

S AM FOUND THE DIRECTIONS EASY TO FOLLOW. The flier was the same as the others — a silver four-seater with windows. Greenery below was sparse, and she wondered why no one had planted anything on their silvery roofs. The other sectors they passed over were green with trees and smaller plants. The flier docked at a port similar to the one where Todd kept his ship. She departed, found the down-tube, and stepped onto the platform.

At the bottom of the tube way, Sam passed through the smaller door and stopped. She could barely see in the cave's dimness, but a blob of light straight ahead drew her.

This led into a bigger, brighter cave with a wide entrance. Just outside, a large, silvery animal with a long narrow tail lay stretched out nearly as long as Sam was tall. Female, Sam sensed. The creature's triangular head swiveled toward Sam, and she yawned widely, displaying a lot of long, sharp teeth.

Sam stopped. *Was this a Felce?*

In one smooth motion, the being swooped to her feet. Standing on her hind legs, she looked Sam in the eyes.

Sam shook inside, but kept eye contact. The creature's pale blue eyes displayed a vertical pupil. The Felce dropped down onto her front feet and sat on her haunches. Lifting a paw, she licked it and swiped it across her face. The fur-covered paw revealed fingers with retractable claws and a separate thumb.

"Me, Maya," she said. "Oo?"

"I'm Samanda from the Terran sector. What can I do for you?"

Maya rose to her feet, stretched her whole body, front and back, and moved along the trail that led downward through a tunnel of trees. Sam had to trot to keep up. Again, leaves and limbs reached for her.

After several minutes, they stopped at an open area in front of a cave overlooking a wide space below. Several creatures like Maya worked on something — Sam couldn't tell what from up there — on low tables as they sat on the ground. Others prowled in the shadows.

GETTING READY TO HUNT, came into Sam's mind. *PREY NOT REAL.*

Somehow, she was not astonished at hearing the creature's voice in her head.

"But you eat it."

Maya nodded.

FAKE PREY WITH MEAT INSIDE. NOT PREY MEAT. KITS NOT GROWING WELL. Apparently, she was unable to speak more than a few sounds aloud.

"I see," Sam said. "Our people are not as tall and do not live as long as our ancestors. That's happening in other sectors, too." How was she able to hear Maya?

IS THIS WORLD. HOW WE FIX?

"I don't know yet. Are you having any problems with your land?"

TREES FEEL LIKE TREES, BUT NOT REAL. CAVE AT BOTTOM COLLAPSED.

"Our City is collapsing, too. No one seems to know what to do about it."

Maya switched her tail. *NOT GOOD. YOU EAT MEAT?*

"We get proteins made up to look like meat. There's no place for animals in our City. All caves, no trees." Sam looked at the trees around her. They appeared real.

SAD.

Sam nodded.

They sat together in silence, under the trees. Warmth and peace wrapped around them.

This isn't real, like at Liia's, but it's a lot better than my place.

ALL HUNT, EXCEPT VERY OLD, VERY YOUNG, MOTHER WITH NEW KITS OR READY TO BEAR YOUNG. I GO LATER. ALL GROW PLANTS; OLDER FEMALES MAKE MASH WITH NUTS FOR KITS BEING WEANED. She flowed to her feet.

Sam rose and followed her into the cave.

A small fire flickered inside, and a series of stones on edge with flat ones across the tops made shelves. An assortment of pottery pots, plates, and figures lined them, some in blue or purple.

WE MAKE. She picked up a little purple pot with her thumb and paw-fingers and held it out to Sam. *COLOR FROM BERRIES NOT GOOD TO EAT.*

Sam took it and turned it in her hand. "It's beautiful." She tried to give it back.

NO. YOU KEEP SO YOU REMEMBER. YOU TELL WHOEVER IN CHARGE WE NEED REAL PONGO MEAT. COME BACK SOMETIME.

"Okay, I will. Thank you."

They left the cave and ambled back up the trail. Maya told Sam her people had been brought here because the pongo on the island on which they lived were dying out, because the pongos' food was no longer good. She accompanied Sam into the big cave and, at the exit to the tube cave, sent, *FAREWELL. WE MEET AGAIN.*

"Yes," Sam said.

Sam tubed up, flew back to Spaceport, and arrived down at Todd's just in time for late meal. He had already fetched food. Brad and Max's location had not changed. She told him about the Felce.

"Felines," Todd said. "That's different. And you heard her in your mind?"

"Yes. After I got used to it, it felt natural." Sam smiled.

"I don't remember hearing about that."

"On the screen, all it said was what they looked like and how they lived. Nothing about their culture."

"Not surprised." Todd picked up his napkin.

After they finished eating, she called Dondo and reported.

"I don't know how we can get their pongo meat, unless you can go back to their world and get some," Sam said. "Have I got to all the sectors yet?"

"No. I will pass your request along." He disconnected.

"Well," Sam snorted. "How are your assistants?" she asked Todd.

"They are still trying to find a way down. All tubes they've found so far only go down to the ground level."

Todd showed her a notice on his screen.

All levels below ground level are closed. If you reside in levels 1-5, the first five above ground, you must monitor news regularly. We do not anticipate any damage there, but you should be prepared.

"Oh, no." She prayed to the Oneness for Brad and Max to be safe.

*   *   *

World reached out to the one.

20

S AM SHOWED TODD THE LITTLE PURPLE POT and put it on the shelf with the figurine from the Ghind, next to her little plant. It had three sets of leaves now. That reminded her of the seeds Liia had given her: there were three of them, a little bag of dirt, and instructions.

Max was supposed to have planted them, but he wasn't there. The knot inside her tightened. She felt helpless. There was nothing she could do find him and Brad right now.

"Todd, I need some pots for the seeds Liia gave me. Do you have anything like that?"

"I don't think so. I'll look." He poked around in his cabinets, but did not find any. "I'll see if I can pick up a couple tomorrow."

Todd's comm pinged.

"Hey, Bill," he said.

Pause.

"Not anywhere? Okay, keep looking."

Todd ended the call.

"That notice was right," he told Sam. "Below is totally closed off. Good news is Brad and Max are moving up again. All they need to do is keep going until they hit Ground Level."

"How long?"

"Depends on how many levels they can go up in a day, and if they can find food."

"Food," Sam echoed. "Oh. Max needs a lot to keep his man shape." Icy coldness gripped her chest.

"There's a severe shortage down there. Most of the caffs are closed. Don't worry. Brad will figure something out."

"I hope." *Oh please, help them find a way up and food soon.*

*   *   *

In the morning, Todd got a call from his office. "I have to go in. You stay right here. I don't want to have to go looking for you, too."

After Todd left, Sam tidied up the place and put her clothes in a drawer he had emptied for her. The tracker showed that Brad and Max had not moved yet.

Maybe they found a good place to sleep.

On the news, more capsules had slipped Down Below but, quote, everything was being taken care of, end quote.

Sure, Sam thought.

Dondo called. "Explain your message."

"Maya, the one I talked to, said the fake meat they put inside the fake pongos does not have all the nutrients they need. The kits are not growing properly. She wants real pongo meat and real trees. Is it possible for someone to go to their home world and get some?"

"I see." He paused. "I will pass your message on to the Volen. They will decide. It may not be possible. Now. We don't expect your location to receive any damage, but you must consider finding an alternate location closer to the mountains and higher."

"We have. What are you doing to take care of the mess in Down Below? Brad and Max are still there."

"It is being taken care of. I will call you when I have another assignment." He cut off.

116

"Well," Sam snorted. She was beginning to sense that Dondo had some other plan he wasn't telling them about. She wondered whether he was human ... or something else. In the database, she found a single sentence.

Dondo, of unknown background, is liaison between City and the Volen.

Unknown background, huh, Sam thought. She looked up Volen, but all she could find was a notice saying:

Information not available.

Sam sat and glowered at the screen. If Dondo wasn't human, as she suspected, then their world and City were being run by aliens — aliens they didn't even know.

How much did they care for our welfare? Our world is falling apart, and what are they doing about it? For all I know, they are causing the falling apart, for some reason of their own.

Sam recalled what she'd read just before her personal world fell apart — something about Volen material not lasting forever.

Sam slammed her fists on the table. All this on top of the monster knot of worrying about Brad and Max in her innards. She jumped up, ran around the apartment, and tried the door. After she figured out what kind of lock he had, she got out her tools and opened it. She ran out, slamming it behind her, and ran and ran down the street. When she finally stopped and bent over to catch her breath, she realized she had no idea how far she'd come.

Sam turned, started back, and became aware she didn't know which place was Todd's apartment. They all looked alike. She'd never noticed the address number above the door; she'd only been there a few times. She kept going. When she crossed the second street, she saw Todd headed toward her.

He broke into a run. "I told you to stay in the apartment. How did you get out?" he yelled when Sam was within hearing distance.

Approaching him, she said, "I'm an inquiry agent, remember? I have tools of the trade. I'm sorry, I just had to get out of there."

Todd held the door open, Sam walked in, and he let loose. He called her every name from "idiot" to "earthrat". Sam had never seen him this furious. She was learning a lot about Todd.

When he ran down, he pulled her into a hug, and she didn't try to fight him.

"Don't you see, Sam? I love you and I can't stand the thought of losing you, or even you getting seriously hurt."

"Oh, Todd." Sam hugged him back. He was all she had, now. "I'm sorry, this situation is driving me bonkers."

"I know." He let her go. "I have to go back for a while, but I wanted to grab something to eat, and check on you."

"Oh. Dondo called, and when I asked about Below, he said they were working on it."

"Sure." Tod snorted.

He led her to the seat. They ate a bit, and he told her that everyone in the office was wondering when their capsule was going to fall into the pit.

"I told them we were nowhere near the danger zone, but that was all they could talk about."

"The Volen knew about the aquafer, right?" Sam asked. Todd nodded. "So why did they build so much stuff on top of it?"

"I've wondered about that. I do know that once they got up to twenty levels up or so, all the way across, they had to keep the roof even because of the solar panels. And the more people who came along, the more levels they had to build."

"But couldn't they have dug the Below levels away from the aquafer?"

"The areas at the east and north sides are solid rock, and, since the Ambaak sector has no Below, the Volen couldn't go too close to their side. And the Volen material is very light. Maybe it can only last a certain length of time and its time is up."

"Hunh," Sam grunted. "I guess they didn't count on all the heavy stuff inside the block capsules."

"Right."

He booted up his screen. There was nothing new. Just, "It's being taken care of." He set his screen so Sam could research the ancestors' early history and returned to work.

Sam went back as far as she could. The first ship's crew were people who wanted to come; the colonists were unwanted on Old Earth. The second ship carried people who wanted to come. Most of the unwanteds were glad to be here and have a new life, even though it meant hard work.

She was fascinated, and the time sped by until Todd returned with a couple of people. He introduced the tall, skinny guy with caterpillar eyebrows as Bill, and the older woman as Susan.

"This is Samanda, a spyshop keeper and inquiry agent," Todd announced.

"Oh my. I've been wanting to meet you," Susan said with her little triangular mouth. "Todd has talked so much about you."

"Welcome to our place," Sam said. She smiled.

"Susan keeps all our files organized and up to date." Todd put a bag of food on the table. The other two had also brought bags of food.

"I do research Todd doesn't have time for ... or doesn't want to do," Bill said with a grin.

"He's a big help, and so is Susan." Todd pulled containers out of his bag, and they all sat down.

As they ate, Todd said, "I brought Bill and Susan here to meet you, Sam. They are going to arrange and lead teams to go down and do whatever they can. It doesn't appear that either the government or Security is doing much."

"How are they going to get Down Below?" Sam moved a plate around.

"There is one stairway we can unblock, at the east end," Bill said. "The car on level four down is running for several blocks. We'll take that over as far as it goes."

"How soon will you go? Can you look for Brad and Max?" Sam wanted to ask to go with, but knew the answer would be no.

"We're planning on three days from now." Susan smiled. "We've got most of our people, and we're arranging a place to meet. We're still collecting supplies. And we will look for your brothers."

"If you need anything from my tec shop, I'll gladly donate it." *Finally, a ray of hope.*

"Thanks," Susan said. "Can we go look now?"

"Yes," Todd said.

The four of them tubed down to Sam's shop. Bill and Susan collected a few tools and an explosive kit. Sam checked her office, dumped a few more items in her bag, plus all the food she could find. When they returned to Todd's, Sam made a list of what they took.

Susan and Bill left the next day. Sam gave her an image of Brad, described Max, and told them he was probably in his furry natural form. They promised to keep in touch, calling three times a day.

"Dondo better not call me," Sam said, as Todd closed and locked the door behind them.

"Dondo," he repeated. "Did you sense anything non-human about him?"

Sam stopped and turned to him. "Yes. I've wondered about that. There's something odd about him, but I can't put a finger on it."

"I think he's an android. His voice and movements seem unnatural."

"An android?" Sam asked.

"A man-shaped robot. I looked it up. The Volen created them for unspecified purposes."

"Uh-huh. So they could do anything." Sam rolled her eyes. "Anything the Volen wanted."

Todd grinned. "Exactly. But I haven't heard of any others."

They wandered over to his screen. "Look, they're heading north."

"Good."

*　　　*　　　*

World watched.

21

B RAD, MAX, AND THE CHILDREN tubed up to Twenty, but the car service was down for repairs. Or so the sign said.

"Let's go this way," Brad started down the northbound street, along lighter gray buildings with less trash than Below, and the others followed.

A few blocks later, they found a rest area. Brad led Max down the walk between gray-green floor with gray seats under fake trees to the front entrance of the building. A few people sat on the benches: a gray-haired man apparently asleep, a young woman watching two little boys playing in the fake grass.

Inside, he saw gaming screens lining the front wall, with young men at most of them. Brad and his group proceeded down the hallway between the sleeping room and the dining area to the food in the rear. He got them some food at the back counter, and they found a table. After they ate, Brad made arrangements for beds for them.

* * *

In the morning, the car service was still down. Brad decided to tube up to Thirty-Five and call Todd. But when they got there, Brad couldn't remember Todd's number. He had it programmed into his comm, which he no longer had.

Brad found a caff and, after a midday meal, Brad decided to go to Liia's. They tubed up to Forty-Eight, walked a block over to the portal and through, to Ambaak's top level.

Since the Ambaak car system would not accept Jim's Terran credits, they walked down the car tunnel.

"They could at least have some benches along here," Brad muttered.

Although he didn't know exactly how far it was, he knew this sector was less than half as wide as the human sector. And Liia's was at the far end. Doors along the south wall led to other clan blocks.

Brad knocked at the next one they came to. No response. Same thing at the next door. At the third door, a young woman with dark hair opened the door a crack and peered out.

"Hello." Brad smiled. "My name is Brad Lar. We need to get to Liia's place at the far end, and our credits won't work here. Could you loan us enough to take the car?"

"Why should I?"

"Because the children can't walk that far, and my friend Max here is sick. I'll see that you get paid back. Also, you need to know, if you don't already, that this world is having serious problems. The bottom layers are falling apart."

"No!" She put her hand to her mouth.

"Yes, I'm afraid so. You need to get with Liia and the other clans. Your people need to work together."

She slammed the door shut, then opened it a moment later with a small, black box in her hand. He backed out of the way as she stepped over to the ticket machine. "I am Dori. Tell Liia I am in unit 4803. Good luck."

Brad and his group waited for the next car and piled on.

"Real windows."

The boy ran to a seat and stuck his nose on the glass. His sister pushed in beside him. Brad and Max took the seat across from them. A rolling screen of scenery made it appear they were riding through the countryside.

At the end, Brad and his companions left the car, and he led them to Liia's door. After a moment, a slot in the door opened, then the door itself swung wide.

"Brad," Liia exclaimed. "Where's Sam?"

"At home. Max and I were kidnapped. It's a long story."

"Come in, come in. Who are these children?"

"I'm Jim. This is Betty, my sister," Jim announced.

Betty stared around at the place. "Flowers," she said.

"We found them at a car station Down Below. They'd been waiting for their parents for two days," Brad said as they walked into the courtyard. The children gaped at the place.

"Where's the walls?" Jim asked.

"Only inside rooms," Liia said. To Brad, "We take care of these young ones."

Two other women emerged from nearby rooms. "This is Jone and Ana. This is Brad, from human sector."

The women nodded.

Betty mumbled something to Jim.

Jim said, "My sister needs a toilet."

"I'll take them," one of the women said.

"Thanks, Jone," Liia said.

The woman took the children into her room.

"Max?" Brad looked at his companion.

The alien shook his head, huddled up. His human face had slipped away.

"Food?" Liia asked Brad.

"Yes, please."

She fetched bread and a bowl of beans. Max ate most of it.

"He needs it more than I." Brad patted Max.

"Evening meal be soon. You eat all you want. We have plenty of food here."

"Good."

"Now tell how you got here."

Brad, his hand on Max, now curled into a ball on the bench beside him, told her of their kidnapping, escape, and adventures.

As he was telling Liia about finding the children, the place shook. Brad grabbed the bench arm and Max. The vines above swung wildly. Slowly it settled down. All the benches and tables were part of the block, but things that weren't held down tumbled around.

"Just another small one," Liia said. "Are you well?"

Brad patted Max. "I think so. If that's a little one, what's a big one like?"

"I hope not to find out." Liia paused, scanning the courtyard. "So the children. What are your plans for them?"

"I haven't had a chance to think about it. Probably take them to Todd's and try to find their parents. I couldn't just leave them sitting there."

Liia nodded.

Jone and the kids came out of her room.

"You all right?" Brad asked.

"We hid under the table," Jim said. "Are we going to stay here?"

"For a while." Brad knew they all needed to rest.

Betty, still holding Jone's hand, asked her, "Are you our new mommy?"

"Liia, do you think ..." Jone wore a hopeful expression. "I have room."

Liia thought a moment. "Okay, they stay with you for now. What about you two?"

"I need to contact Sam," Brad said. "They took my comm, and we can't use Jim's credits over here. Do you have a comm?"

"Only to Central. I ask them to contact her. What is her number?"

Brad gave Liia the office number, and she went away.

When she returned, she said, "That number is out of service. Do you have another number we can try in a few days?"

"A few days?" Brad stared at her.

"Can only do personal calls every three days."

"Oh shit. She never uses her personal one. I don't know Todd's; it's programmed into my comm."

But that must mean she's with Todd, he thought, and felt a little better.

"You must be very tired. Stay here a few days and rest. We figure out how to find them. The chimes sound when meal ready." Liia showed Brad and Max to a room on the south side. "You stay here. A meal be served soon."

"Thanks." Brad led the way in.

The first room contained a wide yellow couch and a pair of matching chairs, with small tables next to each, and a screen on the wall. In a corner, a spiral staircase led up to a second level. Behind it was another room with a large table painted with flowers, matching chairs, and cabinets lining the walls. A toilet room and storage closet sat at the rear.

"Vines," Max said, pointing to the wall.

"Yes." Brad led the way upstairs. "Nice."

The small front room appeared to be a storage area, and the middle room had a bed on each side with bright covers, and more vines on the walls. Built-in drawers beneath the beds and at the end of the room provided storage. Both rooms had skylights. At the rear was a full bathroom.

"I'll take this one; you can have that." Brad sat on the right-hand bed.

"Sky," Max said, looking at the skylight. "Out, we go?"

"Maybe. I guess we'll stay here a few days until we get rested up," Brad said. "I feel like just sitting for a while."

"Too, me." Max crawled around on his bed and found a corner to curl up in. "Sam, call?"

"I don't know her number, and Todd's was in my comm. Besides, I can't try again for three days, according to Liia."

"Nice, Liia. Phone number know, I."

"Max! Why didn't you tell me?"

"You knew, I thought."

Brad reached for him, but Max ducked back into his corner.

"You knew." Brad pounded on the bed. "Now we'll have to wait three more days."

*   *   *

As Sam was heading for the bedroom, the apartment shook. She grabbed the doorway and held on. Fortunately, the shaking didn't last long.

"What was that?" she gasped.

"Earthquake," Todd said. "You all right, Sam?"

"Just a little shook up." She grimaced.

"Come sit down." He patted the long seat across from the screen. "Probably no significant damage in our sector except for the areas at the west boundary."

"Liia?"

"The block capsules and attached furnishings are indestructible. Loose stuff will be floating around, through."

"Where's Brad and Max?"

"Stopped. Far west and north. Could be at Liia's."

"That would be great. She'll take care of them." Relief flowed through her. "I wonder if their cars and tubes are running,"

"Probably. They're on a different system than us."

But now Sam had a new worry. *Had Liia's place been damaged?*

Her thoughts were interrupted by a message ping. Dondo. *What did he want now?*

Sam called him back.

"I have arranged a meeting of you and representatives of the other sectors you have spoken with, to be held in three days, at the meeting place above the Hive. They do not travel far. You, Brad, and Todd be at the local port at Complex at Ten hours on Thirday next. The meeting will last two or three days, so bring what you need."

"What if Brad and Max aren't back? Why not the governors?"

"They will be found. The governor does not believe the damage will affect him. You are the important one. You will come."

Sam was getting tired of this. "What's this all about?"

"The future of your world."

Ha, she thought. "Okay." *'Your world', he said. Did that mean he's leaving, too?*

"Good." He clicked off.

"Now what?" Todd asked.

126

Sam told him.
"I guess we better go, then."

*   *   *

World grew alert.

22

THREE DAYS LATER, Sam and Todd packed their bags and hiked up to Forty.

"The tubes are only functioning sporadically," he said. "I don't want to take a chance we get stuck somewhere."

Todd used his pass to get them into Complex, and over to the up-tube. At the top, he led the way to the stairway up to the Complex port. This one was larger than the port where Todd kept his ship, but with the same gray walls and no windows. Todd showed his ID, and they trotted down the tube to the ship when they were called.

Dondo stood in the corridor outside the airlock and showed them into the first cabin behind the airlock. Pale blue walls lined the large room with comfortable seats, with a bedroom and head at the rear. A table, with fruit and meat tarts, and chairs sat near a screen.

"Prepare for takeoff," he said.

They buckled themselves in, and the ship eased away from the port.

Sometime later, they pulled into another port, and someone else boarded. Sam wanted to see who it was, but their door wouldn't open.

She heard a little voice, and a woman's asking, "What makes this go?"

Must be Mantz and his family.

Dondo's ship picked up the others as they circled the continent. The wall screen showed what they were flying over: their silver roof, the Noreg tree tops, the Itza tan stones. Sam heard the Itza chittering as he boarded after they stopped there.

Sam and Todd watched the screen, checked on news every once in a while, and ate the food that Dondo brought from time to time.

If Liia's group got as much food as they did, Max had plenty to eat.

Later, as Sam was digging out her nightshirt, she heard the Ghind Elder, out in the corridor, murmuring something she couldn't make out.

*   *   *

In the morning, the ship stopped while they were eating, and Sam heard Maya hissing out in the corridor. Maya's trees were completely different from the Ghinds' trees, which were nothing like the Noreg's.

Finally, the ship landed in a round valley near a round building. Dondo opened their door and led Sam and Todd down a covered ramp to the ground.

They stopped just outside the ship. Maya came out first, and she and Sam exchanged nods. Joba carried the Elder, who smiled at them. Koz, the Itza, ignored them. Mantz and his family greeted them. The little girl carried her Katta, and her older brother stomped along, head down, apparently ignoring everything around him.

Brad bounded out and gathered Sam in a big hug. Max joined in, and Liia smiled.

"Brad, you're so thin."

"We didn't have a lot to eat until we got to Liia's. You are staying at Todd's?"

"Oh, yes." Sam grinned.

Dondo directed his passengers to their various places in the round building — long, narrow triangular apartments with a small, clear-walled room at the inside. This wall looked out into the center of the building, and Sam could see the others standing in their clear rooms. Some were empty. One room, across from her, held a large black ball hanging in midair.

Todd stood behind Sam. She saw Brad and Liia in the next room.

Where was Max? Was he all right?

The knot inside her tightened.

"Welcome, all," Dondo began as he strode into the center area. "We must all work together to save this world. The Volen will no longer be available to help you. You are on your own."

"What?!" Sam cried.

Others exclaimed. Maya hissed. From The Elder, in a piercing voice, "Explain."

Sam grabbed onto Todd. He was the only thing she knew for a fact was real.

Dondo put his hands up and turned slowly in a circle, so all saw his face. "When the Volen discovered this world, the Terrans and the Ambaak were already here, with thriving colonies. The Volen knew the Ghind needed a new home, so they brought them here, as it closely matched the Ghind home world."

The Elder nodded.

"Then it became a home for other unwanted species," Dondo continued. "As the Volen brought others, over time, they gave the newcomers the knowledge of Standard — a form of the Terrans' language — so the species could communicate with each other."

"Ah," Todd said.

"As the colonies grew, and building materials became scarce, the Volen provided housing and other structures with their indestructible material. No one knows, except them, what it consists of. The Volen knew of the aquafer, but the original human colony had been built over it to access the water. Since their material is very light, and the two-block cubes were mostly full of air, the Volen apparently figured there would be no problem."

Ha, Sam thought, and shifted to her other foot.

"The Volen knew of the plate tectonics and warned the Ambaak not to build close to the coast, but the Ambaak insisted on having their buildings by the sea."

Liia grimaced.

"The Volen material will disintegrate over a period of time. You have one week to prepare lists of items you will need to reconstruct your homes. There is room in the hills above your sectors for you to live, until Volen material is gone and you can rebuild on the plain."

Sam looked at Todd, and he nodded. The place seemed to be growing cooler.

"Samanda, come out here," Dondo said. The wall in front of her peeled back and she stepped out. "You have all met Samanda. She and her brothers," he nodded at Todd, and Brad in the next room, "are the nucleus of the group who will oversee the change. Now for the rest of you. Ambaak?"

Liia stepped out, glancing at Sam, followed by Brad. Only iron will kept Sam from running to him.

"This is Liia from Ambaak. Her people's building suffered a little damage in the lower levels, but when the big one comes, there will be much more damage."

Liia sucked in her breath, and Sam felt her distress.

"Samanda's sector has much damage in lower levels. Now Mantz of Noreg. We did not detect any damage there."

"We felt shaking," Mantz said as his wall scrolled aside. "What will happen to our trees?"

"They will go. We will find the largest trees on this world and plant them above your sector."

Mantz and his woman exchanged looks and sighed. "Cannot be helped."

"Koz of Itza." The lizard-like being stepped out and looked straight ahead.

"Since you favor heat, we will relocate you to the southern desert continent." Koz blinked his eyes.

"Elder of Ghind." Joba carried her out and held her.

"We do not need much. We have real trees," she said.

"Maya of Felce."

The big cat stalked out on two legs, switching her tail and clenching her claws. *GIVE US REAL GROUND, REAL TREES, REAL PONGO MEAT*, she snarled through her translator.

Dondo nodded. "And last, people from the Hive."

A black, buzzing ball sailed out and hung in midair.

"Now we all know each other. There is a group in the high mountains who cannot breathe the thick air down here, and another in the sea in the smaller archipelago. Their homes are of natural materials, and they are already self-sufficient. Samanda, begin."

Dondo stood still.

Sam's mind went blank for a moment. She took a deep breath. "Are you all as stunned as I am?"

Nods, growls, and buzzes came from the others.

"First, I think we need to have questions answered. I'm sure we all have questions."

"Yes," said the Elder. "Let us go to quarters and make lists of questions. Take time. Perhaps we get answers."

"Is there any you want to ask right now?" Sam asked.

They all looked around at each other. The buzzing ball retreated into its room.

"We need to know what is Volen that will disappear and what is not, that will stay." Todd looked around at us.

"You will receive a list." Dondo eyed us all. "Very well. Make your lists. A meal will be served to your quarters shortly. We will look at the lists in the morning. That is all. Samanda, stay."

All, Sam thought, rolling her eyes. *My world's being turned upside down, and 'That is all.'?*

"Yes," she said. "So when is this going to start? Are we going to get any more offworld supplies?"

"You will have seven days to present a list of items you will need. The Volen will arrange to send us as many items as they can. I will pick the lists up at Complex, and at the ports of the other sectors."

"What we really need is a communication system between sectors, so I can call the others if I need to, and the others can call me, instead of all this running around in fliers nonsense. Mantz is the only one who has a comm and can call me. I think The Elder has one, too, but I don't know whether she can call me direct. Maya needs one with a mental translator." Sam's mind was still trying to process all this.

"You have problem with fliers?"

"They take too long. Leaving my place, going up to the port, and flying around, it takes most of a day just to get over to the other side. So I have to stay overnight and spend the next day getting home. Not worth it for an hour's talk. We need to be able to talk to each other instantly. Also we need to be able to connect more than two of us together when necessary."

"Enough. We will talk later." Dondo turned and left.

Sam stuck her tongue out at his back and returned to her quarters, to find Brad, Max, and Liia there.

"What's up?" Brad asked, pulling her down beside him on a couch.

Sam cuddled up to him, patted Max on her other side, and finally relaxed. The knot began to dissolve.

"How are you, really?"

"Tired. I could sleep for a week." He gave Sam a squeeze. "What were you talking to Dondo about?"

"I'm trying to get him to set up a communication system so we can call each other direct."

"That'd be great," Liia said. "Half the time Central doesn't patch calls through just because they don't feel like it. I'd love to be able to talk to you directly."

"Questions," Todd said. "My first one is to find out what is made of Volen material and what isn't."

"He said he'd give us list," Sam said.

"When?" Brad asked. "We know the walls, ceilings, and floors are. Furniture, doors, cupboards."

"Those can be rebuilt. What about machines, conduits, the tubes and cars?" Todd shook his head.

"Let's put that at the top of our list of questions." Sam was going from a state of worry, to shock, to planning an unreal future.

"Sam, I have female questions," Liia said. "May we go to my quarters?"

"Sure." Sam followed her over.

"Do you think we get what we ask for? To rebuild, we need many materials and tools," she asked.

"I hope so. Dondo seems honest. His directions were always right."

"Yes, but will the Volen let him? They don't seem interested in us anymore. I'm concerned about my people. My clan be all right, but the others down below. What can I do about them?"

"I take it your Central won't do anything."

"Right. I think they just do what they feel like."

"I suggest you start exploring outside, up in the hills, for a place to move your clan. Then when you move out, another clan can move into your block. Also, you need to set up a way for you to communicate with the other clans."

"Yes. My mate and others are working on it."

"Good." Sam paused, thinking. "I just remembered, I have a communication device in my shop that I think will work between our sectors. I'll go dig it out and have Brad bring it over and show you how it works."

"Great. Thank you." She smiled briefly.

Maya stalked in and sat on her haunches. *WE FEMALES MUST RULE,* she said to them in their minds.

Sam saw Liia jump and wondered again how Maya did that.

"I agree." Sam pushed her hair back. "Our councilors are all men, and the governor thinks he's an emperor. They do what the men in their districts want and ignore us women."

Liia nodded.

Maya switched her tail. *MALES ONLY INTERESTED IN THEIR PROWESS. TIME WE TAKE OVER.*

"How?" Sam asked.

WE MAKE RULES FOR OUR CLANS AND IGNORE MALES, Maya sent.

Juba carried in The Elder and set her in a large, stuffed chair.

"We're talking about women taking over and ruling our various clans," I told her.

"Good." The Elder settled herself. Joba moved to the other end of the room. "Although Elders can be either female or male, females live longer, so most Elders have been females. We have few problems. Once, long ago, we had a male Elder. He made too many rules, many difficulties. He did not last long."

Sam nodded. "I'm trying to get Dondo to set up a communications network among us, so we can talk to each other without having to leave our sectors. That way we can keep in touch."

"Yes." Liia pounded her fist into her other hand.

Maya nodded her head and let out a tiny growl.

"Give me your comm number," The Elder said. "I have one."

"With you?"

"I did not think to bring."

"Good. That's two. Mantz has one."

The meals arrived, and the meeting broke up as they each returned to their various quarters. Sam, Brad, and Todd sat around the table; Max came out of his corner to join them.

"How are you doing, Max?" Sam asked him.

"Okee."

He didn't sound 'okee' to her, but he was eating, so she didn't worry too much.

After their meal, Todd, Brad and Sam met with Dondo again. He said fliers were Volen; Spaceport would stay. Occasional ships from other worlds would arrive. All the conduits, power and water equipment, and air ducts were Volen. The screens and comms were Volen, but he would provide us with a way to save our data files. Factory equipment was part Volen and that part could be rebuilt with other materials.

It would over a year before all Volen materials were gone.

"Are these breaking up into little pieces, molecules or atoms? And are there any chemicals in this stuff that would be harmful to any of us?" Todd asked. "Is this going to be in the air, water, or ground?"

"I do not have answers. Only Volen know what in materials. Probably harmless. You have been here many hundreds of years."

"That's not the same. Small particles can be breathed in or gotten into food. And we have changed. That's what you told us at the first meeting." Todd stared at Dondo.

"I will ask Volen," Dondo said. "Go to your quarters. I will take you home in the morning." He turned and walked away.

They looked at each other.

"Could we have been ingesting it all along?" Sam asked.

"Possibly," Brad said. "Molecules could detach into the air. Todd, is there any way to find out the thickness in early days as compared to now?"

"I'll check."

*   *   *

World became aware of beings on its surface.

23

"LET'S GET THE OTHERS." Todd strode to the clear room and raised his voice. "Folks, we need to talk while we're all together."

The others moved out.

"I see our people begin preparing shelter outside," Liia said.

Everyone gathered around. Hive buzzed on the outskirts.

Todd led the group to a huge screen on the wall of the inner circle and booted it up. "Sam, do you have anything you want to say first?"

"Yes." She had been thinking rapidly. "We all have to work together to save our world." Heads nodded. "For those of you I haven't told yet, I'm working with Dondo to set up a communications network among all of us. We need to be able to reach each other easily. Todd?"

Todd brought up a map of their continent — two rough ovals, one inside the other, with a dark mass down the long axis. Sectors were marked off between the two ovals. "This is our world. As you all heard, the Volen have deserted us, and their material will gradually disintegrate. It's already happening in our sector.

"This area," he pointed to the ring around the dark mass in the center, "is mainly hills and valleys. Those of us who live in cities will have to move up into these areas and make our homes there. Those who have a lot of Volen material will have to plan how to live without it."

"Our trees," Mantz said.

"Do you have any seeds of your real trees?" Sam asked.

Mantz and his mate, Essie, shook their heads.

"Oh," she said suddenly. "Great grands' pouch."

"Maybe." Mantz nodded.

"Yes, check that out. We will search for the biggest trees on this world," Sam said.

"We have real trees," the Elder said. "Some hills they made."

HOW YOU HAVE REAL TREES AND WE DON'T? Maya sat up and snapped her tail back and forth.

"Trees always there."

"Are your trees a special kind? I noticed they were different than the others," Sam asked Maya. "Maybe they won't grow on this world."

"Ssss." Maya crouched back down.

From Hive, everyone heard in their minds, *WE PREPARE.*

"Good. Work on your questions and lists of things you need, and start planning your new life. See you all in the morning."

Sam headed back to her quarters. Her mind was spinning with more thoughts than she could handle.

As they sat, Sam asked Todd, "Is there any way out from Fifty?"

"Two in Complex," he said. "Governor's house next door is outside, actually Level Fifty-One, but even I can't get in there. But what we need to do first is move up. One of the councilor's assistants I work with is keeping an eye open for any apartment that might become available. He has a three-bedroom apartment, but only uses one, and said we can move most of our stuff up any time. Sam, you and Max can stay there."

"I need to get my things from my shop, first. Is everything still running in Above?"

"As far as I know. You'll have to give up your shop. Can you sell your stock?"

"Probably." Sam wasn't sure at all. There weren't that many spyshops.

"I'll handle all the official stuff about you moving up there and see you get a new comm. I'll check around and see if I can find someone on a lower level to take over your place."

They talked some more and finally went to bed.

Now that Sam was getting out of that place, she was going to miss her comfy little sanctuary.

*   *   *

In the morning, after another meal, Dondo brought them all together again.

"Do you all understand the changes that are coming? Do you have questions I can answer now?"

"Why is this happening?" Sam demanded.

Dondo looked blanker than ever. "Volen need resources for other peoples on other worlds. Not enough Volen for all, anymore."

"So they are shrinking, too?" Sam asked.

"Their number shrinks. They are ancient race and live long, few replacements. They are coming to the end of their span of life. I must tell you this. I am not a living being like you. Much of my body is made of Volen material. I, too, will go. Volen changing, their material changing, everything changing."

"Oh." So he *was* not human. She wasn't sure how she felt about that.

"Not good," added The Elder.

Others murmured.

Todd spoke. "I have a question. We need to know what is Volen and what isn't, so we know what we have to replace."

"You will receive a list. This is not what we would have wished, but it is what we have, and we must deal with it. At least, we have time to prepare. Now we must leave."

Sam, Todd, and the others returned to their quarters, gathered their belongings, and proceeded out the back door to the ship. As Sam settled into her cabin, she thought about changes that had already happened and what was ahead.

How am I going to deal with all this?

✳   ✳   ✳

The ship traveled around in the same direction that they came from, so Dondo let Liia off first, and Sam's group next. At the port, Sam and the others found the down-tube, and trudged back to Todd's apartment. Inside, they dropped their bags and sat.

"What in City are we going to do now?" Brad asked the air.

"Make a list of what you think we need to do, what tools we need to do them, and a timeline, what do we do first, what do we do next, and so forth." Todd pulled out his comm and plugged it into his screen. "That goes for you, too, Sam."

Sam took her comm out of her bag and stared at it. "I guess I need to get the rest of my stuff out of the shop and get that phone to Liia first. Who knows what Dondo will do about my communications network."

"Hey, Todd, thanks for taking Sam in." Brad leaned back into the cushions.

"I couldn't leave her down there alone." He tapped a few keys. "Look at this."

> Attention all Upper residents. Because of the continuing destruction of Lower, we are requesting that any of you who have room take in a Lower citizen. Many have gone to the factories outside the problem zone, but many more are losing their homes. Call this number.

"Well, Sam," Todd turned to her. "Shall we look for someone to take over your place?"

"Of course, but I have to get my stuff out first."

"Okay, I'll arrange it, and we'll all go down the day after tomorrow. I've got to make some calls tomorrow. Let's go get something to eat. Coming, Max?"

Max's head jerked up, and he unrolled himself. "Ready."

Sam, Brad, Todd, and Maxee walked to the caff, ordered, and Brad began to tell us of his and Max's adventures. Max nodded now and then, until the food came.

"When we came off the car at the end of Lower One, I saw the children." Brad said.

"Children?" Sam's hand stopped in midair.

"They're with Liia's friend, Jone, now. She doesn't have any of her own."

"So, tell." Sam's spork continued to her mouth.

Brad told us how they used the boy's comm to get a meal and a car in Above.

"We need to get him those credits back." Sam sipped her drink.

"I need a new comm. I feel naked without it," Brad added.

"We'll get you one soon," Todd put his mug down. "You can use mine or Sam's, if you need to."

"Thanks. Then Liia got the message about the meeting, and the three of us went up to the roof and climbed walls between clans over to the port above Central. We had to go south several blocks to find one close enough to the next one east. I knew you would be at the meeting. That was better than trying to walk all the way home. And so here we are, all together again." Brad smiled at Sam.

They returned to Todd's place, started on their lists, and eventually retired for the night.

*   *   *

The next day Sam checked her messages and answered a question for a client. She sat back and stared at the screen.

First, find a place to move to. Second, people. How to let them know, tell them what to do. Could they use the screen broadcasting system? Third, get people from here to there. What people? Who were they?

Sam sat up and touched keys. She found a database of all the current residents of City. It gave name, ID, address, age category. She set up a spreadsheet and copied the data into it, creating a new column.

While the data was downloading, she went out and sat on the couch next to Max. He slept most of the time. He'd get up for meals, stuff himself, and go back to his closet or on a couch if the men weren't around.

Brad had gone over to the lab to get more nutrients for Max.

"What are we going to do about Max's nutrients?" Sam asked Brad after he returned and joined Max and her on the seat.

"I told Jill what was happening, and she said she would figure out how to find the ingredients here, without the Volen' imports."

"Good." Sam made circles with her toe.

"What's going on with Max, anyway?" Brad asked.

"I don't know, but something's changing. Puberty, maybe?"

"Oh, no. That's all we need now, Max turning into something unknown."

Max stuck his head out of his curled-up body. "Becoming female, I am." He grinned. "Maybe Baby Max I make."

"What?" Sam couldn't believe her ears.

"Um, Max," Brad stuttered.

"Become female, child. Make more child, female. When no more, male become."

"How do you know?" Sam stared at him. This was a whole other problem, on top of everything else.

"My head, in." He curled up again. Brad and Sam looked at each other.

"A baby Max," Brad said. He looked stunned.

"I hope he knows how to handle it. Don't tell Todd yet. He's got enough worries."

"Okay." Still gaping, Brad went to look for something to eat.

✳   ✳   ✳

At late meal, Todd told Sam and Brad he'd found someone to take over her place.

"We'll meet her there tomorrow when we go down to clean it out. You two get a good night's sleep."

When they left in the morning for Sam's shop, they all carried bags. Sam had her big bag along with her everyday bag; Max carried Brad's duffel. Brad had his large bag, and Todd a huge contraption on wheels. Todd took one tube platform, Sam and Max the next, and Brad on the third platform.

At the shop, Sam dropped her bag and fished out her unlocking gismo. The place smelled musty and flat. Brad went upstairs to collect his belongings.

"I wish we could take the recliner," he said.

"Not a chance." Todd looked at Sam. "Show me what you want to take of your stock."

They went up and down the rows. Sam found the phone system and tucked it in her small bag. She took at least one of most every kind of non-Volen gadget. Todd's carryall on wheels was almost full when they were done.

Max stuffed all his things from his cubicle into the duffel. Todd checked Sam's screen. Everything of hers was gone.

Sam climbed the spiral staircase and collected the rest of her belongings, checking every drawer and corner twice. The bed was solid, so nothing could get under it. The place looked bare and blah without her pictures on the walls.

They were just about packed up when the shop bell rang. Sam ran downstairs. Susan and a young woman with two little girls entered, each carrying a small bag.

"Hi. I'm Sam, the owner. These are my brothers."

"I'm Connie. This is Doreen and Alice. This is a lot bigger than the place I had down below. The whole block down there is practically on its side."

"Oh, no."

Sam showed Connie to Brad's chair. "Here's the office comm. Todd will set it up for you."

"This is nice. Does this chair come with the place?"

"Yes."

"So comfortable." Connie smiled widely.

"The apartment is upstairs." Sam led her and the girls up. Susan followed. "The recliner is comfortable to sleep in, and the girls can have the bed. My brother, Brad, slept in the recliner all the time."

"So much room. I feel so lucky. I didn't know what was going to happen to us." The girls bounced on the bed.

"You do know this is only temporary, don't you? In a few months, we'll be moving you up to the new place in the valley."

"Yes, Susan told me. I don't know if I can handle it." Connie inspected the closet and bathroom. "Girls, stop bouncing on the bed."

The two little girls stood still for about five seconds and began to bounce again.

"You will. Have you been in the business long?"

"I took over from my grandfather two years ago. I like being able to solve problems. Are you taking all the stock in the shop?" Connie sat back in the recliner.

"No. I've packed up what I'm going to take. What's there is yours. Also, I'm leaving you a few sheets and towels."

"Thank you. Girls, I told you to stop bouncing on the bed. Now. Sit down."

The little girls sat down on the bed and sighed.

"How bad is it down there now?" Sam asked.

"Awful. No power, no tubes, water is hard to find and food even scarcer. Nobody knows what to do, except for the people who found us, and Susan was very helpful."

"Thanks, Susan." Sam motioned toward the stairs.

They all went down, and Connie and Todd took care of the paperwork.

"How are you doing?" Sam asked Susan.

"Not good," She leaned against the wall. "We have been getting some people out, but not nearly enough."

Sam told her about their meeting, and what Dondo had told them.

"Oh, no. What are we going to do?"

"We'll look for a place up in the hills. You keep doing what you're doing down here. Are you hungry?"

"We all are."

"Todd, let's go eat."

"Okay."

Sam took the others to the caff and introduced Connie and the girls to the caff owner. "They're taking over my place. This one's on us."

While they waited for their meals, Sam gave Connie their comm numbers. "In case you need to get ahold of us."

"Thanks again."

The three of them ate as if they hadn't had anything for days.

After the meal, they returned to the shop, and Sam gave Connie the keys.

Susan left to go back down to Below.

Sam, Todd, Brad, and Max collected their bags.

"Good luck." Sam smiled.

"That's one," Brad said as they left and crossed the street to the tube.

"How many more?"

"We'll do what we can." Todd said.

The return trek took a lot longer, carrying all that stuff. Todd had to have Max hang on to his carryall, because the up-tube couldn't handle Todd's weight too. He went up last. When they reached Todd's place, they dumped everything inside the front door and collapsed.

"Okay, that's step one," Todd said. "My legal job now is to dig up everything I can find on how to build a new colony. You two need to work on your lists. I've started mine."

"I have, too," Sam said. "I think we need at least one day's rest before we go anywhere else."

"Of course."

*   *   *

World examined these beings. They did not belong.

24

MAX HAD TAKEN HIS BAG and disappeared into the closet. Sam looked at her big bag and decided she didn't need anything in it anytime soon.

Brad shoved his bag out of the way. "We'll have to make more than one trip up to Hal's, you know."

Sam groaned.

"I'll probably need three." Todd kicked his carryall. "Sam, you and Max can go up once and stay. We'll bring the rest of our stuff up."

"Are you sure?"

"Yes. You need to get settled so you can get everything organized."

"Okay."

What 'everything'? I get to do the organizing?

Sam shrugged and fished the phone out of her bag. "Brad, after we go up, take this over to Liia and show her how it works."

"Sure. Let's play with it tomorrow. I'm beat, and hungry." He put the phone on a table.

They trudged to the caff, ate, and brought home a meal for Max. After Sam gave him his food, she went to bed, leaving the men in the living room talking.

*   *   *

"You people ready to go up today?" Todd asked during breakfast at the caff on the second morning after they returned from Sam's place.

"Sure." Brad picked up his spork. "Yesterday was easy. I didn't have to carry anything."

"I'm fine. Max?" Sam nodded.

"Go, I."

When they returned to Todd's and checked the screen, there was another announcement from Security. The tubes in their district were down for maintenance. For two days.

"Not now." Sam groaned. *Anything to make things worse.*

"What idiot thought of that?" Brad thumped the seat.

"Maybe they want to make sure everything's working." Todd studied the district map. "We're smack in the middle, below Complex. We'd have to go up two to get a car."

"Are they running?" Brad asked.

"As far as I know. I think our best bet is to go up to Complex, the tubes inside will be working for sure."

"Yeah, those guys aren't going to walk up even one set of stairs." Brad smirked.

*   *   *

The next morning, Sam and the men hauled their bags up five flights. They stopped every third step and rested for ten minutes between stairways. Todd got them into Complex and up the tubes. They caught the car at Forty-Eight. Then they had to haul their stuff up two more flights to Fifty, to Hal's apartment. Which was half-way down the block, of course.

Todd had called Hal, so he was waiting. Todd introduced them as Sam looked Hal over. All Sam saw at first were his great brown eyes. Not as tall as her brothers, but heftier, he also had a delicious smile.

"Come in, come in," he boomed. They trooped in and dropped their bags. "Sit down, sit down."

"Oh," Sam murmured.

The main room, with pale blue walls, was larger than Todd's. Two dark blue couches and matching stuffed chairs left plenty of room for a round table and chairs, and the wide screen table and chair. His screen was larger than Todd's and displayed mountains.

A line of cabinets, with a counter and shelves, matched the wall at the rear. Little round tables accompanied each seat. Pictures of mountains and lakes adorned the walls.

Sam dropped into the nearest chair. The others joined her in various seats.

"Did you know the tubes were down?" Todd asked.

"Yep. Oh, you had to lug those things up the stairs?"

"Yeah." Brad leaned back in his chair.

"Let me get you something to drink." Hal strode to the rear of the room and returned with a tray of mugs. "This is what we call joy juice."

It was cold and refreshing, with a tangy taste.

"Let me show you around."

In a short hallway at the side of the room, Hal showed them the bedrooms. They were each larger than Sam's office, one green and one yellow. Sam chose the green one because it had a large closet for Max.

"This is our room, Max."

He trudged in with his duffle and disappeared into his new quarters.

"This room is for you men."

It was smaller than Sam's, and there was a bathroom next door.

"I'll take it," Brad dumped his bag in there. "Todd can sleep on the couch."

"That's my room, my room." Hal pointed to the door at the end of the hall. "I need to go back to work. Make yourselves comfortable. Todd, you may use my screen. I'll be back in a little while with food."

They settled in. Sam sat and stared at the screen in her room. This place reminded her of the place they'd lived in before Mother left. She was too tired to do anything, even comprehend this move. She stretched out on the bed and slipped into sleep.

When Hal came home, he brought a large bag of food and two comms. "Hey, people," he called.

Sam woke, went out to the living room and saw the bags on the table. Brad sat up on a couch, rubbing his eyes.

Hal passed out the new comms.

"Good," Brad said. "I've felt naked without one."

Sam had left her office comm with Connie. "Why do we have to change comms every time we move? It's such a hassle."

"We get a lot of complaints about that." Hal pulled boxes of food out of the bag. "I think when they first had them, they were physically connected to the apartment screen. There's been a committee discussing changing that, for about five years now."

"Whoopee," Brad muttered.

"But the good news is," Hal paused and grinned, "the place next door is vacant, and it's yours, it's yours."

"Already? That was fast." Todd sat up.

"The old man died, and I grabbed it."

After the meal, Sam excused herself and went to bed. If the men wanted to sit up and talk, fine. She was too tired to care.

*   *   *

In the morning, Hal gave Todd the keycodes for his place and the new apartment. They went over to the new place, and Hal hooked up their comms. It was the same size and layout as Hal's, but the main room was pale green. Sam took one look at the big yellow back bedroom and claimed it for her own. Brad took the one with the big closet for Max, and Todd the other.

The men and Sam moved one load and Max over, then Todd and Brad went with Hal to their various jobs at Complex. Max got himself set up in his closet, and Sam went back to Hal's for more of her stuff.

At the new place, Sam unpacked and went through all the drawers and cabinets. They had been cleaned out.

Max came out. "All, where?"

"They all went off to work."

"Okee." He disappeared again.

Sam sat and stared at her lists.

How am I supposed to know what I will need a year from now? We don't even know what all is available on this world, food or anything else.

She felt overwhelmed.

Why did Dondo choose me to lead? I'm no leader. As a child, Todd always led us. When I worked for Dad, I did what he told me. When I worked for Uncle Joe, I followed his instructions. Oh, sure, I was good at figuring out things and dealing with people, but that didn't make me a leader.

That evening, after they ate, Sam called Dondo and told him they had their lists ready.

When she went back to her corner of the couch, Hal, who had eaten with them, sat beside her.

"I didn't know Todd and Brad had such a beautiful sister," he said.

"Now you know." Sam edged away. "How long have you known them, anyway?"

"Let's see. I met Brad when he brought a request from the xenolab to my Councilor who shoved it on me, as usual. Brad was the regular messenger for a while, and we got to know each other. He never said anything about a sister, though. Todd was our connection with Legal. He never said anything, either."

"He had his reasons. Have you always worked in politics?"

"Yep." He smiled, and my heart thumped. "I wasn't that good at math or sciences, and I flunked the space test."

Sam nodded. At age twelve, teachers shepherded the children to a partially open space to see how they dealt with being out under the stars. Sam and her brothers thought it was fantastic, but few others could handle it.

"Uh oh," she said.

"What?"

"How are all these people who live in these little places going to handle living in the wide outdoors?"

"Oh." Hal paled. "I went up top once. There was too much, I couldn't comprehend it."

Sam had another thought. "Is it just from what you see, or is there more to it?"

"Mostly vision, I think."

"We could build little apartments with no windows. But getting there would be the biggest problem. Maybe some kind of blinder?"

"We'd have to see where we're going." Hal jumped up. "I need to be getting home. Things to do." He spoke to Todd and Brad and left.

"Well," Sam huffed. She marched into Brad's room. "Brother, we've got a problem."

He turned in his seat. "What now?"

"Most of the people have always lived in these tiny boxes. They are not going to be able to cope with wide open spaces. We can build them little boxes in the valley, but how are we going to get them there without them freaking out? Hal got upset just talking about it."

"Oops. Hadn't thought of that, but you're right. Maybe blindfolded and tied together?"

"Over all those hills?" Sam waved her arms around.

Brad glanced at his screen. "Let me think about it."

"Well, think hard. We've got to do something. Goodnight."

Sam crawled into bed, but couldn't sleep.

Too many things to deal with, and we keep finding more. What will happen next?

*　　　*　　　*

The next day, Brad and Todd returned to Todd's apartment to collect more stuff. They dropped off the lists on the way.

Sam moved the rest of her belongings over to the new place and sorted them out. It took a while; they'd just thrown things in the bags every which way. Meanwhile, her mind buzzed along faster than the cars.

First, they had to find out what was made of Volen material and what wasn't, answers to their questions, and if the particles would affect them. They had to wait for Dondo to get back to her for that.

Second, they had to find a place to move to — somewhere with trees, water, and a place to grow food. Then they had to plan the move. Sam thought she could start with that. Like how to get all their stuff over there.

Todd had said there were more of those carts like his, but how would we move really big things, like lab equipment that I knew was ours? Could we build carts? Would they fit in Todd's ship?

So many questions and no answers.

And then there was Max. He seemed to be doing okay, the process was innate, but would they need anything new for him? And what about Baby Max?

Sam still couldn't believe that. She started another list of things she thought of. Finally, she drifted off.

*   *   *

World gave a great shake.

25

T HE FOLLOWING DAY, Brad took the inter-sector call device to
Liia. Jone answered the door, with Jim and Betty behind her.
"Well, hello," she said. "Come on in."

"Hey, Brad," Jim grinned. "Did you find Dad and Momma?"

Betty smiled at Brad.

"No, but we'll keep looking."

Jim's face fell. "Okay."

"Getting enough to eat?"

"Oh, yeah. The view from the windows is great. A real ocean."

Before Brad could respond, something like a giant hand picked
up Liia's clan's block cube, shook it violently, and dropped it. Brad
grabbed the boy as they fell and bounced to the ocean end of the
courtyard. They huddled in a corner until the shaking stopped.

Brad took a deep breath and hugged a shaking Jim. "You okay?"

"What happened?" the boy asked, round-eyed, rubbing his
elbow.

"Earthquake. Big one."

Brad pushed a few plants and a trowel off his legs and sat up against the wall. The whole block cube slanted at about thirty degrees to the south. People began untangling themselves, some moaning. Brad had read about earthquakes, but the articles hadn't mentioned the total disorientation and shock.

"Let's just sit here a minute."

"Okay." Jim leaned into him.

Brad watched as people staggered around aimlessly, asking, "What happened?"

Others lay as they fell, next to tables. Women appeared in doorways, clinging to the frames.

Where was Liia?

Finally, it hit Brad. *How did Sam, Max, and the others fare?*

"No," he whispered, an iceberg around his heart. He closed his eyes. *Sammie, are you all right?*

Something with a faint scent of Sam came into his inner being and thawed the berg.

Liia limped over to them. A scratch lined her face and a big bruise darkened on her lower arm.

"Where's Betty?" Jim asked.

"With Jone, in her rooms. They're all right."

Brad climbed to his feet and helped Jim up. They were in the doorway of the dining room.

The place shook again, and they all sat down.

"How long will this go on?" Brad asked.

"Days. Weeks, maybe." Liia curled up into herself.

When the shaking stopped, Brad grabbed the doorway, pulled himself up, and turned to look down out the window. He saw the ocean pulling back.

"Oh, my Oneness," he muttered and turned to the others. "There's going to be a tsunami."

"What's that?" Liia sat up.

"The earthquake is moving the water away from us, then it'll return in huge waves. Can you call Central to warn the people of the bottom clans to get out? It could break the windows and flood their places. Don't worry, it won't come this high."

"Liia, Liia," cried a man, stumbling over to us.

"Giil." Liia reached up for him.

He picked her up in a hug. "Are you all right?"

"Mostly."

"This is my mate," she said, and introduced Brad to him.

"So you're the ones Liia told me about. Welcome to our mess."

"Giil, he says there's going to be a tsumani. I've got to call Central to warn the people in the lowest levels. Look."

She pointed to the window. Bare, wet sand and rocks stretched into the distance.

"How long before it comes back?" Giil asked.

"Not long," Brad said.

The two hurried off to the comm room.

Brad turned to Jim. "Let's go find your sister."

Some people were up and moving around; others lay and groaned. Plants, tools, and other items covered the floor. Brad picked up one plant and stuck it into a nearby box. He toddled on shaky legs across the courtyard, Jim clinging to his arm.

At Jone's, Betty yelled, "Jimmy," and hugged him.

"It's a mess, but come on in," Jone said.

"We need to go help the people out there."

Brad told the kids to stay in Jone's rooms and pick things up.

As he and Jone went out to the courtyard, a bullhorn voice announced, "People are hurt. Everyone who can, please help them."

Brad kept thinking about Sam as he picked up mugs and writing tools.

Was she okay?

When the tsunami hit, the building shook and settled. Brad trotted to the dining room window. Jagged waves splashed up to windows a few blocks down. He watched as the water drew back, carrying people and things with it. A four-legged chair bobbed along, and he thought he saw a table.

The windows, if not the walls, are broken, he thought.

*　　*　　*

Sam was reading a page on her screen when something yanked her chair back and dumped her on the floor. She huddled right there, heart pounding, until the shaking stopped.

"Max?" she called, crawling toward the closet in Brad's room.

"Sam?" a small voice cried.

Sam crawled in with Max, and they clung together, shaking.

"Shakes, like not, I," Max whispered.

"Me, neither." Sam was still quivering, heart racing, waiting for the next quake. Her mind was blank. All she could do was huddle in a corner, hold on to Max, and wait. Aftershocks rattled them from time to time.

A while later, she heard Todd and Hal come in, talking.

"Sam, Max," Todd called.

"I'm here." Sam crawled out of the closet and Todd helped her up into a hug. This time, she let him hold her. This time, she needed it.

"You two all right?" Hal asked, hanging on to the door frame.

"No. There's a bruise on my arm where it hit my table when the quake threw me out of my chair." Sam felt Todd shaking, too.

With one arm around her, Todd looked around at the mess. "I'm keeping everything in drawers from now on."

"I want to check my place, but I'll be back." Hal left.

Sam held on to Todd and barely noticed when the lights went out.

Todd turned his head to his screen and swore. "Power's out."

He led Sam to a couch, and they dropped onto it.

Sam leaned back, her head resting on his shoulder. She'd never been this rattled about anything in her life. Every time she tried to hold on to a thought, it slipped away. The whole atmosphere of the place felt different, unreal.

"How is it out there?" Sam asked, glancing at the mess on the floor.

"Not good. Everything not part of the block is on the floor. Like here." He let her go and swept his hand around. "And with no power, it's dark everywhere." He looked up at the skylights. "Except all of us on Level Fifty."

A little later, Hal returned. He showed Todd where the backup power was and how to turn it on. Back at the screen, they found a single message, red on black:

Everyone stay in your apartment until further notice.

"How are people supposed to read this if they don't have power?" Sam asked

"It's automatically sent to everyone. Looks like the whole web is down, except for the emergency messages." Todd played with the controls.

"What good does that do if there's no power?" Sam repeated. Todd shrugged.

Hal, Todd, and Sam sat on the couch and stared at the pictures on the wall. Although close to sunset, there was still enough light from the skylights to see them.

Sam was still numb, unable to put two thoughts together. She jumped at every little aftershock. Hal's foot twitched, and Todd's hands played with themselves in his lap.

Finally, a thought pushed through the fog. "What are we going to do about the screens when these are gone?" Sam kicked her heels.

"I talked to Gale, who runs the screens, and he is going to build an old-fashioned computer and put all our data on it. He's got all the specs. We'll figure a way to make power. Ken in water management is going to make copies of their plans and the water pumps. We'll have to figure out what else of the Volen stuff we can make copies of." Todd looked at his hands.

"How bad do you think the quake was?" Sam crossed her legs.

"Pretty bad. If it shook this bad here, it must have been even worse for the Ambaak sector," Todd added.

"Brad!" Sam sat up. "He's over there."

"I know. The blocks won't come apart, and the furniture is part of the block, but everything loose will be all over the place. They'll have bumps and bruises, but probably no worse. He's all right."

"How can you say that?" Sam jumped to her feet. "You don't know, you can't!"

"Calm down. Educated guess based on what we felt here." Todd glanced at the screen. The message had not changed. "We'll just have to wait 'til they get things going again."

"Okay." Something inside her told her Brad was alive and not badly hurt. "What about Below? Bill and Susan are down there."

"Probably a mess. Why don't you see if Brad's got that phone hooked up over there?"

Sam tried but didn't get anything. Maybe he hadn't time to do anything with it.

*　　*　　*

The next day, Todd had to go back to Complex.

"Are you going to be okay here alone?"

"Sure."

He gave Sam a quick squeeze and left.

Sam attempted to clean up the place, mainly piling things on the tables and counters.

Max wouldn't come out, so she took him some food. After that, she sat and stared at her screen. There was no word from Dondo, and she wondered where he was. She tried the phone again, and got Brad, faintly. He was okay and would be home in a few days. He was helping Liia's people get sorted out. Sam told him about their mess.

"Thank Oneness all the furniture and stuff are built in," he said. "Think what it would be like if all the chairs and tables were loose."

Feeling much relieved, Sam tried not to think about loose couches careening around. Then a large aftershock knocked her off her chair.

"How much longer is this going to go on?" she asked the room, as she crawled in with Max.

Later, Sam managed to stagger out and curl up on the couch facing the screen.

When Todd came home, he asked, "How are you doing?"

"Still here, more or less. Brad called. He's okay. He's going to stay there a few days to help them get straightened out. Their block is tipped way over."

"At least we know he's safe." Todd dumped his case on the screen table. "I went out on the roof to check for damage. There are escape hatches for every apartment on Fifty. Let's find ours."

It was in Brad's room, in the back corner. They found the gadget to open the hatch on a closet shelf. The ceiling slid open followed by the roof, and a rope ladder dropped down. Sam climbed up and stuck her head out. A wall of gray rock loomed up in front of her. She pulled herself out and looked around.

The wall extended as far as she could see, in either direction. No way could they climb up there. The silvery roof stretched out to either side, except for the massive building that housed the power and water stations above Complex. At least the air was better than what they had inside.

"Why is our roof silvery when Liia's is green?"

"Solar panels. That's where we get our power from."

"Oh." Sam climbed down and let Todd stick his head out.

"Air's good. Let's leave this open."

Sam went to check for a hatch in her bedroom. No luck. Or else she was blind.

*   *   *

Later, Hal came over. "Did you know, our whole sector dropped?"

"So that's where the hills went." Sam sighed.

"How did the area on solid ground move down?" Todd asked.

"I don't know. Once they get transport working, they'll send people down to take a look."

More waiting, Sam thought. "Will it slip anymore?"

"Not right away. Eventually, when the Volen material starts dissolving."

"Oh, dear." Sam looked at Todd. "That'll make it even longer to walk up into the hills."

"Yes."

Todd went through a pile on the counter and put things away.

*   *   *

The next day, Sam cleaned the place thoroughly, and caught up on reading the stack of information she'd downloaded a while back and never got around to reading. She wanted to know as much as possible about this sector and how it was run. She didn't let a couple of aftershocks bother her. Much.

*   *   *

In Ambaak, Brad carried some of the injured to their rooms and helped the medics treat them. He ate with Jone and the children in her place. The dining room was off limits, and Brad and a couple others had leveled the food prep area with a lot of boxes and odds and ends.

A few nights later, Jimmy asked, "Are you going to be our new dad?"

Brad blinked. He didn't know how to answer that. Jone looked at him hopefully. He'd had a lover, Alane, on the world of Bardack, but her custom decreed that the wife live with her husband's family, and she refused to leave her homeworld. Brad had thought of his parents, how his father had brought his wife to City, but she returned to her homeworld. He couldn't face that.

But he needed someone.

"I don't know," he said finally. "I have all my family and friends in City, and I know you wouldn't want to leave Amabaak, Jone."

She nodded and her face fell. "You could go back and forth," she said.

"Please," Jimmy said.

"I'll let you know."

Brad felt caught in a trap. He loved the kids, felt they were his now, and he liked Jone, but he couldn't conceive of living here.

"I'm sorry." He jumped up and left.

*   *   *

The next morning, after they ate, he told the children, "I'm going home, and we'll keep looking for your folks. You take care. Don't be afraid to ask for help. I'll be back one of these days." He turned to Jone. "Take good care of them. They're yours now."

"Oh, I will. Here's Liia."

"Leaving?"

"Yes. I have to get back to my place. Take care, I'll be back."

When he opened the door to the car way, there was nothing. The car track dangled in the open area between the door and the next clan block.

Brad looked up at the distant block, returned, and reported to Liia. "This block is down and away from the next block, and the car track broken."

"Churtle," she swore. "The way we went up before is gone. You can go up the stairs," she pointed to the green cylinder, "but there's a wall around the roof. You can check it if you wish."

Brad took the stairs and stepped out. A cliff rose behind the cube, and a great gap separated Liia's cube from the next one. A smaller, but too big to jump across, gap sat between Liia's block and the next one south.

"Shit."

He turned and retraced his steps. Liia was working at a table near the door from the stairway. He told her what he'd found.

"Shouldn't there be stairs down near the tube?"

"Yes." She went with him. They found the stairway on this side of the gap. Brad opened the door and looked down. "They look okay. I'll try them. Thanks for all your help."

"Thank you."

After the first stairway he lost the light from above and dug out his lightstick. He jogged down a half dozen stairways and stopped to rest. To his left he found a door. He opened it and saw a long hallway.

"Shit," Brad said, remembering the trip west on the car. He would have to walk back across the Ambaak sector before he could reach his own. Maybe there was a working car farther down.

He continued descending and opening each door. Three doors down he found cars. Liia had given him a ticket, so he was able to ride.

When the car stopped at the far end, Brad stepped off. He had no idea how long the trip had taken; he had napped part of the way. He used the rest station and turned to the portal. Inside, the stretch tube to the human sector had been torn away from the farther opening. No way he'd get across here.

Brad continued down the stairs. When he reached the next portal down, he found the interior was also torn away from the wall. He thought about jumping across. He was sure he could do it, but he heard Sam's voice in his mind asking, *"What if you don't make it?"*.

He yawned. His feet felt like he was wearing lead boots. He curled up on the seat in the portal and slept.

*   *   *

The second day after Brad called to say he was leaving, Sam grew tired of worrying and called him.

No answer.

Questions sprouted. *Was he all right? Had he fallen and hurt himself? Was he somewhere the phone didn't reach? Lower down? Where? Why?*

"Please, Oneness, take care of him," she said aloud.

She returned to her spreadsheet. She had marked off her group, Susan and Bill, and a few others she'd talked to about the upcoming changes, but there were so many others. The governor and Security refused to allow them to make a general broadcast, so it meant going door to door.

Sam sighed, and wrote up a message to tell people.

*   *   *

Brad woke and stretched. Hungry, he ate the last of his food. He tried to call Sam, but couldn't get through.

Maybe when I get closer, he thought.

He headed down the stairs.

Three flights later, the place shook. He grabbed the rail and heard a deep groaning and twisting.

After the quake stopped, Brad stood holding the rail and did some deep breathing. Then he continued on downward. The stairway slanted even more, and doors to the levels hung off their hinges. At the next portal, he was able to get across to his sector, only to find more darkness. He wondered about the extent of the power outage.

Was it just here on the west side? Or the whole sector?

Brad shone his lightstick around. The streets slanted here, too. The nearby tube was jammed so he couldn't reach the stairway. He headed east. Two blocks later, he found a stairway he could squeeze into, and hauled himself up to the next level. He stopped to catch his breath and called Sam.

"I'm on Level Seventeen, at the stairway two blocks east of Liia's. I'm on my way home."

"Thank goodness," Sam said, sounding relieved.

Up took a lot longer, but the stairways here were in better shape. He tried the tube every few levels, but they were all dead. After every third stairway, he went east a block. Occasionally he saw a speck of light down the street.

So other people were out looking around.

Brad had gotten used to the dark and hoped his lightstick would hold out. He ignored fatigue, focusing on Sam.

If he kept going up, he'd get to Fifty eventually.

*   *   *

World allowed the sea to scour out the lowest levels of construction at west end of continent.

26

"**T**HANK GOODNESS," SAM SAID, relieved, and dropped into her chair. Now all she had to do was wait. Again.

She laid her round stylus on her table and watched it slowly roll off. At least the power was back on. She jumped every time the place jiggled.

Sam still hadn't heard from Dondo and was beginning to wonder whether she ever would. A basic version of the web had come back up, but information was still sparse. Only tubes inside Centrex, and the Level Forty-eight cars, where most of the top brass lived, were working. Citizens were limited to two meals a day until arrangements could be made for more production. And limited water until the link to the reservoir was repaired.

Every time Sam checked on Max, he said he was 'okee', but he only came out for meals.

When Brad arrived late that afternoon, Sam jumped into his arms.

"Hey, sis," was all he could get out as he held her tight. Sam felt him shaking, too.

"How was it over there?" she managed to ask.

"Not good. Stuff all over the place. It's slanted. Liia's okay. How's Max?"

"Soso, still in his corner in the closet. I crawled in there with him until the shaking was over."

Brad gave her a squeeze, let her go, and dropped onto a couch. "Have any food in here?"

"Yes." Sam dug out a large roll, a packet of protein, and filled Todd's largest mug with water.

"Thanks." He took a big bite of bread and glanced at the screen. The messages continued to flash and scroll. "Is that it?"

"Yes. Hal showed Todd the backup power, but the regular power came back on last night."

Brad put down his roll. "Excuse me." He headed for the bathroom.

When he returned, he repeated, "'Backup'?"

"Rows One through Six from the north on Fifty all have backup power."

"Why? The lower levels without skylights need it more."

"The government strikes again."

"Yeah," he said. "I didn't see any light until Level Forty-Five." Brad took another bite.

"Oh, by the way, we found a way out to the roof in your room."

"Great," he mumbled between bites.

After Brad finished eating, Sam showed him the escape hatch. He stuck his head out.

"Wow. We'll never get up into the hills from here."

"I know."

Sam and Brad sat and talked. He told her what had happened in Liia's clan home.

When Todd arrived, he slumped into a chair. "They put me to work cleaning up." He heaved a sigh. "Every paper in every file in every cabinet was dumped on the floor. Plus spilled mugs and all the stuff they keep on their desks. At least, the furniture didn't move. Hey, Brad. Glad you're back."

"Me too," Brad said. "At least it's still level, here."

"More or less," Sam said, remembering her stylus.

"Liia's place is tilted almost thirty degrees." Brad leaned back.

"Oh, wow. How do they get around?" Todd stretched out his legs.

"We strung ropes between plant tables and doorways. Better than crawling. We were able to level the food prep area with books and prop boards."

"How's Liia doing?" Sam asked.

"Frustrated. Their Central won't do anything or give them supplies. I told her about Dori in 4803, and she's going to walk along and invite everyone to a meeting."

"Good." Sam sat up. "You two hungry?"

"Yes," Todd put his feet down. "Hal won't be home for a while. Let's go."

After we ordered at the caff, Brad told us of his latest adventures.

"Going over was a cinch. But after the quake, I had to go down several levels to find a working cross-sector car. Then I had to go down more stairs down to Sixteen where I finally found a portal I could cross through. Some of those doors lower down were jammed." He took a bite. "The children are doing fine. A gal named Jone has adopted them; she doesn't have any of her own. Being from Below, they're fascinated with everything up here. They help out, too."

"What about the plants?" Sam picked up her mug.

"Most are okay. Some of the ones at the lower ends of the plant tables were shaken out, but we were able to replant most of them."

"Oh, good."

They returned to their place and checked the screen. Same old messages.

Maybe something will happen in the morning.

Hal came over. "I have put in a request to see the governor. All four of us, about the meeting with Dondo."

"Will he listen to us?" Sam asked skeptically.

"Come over tomorrow afternoon at fourteen hours. Brad, can you come help us in the morning?"

"With what?"

"Mainly sorting papers." Hal sighed.

"Okay." Brad shrugged.

✳   ✳   ✳

After the men went off to work, Sam checked on Max, then locked up and went out the hatch. She walked down to Complex, took the walkway along Centrex south to the bottom end, around and back up, and over a few blocks. In the distance, the cliff dropped down to hills.

So we could get up that way.

She wanted to go farther, but didn't want to leave Max alone too long, so she headed home.

Sam had left the hatch open, so she could find it, and climbed down. People could get out, but nothing big. The carts surely wouldn't fit.

Max came out of the closet when she jumped down.

"Outside?" he asked.

"Yes, Looking for a way up into the hills. There is one, at the far end. How are you doing?"

"Okee. Longer, not much." He patted his belly. Sam couldn't see much difference in him, except his fur was slightly lighter. His face also looked softer, somehow.

The men came home for the midday meal at about thirteen hours, and Sam walked back with them. She waited with Brad 'til fourteen, and they all tubed up to the governor's office.

Paneling made of a dark, wood-like substance covered the walls of the receptionist's area. Sam wondered where they had gotten it.

Hal introduced them to the governor's executive assistant, Arlene. "I told him what you said about the meeting with Dondo," she said, "but he didn't seem interested in it. He said he would see you for a few minutes. He has to live up to his open-door policy." She grinned. "I believe you, and I'm talking to others already."

"Good," Todd said.

Sam wondered what the governor was like in person. He only spoke in prewritten scripts in broadcasts. She didn't have much hope that he'd actually do anything

After a short wait, Arlene ushered them in. Governor Jackson was studying something on his desk-screen. The huge desk, a table and chairs, and walls of cabinets were also of the same brown woody material as the paneling in the waiting room. A large wall screen hung at each end of the room. Green couches and chairs made a gathering group at one side, and a row of cabinets lined the other end of the room.

Finally, Hal said, "Good afternoon, Governor."

The man looked up. His images on the screen didn't show the lines in his face and the grey of his sideburns.

"Yes?" he said.

"These are the people I told you about, who had that meeting with Dondo," Arlene said.

Governor Jackson looked at each of them in turn. "You work here," he said to Hal.

"Yes, sir. For Councilor Burns. This is Todd, Brad, and his sister Samanda. Brad works in the xenolab, and Samanda is an inquiry agent. Todd is in the legal office."

The governor nodded. "And what do you wish to speak to me about?"

"Dondo met with us and representatives from the other sectors. He told us that the Volen are leaving us, and that all the Volen material will disintegrate within the year." Hal paused. "That means all the buildings and attached furniture, tubes and cars. We need to move out up into the hills so the people won't get hurt in the collapse."

"Centrex won't," Jackson said. "It's built to withstand anything. I think that's nonsense, anyway. If you want to move up into the hills, go ahead, as long as you come into work every day."

"What about all the people down below who make our food and clothes and everything else?" Sam demanded.

"They are being taken care of. The factories are safe. The earthquakes don't hurt anything underground. If that is all, I have work to do. I've heard you out, you may leave."

Sam was speechless. *How could the man in charge of the sector be so ignorant?*

They left.

"I'm sorry," Arlene said. "I have a break in ten minutes. Meet me in the Forty-Nine caff. I need to talk to you."

"Sure," Hal said.

At the caff, they each got a kafo drink and gathered at a table near the entrance. Kafo was a stimulant made from berries that grew in the Felce sector. The kafo in the upper half of Upper was decent, but Sam thought this kafo was much richer. Larger and lighter than the ones in the streets, this caff had pale green walls. The tables were round, and there was more space between them. Sam wished her caff could be like this.

Arlene arrived and sat with them. "Thanks for coming. Tell me more about this meeting. He won't do anything, but maybe I can." She smiled. "Actually, I do more than he does."

"Good." Sam grinned. "We women are going to be running this world. Females from other sectors agree."

One of the men, *Todd,* she thought, choked.

"You know about the problems down below, I'm sure," Sam said. Arlene nodded. "We are trying to get a program going to bring people up here."

"Yes, the welfare program is trying to do that," Arlene said. "I'll get you a contact with them. But they're having problems. A lot of people who have extra rooms don't want strangers in their homes. And those who have safe-for-now homes and jobs don't want to leave."

"Are you focusing on the ones who have already lost their homes?" Sam asked.

"Yes, and we've brought some of them up. They're mostly staying in rest areas." Arlene picked up a spork.

"Why don't you have get-togethers with those people and the uppers with rooms. Maybe if they get to know each other, they'll be more likely to welcome them in." Sam took a sip of her drink.

"What a great idea. Thanks, Sam. Tell me about this meeting you had."

"Dondo picked us all up, people from each sector, and took us to a meeting place up in the hills," Sam began. "He told us that the Volen were leaving, and that all the Volen material, all the buildings and structures, the transportation systems, and the water system would disappear."

"Also the screens and comms, the power systems, and the air ducts. But we won't need the air system when we're living in single houses," Todd added.

"Oh, wow," Arlene said. "Not all at once, I hope."

"No," Sam replied. "He said it would take at least a year, so plenty of time to make our new homes." She hoped.

"The first thing we need to do," Todd said, "is to get the word out to everyone so they know what to prepare for. We need everyone to look through any old boxes and containers handed down from ancestors and find anything useful for our new settlement. The Volen will be sending three more monthly shipments, and the stuff we made lists for, such as building materials and tools. After that, we are on our own."

Arlene sighed. "All right. I can talk to everyone in Centrex except the Councilors. Most of them wouldn't listen anyway."

"It would be nice if we could get on the broadcast system, but it's only for government and Security messages," Hal said. "I'll talk to Burns, but I doubt it will do any good."

"How long have you had your position?" Sam asked Arlene.

"Forever." She grinned. "Actually, more like thirty years. I started out as a clerk, was assigned to the governor's assistant for a project, and when she retired a few years later, he picked me to replace her. Don't tell anybody, but actually I run this place."

The two women giggled.

"Can you access our comm numbers?" Todd asked.

"I can, but why don't you just give them to me now?"

They did, said their goodbyes, and left. The men went back to their tasks, and Sam trotted home.

Max, curled up on the couch, jumped up when Sam came in. "I Maxee," she crowed.

"What?"

"All done." She sat and Sam dropped down beside him. Her.

"You don't look much different." Sam grinned, sharing Maxee's joy.

"Inside." She patted her belly. "Baby Max come after a while."

"You're talking better." Sam smiled at her little sister.

"I learn. When Brad home?"

"It'll be awhile. Let me check the screen. Come on."

Finally, something good happened.

Maxee followed Sam to her room, sat on the bed, and bounced gently. Sam found that the messages were the same: Stay home, two meals a day, use water sparingly.

Back out in the main room, Sam picked up a pile of papers. "Help me get this stuff sorted out."

She had piled everything on the counters and tables without even looking at them. She had already straightened out her room.

They had most of the papers in neat stacks when another earthquake hit, and everything went sailing back onto the floor.

"Oh, shit," Sam said.

"Bad word." Maxee stooped to pick up a handful of papers. "I pick up."

"Thanks, Maxee. You're a good girl."

Maxee smirked.

*   *   *

World relaxed.

27

WHEN THE MEN CAME HOME FROM WORK, they were starving, so Sam, Maxee, and the men went to the caff. "Good to see you up and around, Max," Brad said.

"I Maxee," she announced. "Female, I am. Hungry, I am, too."

As they ate, they discussed their situation. "I talked to Burns about what was going on Down Below, and he said it was being taken care of ... whatever that meant," Hal said.

"I need to go down and get the rest of my stuff." Todd sporked up a bite. "When can we do that?"

"Day after tomorrow is our day off." Hal wiped his chin. "Let's do it then."

"Okay," Todd said. "Sam, you and Max will stay here."

"I Maxee," Maxee put in. "I female now."

"Okay, Maxee." Todd looked at him/her. "You what?"

"Max, the child, has grown up into Maxee, a female." Sam gestured toward her with a breadstick.

"Oh." Todd's jaw dropped and his eyebrows hiked up.

Sam had never seen him this flustered.

"Anyway, she's fine now. I suppose I can go out and talk to people."

"Why don't you make up a message you can give people?" Hal suggested. "That way they'll have something to look at, look at."

"I have."

*   *   *

The next morning, Sam sat at her screen and looked at what she had written up the other day, about what Dondo had told them, and what they were doing about it. She rewrote it five times before she got the message in a form that she felt comfortable with.

Sam downloaded it into her portable comm, got up and stretched, and went into the other room.

Maxee watched an entertainment on the big screen. To Sam, it was great to see him — no, *her* — out here enjoying herself. Sam got a mug of water.

Maxee turned. "Go out?"

"Sure, why not."

They went out the hatch in Brad's room; there was nothing but hallway outside the front door. Sam climbed to her feet and breathed in the fresh air.

"So good." Maxee followed her out and looked around. "How we go up?"

"Not here. We'll have to go down to the far end where there are hills." Sam pointed east.

"Long way?"

"Yes. After Todd and the others go down to get the rest of his stuff, we'll have to go explore."

"Come, I?" She bobbed up and down on her toes.

"Maybe. I'll check with the others."

They walked along the bottom of the cliff west to the cross street. It ended at their street, and in between that and the block cubes, a small area held controls for the conduits. Sam looked out over the silver sea of solar panels.

Were they Volen or not? She wasn't sure. *If they were, what would they do for power?*

Back at the hatch, Maxee stretched. "Good to walk."

They climbed back down inside and got drinks of water. Soon, Brad and Todd came home for the midday meal. Sam told them about their expedition.

"We have to go all the way to the end before we start up," Todd said. "Great." He snapped a breadstick in half.

*   *   *

In the afternoon, Sam walked down her street knocking on doors. Only one person answered — the mother of a Councilor. She listened to Sam's spiel, shook her head, and let Sam download her message to the woman's comm.

Sam returned home and dropped into a chair. Probably the people who didn't answer their doors were at work. At this rate, it would take forever — and they didn't have forever. Of course, if everyone she talked to talked to as many other people, it might work. She sat up. The caffs.

Could we meet with people or post something there?

That evening, when they went for their meal, Brad talked to the manager. She had a board with local announcements and told them that they could put something there. She would talk to other caff managers; they had a private network.

*   *   *

The next day, Todd and Brad went down to get the rest of Todd's belongings. Hal accompanied them, with another large carryall cart.

Sam returned to her canvassing, down six more blocks, around and back on the next street west. About a third of the people were home, and most of them accepted her message. One elderly fellow, a retired councilor, said it was all nonsense and demanded to know why she wasn't home raising babies. Sam put a big "X" on his apartment number on her list.

When the men returned that evening, they had three heaping carts, bulging backpacks, plus two hefty young men with two large bags each. After they dumped it all, only a narrow route was left through the main room, which felt a lot smaller.

"Where are you going to put all this stuff?" Sam asked.

Todd shrugged. "This is Bob and Will Cousins. They are taking over my apartment. They came up from Level Two."

The brothers gawked around at the room.

"Welcome and thank you for helping Todd," Sam said.

Bob, the taller one, looked at her, and his eyes widened.

"She's taken," Todd said.

Sam glared at Todd. "Let's go eat."

After the meal, Bob and Will left to stay with Hal. At Sam's place, the men started unpacking, making an even bigger mess. Sam and Maxee stayed in her room.

*　　*　　*

The next day, Sam sorted stuff in the morning and canvassed more people in the afternoon.

Brad came home early. "Tomorrow you wanna look for a way out?"

"Way out?"

"Up into the hills."

"Oh. Yes. We'll have to go down to the east end to find the hills."

"I have four days off. That should be enough time to find a place."

*　　*　　*

In the morning, Brad, Maxee, and Sam packed their bags, walked down to Forty-Eight, and caught a car across. This car line was working because most of the councilors lived in the top two levels. At the stop in Centrex, a security guard hauled them off and grilled them about where they were going.

Sam fumed.

"Visiting friends in the East End," Brad replied. He came up with a name and address.

The security guard verified it and said they could go. They had to wait for the next car.

At the portal to Noreg, the tree branch walkway had snapped off, but the ground was not too far below the exit. Brad dropped down and caught Sam and Maxee. The slope up here was not bad.

Sam breathed deeply of the fresh air. *Outside at last.* She looked down at the Noreg trees and prayed that they could find the Noreg good trees. The thought of living out here all the time made her want to yell with joy.

Maxee jumped up and down and squealed. "Good, good, good," she cried.

Brad entered an image of the portal in his comm so they could find their way back. They took off with matching grins.

The hills stretched from west to east in pleasing green and brown curves with scattered patches of green trees. Greenish plants clustered in the gullies between them. A light breeze tickled Sam's nose, bringing an earthy aroma, much like she had smelled at Liia's outdoor place. The first valley was barely a dent, so they climbed the next hill.

"Rest, me," Maxee said as she dropped to the ground.

Sam followed and looked back the way they'd come. Beyond the first hill, the silver roof stretched to the sea next to the mass of green of Mantz' trees.

How many people lived under that silver roof, and how many could we save?

They stopped to eat. Sam sat and wondered at the world around her. Maxee pointed to various items, grass, rocks, a little red bug, and asked Sam what they were. Brad lay back and gazed at the sky. The narrow valley below had a trickle of a stream. Something inside Sam blossomed. A brief whiff of the presence sifted by.

"Too small," Brad said as they prepared to move on. "Let's see what the next one is like."

The hill beyond was much higher and topped with trees. Their shadows stretched to the east when they reached the top. In between the trees, Sam saw a wide valley with a sparkling river below. The sky turned pink. Sam looked to the west. The sun was a fireball in the west.

"Is that natural?" Sam asked.

"Yeah." Brad turned. "It's called sunset. That valley down there looks good," he added.

"Yes," Sam breathed. It was what she had dreamed of.

"We go there?" Maxee asked.

"Tomorrow. Time to stop and rest now."

Brad unslung his back bag and led them down into a circle of trees. These had large, three pronged leaves. An open space let them get a glimpse of the valley.

On one side, by themselves, three tall bushes sparkled with tiny white flowers. Real flowers. Sam walked over and gently touched one. It was so soft. She leaned over and sniffed. Sweet and spicy, like one of Liia's flowers. She wondered whether these plants grew down in the valley.

Sam sat down next to the bushes and let their aroma wash over her as the branches reached down to her. She sensed that otherness again. Maxee dropped down beside her and sniffed a blossom.

"Flowers nice."

"Yes." Sam hugged her.

Brad plopped down beside them. "This looks like a good place to camp." He plucked a blade of grass and chewed on it. "Say, your face is red."

Sam touched her cheek and it was painful. "Yours is too."

"Sunburn. Living indoors all our life, our skin has no protection from the sun. We need hats."

"Hats?"

"To keep the sun off our faces."

Sam yawned. They ate and went to sleep not long after dark.

✳   ✳   ✳

In the morning, Sam woke as it was just beginning to get light. A presence emanating from the bushes and ground surrounded her for a brief moment. Then it was gone.

What was that?

She shook her head and rose. On her feet, she felt like a whole new person, one with this world. Sam danced around.

Me, dance? I haven't done that for years.

Maxee jumped up and joined her.

"Hey, girls." Brad sat up and stretched. He rose and passed out hunks of bread. "I'm ready to go."

They grabbed their back bags and started off. Sam wanted to run, but there were too many trees in the way. A trail of sorts zigzagged through the forest and, as long as it kept going downhill, they followed it.

After a while, they found a little spring leaking a trickle down the hill. They knelt and drank their fill. The water was cool and sweet, with none of the chemical taste of City water.

Brad found a bush with large leaves and pulled off a couple. "These will do for hats for now." He handed one to Sam. "Hold it over your head."

"You think it'll do any good?"

"Yes, sweet sister."

The sun was high when they reached the bottom and stepped out of the trees. A line of green marked the river. The little stream ambled to meet it. The valley itself was grassy, with clumps of bushes and tall trees. The river drew them, and the presence held Sam. She felt no need to fight it.

"Well, there's our water," Brad said.

The river was wider than twice the length of their apartment. They rested and headed downstream. Bright yellow flowers on the bushes along the water gave out a sweet aroma. Trees dangled feathery branches in the water.

Soon, Sam saw a high hill ahead. They climbed it and sat on top. The flat top was as long as several blocks, and at least four blocks wide, facing the river. Many trees were scattered about.

"This is the place," Sam said, leaning back on her elbows.

"Yeah," Brad said.

"We live here?" Maxee asked, sprawled in the grass.

"Yes."

After a while, they wandered around, studying the place.

At a corner facing the river, with several trees, Sam said, "Here's where I want my house."

She could visualize sitting on her porch overlooking the river, gazing at the distant mountains. Out here, she felt much more alive than she ever had before. This was her world.

"Flat top is mesa," Maxee said. "Is good."

"How do you know that?" Sam asked.

"Read a lot."

Once again, Sam wondered what Maxee's world and her people were like. Spacers had discovered the place after a battle between two unknowns and found everyone dead. Per standard instructions, the spacers had brought back one of the dead. Sam's dad had found Max, a living infant, in a female's pouch.

That night, Sam slept under her trees. She dreamed of this plateau lined with houses along the river, government buildings and labs behind, and houses spread out all over the valley.

She also dreamed of an unsullied world. Unsullied by people.

*   *   *

World watched.

28

IN THE MORNING, SAM WOKE to blue skies peeping through the green tree leaves and a feeling of being tested. Beside her, Maxee lay curled into a ball, a fan of small branches over her. Sam shrugged off the feeling and rose.

She found Brad at the next group of trees, stretching. He put an arm around her.

"This is incredible," he murmured. "I wish Dad could have seen this."

"He probably did see something like this on Mother's world."

"That's right. He was there for about a year, right?"

"Yes."

A memory came. Mother had held her auburn hair next to Sam's and said, *"See, we match."* Sam blinked away the tears and watched the river.

After they roused Maxee, and had a bite to eat, they found an easier place to get down to the valley and walked downriver. Sam absorbed the burbling and swishing sounds of the water, music to her ears. When they reached a place where the hills came down to the river, they stopped and rested.

"Oh, man," Brad said.

"I know." Sam couldn't keep her eyes off the river. This was the real jewel.

"We live here." Maxee sprawled on the grass.

"Just a few little things to take care of." Brad patted the grass. "Like building homes and other places, providing for water, power, food and clothing, providing protection from weather."

"Spoilsport." Sam grinned at him.

Sam, Brad and Maxee dragged themselves away from the valley and headed back to City. They had no trouble finding the portal, but only Brad was tall enough to reach it. He hauled the broken-off part of the walkway over and propped it up against the entrance like a ramp. Brad went up first. It slipped off and he fell.

"Brad!" Sam's heart twisted.

He jumped up. "I'm okay." He propped up the boards again and he pushed them farther in. This time he made it to the top. Brad held onto the ends and, braced with his feet against the inside door rim, said, "Come on up."

Maxee crawled up first. "Easy."

Sam followed, and stood, holding on to the door frame. "We'll have to do something about this."

"I agree. Let's leave this up like this for now." Brad turned.

They went through to the car terminal.

Something else to figure out, Sam thought. *How much more are they going to pile on me? I didn't ask for this.*

*   *   *

At home, they found most of the comm web up, so Brad tried to contact Bill and Susan. He could not reach Bill, but he got a response from Susan. She and two of her group were at the museum, and no, she hadn't heard from Bill since the big quake.

"The museum," Sam said.

She'd forgotten about it. One cube block on ground level covered one of the original houses and a few outbuildings. The whole block was a museum which held a lot of ancient artifacts, and was open to anyone, Upper or Lower.

"I hope they can save some of those things. It's our history." *Something else I have to deal with, but we need to know where we came from.*

*   *   *

After the men went back to work, Sam took the Forty-Eight car west. It stopped several blocks before the end. At first, she wondered why, then she remembered Brad telling them about the broken cars at Liia's place.

Sam did a circle of two blocks south, two east, and two north, again only finding a little over a quarter of residents who answered the door. She caught the car home and collapsed into a chair.

This was hard on her feet. She wondered if she could get better shoes. All they had was several layers of heavy cloth wrapped around their feet. All the original footwear brought from Old Earth was long gone, and there was nothing here to substitute for leather.

When Brad and Todd came home, Hal came with them.

"Hi, beautiful," he said when he saw Sam.

"Hi." Sam blushed in spite of herself.

The men dropped their cases and they all went to dinner. After they'd ordered, Hal announced, "I've found someone with the council who's ready to listen, and he wants us all for a meeting, tomorrow."

"Will they listen to us?" Sam asked.

"Some will. We have to try."

"True." Sam took a bite of stew.

*   *   *

The four of them, Hal, Todd, Brad and Sam, went to Arlene's office, and she led them over to the council chamber. They stood in the center of a square of tiers of high-backed chairs with arms, mostly filled with councilors. All the brown walls of the chamber held screens.

187

Arlene introduced them and added, "They have something really important to say, so please listen."

Todd told of Dondo's message and what they'd found out later.

"And you believe this?" someone on the left side asked.

"Yes, because it is already happening Down Below," Sam said.

"Down Below has nothing to do with us," he retorted.

"What do you think we're sitting on?" Sam asked. "Where do you think your food and clothing come from? When it goes, we'll sink. Which is already happening. Have any of you looked outside lately?"

"Outside? Of course not. Everything we need is in here." Someone on the right.

"Everything except real air and plants and trees."

"Sam," Todd said. "However, gentlemen, Dondo did tell us that the average man is two inches shorter today than our ancestors were. That means we are missing something. And we're going to be missing a lot more when the Volen leave."

"They wouldn't dare." A voice from the rear.

"How are you going to stop them?" Sam moved from one foot to the other.

"Gentlemen, we need your help, to get the word out. Many of us have boxes of stuff handed down to us by the ancestors. We need everyone to check their boxes for anything that will be useful in our new colony. The Volen will not send us any more materials or the usual items we get from them," Todd said.

"I don't believe it." The voice from the rear.

"Where is this supposed new colony supposed to be?" Someone from the left.

"In a valley up in the hills in back of us," Sam said.

"Outdoors? Over my dead body." Several chimed in.

"If you wish," Todd said. "We are going."

"Have you seen this place?"

"Yes." Sam smiled. "It's beautiful, along a river."

"Get these crazies out of here," someone yelled.

Sam backed into Brad and Todd.

Arlene led them out. "Just a bunch of little boys."

"How did they ever get their positions?" Brad asked.

"Hereditary," Hal said. "From their fathers, grandfathers, and those before them."

"Not in our world," Sam said.

"Wait here." Arlene stopped us in an angle of the hallway and trotted off.

She returned with a young man with long, black hair.

"I just became a councilor when my dad retired," he said.

"Which district?" Sam asked.

"Southwest One. Next to the museum."

"Uh oh," she said. "How are things down there?"

"I've sent someone down, but haven't heard from him yet."

"Then your district will be one of the first affected, if it isn't already."

He nodded. "I believe you. What can I do?"

Todd took him aside.

Sam looked at Brad. "How can they be so dense? Weren't they even listening?"

"I saw a couple old guys asleep in the back. They don't want to believe because they're in their nice, comfortable ruts and they want to stay there. We'll just keep doing what we need to do."

"Well, one of these days, their ruts are going to collapse."

Brad grinned at her. "You're so right."

At home, Todd unpacked boxes. Sam had a few things from Uncle Joe. Brad had Dad's treasures.

Todd laid out several flat packages wrapped in old-time plastic. He peeled off a layer and said, "Come look at this."

Sam and Brad looked over his shoulder as he peeled off more layers. The thing was a book, a very old book. They could not decipher the words on the cover, they were so worn. Todd lifted the cover, revealing a map on the page underneath.

"Wow," Todd breathed. "This is a map of the original colony."

The edge of the page crumbled where he touched it. He quickly wrapped it back up. The others were wrapped in the same old plastic. He piled them back in the box.

"I've got to find a way to copy these."

"Would it have information on building the colony?" Sam asked.

"Most likely. This is indeed a treasure."

"I wonder how many more treasures there are in City." Sam stretched.

*　　　*　　　*

The next day, Dondo called Sam to come to Complex, where he gave her a new, smaller comm unit that fit in the palm of her hand. He appeared thinner than before.

"This device will connect you to one or more of the other sectors. It is a communicator only. You can still use your regular comm."

"Thank you. Can you have the Volen deliver our building materials directly to our site?"

"You have one?"

"Yes." Sam described how they got there and the little mesa with their markers on it.

"I will ask them."

Sam went home and tried to call Liia on the new device, but apparently she had not received hers yet.

*　　　*　　　*

World shook clouds, sent out bugs.

29

S USAN SHOWED UP WITH TWO LARGE YOUNG MEN carrying huge bags.

"What's all this?" Sam asked.

"Artifacts from the museum." Susan grinned at me as she dropped her bags.

The men put down their loads and the shorter one helped Hank, the larger man, remove a huge crate in a sling with wide black straps over Hank's shoulders, another around his waist, and two other straps connecting the shoulder and waist bands, crisscrossed across his chest.

"This is Ronny and Hank. They've been a big help. We'd like to stay a couple of days to rest before we go down."

"Sure. Have a seat. What in City is in that crate?"

"Some kind of machine with a motor. I'd like a shower, if you don't mind."

"Sure, Susan." Sam showed them the bathroom.

The men used the facilities first, then turned it over to Susan.

During their evening meal, Susan told them what things were like down below.

"They said it was closed off." Sam waved a breadstick.

"They're wrong. We have two stairways open at the northeast corner. Only the top two or three levels are livable, even though they have little power and water. We're moving people up as fast as we can; the rest areas and museum area are full. Ronny has a fancy image capturer in his comm and took a lot of images of the museum and the area."

"Oh, good." Sam took a sip of her drink.

Ronny grinned, showing a space between his front teeth. "I'm the official imager. I'm taking as many images of everything that I can."

"Very good. How are you going to show your images when your comm is gone?"

"I'm working on that."

*   *   *

Susan and Sam sorted through the artifacts from the museum. They organized and found places to put each of the items.

"Look at this doll," Susan said.

The doll's long dress was faded to a yellowish white, and her hair had fallen out, but her face was beautiful, with big blue eyes and red bow mouth. The box she lay in was yellowed and scratched.

Sam took the box and turned it over. A tag provided a date: 7/9/130. "Susan, this doll is a thousand years old."

They stared at each other. Sam emptied a box of food packets and put the doll box inside it. On the outside she wrote, *"Doll. Earliest ancestors."*

"This is our history. We have to save this."

"Yes," Susan said, breathless.

Sam set the box on a shelf in the corner of her room. They kept going, packing small items in boxes. Sam kept an itemized list in her head, and later wrote it down. By the time the men came home, every cabinet and cupboard in the place was stuffed.

That night, Todd told them he had four days off. "Who wants to go up to our site?" he asked.

They all did, even Maxee.

In the morning, Ronny and Susan got Hank harnessed up with the machine box, and Ronny carried a couple of bags. Todd and Brad carried bags of their belongings, and Sam took up some tools and the food. Maxee carried her tote, and Susan carried her own back bag.

The group had to wait for an empty car, for they took up seven of the eight seats. In Centrex, they were hauled off and grilled again. Brad told Security they were taking stuff from relatives lower down to his East End friend. It took a while before the security guard bought it. The next car only had room for Sam, Maxee, Susan and Brad.

"Get off at the last stop. We'll meet you there," Brad told the others as they boarded.

At the terminal, Sam paced around, waiting for them. Only Hank and Ronny showed up.

"Where's Todd?" Sam demanded.

"They made him wait, even though there were empty seats. He'll be on the next one."

"They're running every twenty minutes now," Brad said, looking at his comm.

This wait was even longer. Sam heaved a sigh of relief as Todd stepped off.

"Security thinks they own the place," Todd growled.

Sam led the others through the portal. The walkway had slipped off. Brad dropped down first and moved it out of the way. Then, one by one, they dropped themselves and let down the bags.

Hank glanced around, shut his eyes, and trembled. "I can't," he said. "It's too big out here."

"Uh oh," Sam said.

"Agoraphobia," Todd said. "Fear of open spaces. I looked it up." He took a deep breath. "Aah. This is great. The sooner we move out here, the better."

"Right. Another problem." Sam took a breath. "Susan, are you all right?"

"I think so. If I keep looking at my feet."

"Walk with me. Ronny?"

"I'm okay. I'll pretend I'm looking at my images."

"Brad, keep an eye on him."

"Okay." He moved next to Ronny.

Sam pulled an extra tunic out of her bag and made a makeshift blindfold for Hank. "Todd, you get to lead him."

Sam led the way, holding Susan's hand.

It was harder going, carrying their stuff, so they camped by the stream in the second valley. Hank huddled under a tree. Sam realized this was going to be a big problem for the people. They would have to make blindfolds or hoods for those who couldn't handle the space until they got the people into their new homes. Homes without windows. And lots of blindfolds and hoods.

Yes, Sam thought. Hoods open at the bottom, so they could see their feet. Sam wondered if she could get the records of everyone who passed the outdoor test at age twelve. Those people could lead the others.

Sam looked for the sunset, but only saw the sky go to pale blue. She tried to sleep, but creatures in the trees kept making *tweep*ing sounds.

*　　　*　　　*

The next day, they headed up the incline and, after a couple of rest stops, arrived at the top.

"Oh, my," Susan said, looking at the valley below. Her hand gripped Sam's tightly.

"Beautiful, isn't it?" Sam said.

"I can't believe the difference from inside. Oh, Sam, thank you for bringing me here."

"We still have a ways to go."

This is the place, Sam thought. *But oh, the work to make it livable.*

After a few moments, Brad said. "Let's keep going. There's still plenty of light." He found their trail and led the way.

They camped in the trees partway down. Sam lay and listened to rustling and other unidentifiable sounds in the forest — her new world. The otherness soothed her.

In the morning, when they left the forest, Sam angled over toward the mesa. Todd stopped and looked around.

"Fantastic," he said. "You two did a great job finding this place."

Sam grinned. "Thanks."

She looked at Susan, who also had a grin on her face. Ronny was imaging everything in sight.

"Come on," Sam said, starting off.

Under a group of trees near the base of the mesa, Hank lifted his blindfold. "A river," he said, and stared at it. "If I can see that … yes. I can do this."

"Thank you, Oneness," Sam whispered.

After they rested, Sam took them to the mesa. A great pile of boards and barrels lay nearby. Their Volen delivery. Sam started up.

"No," Brad said. "Let's go sit by the river."

Sam sat between Brad and Susan, and the others along the edge, under the trees, and watched the gurgling water roll by. The world waited for her.

"If the people could only see this, they'd come in an instant," Susan said.

"I know."

Maxee lay in the grass playing with several small river stones. The men sat with their own thoughts.

Little invisible bugs buzzed around them. Sam swatted at them. She hadn't figured on this. Maxee was the only one the bugs did not attack.

Someone's stomach growled. Todd passed out hunks of bread. They tried to keep the bugs out of their mouths as they ate.

The breeze grew stronger.

Sam rose. "We need to plot a place to relieve ourselves."

"Yes," Hal said.

They found a place downstream and away from the river. Then they climbed the mesa and wandered around on top.

Sam showed them where she wanted her house, and Brad's and Todd's. "Government and labs over there." She waved toward the side away from the river.

"Good," Todd said. "But it'll be a lot of work."

"We need to get people up here. People who can work out in the open." Brad turned around.

"Well, we've got supplies." Sam walked around. "Over here. It looks easier to get up and down on this side."

They made that their pathway down and began hauling their belongings up to the top of the mesa.

The wind picked up, clouds blew in from the west, and it grew darker.

"What is?" Maxee asked.

"Weather," Brad said. "Looks like it might rain."

"Rain?" Sam asked. *What happened to my beautiful, sunny outdoors?*

"It does sometimes." Brad grinned at her. "I've been studying it. Let's get our stuff under trees."

"And us," Todd added.

Drops of water began to fall. Sam and the men huddled under the trees, but Maxee danced around trying to catch the drops. Susan found a wide bucket and set it out.

It rained harder, and Maxee ran in under the tree.

"Water come down from sky." She giggled.

Sam realized they needed the water to keep everything green, but this had not been in her picture of outdoors. The rain didn't last long, though, and a gorgeous arc of colors glowed against the clouds.

"I want," Maxee cried, reaching for the rainbow.

"Sorry, kid, it's not real," Brad said.

Ronny clicked away with his imager.

When the colors faded, they shared the water in the bucket and went back to work.

"We need to make collectors like this," Todd swung the bucket. "What have we got?"

He pawed through the pile of items the Volen had left them. After emptying a barrel, they found that it was lined with some kind of impermeable material.

"This will work."

They took more boards and other items up, fighting off more bugs. As darkness fell, the bugs disappeared.

Thank goodness, Sam thought. *Now we can sleep peacefully.*

*   *   *

World caused soil to compact. City shifted.

30

S AM WOKE TO A SENSE OF AWARENESS of the planet beneath her. The world was a living being. She realized she and her people had to work with it, to share this space.

"We must have shelter," Sam said aloud, sitting up.

She sensed agreement. As she prepared for the day, she decided not to tell anyone about the world yet.

The group built a crude lean-to against some trees in the middle of the mesa and put all their stuff in it. Sam took some boards and outlined her house, then she, Brad, and Todd moved more boards up the mesa. It was cooler now, and they had to keep working to stay warm.

"We'll need warmer clothes out here," Sam noted.

"Yes," Susan agreed.

They marked out the rest of their places and a line of apartments. Sam was pleased to spend another night under her trees, but only Maxee's soft fur kept her from freezing. This move was not going to be nearly as easy as she first thought.

Even cooler in the morning, they left as quickly as possible, Sam with mixed emotions. On one hand, she loved breathing the fresh air, drinking the mountain water, and living with real grass, flowers, and trees. On the other hand, things like sunburn, rain, and bugs made outdoors less than perfect.

As the group returned to City, Sam told Susan to let people know where the valley was, and how to get there. The main buildings were to be built up on the mesa and the housing below.

"I don't know when I'll be able to get back up myself, and we need to get the place started. Anybody you know who knows anything about building?" she asked.

"There is one couple I've met who have done some lovely cabinet work. I'll see if I can find them." Susan smiled.

*　　　*　　　*

At home, Sam called Liia.

"We're ready to go, but there's no way to get up into the hills from here," she told Sam. "The way you and I went is gone. There's a big gap at the back of the roof, and no way over to the next clan square. Is there anything you can do?"

"I don't know, off-hand. Let me get with the men. They may have an idea."

Todd and Brad listened. "I don't see how," Brad said.

"I can't take any more time off," Todd said. "Brad, you can fly my ship, can't you?"

"First ship I learned on."

"Tomorrow, take my ship and fly over there. I'll fix the paperwork. See what you can do."

"Your ship," Sam said. "Is it Volen?"

"No, I bought it from an offworlder."

Sam relaxed. "So we'll still have it when the fliers are gone."

"Yes. I have someone looking into whether we can get our hands on another one. It's solar-powered, so we don't have to worry about fuel."

*　　　*　　　*

After a day's rest, when Susan and Sam did some planning. Susan prepared to leave.

"Oh, here it is," she said, holding up a locket. "I wondered where it went. I meant to give it to you earlier. Maybe you can find these children somehow." Susan gave the locket and a pair of rings to Sam.

It held images of a boy and a little girl. "I'll see what I can do." Sam sighed.

Not likely in all this mess, and something else I have to deal with.

"Thanks. It's been good seeing you."

"You're welcome any time." Sam smiled.

"Thanks. You'll get everything taken care of. Just keep doing what you're doing."

Sam went to her spreadsheet that listed all the residents. She'd marked her family and ones she'd told about the upcoming collapse and move. There still weren't very many.

That evening, Sam showed the men the locket with the images. "Susan brought this; she found it on a dead woman. She thought maybe we could identify the kids."

"Oh, my Oneness, that's Jim and Betty. Was there a man with her?" Brad demanded.

"She said there was one, mostly buried. These are their rings."

Sam gave Brad her comm device so he could call Liia.

"A friend working down below found a locket with a picture of Jim and Betty. The woman and man were dead. I'll bring the locket and their rings when I come over tomorrow. I'm borrowing Todd's ship and flying over to see what I can see. About midday, if you want to be up top."

Sam wanted to go with him, but Todd said no. "Max can't afford to lose both of you."

"Maxee," Sam said. "All right."

*   *   *

The next day, Todd came home with the news that he had acquired another runabout ship. On his next day off, he taught Giil and Liia how to pilot it, and leased it to them.

Meanwhile, Sam decided it was time to check in with everyone and dug out the new comm device. The device had a button for each of the other sectors, and one below to call them all. The screen, a translator, showed words as they were spoken.

Liia answered first. "Sam, thank you so much for the little ship. Our clan is moving up quite quickly now, and many of the top clans are ready to go. We're building places for several clans together."

"Glad to hear it."

Mantz signed on. "Lowest trees fall over, smash houses and people. We are moving up, living on ground. New trees not big enough for tree houses."

"Well, you don't have your big bad beasties to worry about, so you don't have to live in trees for safety. But the treehouses did look nice."

"We found great grands' seeds, but only tiny sprouts so far."

"Okay, good. Hang in there." Sam took a breath. "Elder?"

"No problems yet. Making dirt hills. Need to make them stay together."

"Do you have any clay soils anywhere?"

"I will check."

"Okay. Maya?"

"Fake ground gone. Waiting for other. Lower trees falling. Making new caves higher."

"Good. Hive?"

"We prepare."

"Okay. We have a place in the hills and are beginning to build. I still don't see how we're going to get all this done in a year."

"Do what you can," The Elder said. "If you need help, we can send people."

"Thank you. I'll let you know."

"We, too," said Mantz. "Use our land as you need."

"Thanks. I'll call again in thirty days,"

Sam signed off and sighed

So much to do and so little time. 'Overwhelmed' is an understatement.

Her next project was to head to the fabric store two blocks down. One side of the store was lined with racks of readymade clothes, the other side had counters with piles of cloth. Thread, needles, and other notions lined the rear.

Sam pawed through the piles looking for dark cloth. A large piece of black and a smaller piece of dark blue surfaced, and she also found some dark green. Those items, along with needles and thread, took most of her credits. She'd have to do something about that.

At home, Sam laid out the pieces and tried to figure out how to make hoods. Aunt Linda, Todd's mother, had taught her how to thread a needle and do basic stitchery, but she needed some kind of pattern. She had no spatial talent at all.

When Brad came home, Sam showed him the fabric and said, "I need a way to make hoods out of this. Do you have any ideas?"

"Easiest way is to make cones. Do you want eyeholes?"

"No." She stared at Brad. "The whole purpose of the hoods is to cover the eyes."

"Oh." Brad turned away.

He found a large piece of paper, drew a circle on it, cut it out, and cut out a triangle. Then he brought the two edges together and, behold, a cone. He popped it on her head.

"It's a little wide."

"Yeah, the wind could catch it. Here." He grabbed the scissors and cut off the point. After pulling the two sides of a triangle around farther, he pulled the hood down.

"Much better," Sam said.

"There's your pattern. Go to it."

The next morning, Sam managed to make one. It took more than an hour. "There's got to be a faster way."

"I do?" Maxee asked.

She'd been watching Sam, so Sam showed her how to do it. She picked it up quickly, and her long agile fingers moved much faster than Sam's. By midday, they had four done.

At the caff, Sam ran into Wanda and Carol from down the street. Sam had an idea.

"Wanda, you make doll clothes. Would you be willing to help me make hoods? We need them for people moving up to the new place, so they won't get overwhelmed by the outdoors."

"Do you have the material and things?" Wanda slung her long dark braid over her shoulder.

"I've got some. I need to find another fabric store. I bought out all the dark material in our local one." *And I need to get some more credits, too.*

"I've got a bunch of navy blue the Volen sent a while ago. Little girls like bright colors on their dolls, so I never used it."

"Good. Come by after we eat, and I'll show you the pattern."

"I can sew too," Carol added. "I'll help." She touched her gray curls.

"Thanks."

At Sam's place, later, Wanda looked at the pattern, made some notes, and she and Carol left.

✳   ✳   ✳

World watched as beings went back inside.

31

I N THE LATE AFTERNOON, Hal came over.
"Have you heard? No non-employees will be allowed in Centrex, not even on through cars. Only the public offices on the lowest level will be open to citizens."

"What?" Sam exclaimed.

"We'll be allowed through since we work there, but you won't be able to ride the cars through. Sorry, Sam."

"So how am I supposed to get out now?"

Hal shrugged.

"We'll figure a way," Brad said.

Sam didn't see how, but she knew he would come up with something. "That reminds me. I'm getting low on credits. Doing all this other stuff doesn't leave me any time to do my regular job. Any ideas?"

"I'll get the council to reimburse you for the cloth," Hal said.

"Thanks." Sam smiled at him, and he smiled back. Her heart thumped.

Sam and Maxee made hoods until the material ran out. Wanda gave her some more; she had piles of navy fabric. She also talked a couple of fellow doll sellers into making hoods.

Sewing was not one of Sam's talents, but Maxee loved it. Sam soon went back to canvassing.

Most mornings, Sam, along with many others, went door to door to talk to people. She tried to get people up here to take a stranger into their spare room. Occasionally, she came across someone who had seen the information in a caff and was already preparing to leave.

*   *   *

One morning, Sam felt a need to go down to a lower level. After a couple of no answers, Sam heard a tiny voice say, "Come in."

She tried the door. It was unlocked, and she pushed it open. In the dimness, all Sam could see was someone huddled in a big chair and piles of stuff on the big table, bed, and floor.

"Hello," Sam said. The person in the chair murmured something. "Gloria Smith?" Sam asked, checking her comm.

"Yes. Food? Water?" the tiny voice whispered.

"Just a minute."

Sam turned up the light just enough so she could see what she was doing, went to Gloria's sink, and pushed the lever. No water came out. Sam filled a mug from her water pouch and held it for Gloria. She drank half of it.

"Better," Gloria said, more clearly. "Pardon me for not getting up. If you would, please, carry me to the bed and empty the pot. My aide did not come yesterday."

"Sure."

How could someone not come to help this little old lady?

Sam cleared a space on the bed, picked up the tiny woman, carried her over, and laid her down. Sam found a bucket in the seat of the chair, full of Gloria's waste. She pulled it out, dumped it in the toilet. and pushed the button. The toilet bowl emptied, but she could still smell it. Probably stopped up and couldn't go down too far anymore. Sam found a clean cloth and cleaned Gloria's bottom.

Then she cleaned the chair seat, all the while wondering where Gloria's family was and how could they let her live like this.

"Do you have any children or grandchildren?" Sam asked, as she carried the tiny woman back to the chair and arranged her skirt so that it did not cover the bucket.

"My children died young. Thank you."

"Here." Sam gave her a soft food bar.

She wondered about the children. Most people here died of old age, but didn't think it was appropriate to ask about them.

Gloria sat up straight and ate the bar quickly, just short of gobbling. "I have a neighbor who brings me food every day, in the morning and evening. After I eat, she carries me to the bed and cleans up. But she did not come yesterday."

Little shocked Sam anymore, but that certainly did. "Do you have any relatives who can come take care of you?"

"No. I don't know what I'll do if she doesn't come tonight."

"We'll find someone. I'll stay here until we do."

"Oh, would you?" She reached out for Sam.

Sam hugged her gently. Tears ran down Gloria's wrinkled cheeks.

"Don't worry, we'll find someone." Sam keyed her comm with one hand, holding the woman with the other.

"Ah, here it is. I'm going to make a call."

Sam tapped the number of a woman on the empty room list. "Hi, Judy? This is Samanda Lar. I talked to you the other day. Do you still have that room available?"

"Yes, did you find someone?"

"Yes, an elderly, chair-bound woman. She needs to be looked after, but she's very alert."

"I can handle that. When can she come?"

"As soon as possible. You will need a couple of husky young men: one to carry her, and one to carry her belongings."

"Okay, let me get back to you. You are staying with her?"

"Oh, yes. I couldn't leave her now."

After Sam hung up, she turned to Gloria. "A Judy Wilson, with two grown sons, has a room for you in her apartment. She and her sons will be down to take you up. She's on the twenty-seventh level. I'll stay here until they come."

"Oh, bless you, you're an angel."

She began to weep. Sam held her and found a handkerchief on her side table.

"You don't know what it's like to live like this, unable to move. I watch my screen, but it gets boring after a while. The Oneness must have sent you."

"Yes, I had a feeling I would be needed down here today."

Gloria wiped her eyes. "Maybe you can help me go through my things. There's a large bag in the closet."

"Sure." Sam dug out the carryall and pulled it out into the room. "Now what do you want to look at first?"

"Bring me those things on that shelf."

Sam took her several carved animals; a couple of small, worn dolls in a yellowed box; and an image of a handsome young man. Gloria fingered each item as she reminisced. "This was my mate, Rodney. He carved these figurines. The dolls were handed down from I don't know how many greats."

Sam looked around, found a small box, and put the figurines and the dolls in it. Gloria wanted to keep the image on her side table for now.

They continued to work together. In the back of the closet, Sam found a battered old red box and brought it to Gloria.

"Do you know what's in it?" Sam asked as she looked it over.

"No. It was Rodney's. Open it."

A new cookpot lay in thin papers. Sam held it up.

"What is it?" Gloria asked.

"It's a cookpot. If you don't want to keep it, we can use it." Sam told her about what was happening to the city.

"Take it."

Sam repacked it in the box and put the box by her bag beside the door. They had the carryall half full, and the bed and big table cleared, when Gloria asked Sam if she could go get some food.

"Sure."

Sam went to the nearest caff. When the frowning woman would only give her one small meal, Sam told her she needed food for Gloria in 254. "Her neighbor who gets it for her never came the last few days."

"She's gone. Went up to a cousin."

"And left that poor woman to starve?" Sam was appalled.

"Some people." The woman shook her head.

"You won't have to worry about Gloria. I'm having her moved up to a higher level to live with someone I know."

"Good." She gave Sam another meal.

Back at Gloria's, Sam helped her eat, then turned to her own meal.

Shortly after Sam finished, her comm buzzed.

"Judy here. My sons and two of their friends are coming down in the morning. I'm getting her room ready."

"Thank you. I'll be here." Sam told Gloria

"How can I ever thank you?" Gloria said, clutching Sam's arm. "You sleep on the bed, I'll be fine in the chair."

"Okay."

Then she called Brad to let him know where she was.

*   *   *

Sam had Gloria's belongings packed when the men showed up in the morning. They brought big bags; one had a basket contraption on his back. He set it down on the bed.

"Let's see how this works," he said to Gloria. "I'm going to pick you up and put you in the basket."

Gloria settled in, her shriveled legs curled in the bottom, and leaned against the high back.

"Oh, this is very comfortable." Gloria shifted around. "Thank you." She smiled up at him.

The blond man, Judy's son Ed, took the seat and bucket out of the chair. After emptying the bucket, he packed them in a large bag.

"We'll take this and put it in Mom's chair."

Ed lifted Gloria out and put on the basket, pulling the wide straps over his shoulders and another around his waist.

"Just a minute," Sam said.

She fashioned a diaper out of an old sheet and put it on the old woman while the men went outside. Gloria smiled her thanks.

207

"Okay, you can put her in now."

Ed squatted. One of the others lifted Gloria into the basket and got her settled. The other men divided up the bags.

"Thank you again," Gloria called as they left.

After Sam scrubbed the apartment and put the regular seat back into the big chair, she rested briefly. She double-checked drawers and corners for anything left behind, then departed to continue to work her way down the street. At a rest area packed with people, both inside the building and outside on the grounds, she found a young woman with small twin boys and took her to Gloria's apartment.

"Thank you so much. This will be a lot more comfortable than anything I've had before. I wish Lane was here."

"Lane?"

"The boys' father. He went to help and never came back." She choked back a sob.

"I'm so sorry. So many have been lost already. At least you have your little ones. Don't be afraid to ask for help. Anyway, enjoy this room while you can. You will be moving up soon."

Sam gave the woman her spiel. The young mother had lost her comm, so Sam told her that people would let her know when it was time.

Sam left the woman to explore her new room.

Back home, Sam marked off Gloria's room with the new name, and noted Judy's room. A few others had been marked on the master list.

This was going way too slowly. We have to find a way to reach people who are not at home during the day.

Both Brad and Todd refused to let her go out at night. Sam didn't want to, anyway. The streets weren't lit very well, and she hadn't forgotten her ex's goons.

*   *   *

World moved soil at edges of aquafer into the water.

32

EVERY DAY SAM WENT OUT to a different area and talked to people. Only about one in three believed in her warning. Those promised to go through their belongings and call her if they found anything they could use in the new place. About a third of the believers offered to help. *I'll believe it when I see it.*

Every evening she came home, collapsed, and after late meal, went through her lists and tried to think of what else she could do.

A few people called, saying they had found old tools or books in their ancestor boxes. The next day Sam would go down, pick up the artifact, and go on to her next group.

*   *   *

One evening, Brad said, "You've got to take a day off. You're wearing yourself out."

"I can't just sit around all day."

"Go up to the valley."

"That's three days."

"I'll take you tomorrow."

Todd burst in, waving a paper. "Did you see this, Brad?"

Brad grabbed it and read. "Oh, shit."

"What?" Sam demanded, trying to see over his shoulder.

"It's an edict from the governor," Todd said. "From now on, if anyone who works in Centrex is absent, except for preapproved days off, that person will be terminated."

The three of them looked at each other. "Why?" Sam asked.

"Too many people have been taking time off to save the world." Todd snorted.

"But we need them." Her heart sunk with a thud. *How were we going to get people up there now?*

"I've already used up my vacation," Todd said.

"And I don't have any yet," Brad added. "And we can't go up and back in one day."

How are we going to get people up there now? Sam clenched her fists.

Hal knocked once and burst in. "Did you see this?"

"Yes." Todd said.

"I'm sorry, I won't be able to do anything for you. I can't risk losing my job. I don't want to lose my apartment. I'd never get another job in Centrex."

The requirement to keep an apartment was to be productive in some way. Lose your job, you have five days to find another. No job, no apartment.

"That's okay," Brad said.

"Let's sit down." Sam groaned. "I've been on my feet all day." She sat, and the others followed suit.

"I have an idea," Todd said. "Maybe I can get the firm to set me up in an office outside of Centrex. I think there's a way we can do it, so I'm not legally bound to the Centrex office. As long as Brad is working there, we can keep the apartment."

"What about Arlene and the others?" Sam asked.

"She's furious and ready to quit, but even if she found another job right away, she couldn't keep her apartment. She'd have to move down lower."

"Or move in with us. Brad, you move in with Hal, and she can have your room." Sam leaned back.

"No. I'm staying right here," Brad said.

"Why? She'll be my chaperone."

"Just what do you think I'll do to your sister, Lar?" Todd glared at Brad.

"I'm a big girl, I can take care of myself."

"Okay, okay." Brad put his hands up.

"Arlene won't live with anyone else, anyway. She's going to keep her job and her apartment. She said she would be more useful working from the inside." Hal stood. "Let's go eat."

Maxee came out of the bedroom from where she'd been peering around the corner.

At dinner, we discussed the situation. "Todd, you and Hal don't risk losing your jobs," Sam said. She knew their apartment was in Todd's name. "Brad, is there any way you can use your position in the labs to go up to the valley to see about installations or something, so you can go up and be working?"

"My smart sister strikes again. Let me think about it and talk to people."

"Good. We're not going to let those goons stop us." Sam took a sip of her drink.

"I heard someone talking about vacation today. Let me see if I can find him and if he can go with you." Todd put his spork down.

They returned home with a little more hope.

*   *   *

The next morning, Sam went on her rounds, and ran into an older man who was also canvassing. She introduced herself.

"So you're the mastermind behind all this," he said with a smile.

"No, I just happened to be in the wrong place at the wrong time," she replied with a wan smile. "How are you doing?"

"So-so. One woman took an hour to find her ancestor box and go through it; nothing useful. Three doors slammed in my face, and two who took the information. One of them will do some canvassing. I'm Doug Green." He took a breath. "I've heard about the valley. Any chance I could go up and see it?"

"Maybe. Where do you live?" He gave me his address, and Sam saw it was checked off.

"Oh. That's not far. Okay, go get your stuff, enough for three or four days, and meet me back here. I'll go down that street and come back. We'll find a place for you to stay."

"Great." He trotted off.

Sam looked him up. He was a plumber with good ratings.

Great, we could use one to do the waterworks. He would be useful in the valley.

She went along and collected a few more people who were concerned, and one helper. The older woman said she would go sit in the caff and talk to everyone. That made Sam feel better.

If only there were more like her.

By the time Doug returned to the corner, Sam was beginning to wonder if he would come back. He arrived lugging a huge bag beside his back bag, gloom on his face.

"They fired me because it was not my day off." He dropped his bag. "I don't understand. I never had any problem before."

Sam told him about the edict. "Probably because you work for the water department, which is up there, they included you in the list of people who worked in Centrex."

"Okay." He let his head drop. "But it wasn't on the screen before I left." He looked at Sam. "I've worked there thirty years. What kind of nonsense is this, anyway?"

"The government is going crazy." Sam smiled. "I thought you had five days to find another job before you had to move out."

"Not anymore, with the housing shortage. There was a notice on my screen and my comm didn't work."

"Okay, come with me. We'll find you a place to stay. Is there something I can carry?"

He pulled out a small bag, medium weight. "My ancestor box and a few books. I brought everything I really wanted."

They tubed up to Fifty and walked over to her place. Inside, Doug dropped his bags and collapsed on a couch.

Sam put the bag she'd carried on a table and her comm beside it. "Make yourself at home. You can relax now."

She showed Doug around and found him something to eat. They all saved a little from meals at the caff for snacks.

Sam called Todd and got the message: No Private Calls Accepted.

"Shit," she muttered under her breath.

She called Brad, with the same result.

Then she tried Arlene. "I need to contact Todd or Brad," she said quickly.

"Sorry, the governor is not available." Arlene hung up.

"Bugs."

"Problem?" Doug asked.

"I share this place with my twin, Brad, and my other brother, Todd. They've done something to the phone system in Centrex and won't put private calls through. You're an employee, can you call your boss?" Sam handed him her comm.

"Sure." He punched in the number. "This is Doug Green. What's this about days off?"

Pause.

"Okay, but why wasn't I told before today? I'd have gone to work if I'd known."

Pause.

"I'm staying with Samanda Lar and her brothers in 5023W."

Pause.

"She is not a kook! She's a brave, smart, take-charge lady." Doug abruptly ended the call.

Sam blushed.

"I guess I'm stuck here," he said.

"Hal, next door, has an extra room. You can stay with him for the time being. They'll be home soon."

"Fine." He returned her comm and lay back.

"Just relax. I've got to do some work in the other room."

"What's that?" Doug sat up.

Sam turned to see Maxee peering around the doorway.

"Come on out, Maxee. This is Doug, a new friend."

She tiptoed out, but stayed by the doorway.

"Maxee is our alien sister. My father ran the xenolab, and a spacer brought her in as an infant. She grew up with us. Don't worry, she's friendly and very curious."

"Oh. I knew there were aliens in other sectors, but I'd never seen one. Hello, Maxee."

"Hello, man. Live here, are you?"

"No, he'll stay with Hal."

"Okee." She disappeared back into Brad's room.

"Well." Doug said. "This is the most unusual day I ever experienced." He lay back again.

Sam returned to her room, booted up her screen, and uploaded the day's information.

*   *   *

Later, Sam heard from Brad. "Did you try to call me?"

"Yes. They said no private calls."

"Yeah, something else new. We're also not allowed to leave Centrex for midday meal, either."

"Can you talk to Todd there?"

"Only when he's waiting for an assignment, but I have no way of knowing when that is. I'll arrange to have him call me."

"Okay. Why I was calling: we have a new associate." Sam told him about meeting Doug and bringing him up here. "He's a plumber, so that'll be useful. I told him he could move in with Hal. I hope that's okay."

"Sure. I guess. I'll be home shortly."

When Brad arrived back home, Sam introduced them.

"You have a very bright sister," Doug said.

"Yes." Sam sensed Brad bristling. "She says you're a plumber. How long have you been doing it?"

"Thirty-odd years. I understand you will need a plumbing system set up in your new place. I believe I can handle that."

"Great," Sam said.

Brad nodded. "Do you know Ken, the waterworks manager?"

"He's my boss."

"Good."

Todd and Hal arrived, and Sam noticed Todd's new briefcase as she made the introductions.

"Welcome aboard." Hal grinned. "Sure you can have my extra bedroom. Let's get your stuff over and go to dinner." They left.

"What's with the new case?" Sam asked.

"This is a very important case," Todd said, laying it down carefully. "This contains the copies I made of those ancient books I found. I didn't get all of them, some pages crumbled before I could get them copied. I did get the map and most of that book."

"Great. Thank you." Sam grinned.

"I also made copies of the copies and they're in with the most important legal papers."

Hal and Doug returned, and they all headed out for late meal.

At the caff, Sam said, "Okay, you three. What can we do so I can get in touch with you while you're at work, if I need to? Can you call from your caff?"

"I don't know."

Brad looked at the others. Todd shook his head.

"It's frowned upon, but a lot of people do it on the lower levels," Hal said. "If we do it too much, they're liable to ban it altogether."

"They wouldn't," Sam said.

"Oh yes they would." Hal took a bite of stew.

"Do you have to eat on your work level?" Sam asked him.

"Technically no, but almost everyone does because it's simpler. But again, if Security sees people going to other levels, they may shut that down too."

"What is going on with those people, anyway?" Sam jumped up and began to pace.

"It's the governor and his cronies on the council." Hal crossed his legs. "They don't want to believe your story, but they can't help seeing what's happening, and are trying to shut it out."

"Well, they won't be able to forever." Sam plopped down in her chair.

"Yeah, we know." Brad stroked his moustache. They'd run out of depilatory. All of the men now sported facial hair.

"So what are we going to do?"

"I don't know, Sam," Brad said. "We need a lot more people like Doug here."

"It's frustrating, knowing what's going to happen, and all these people don't want to hear about it," Doug remarked.

"Well, maybe, as someone said a long time ago, we'd be better off without them." Hal said.

"Hal!" Sam stared at him, shocked.

"We've already lost half of Below," Todd said. "And we're going to lose a lot more. We just have to accept that we're not going to get everyone out. We just have to try to get as many as we can."

"You're right," Sam said, but she thought, *I want to get everyone out. No one deserved to die in here.*

"We'll see what we can find out tomorrow," Todd said. "Doug, are you up to climbing up into the hills? You'll only have to carry your little bag."

"Sure. I've wanted to see the valley ever since I heard about it."

"Will being outside bother you? I've got plenty of hoods," Sam asked.

"No. I passed the space test, but I was more interested in plumbing. My dad and grandfather were plumbers."

"Good," Sam said.

*   *   *

World continued to pull City block cubes down.

33

A FTER THE OTHERS LEFT FOR WORK, Sam, Doug, and Maxee donned their back bags and headed out. Since Sam and Maxee couldn't go on the Forty-Eight car through Centrex, they walked over to and around Centrex, and caught the car on the other side. This time, the Noreg ground was just below the doorway from the portal, so they stepped out.

"Wow," Doug said, looking around. "What are all those trees?"

"This is the Noreg sector. They live in the trees. Come on." The trail was growing clearer as more people used it.

"This is great." Doug did a little hop and skip. "This air is so clean and crisp."

When they made camp that night, Doug thanked Sam for finding and bringing him.

"I feel so alive out here. I never realized how dead it was in there. I feel years younger."

"I know. I get a new rush of energy every time I come out."

"Us, too," Maxee put in, standing on her toes.

Again, Sam felt the presence of the world, and found comfort in it.

*   *   *

The next day, the group kept up a good pace, and camped in a little glen in the lower part of the forest.

Doug raved about everything he saw. "How did we ever get trapped into that place?"

"It just grew over the years, and people forgot what it was like to be out in the real world."

When the three of them came out of the trees in the morning, Sam felt again the awe of the open valley, river, and hills and mountains beyond.

This was the real world. How had I ever lived in that dingy little place inside?

Doug stopped and stared, jaw hanging open.

Sam pointed to the left. "This is our new home. Come on."

Maxee danced ahead.

They passed by a partially built log building on the way to the mesa.

"What?" Sam said. "Who's been here?" *Did Susan find someone already?*

"New people," Maxee said.

"This is new?" Doug asked.

"Yes. There was nothing here when we came before. Come on."

Sam led the others to the mesa and up the back side. The lean-to was gone. A square building now sat in its place. They found several people inside.

"Hello," Sam said. "I'm Samanda Lar, this is Doug Green, a plumber, and Maxee. How did you get here?"

"Susan Cobb told us," said a tall young woman with black hair. "I'm Glenda. Do you know her?"

"Yes." Sam looked around. "Glad to see you. What are you working on?"

"Constructing walls in here." Glenda waved her arm around.

"This is great. Did you have any problems getting here?"

"Only that some of my group couldn't handle outdoors and we had to make makeshift eye covers." Glenda pointed at people huddling away from the doorway.

"Right. I should have told Susan to mention that."

"No problem."

"So, do you have everything you need?"

"So far," she said. "We brought a lot of food. I didn't know what was up here."

Sam nodded. "I'll show these two around and we'll have a meeting after the midday meal."

A husky fellow with a red beard came out of the shadows and said. "I'm Gus."

"My mate," Glenda added. "He's the head builder."

"Glad to meet you. We need to get this place going."

"Right." Gus and Glenda looked at each other.

"See you around."

Sam and Doug, with Maxee trailing along, left and walked around the top of the mesa. The meeting house was the only building completed, although a few other buildings had been marked out along the back side. The boards Sam had used to outline her house were still there.

Sam and Maxee sat under the trees. Doug wandered around.

Sam was pleased that someone had come here and started building, but wished she'd known of it before she got here. They needed a more extensive communication system than just between her and the other sectors.

When they met for midday meal, Glenda said, "We're so glad to get Doug's help. It's not fun to have to go down to the river every morning to get a bucket of water. We wash our clothes downstream. What we need is more people. Do you have any idea how many people there'll be all together?"

"No. Too many don't want to come," Sam said. "Either they don't believe there's a problem, or that someone will fix it before it gets to them."

"That's because they don't see it. Everything's fine in their neighborhood, so what problem?"

"I know, I run into that all the time. Now that some of the lowest levels in Upper are having problems, they want help right away, and we don't have enough people to help."

*   *   *

The next day, Sam saw a stream of people come down out of the forest, all carrying large bags and wearing back bags. She went to meet them and found Susan in the lead.

"Susan! What is all this?"

"This is a whole food factory." She indicated an older woman behind her. "This is Louise, who runs it." Everyone dropped their bags, as more followed. Most were wearing hoods that ended at their noses.

"Welcome," Sam said. "Where do you want to build the factory?"

"Near the river," Louise said.

"Some of your people are going to have to build living places. We'll get you with Glenda and her group. You'll need to put up a building before you can set up."

"Yes. Jon here is in charge of construction."

Sam led them over to Glenda's group and watched as Louise and Jon looked around for place to put the factory. The two gathered their people together, piled up the items they'd brought, and made a camp behind the mound. Many of the people went up into the forest.

*   *   *

After Sam made sure everyone was settled and had a good night's sleep, she and Maxee returned to City.

They received hugs from Brad and Todd, and then Todd asked, "Where's Doug?"

"He's staying up there to start on the water system."

"Good."

"Maxee wanted to stay, but I said not this time."

At late meal, Sam told Brad and Todd about her trip, and the factory people.

"Great," Brad said. He grinned. "Way to go, Sam."

Back in her room, Sam checked her screen. Nothing much new. Reports from the field workers the same. Still only about one in three people took their message seriously.

One thing Sam wasn't happy about was that she couldn't call Brad or Todd from the valley. Too many times she'd wanted to ask one or the other of them something, but no way to do it. She wondered if Dondo could make a link on the phone for the valley. She left him a message about it.

Sam talked to Liia every few days. Liia was frustrated because, although they were able to move her clan up quickly, the others were showing a lot of resistance. Survivors from the lowest clans had moved in with other clans, but too many were afraid of moving outside.

"Do you want me to come over and talk to them?"

"No, because they wouldn't listen to you because you're not one of us."

"Okay. If you change your mind, let me know."

Sam called the others. Mantz said more trees had fallen, trapping some people, and many were getting the idea that they should move.

"We are working on places above. Someone had planted three big trees at bottom of the hills, but they not even a third the size of ours. Great grands' seedlings only knee high. Will be way too long before we can build in them. Even little Matti be too old to live there."

The Ghind were doing all right, according to The Elder. "My hill cave still good," she said. "No clay soil. Some building caves in hills above."

"Try in Itz, if they're gone."

"We will."

Maya reported that low trees and caves were collapsing. No new trees or pongo yet.

*   *   *

World watched as beings came out again.

34

TWO DAYS LATER, the block to the south of the museum on Ground slid into the mess below. Half the people who lived there were in other blocks, mostly at work. Of the other half, only a few managed to get out before it flooded.

Sam called Arlene and asked to speak to the governor.

"Sorry, he's not taking calls."

"Tell him thirty more people just died because he and his cronies won't do anything. Is he going to wait 'til Centrex is sitting on the ground to do something? People are dying every day because of his inaction."

"I will tell him. Don't expect any positive results."

"I won't, but I had to say it. How are you doing, Arlene?"

"Coping. I've talked to everyone on my block, but most of them don't believe me."

"I know what you mean. I'm out there every day, Do what you can, and thanks."

* * *

The next morning, when Sam went to boot up, instead of her home page, there was a message in red:

Your comm is no longer available for calls. Your screen is shut down except for entertainment. You are under house arrest.

"What?!" Sam screamed. "How dare they?"

She stared at the two red buttons, the only things on the black screen. One said, "Shut Down"; the other said, "Entertainments".

Maxee ran in. "Hurt, Sam?"

"No, furious." Sam pointed at the screen.

"Sam bad?"

"No. It's all right, Maxee. Go back to whatever you were doing."

"Okee."

Sam grabbed her comm and punched in Brad's number.

Completion of call not allowed.

Same thing with Todd's number. She tried Brad's and Todd's screens. They both said Permission Denied when she entered her pass code.

Maxee followed her out to the big screen in the main room. "Sam okee?"

"No, still mad. They shut down my screen and I can't access the others. And they won't let me call Brad or Todd." Sam stomped her foot.

"Why? You bad?" Maxee smirked.

"Maxee," Sam said, trying to keep her voice under control. "All I did was call the governor to ask him if he was helping the people Down Below."

"Gov bad?"

"He won't do anything to help his people."

"Bad."

Sam tried the big screen, with same results. Nothing. She clenched her teeth to keep from screaming, turned, and saw the front door.

Yes.

But it wouldn't open either. She tried her door opening tool. It didn't work. She could blow the door, but then they wouldn't have a door.

While Sam was deciding what to do next, her comm beeped. "Hello?"

"It's me, Brad. What happened to your phone?"

"You're calling on it, aren't you?"

"Yeah. After I got outside Centrex."

Sam took a deep breath. "Brad, the governor put me under house arrest. I can't call out, and I can't use my screen except for entertainment."

"What? What did you say to the governor?"

"I just asked him what he and his people were doing to take care of the people on lower levels." Sam sighed. He knew her too well.

"Is that all?"

"That's all I remember."

"Okay, we'll talk when I get home."

Sam didn't like the sound of that. She threw whatever she could get her hands on around the room. Maxee crouched in the hall doorway and, after Sam collapsed on the couch, picked everything up and put them back where they belonged.

Sam stomped back to her room and tried to work on her paper files, fuming.

When Brad came home, he strode into her room. "Tell me what you did."

"I beg your pardon?" Sam hated it when he assumed that she had caused whatever had happened.

"You said you called the governor. Why?"

"I was mad because we lost another block cube and a lot more people. I only talked to Arlene. I don't know what — if anything — she told him."

"As I understand it, she is required to pass on any message. What did you say?" Brad stared down at Sam.

Sam jumped up. "I only asked what he was going to do about those people down there."

"He's trying to forget that, remember? Maybe he just didn't like to be reminded. I'm sure he knows you are the one running this business."

"Well, I had no idea he'd do something like this."

"Okay. But now we have to figure out how to get you out of here. I assume you tried the front door." Sam nodded. "Have you tried the hatch?"

"Oh. No." Sam ran into his room and opened the hatch.

At least that opened for me.

Sam climbed up and stuck her head out. "Okay, so I can get out. How do I get back inside, into the street?"

"Good question."

Todd marched in. "Sam, I hear you stirred up things with the governor."

Not again.

"I just sent a message asking what he was going to do about the people in the lower level."

"Right. And?"

"I explained it to Brad." Sam thumped the table and marched back to her room.

She dropped into her chair and tried to get her mind back into its working space.

Brad and Todd followed.

"I'm not finished," Todd said. "Sam, this will be on your record, and you may be stuck in here for a long time."

Hal barged in and they tried to explain everything to him. All at once.

"Okay," he said after things had settled down. "Let me get this straight. You cannot call out on your regular comm, but you can receive calls on it from outside Complex. The only thing you can get on your screen is entertainment and emergency messages. And you can't get into Todd's or Brad's screens."

"Or the big screen," Sam added.

Hal paused. "Have you tried going out the front door?"

"Yes, and it won't let me."

"Let's try you going out with one of us."

Sam walked with him. He went out first, but when she followed right behind him, the door stopped her.

"Let me," Brad held her tightly to his chest and tried to go through. The door refused and made clicking sounds. "It must be your chip. They used it to lock you down."

"So the hatch doesn't have a chip detector."

"Yeah."

"Okay." Sam sighed. "But I need my files so I can keep them up to date. My pass codes for Brad and Todd's screens don't work, either."

"Is there any way you two can access her files from your screens?" Hal asked.

"Probably," Todd said. "My screen is set up to be the primary screen in the apartment, and the others are tied into it. Let me see what I can do." He looked at her. "Sam, don't ever talk to the governor again, unless he asks you a question in person, and, even then, be very careful what you say."

When he left the room, Sam stuck her tongue out at him.

Todd was able to pull up Sam's files on his screen and showed her how to do it. He said she could use it during the day while he was at work.

Sam saw new entries today, so the people in the field could still send their data to her screen.

Thank Oneness for that. Hers had the master copy.

∗   ∗   ∗

World was displeased as more beings trailed up to valley.

35

ONE DAY, DOUG AND A COUPLE OF THE FACTORY PEOPLE showed up. "Sam, this is Jade, a line supervisor, and Allan, a maintenance tech."

"Welcome," Sam said, motioning them in.

Doug gave her a report on progress, and Sam explained her situation and asked if he would be willing to come down a couple times a month. He agreed.

Jade said, "The place is going up fast, and we've got one line working. A couple people went back for more foodstuffs. Louise wants to know if you have some kind of gadget we can use to test the local flora to see if it's edible. There's a lot of different plants, but we don't know if they're safe to eat."

"I have one, but I need to keep it." Sam said. "Brad, are there any in the lab?"

"I think so. You people stay over, and I'll check in the morning."

*   *   *

The next day, Brad brought a tester from the lab, plus various lab supplies for Doug to take up. As they prepared to leave, Sam received a call from an extended family on the east side who wanted to go to the valley.

"You can go today," she told the grandfather. "Three people are leaving here shortly and will come by your place and take you up. Do you need hoods?"

"We have some, thank you. The local fabric shop handed them out."

"Take everything you want to keep, and as much food as you can. There's food up there, but we don't want to waste any down here."

"Thank you. We will be ready."

"Everyone helps," Brad said.

"It's still not near enough." Sam fisted the arm of the couch.

The more time Sam spent with her spreadsheets, the more depressed she became, seeing how little had been accomplished in the first couple of months. Liia reported sporadic progress, and the Noreg were losing more and more trees.

The Ghind were having trouble creating hills from soil that would not stay put.

Maya said her world was in chaos. *VOLEN TREES COLLAPSE RANDOMLY, AND MANY FALL OVER AS ROOT SYSTEMS DECAY. VOLEN PLANTED YOUNG TREES, BUT SOME OF THOSE CRUSHED BY VOLEN TREES.*

The Hive reported that the Volen had provided them with a skeleton of a hive and they had built over, around and through it. They were afraid the natural part would collapse when the Volen part dissolved.

"Build your hive material around the Volen material. Surround each strand with your material. Start with main structure components. When the Volen part starts to collapse, fill in the empty spaces. Do you have people checking all the parts of your hive? If not, do so."

THANK YOU. WE WILL.

At least, I could help a little.

* * *

One evening, Todd called out from his screen.

"Hey people, here's a message from Bill. He's on Level Three, he'd brought a group of people up from Below. His comm's dead and there's no power down there to recharge it. He's okay and looking for a working power point so he can charge his comm."

"Great," Sam said, with a sigh of relief.

They hadn't heard from him for so long, she was worried about him, too. Susan checked in every few days. She told us that the water had stopped rising, but there was no power, lightsticks were fading, and lanterns giving out. Someone had figured out how to make fire, and small fires burned in the streets on many blocks. Everyone supplied anything that could burn.

"My group and I are working as fast as we can to get everyone out," she added. "But too many refuse to leave, and we tell them we can no longer help them. Their lives are in their hands. Those are the ones I marked with a purple 'X'."

"Okay," Sam said. "I hate to leave them to their deaths, but we need to save the ones we can save. When was the last time you had a good night's sleep?"

"I don't remember. Actually, I get around four or five hours a night. But I can't stop, with all these people looking to us for help."

"You might as well stay down there. You're out of a job up here."

"Yes," Susan said. "Todd told me. Actually, I'm glad to get out of that mess."

We're losing too many people, but I don't know what I can do about it, other than what I'm already doing.

Sam thought of the one thing she hadn't tried. *The hatch.*

It was open. She grabbed her comm and call device and climbed out. She accidently hit something and the hatch cover slid closed. She could not get it open again.

"Oh, shit."

She tried to call Brad and Todd and got nowhere. She walked over to Centrex, down the outside stairs, and waited for one or the other to come out. Brad usually came home first.

When he appeared, he said, "What are you doing here?"

"I went out the hatch, and it locked behind me."

"Oh, Sam." He shook his head. "I'll let you back in."

"No." Sam had been thinking about this. "I want to go to Hal's, so I can get out."

"Okay, I'll call him."

After Brad got the go-ahead, they went to Hal's place. He still had Hal's keycode and let them in.

* * *

Later, when Hal and Todd arrived, they all had a meeting.

"Now that I'm out, I want to go up to the new place," Sam said. "I think it's time we named our new place. How does 'Starview' sound?"

"Fine with me," Brad said. Todd nodded.

"Brad, you go get what I need to take, and one of you will have to go with me on the car to pay. How late does it run?"

"Midnight," Hal said. "But we don't have to go to the end, we can get off before and catch one back."

"I don't want you going up there by yourself," Brad said.

"Well, none of you can go with me. Do you know of anyone else?" Sam waved her hand.

"Not off-hand."

"Okay, I'm going."

Sam scribbled a list and handed it to Brad. After he brought back her bags and Maxee, they went to eat.

"You go up?" Maxee asked. "I go, too?"

"Not this time." Sam smiled at her. "Next time, maybe."

Maxee sat back and screwed up her face.

"Sorry, Maxee," Brad said. "It's dangerous out there, and we don't want you out unless there's one of us men along."

"Sam go alone."

"Sam can take care of herself."

Sam snorted.

After they ate, Todd took Maxee back to the apartment, and Brad and Hal took Sam to the car. Hal sat next to her, and a sense of belonging swept over her.

Because it was after working hours, Hal managed to talk Security into letting Sam go through Centrex. Brad and Hall got off three blocks from the end, after the car emptied of other people. Sam rode the rest of the way and slept on a comfy couch in the portal.

*   *   *

Sam took a deep breath and started up the hill. Going by herself felt strange, but she also enjoyed being alone. She was able to go at her own pace and take in the countryside, the brown hills, the clumps of trees with long, gray seedpods, the orange flowers.

She camped in the forest and woke in the morning to see a tiny gray creature, sitting up, watching her with great black eyes. It had large ears and long, stiff hairs around the black, twitchy nose. It carried the essence of the world.

"Hello," she said.

The creature let out a squeak, scampered away and up a tree, disappearing into the leaves. It moved as fast as a car. Sam knew about animals, that was part of her Old Earth history, but she'd never seen one in the flesh.

*   *   *

World sent its creatures out to observe.

36

SOMEONE HAD STARTED ANOTHER TRAIL that went more directly to the mesa, mostly skirting the trees. Sam followed the trees; she enjoyed walking beneath them.

As Sam hiked down into the valley, she saw ragged rows of apartments behind the mesa.

What was going on?

She asked one of the people working on them, "Why are the apartments not lined up?"

"There's big stones in the ground."

Sam sighed and climbed up the mesa.

Another unexpected problem. How many more will I have deal with? When will this all be over, and I can relax on my porch?

Houses stood along the river side. Hers was a bare wall structure, no roof, with one wall partly built between front and back rooms. Someone had built a platform for a bed in the front room, but there were no openings in the front wall.

"I guess I'm going to have to stay here and supervise those idiots," Sam said to the house, kicking a wall. She dumped her bag, found her laser, and cut an opening in the front wall, wide enough for her and about four feet high.

Then she stepped out and almost fell off the cliff.

"Whoa," she cried. That was way too close to the edge. Sam stormed off to find Glenda.

Why couldn't people do things right?

Glenda and Gus were in the meeting house going over plans. "Hi, how are you?" she asked when Sam stomped in.

"Furious. Somebody built my house, and probably the others, way too close to the cliff's edge. I want to know who's responsible, and for my house to be moved back so I have room in front for a porch and a yard."

"How close?" Gus asked. "They just finished last night. I haven't had a chance to go over there and check it yet."

"One foot."

"What?" they said together. "I told them ten feet back," Gus added. "Glenda, you go take a look, and I'll go find those two."

When Sam and Glenda returned to Sam's house, they found that not only her house, but all the others, were perched on the edge of the cliff.

"I'll be." Glenda clenched her fists. "Those two, Bud and Boog, are off house building as of now. I'll find some grunt work for them." She grimaced. "And I thought we were doing good, getting those houses up so fast."

They headed back to Sam's place, looking inside each of the others. Only Brad's, next to hers, had anything inside, the beginnings of an interior wall.

Back at Sam's house, they met Gus and two skinny fellows.

"They say the plans said one foot. My plans say ten feet. Show Glenda yours." Gus waved his hand.

The taller fellow pulled out a wad of paper. Although the number was obscured by a blot of dirt, the plan clearly showed a large room's width between the edge and the closest part of the house.

"You call that a foot?" Glenda demanded. "I've a good mind to send you back down Below."

"No, please. Don't make us go back."

"Go clean the sanitary relief station. I don't ever want to see you again." Glenda pointed toward the forest.

"Do we have to?" the smaller one squeaked.

"Yes. Go." Glenda glared at them.

They trotted off.

Gus said he would try to find someone to move her house back.

Glenda apologized profusely. "I'm so sorry, Sam. There's just so much going on and we can't be everywhere at once to supervise. We've had other problems. We need more supervisory people, but it seems like everyone who shows up are only workers. We will get your house and the others moved back, I promise."

"Apology accepted. I know there's always going to be problems with projects like this." Sam paused. "You look tired. How much sleep are you getting?"

"Not enough. Every night I lie down, and all this stuff keeps going through my head."

"I know. What I do is the alphabet thing. Right now, I'm doing people's names. I start with 'A' and try to think of all the people I know or have heard of that start with 'A'. Then I go to 'B'. and so forth. When I concentrate on that instead of my worries, I usually get to sleep pretty quickly. You can use any categories or words you want. Just keep your mind focused on them."

"Thanks. I'll try that. I've got to go back to work now. See you around." Glenda trotted off.

Sam went back into her house and yanked a loose board off the inside wall. That gave her an idea.

She hauled the board outside, then yanked off another board. When she got to the bed shelf, she sat on it, and the whole thing collapsed. "Ouch," she yelped.

She wasn't hurt, just mad. She cleared out those boards, the rest of the wall, and made a pile of them outside. After a rest, she took off and found Glenda at the caff.

"Have you found anybody yet to work on my house?" Sam asked.

"Gus will be free for a little while this afternoon and he'll come look at your house and see how to do it."

"Good. I sat on my bed platform and it collapsed."

"Oh, no." Glenda gasped.

"So I pulled out all the interior boards."

"Sam, you didn't." She looked at Sam open-mouthed.

"I sure did. I've waited forever for this house and I'm not going to wait any longer than I absolutely have to, even if I have to do the whole thing myself."

"I'll make sure it's done right this time."

After the meal, Sam returned to her house. Determined to fix it, she studied how it was put together. The two who had built it left some tools, and she found one she could use to unfasten the fasteners. Sam was able to get one side wall down by late meal.

Gus went with Sam to her house after they ate, helped her get another wall down, and the house laid out where it was supposed to be.

Sam slept out under the trees. The presence reassured her. She understood that this world was a living being who was displeased with City. She would have to teach her people how to live with World, not against it.

∗   ∗   ∗

World waited.

37

THE NEXT DAY, ANOTHER GROUP showed up, and Gus brought one of them, a hefty young woman, to work on Sam's house. He went on to inspect the other houses.

"Hi, I'm Abby," the young woman said. She examined the details of construction. "Whoever built this should be fired."

"They've been reassigned to sanitation duty." The two women giggled.

By midday, Sam and Abby had two more walls down and the new floor staked out. Moving walls and boards was easier with two of them.

As they walked to the caff, Abby said, "You know, I'm descended from the original carpenters. The skills and tools were handed down from generation to generation, so my father taught me and my sister how to do it right. Even though we weren't building houses, we still built cabinets and boxes, so we'd learned the proper way to do carpentry."

"Good. We need all the professionals we can get."

*   *   *

Two days later, the two of them had Sam's house done, complete with a porch with a chair on it. Since no other crews had showed up, they started on Brad's house.

After getting one wall down, Sam heard a shout, and turned to see Brad and an older man, laden with bags.

"Brad! I didn't know you were coming."

"Hi, Sam. This is George MacFee, head of the lab department. We got permission to come up and test plants to see what we can use."

"Great," Sam replied. Brad dropped his bags, and they hugged. "You can put your stuff in my house for now."

"Where's the lab building?" George demanded, a frown on his square face.

"Over here." Sam led them to the layout of the lab on the other side of the mesa.

"Why isn't it built?" George scowled.

"We wanted to be sure you approved the layout."

He mumbled something and walked around the area.

"Has anyone noticed I'm not in the apartment?" Sam turned to Brad.

"No." He grinned. "Next Firsday, Todd is going to ask Arlene if your house arrest can be lifted."

"How's Maxee?"

"She's doing fine. She found some games in the entertainment section on your screen and has been playing them. Also, she found a way to send a message to everyone in our district, so I wrote the message and she sent it."

"Very good."

"She does miss you, though. She keeps asking when you're coming home."

"I wish there was a way those of us up here could contact the people down there."

"Yeah, that would be useful."

Glenda approached us as George returned.

"Oh, here's Glenda, the head of construction. Glenda, this is George, the head of the lab department. He's approving this building."

"Not quite," he said, glaring at Glenda. "There's a few things that need to be changed."

Brad and Sam left them to discuss the changes.

Later, George found them and wanted to know where he could set up his plant testing equipment. Sam showed him a corner of the meeting hall.

At the evening meal, George said, "This is not bad up here. What I've looked at so far won't harm us, but on the other hand, there's not much in the way of nutrients we can use. I need more light. Brad, will you build the botany corner first?"

"Sure, boss."

"There's lots more plants up and down river and over by and in the forest," Sam said.

"Good," Brad said.

Sam and Brad worked on the lab until Crew Two finished an apartment house and came over, then Sam went back to finish Brad's house.

Brad worked on the lab in the mornings and searched for plants in the afternoons. He told Sam that he and his boss found a few useful plants, plus one common one with tall leaves and a big root ball that could be used as filler and enhanced the properties of the other vegetables. One group had started a garden. Brad found a tree with ripening fruit that checked out well and was very tasty. They saved the pits and planted them, for more trees later on.

Another group started laying out a row of apartments down along the river, below the mesa, and Sam and Glenda had to quash that pretty quickly.

They held a meeting of all the crew bosses and higher. "The river can flood and overflow when too much water comes down from the mountains, or it rains a lot," Sam explained. "There is something called a flood zone, which is where the water comes up to in a major flood. Brad is figuring that out now. We don't want to build anything in the flood zone; we don't want water coming into anyone's home. Brad will make a map of the zone and pass them out so you'll know where not to build."

"That makes sense," Glenda said. "Crew Four, remove all building materials from below the mesa and go on to your next job."

"Yes, Ma'am."

They all disbursed to their various tasks. As Sam walked back to the house, it occurred to her she hadn't felt any shakes up here.

Was it because we couldn't feel any? Or that there weren't any?

On her break, Sam called the other sectors.

Liia said, "Most of the top three levels are up and building."

"Do your people have a problem with open spaces like ours?"

"A few did, but then we had those open courtyards."

"Oh, right."

Mantz was next. "We do well," he said. "Most people in top half and hills. Many Volen trees down. Our trees up to our waists, but many new trees crushed by others."

The Ghind were still having problems with hills, and The Elder had been moved up to a cave in a real hill near the top of the sector.

"How are you doing, Maya?" Sam asked.

"Big mess. Many trees down blocking trails; new trees not enough. Did get pongos and their food. Mostly males. All females carrying young. We careful not to hunt those. They hide, anyway."

"Great. Glad to hear you're doing well."

Hive did not answer. *Something else to worry about.*

*   *   *

The next day, Brad and George returned to City.

"Do you want to come with us?" Brad asked as they prepared to leave.

"I can't. I can't leave Abby in mid-house." Sam did want to go back and see Maxee, though. "I'll come when we get this house done. Probably a couple more days. I'll get Doug to go with me."

"Yes, he needs to get his bag out of our place. See you soon, Sam. Take care."

Brad's departure left a hole in her being. She went back to work, looking forward to returning to City.

The next day she found Doug. "I'm going back to City tomorrow. I'd like you to go with me. You can get your bag you left in our apartment."

"Good idea. There are things in there I could use." He grinned.

* * *

World waited.

38

S AM AND DOUG LEFT RIGHT AFTER FIRST MEAL.
City had slipped down farther, and someone in the last group
up had told her the top portal was below ground. They had to go
to the next portal south. It was dim inside after the bright out-of-
doors. Sam and Doug took that level's car over to the first stop past
Centrex. Sam paid. She'd received a small reimbursement for the
fabric she'd bought, but not enough to cover what she'd spent.

Doug called Brad to let him know they were coming. The two
tubed up to Fifty and walked back to her apartment.

When Sam and Doug arrived, Maxee squealed and ran to Sam.

"How are you doing?" Sam asked as she hugged Maxee.

"Good, good. Time soon."

"Great news." Todd beamed. "You're free."

Sam dug out her comm. It worked. *Thank Oneness.*

Susan came out of the bathroom. "Good to see you. I'm up
here for a while. Lower is totally gone. One through Ten Upper are
mostly gone. Bill's on his way; we got a message from him."

"Hey, Susan." Sam grinned. "Good to see you. I'm starving. Is it time to eat yet?"

"Yes."

They all went to eat late meal. Hal told them a few of the Councilors were beginning to believe in what was happening, especially the ones in the lower districts. The council was mostly overseeing repairs rather than new, long-term projects.

Todd told them about all the legal stuff his office was working on for the new place, so that everyone would own their own little piece of land and home, plus government procedures. Brad said the med clinic had a bunch of supplies to go up.

Doug described what all was going on up in the valley. Sam reported on her call to the other sectors.

"I see we slipped again."

"Yeah," Brad picked up his mug.

When Sam asked if there'd been a problem getting her house arrest nullified, Todd said, "I think they'd forgotten all about it."

"I'm not going to let them forget about me. Hal, is there any way to send a message to all of the council at one time?"

"I think so."

"No, Sam," Brad said at the same time.

"Okay, Brad, you write it for me. I want it to say, 'I'm here, I'm the leader of the new settlement, and I've been up there the last month.'"

"Sammie," he said, looked at her, and sighed. "All right, I'll do it, only because if I don't, you will."

Sam punched him in the shoulder.

*   *   *

The next day, Sam went back to her canvassing. As Sam left a new helper's apartment and headed down the street, she ran into Jerg.

"What are you doing here?"

"Looking for you."

He grabbed at her. Sam pushed him down and ran back to the woman she'd just talked to.

"Pardon me," Sam said as she barged in, "I just ran into an old enemy, the partner of my ex. I thought they were gone."

"Sit down and tell me."

Sam did. The past had all come back when she saw Jerg. He'd put on weight, but the same steely and narrowly-spaced eyes had bored into hers.

Gladys cracked the door and peered out. "He's in the corner caff." She pointed to the left. "I'll stand here and block his view, you run that way, to the tube."

"Do you have a hat or scarf or something I can put over my hair?"

"Yes, it does stand out. Let me go look."

She returned with a long blue scarf and some hairpins. They put Sam's hair up, and Gladys wrapped the scarf around Sam's head.

"Thanks. I'll return it when I can."

"Don't worry about it." Gladys returned to the door and stepped out.

Sam slipped behind her and ran down the street to the tube. She took the first tube down two, went up one flight of stairs, down the street to the car line, and back home.

Sam dropped into a chair, and Maxee looked at her. "You see bad man?"

"How'd you know?"

"See I, in your face."

"Oh." *What else could she do?* "The one on the ship," Sam panted. "Not the big one, the one that put you in the cabin."

"What he do here?"

"Looking for me. I need to go check something."

Sam went to her room and called Connie, in her old shop.

"Yes, I gave him Todd's number. I didn't know ..." She sounded like she was about to cry.

"That's all right," Sam soothed. "That's his old number. How are you doing?"

"I'm keeping busy. A lot of people tell me how good you were. I like this place. Thanks again."

"Glad to hear it. Take care." Sam disconnected.

The new fellows in Todd's apartment probably wouldn't have given him hers.

So it was a chance meeting. But he'll keep looking. Now I can't go out. Again.

Sam searched for him in the resident database and couldn't find him.

Later, when she told Brad and Todd, they erupted.

Brad cursed, using swear words Sam had never heard before.

"What does he want now?" Todd demanded.

"I don't know." Sam was split between crawling into a corner and running out after Jerg to get rid of him. "He's not in the resident database, so he's probably on a ship."

"I'll have my friend check ships," Todd said. "Of course, he could be staying with someone and using his friend's card for food."

"Thanks," Sam growled.

Todd reported her skirmish to security. "No, I have no idea where he's been or what he's been up to. He's not on the current residents' checklist, so he's probably on a ship at Spaceport. Pause. "Right. I will."

He clicked off and turned to Sam. "You are not to go out by yourself or just with Maxee. Only if Brad or I or Hal is with you. Understand?"

"Yes. Starview ..." *I had to get out of this dungeon soon.*

"No. All he'd have to do is follow people over there. You're safer here, and you need to be here."

Sam was stuck inside again. Of course, she could always sneak out the hatch, but then she'd have to walk all the way over to the valley.

*   *   *

World pushed Volen material to dissolve faster.

39

O NE DAY, DOUG SHOWED UP, with a couple of men that Sam didn't know.

"Hi. Come on in." She waved them in. *Now what?* Not that she wasn't glad to see Doug.

Doug introduced the others, and they all sat down.

"How are things up there?" Sam asked.

"Moving along," Doug said. "We had a rainstorm. Lots of stuff got wet, and a lot of people complained. It was unexpected. We need to know how to tell when it's coming."

"Oh." It had been so nice up there Sam never thought of telling anyone about rain. "Clouds come over, the sky goes gray, maybe some wind. If you see that, it's likely to rain, so get everything you don't want to get wet under cover. Did it rain much?"

"About an hour. Not real hard."

"Well, I can't do anything about that. If there's a breeze and it starts to build up, put papers under cover and put loose things in containers or tie them down. You are outside now; you are going to have weather. Deal with it." Sam smiled. "You might want to find some large containers to collect rainwater in."

"Ah," Doug said. "Of course."

His companions said they were staying at a friend's, would be back in the morning, and left.

"How's the plumbing coming along?"

"Slowly." Doug crossed his legs. "There's not much in the way of plumbing supplies, so I'm having to do a lot of jury-rigging."

Sam and Doug talked for a little while until Brad and Todd came home.

"Hey, Doug. How's it going?" Brad grinned.

"Progress is being made. I'm updating Sam on progress in Starview."

"Okay. Good." Brad dropped into a chair.

"Do you know anywhere down here I can get plumbing supplies? I've practically cleaned out the waterworks department."

"Do you know any other plumbers you can ask?" Sam pushed her hair back.

"A few," Doug said. "I know two who are up there, and they didn't have much. I'll check around."

Hal knocked and came in with a short fellow with pale hair. "This is Ross," Hal said. "He lost his job and his apartment, so I invited him to come stay with me."

"Hello, Ross. Welcome to our group," Sam said. "I'm Samanda, this is Brad and Todd and Doug." Maxee had hid in Brad's room.

"Hi," Ross murmured, looking around. "Nice place." He stayed close to Hal.

"Centrex is starting to empty out," Hal said. "Even some of the Councilors are leaving."

"Maxee, come on out," Sam called.

She tiptoed out with a girl face, wearing one of Sam's girly coveralls. Ross nodded.

"Let's go eat," Brad said. "You can come, Sam. I think you'll be pretty well protected with all of us."

"Thanks, Brad."

He always acted the protective big brother, even though I was born first. Sam smiled at the memory.

Instead of going to the nearest caff, Todd led them to the tube and down, then over a few blocks. They had to eat at two tables and talk across the aisle.

Ross told the others it had been one of those mornings. He couldn't find the shirt he wanted, he missed his usual car, and his boss, who usually came in later, was on time and saw Ross come in late. That afternoon, the boss got a notice to let someone go, and so he picked Ross. When Ross arrived home, he found an eviction notice on his apartment door.

"I called Hal and, after work, he rounded up a couple guys and moved me into his place." Ross looked around at us. "I have to thank Hal for taking me in. I was in a real spot."

"What did you do in Centrex?" Sam asked.

"I worked in supplies, making sure the councilors had everything they need."

"What are you planning to do now?"

"I haven't had much chance to think."

"How about going to Starview and setting up a supplies department. There's stuff all over the place, and nobody knows who has what."

Ross perked up. "How do I get there?"

"Doug will take you up. How do you feel about being out in the open?"

He shuddered.

"I have a hood you can wear. All you'll see is your feet. There's a big building without windows you can work in."

While he was thinking about it, Sam let Maxee tell her about what she had been doing.

When the group left, they took a different route home. Down on Forty-Four, they were ambushed as they got off the car. Several large men rushed at them, and Sam heard Jerg yell, "Each of you get a guy, I'll get the girl."

"Which one?" one of the others asked.

Sam and Maxee stood side by side within the circle of men. Between Brad and Hal, Sam saw Jerg do a double take. Jerg's men stopped.

"Get him!" Sam cried, not moving.

Brad, Hal and Ross surrounded Jerg. Brad grabbed him around the shoulders and threw him down; the other two held Jerg. One of Jerg's men grabbed at Brad, who turned and sent him flying with a punch to the jaw. Hal walloped another man as Brad aimed a karate chop at a third. A group came out of the tube and stared.

Todd called Security. "We have Jerg at Forty-Four 4east 10north car station."

"Tell them to hurry," Brad said.

Jerg wriggled and kicked.

"Help me," Jerg called.

"His men attacked my brothers," Sam yelled.

The group of men from the tube joined in, and Sam knocked out one of Jerg's men with a sleep stick. She lost sight of Jerg.

Other people arrived and tried to break it up.

"I'm holding a criminal for Security," Brad yelled.

But when Security finally showed up, and the mess untangled, Jerg and one of the tube group was gone.

The three officers from Security refused to listen to Todd and Brad, shoved them all into a car, and took them to their lockup.

The Security office was small and gray, like everywhere else in City. Maxee huddled in a corner trying to look inconspicuous. The unconscious man had been taken somewhere else.

To verify their identities, Todd gave them Arlene's number, and Security demanded she come down in person. It took a while.

By the time she finally arrived, Sam was stewing and trying not to scream.

Arlene told them she'd just missed a car, and they only ran every half hour in the evening.

"This woman says she's some kind of big shot," one of the security officials said.

"She's the biggest shot of the human sector, now that the governor has gone into hiding." Arlene smiled at Sam.

"Really?" My spirits rose.

"Yes. Samanda Lar was chosen by the Volen to supervise the humans' move from dying City to our new home up in the hills," Arlene continued.

"Yes," my brothers and Doug said together.

"Okay, okay. What were you doing there?"

"We were leaving the caff after our evening meal." Sam tried not to snarl.

"Why down there?"

"Change of scenery."

After they went through this for everyone, one of them noticed Maxee and hauled her out of the corner. They asked her questions and she just shook her head.

"She doesn't talk," Sam said.

The questioner looked at Sam, back at Maxee, and shoved her away.

"Okay, you can go."

By the time Sam and the others reached the apartment, Sam was ready to drop.

*   *   *

The next morning, Doug and Ross left for the valley. Sam wanted to go, but Brad said not until they knew where Jerg was. Sam was mad, but not at him.

Why did Jerg come back? What did he want of me? Or was it Max, now Maxee?

Sam tried to keep her mind on gathering information they could use in Starview, but that man kept intruding on her thoughts.

My ex is gone for good, but why didn't Dondo tell me Jerg is still around? Why hasn't he gotten back to us? We got the supplies he had said the Volen would deliver. We were given a list of Volen objects so we know what we will still have and what we will have to replace after the material was gone, but there's way to be sure that was all of them. But we still don't know whether the Volen particles are harmful to us.

Sam called him again and left a message.

When Dondo got back to her, he said he never got an answer from the Volen. He wanted to help after she told him the situation.

"I am no longer allowed in Centrex. What can I do to help you?"

Sam told him how to get to the valley and build homes.

* * *

World waited and watched and trembled.

40

S AM TRIED TO IGNORE the almost continual shaking of the building. She had to focus on getting people moved out and up. It was a relief when, that evening at the caff, Hal told her and the others that, after the latest slip, Arlene received a call from the governor. He complained that his house was at a decided tilt, all he could see was cliff, and he wanted it fixed now.

"Arlene told him there was nothing we could about it. Only the Volen could stop it, and they're gone. He demanded to see Dondo. She didn't know where he was."

They all had a good laugh over that.

According to the announcements on the screen, the cars on Four and Eight had quit working, and the cars on Twelve ran only sporadically. The tubes had been reworked so they only went down as far as Thirteen. Services were swamped with complaints, but all they could say was, "You're on the list. We'll get to you when we can." More people moved up, and upper rest areas were full.

Even though Sam knew Jerg was out there, she went back to canvassing in areas that had not been covered. She carried her bag of tricks, with as much as she could stuff in it. More people were listening to her now. They talked about the shaking coming more often and the hitches in the water supply. Sam told people to do as she did, fill containers when the water was on, then they'd have some when it was off.

Every little thing made Sam jump, and the men were no help. Brad laughed when he came up behind Sam, poked her, and she jumped. Until the time she turned and whacked him one.

Sleep was almost impossible, even with her mantra. When she did get to sleep, her dreams were of City falling down or the valley flooding. Sometimes, when she came home in the afternoon, she'd drop on a couch and fall asleep until the men came home.

*   *   *

One evening, Brad asked how she was doing on her paperwork.

"Oh, I've got it up here." Sam pointed to her head.

"Yeah, but other people can't read your mind. You need to have everything on paper. We don't know how much longer the screens are going to last."

"Oh, nuts."

Sam went back to working on her papers.

*   *   *

The next time Doug came down, he told them he'd followed the river down to the reservoir, which was full and overflowing into the ground between the reservoir and City wall.

"Probably under City to the aquafer," Brad said. "Probably because they're not using as much water with Below gone, and broken pipes."

"So what does that mean?" Sam asked.

"The ground under central City is getting soggy. The water level is rising and undermining City. It'll sink sooner."

"Wonderful," Sam snarled.

*   *   *

One morning, Maxee came to Sam and said, "See, you."

She pulled open her pouch. Inside, a tiny pink creature wiggled. "Baby Max." A big grin lit her furry face.

Sam grinned back. "Congratulations. Are you all right? Do you need anything?"

"Only more food. For us."

When the men came home and Sam told them about Baby Max, they eased away from Maxee.

"She's fine," Sam said. "Just be careful of her tummy. We don't want to hurt Baby Max."

"How long will this take?" Brad asked.

"We don't know. We'll just have to see how fast he grows."

∗   ∗   ∗

A few days later, someone reported from Level Fifteen that her mate had thrown something at a wall and made a mark. Later, she noticed that there was a hole. The next day it was bigger.

"Oh no," Sam thought.

She checked their walls; they were okay. She put the word out for everyone to keep an eye on Volen material items and let her know if there was any change.

Liia called in a panic. A half dozen levels had crumbled just like that.

"We can't get down there and Central won't do anything."

"I know how you feel. We just lost four levels. There's nothing we can do either."

Sam sat and worried until Brad got home. Then she dumped her worries on him.

"Stop it, Sam. You've always been a worrywart, ever since you were a kid. There's no point in worrying about things you can't do anything about — like the Volen disintegration. It just wastes energy. And don't worry about things you can do something about, just do it."

"Thanks a lot, Brad. You never worry; you have no idea what it's like." A light came on in Sam's mind. "I'll have you know, the reason I worry is because, back just before Mother told us she was leaving, she told me, 'No matter what happens, I'll always love you and Brad'." So, of course I started worrying about what was going to happen. And have ever since."

"Oh."

"You had Dad, but I didn't have anyone. He avoided me because I look so much like Mother. Aunt Linda, Todd's mom, was nice, but it wasn't the same. She wasn't my real mother." Sam curled into a huddle on the couch.

"Do you think about Mother a lot?"

"Only now and then, when something comes up to remind me of her. You?"

"Same." He rubbed her shoulder. "You probably didn't notice, but Dad stopped laughing after she left. He and I had to literally pry you away from her at Spaceport. You cried for days."

"So did you and Dad."

"I know." He kissed her hair. "How hungry are you? It'll be awhile before Todd gets home."

"Let's wait."

*   *   *

Later, Hal and Ross, Hal's new roommate, came over. Sam noticed that Ross stayed close to Hal, but didn't think anything of it.

"One good thing and one bad thing," Hal said. "Bad thing is some of the top-level Councilors want to close you down."

"How? Why?" Sam wanted to know.

"Why? Because they think you're causing all this mess." Hal leaned back and crossed his legs.

"What? How could I be doing that?"

"That's what I said." Hal looked around. "They said there was something spooky about you."

"Spooky? Me?" Sam gaped, and Brad laughed. "I'll get you later," she told him.

"As for how, what I heard was, they'd move Brad to an apartment inside Centrex so the rest of you would have to move out to a much lower level and be out of their hair."

They looked at one another.

"That is wild," Brad said. "In the first place, they don't even know who owns this apartment."

"And there's not going to be any apartments available lower down. Are we supposed to camp in a rest area?" Sam asked.

"No, we'd just go up to Starview." Brad crossed his legs.

"But I have to be down here to manage things."

"I also heard they want to close the portals," Hal added.

"I'll just call Mantz and he can open one from his side." Sam smirked.

"What's the good news?" Brad asked.

"More and more mid-level Councilors are coming around to our view as they see what's happening down there. I don't think the top-level people will have enough votes to pass anything anymore."

*   *   *

World pulled more of City and Ambaak down.

41

S AM DECIDED IT WAS TIME to go up to Starview again, Brad or
no Brad. Jerg wouldn't think of it; he was always on a ship or
inside here. Maybe she could find some more people who want to
go.

While Sam made her preparations, The Elder called from
Ghind.

"We have a tribe who must leave their home area by the sea.
They build houses. Many willing to go help you. We will bring by
flier. Where do you want them?"

"Oh. Yes, we can use them. Thank you." Sam gave her the
location of Starview.

Two days after Sam arrived with a group she picked up
outside the portal, and the new folks were settled in, a flier sailed
over the mountains and landed up by the forest.

Sam ran down the mesa and over to the little ship. Joba got
off first, followed by a line of his people carrying bundles.

He brought over a younger, lanky fellow with a small scar on his cheek. "Greetings, Sam. This is Owl, the chief of tribe Ottar. I will stay until next group comes."

"Welcome, Joba. Welcome Owl. We appreciate your people's help. Would you like me to show you around?"

"Please."

"First, the sanitary facilities, such as they are, are over behind those trees."

"Trees. Leave all trees here. Only take from forest."

Joba turned and returned to his people. After he spoke, many of the women and children headed for the trees Sam had pointed out, and the rest moved into the forest.

When Joba returned, he said, "We will live in the forest."

"Fine."

Sam led Joba and Owl to the nearest building, so they could see how the places were constructed. Next, she took them up on the mesa, and Owl inspected her house.

"Need more openings."

"I know, but I'm not sure how to do it without damaging the walls."

"I will do."

Next, he inspected the meeting room. "Need more support here and here."

Glenda came in and Sam introduced them.

"She is my second-in-command here in the valley. Her mate is in charge of construction. They'll let you know what needs to be done and where."

Owl nodded. Joba remained blank-faced.

"What are you doing for food? I couldn't eat your food, so you probably can't eat ours."

"We know," Joba said. "We bring some, check some, some here like ours."

"Okay." Sam wasn't sure what to do or say next.

"We go back to people now," Joba said, starting off.

"I will be here in the morning," Glenda said. "Meet me here and we will plan what to do first."

Joba and Owl nodded and left.

"How many were there?" Glenda asked.

"About twenty, but there's more coming." Sam said.

"Wonderful. How much experience do they have?" She sounded pleased.

"They built their own houses in Ghind."

"Great. Thank you."

"Thank The Elder. She arranged it."

Sam went around checking food supplies and clothing. Glenda had had a crew build a storehouse south of the mesa; Ross had set up a table inside, so he could catalogue everything.

There were a lot more people here now, and still problems with not enough food. Sam expected it would stay that way until they could start growing crops. Many, including Sam, wore layers of clothes against the cold, and there were still people going back and collecting more garments.

*   *   *

The following day, Joba and Owl came to Sam's house to show her where she could cut new windows.

Then Joba told her, "You should know. Elder go across soon."

"Across?"

"To further life, beyond her body. Her sister will become Elder. Sister not like Elder. She may want her people back."

"Oh, no." Sam was getting tired of new problems continually popping up. "Will they go?"

"Perhaps. Their homeland no good anymore, so they would have to find a new place there." Joba shrugged

A thought struck her. "Are Jema and Juel here?"

"Not their tribe. They both carry young."

"Which one chose Boba?"

"Neither." Joba smiled. "Boba chose another, so they chose others."

"Good for them. Are they getting along better now?"

"Yes. Like sisters."

*   *   *

Sam spent the next two days checking on the factories and new settlements, referring most questions to Glenda and her helpers, always accompanied by the planet's presence. She became aware through it what was happening in the depths of City, even though she could not put it in words. She became aware of something within herself that was not of this world.

*   *   *

Two days later, Sam went back to City. After the usual effusive greetings, Brad, Todd, Maxee, Hal and Sam went to late meal. She spent as much time talking as eating, mostly about how Starview was growing and would they be able to fit everyone in the valley.

Back in the apartment, Sam, Brad, Todd, and Hal lounged in the main room of their apartment. Maxee disappeared into Sam's room.

Hal announced, "I have a proposition."

"Yes?" Todd said.

"I am getting totally burned out with politics." Hal took a deep breath. "My idea is this, is this: I will sell my apartment to you, Brad, and then quit my job. I will still live there, but I can leave whenever I want. I can go up to Starview with Sam, go exploring, or help out with getting people up there."

"Will I have to move over there?" Brad asked.

"Partially. We would have to move your screen files over there, and you would have to sleep there part of the time."

Brad nodded "That means I'd have to get a new comm. Again."

"Yes. I know it's a pain, but the committee working on revising that has finally passed it onto the councilors to consider."

"Do you think they'll pass it?" Todd asked. "They don't move around much."

"They've gotten a lot of complaints over the years. The comms are going to be gone soon anyway, so there's a good chance they will ... if there are enough of them left by the time they get around to it."

"Anything to look good," Sam said.

"Okay, let me think about it. I'd have to figure out what to do about Maxee, though." Brad touched his moustache.

"She can be here whenever Sam or I are here," Todd said. "Or over there with you when we're not here."

"Maybe."

They retired to their rooms. Sam undressed, climbed into bed, and tried to go to sleep. Her mantra no longer worked very well.

She was still awake when City slipped again as another pair of layers crumbled. Sam sat up and held on.

We have to get everyone out of here now.

She couldn't get back to sleep, so rose and worked at her screen.

✳   ✳   ✳

In the morning, Sam told Brad, "I think we lost another couple levels in the night. Did you feel it?"

Brad shook his head. "Are you okay?"

"Just shook up." She was finally getting used to the movements.

At first meal, Brad told them he had decided to buy Hal's place. After they took care of the paperwork, he settled in over there. It was strange, Sam thought, not having him around all the time.

✳   ✳   ✳

World teetered on the edge.

42

S AM, HAL, AND MAXEE WENT TO STARVIEW three days later. Sam could no longer stand being inside for more than a few days at a time. Hal managed the outdoors by wearing a hood.

A clothing factory with its workers had just moved up to Starview and set up near the food factory. Sam checked it out and helped them lay out a tent city for their workers. The Ghind tribe had been so good at building apartments and houses, most of the food factory people had moved out of their tents.

Sam made her rounds and found everything going well. Doug had rigged up a little water wheel to pump water into a holding bin, and made cisterns out of the barrels the small supplies had come in. He'd lugged one up to the meeting house. He had a crew working with him, and they had their own little patch of tents.

"You are officially head of the Waterworks Department," Sam told him. "Any water complaints will come to you, and you can send along anything you can't work out by yourself. You will also be Chief of Neighborhood of this group and any others that come to work or live with you."

"But I thought Ken was."

"Is he here?" I looked around.

"No. He's staying down there for now."

"Well, you're up here, and this is where the work needs to be done, so you're boss." Sam grinned at him.

"Okay. Only until Ken gets here. I have no desire to be boss. What's that Chief of whatever?"

"I just came up with the name. There's so many people, I can't handle everything. So every neighborhood group will have a chief, like a Councilor, to represent them at settlement meetings, and to take care of any little problems in their groups."

"Got it. I'll tell Glenda or whoever to send any plumbers that show up to me."

"Good."

Sam returned to her house.

"I stay here," Maxee said. She plopped herself into the chair on the porch.

Hal wandered around, peeking out from under his hood.

After dinner, he corralled her. "Sam, this is nice up here, but I don't see any place for me to fit in. I think I'd like to go back."

"Back to what?"

Hal disappeared and, when Sam went by the warehouse, Ross was not there.

An adolescent girl with long blond hair tapped Sam's shoulder. "Excuse me, Miss Sam, but we've got a problem and Miss Louise wants to see you."

"Okay." *As if I need another problem.*

Sam followed the girl to a food factory where Louise waited, standing beside a large box.

"What's up?"

"Some fellows just brought this." She pointed to the open box. "This food doesn't look or smell very good. I tested several samples, and they tested on the border of questionable and not recommended. I hate to throw all that away since we're so short on food, but I also don't want a bunch of people getting food poisoning. What do you think I should do?"

Sam thought. "Why don't you take a few pieces, cook them real good, and test them again. If the tester reads better, keep it and cook it well. If not, try cooking them again in the hottest heat you can get and test again."

"Yes." Louise nodded. "But for a shorter time. We don't want it too overcooked. Thank you, Sam."

"Always glad to help."

Sam returned to her house. There was a second chair on the porch.

"I asked for it," Maxee said.

Sam sat and watched the river burble by below. *It's getting quite high.*

She thought about all the things she had to do, all the questions that came up, how disorganized she felt.

Would we ever get to the point where we could have some fun?

Hal had returned to City, but in a few days he was back. "I didn't realize how bad the air was in there," he said. "What can I do here?"

"Welcome back." Sam smiled at him. "Ask around. Glenda always needs help."

* * *

Sam found Ross at a table in the storeroom, making lists of supplies. "How's it going?"

"Good. I wish I had a screen; a spreadsheet would be very handy."

"I know. The screen guys are working on a computer without Volen materials."

"Good. This is much better than in City. All this fresh air, I can think better."

"Glad it's working out for you. See you around." Sam smiled.

Starview kept Sam busy for several days, answering and referring questions, making suggestions, helping out here and there. With the presence always at her side, she began to feel like an intruder.

*　　　*　　　*

One day, after midday meal, Hal asked, "How would you like to go for a long walk, long walk?"

"How long?"

"Over to Liia's."

"That'll take days. I can't take the time, I have too much to do here."

"You look like you're falling asleep on your feet. You need a break; you need to get away from all this for a few days. Besides, I have time now, and I want to see new places and meet new people. You don't know how good it is to be out of Centrex. I am enjoying doing physical work and not having to constantly explain things to people who are supposedly smarter than me."

Sam found the idea tempting, but pushed it aside. "When is Arlene coming?"

"She's waiting 'til the last minute. She says she has to, since she's the one in charge."

"I can't leave yet either. And there's Maxee. She's in no condition to make a trek like that." Sam pulled her hair back as she spoke.

"She can stay at Starview. We'll get some people to keep an eye on her. "

"Let me talk to her first."

"We stay here," Maxee declared, when Sam told her what Hal wanted to do.

Sam talked to Glenda and a few others, who agreed that Sam needed a break, and that they would look after Maxee and take care of things while she was gone.

"I be fine," Maxee said when they told her. "Nice, here."

"All right," Sam told Hal at evening meal. "I'll go."

Hal and Ross left together.

Sam packed up. She called Liia and told her they were coming overland. She also wrote a message for Brad and Todd for the next group who went back down to City to take.

Sam and Hal left the next morning, after Sam hugged Maxee goodbye, and followed the river westward. Below the surface of her mind, something pushed her onward.

"I think this place will work," Hal said. "I wish I didn't have to wear this hood."

"You'll get used to outdoors. Most of the people who came up first only wear their hood part of the time, if at all."

They stopped in a little grove of trees by the river at midday. Hal pulled his hood up. "Not too bad under trees."

"Good. You'll get there." Sam smiled.

Glad to rest, Sam enjoyed the feeling of overworked muscles. It felt a little odd to be walking with a man other than Brad or Todd, but she enjoyed getting to know him and picking his brain about Centrex and politics.

That evening, they found another grove of trees to camp in. Sam was amazed by the river, how it changed: quiet one minute, all bubbly the next. Places with rocks made waves; other places it widened out flat. A lot of bushes and reedy plants lined it, with groups of trees here and there.

And the smells. All the plant aromas and sweet damp of the earth and freshness of the air. The sound of the river, gurgling, splashing, murmuring.

Sam couldn't get over it. She was out among trees, with a river alongside, walking on real ground, walking all day and no end.

As Sam dozed, the essence of this world soothed her.

*   *   *

World watched the one being.

43

I N THE MORNING, SAM WOKE TO A WORLD OF MIST. Bushes, festooned with their lacy wraps, and the ghostly trees amazed her. Although she could barely see the river, she could still hear it.

"What is going on?" Hal asked.

"Just mist, but isn't it beautiful?"

As they walked along, the mist gradually faded away.

"That river is awfully wide," Hal said. "Are we going to have to cross it?"

"I don't know. Let's just keep going and see what the river does." Sam hadn't thought about that.

The river bent toward the southwest, and she began to worry that they might have to cross it.

Where did it go?

When they stopped at midday, Sam noticed Hal was huffing and puffing.

"Are you all right?" she asked.

"I guess, I guess." He sat and leaned against a tree. "Not as easy as I thought." He pulled his hood off and threw it on the ground. "I did go up and down stairs a lot, as well as gym."

"Well, we're in no real hurry. I'm getting worn out myself. Maybe we should stop more often, even for just a few minutes." Sam dropped down beside him.

Hal dug out some bread from his pack and handed Sam a piece.

For the first time in years, Sam was close to a man who wasn't her brother. She liked it. She felt safe with him, although now she was worrying about his health. Sitting next to him, she enjoyed the cool breeze, and wondered about seasons. She'd read up on them, but never thought about them in real life.

Which season are we in, anyway?

After they ate, they continued on. Sam looked at every plant and tree, listened to the sounds of the river. Neither of them talked much. They came to a place where the river turned south and camped in the little forest in the inside of the curve. Sam heard chirps and flutterings in the treetops, and something moving around in another part of the woods. She felt no fear.

Finally, something I don't have to worry about.

Little purple fruits dangled from some of the trees. Sam checked them with her pocket analyzer. They contained a few things people could use and nothing bad, so she picked one and tasted it.

"Mmm, good." She handed Hal one and picked several more for her bag. "We need to get some of these trees to Starview."

A little later, Sam noticed the river sloped down to City. "Maybe we can cross it there."

They followed the river south to the reservoir and took the walkway that went along the side of the reservoir and across the bottom. At the end, where the pipe came out of the reservoir, steps led down to a doorway in the structure on the roof of Centrex. They passed it by, climbed over a low wall, and walked along the edge of the roof.

"My hatch is along here somewhere. Todd likes to keep it open for the fresh air."

Sam saw an open hatch, went over, and peered in.

Yes, there's Brad's shelf.

She knelt and stuck her head in. "Anybody home?"

"Sam?"

"I'm at the hatch."

Brad bounded in. "What are you doing out there? Come on in."

Sam did; Hal barely squeezed through.

"We're on our way to Liia's," Sam said. "We had to come down to the roof here to get across the river. I think we'll stay here tonight."

"Yes, do. Where's Maxee?"

"Up at Starview. In my house. She loves it up there. Others are looking after her."

"Good."

Sam and Hal had showers, two good meals, and swapped out dirty clothes for clean ones. Both Brad and Todd kept looking askance at Hal.

"He hasn't touched me," Sam said, thinking about his arm around her last night. It had felt so right.

The presence was gone.

At late meal, the men filled Sam and Hal in on the latest news.

"Thirteen and Fourteen are gone," Brad said. "Bill's recruiting people on the west side and Susan is doing the east side. Those people are moving everyone from west to east. They have three portals working."

"Good," Sam said. Only three, she thought, worried.

"The upper level people — the managers and creators — are all doing the most," Todd added. "There are still those who refuse to budge, but I don't feel sorry for them, because they've been told several times."

"Even most of the Councilors have left," Brad added.

Sam was pleased to hear all this.

Progress on getting people to the valley was still slower than she wanted, but she supposed they were doing the best they could.

Back at the apartment, Sam checked her screen.

No one else has reported dissolving walls, thank Oneness.

She caught up on her spreadsheets, to see where they were. Every once in a while, the screen flickered or paused. She asked Todd if his screen did.

"Yes. I think they're beginning to go. Write down everything you need to keep."

Hal told them about the river.

"It would be good if we could make a way up by the reservoir," Sam said. "Then the people from the west wouldn't have to go all the way across."

"I agree. I'll check that out," Brad said.

*   *   *

The next morning, Sam and Hal climbed out the hatch and continued on west, along the tree-lined river. They'd walked over an hour before she realized the presence was back. It was there only in the outdoors, because it was part of the planet. Sam wondered why she was the only one who could sense it.

Hal told her about his family. "My dad is a Councilor," he said. "I'm slated to follow him when he retires, that is, I was. I have no desire to get in on that racket. Mother's a medic, which is a good thing, because she has to look after my little sister, Jan."

"How little?"

"Twenty-two. She lost her feet in an accident. She has these boot things she wears so she can get around in the apartment, but when they go to a caff, Mother has to push her in a wheeled chair. They're trying to find her a mate, but no one's interested in a girl without feet."

"That's stupid. What does she do to occupy herself?"

"She does needlework and reads a lot on her screen."

"There's lots of things people can do without having feet. At least, she can get around." Sam thought of Gloria and wondered how she was doing at Judy's.

"When are you going to move them up?"

"I don't know. Dad won't go, and he won't listen to me. Mother wants to, but doesn't see how she can get Jan up there."

"Where do they live?"

"Forty-Nine east, near the far end."

"I'd like to meet them when we get back to City."

"That can be arranged. What about your folks?"

"Dad ran the xeno lab. He died ten years ago." Sam wasn't ready to tell him the whole story. "Dad met my mother on another world and brought her here. That world was like our valley. She couldn't handle living in City, so she went home when Brad and I were five."

"Rough. How come she didn't take you?"

"The governor at the time wouldn't let her. Said we were born here, we were citizens, we stay here." Sam stared into space.

"That must have been rough on your folks."

"It was. And on Brad and me. We get messages from her every few years. She remarried and had two boys, but she always says she misses her little Sammie-girl. At least, we know she's happy."

"How did you make out without a mother?"

Sam sighed. "Our family was close to Todd's, and we grew up with him. Aunt Linda was like a second mother, but it wasn't the same. Dad said I look just like Mother."

They were silent for a while.

"What about Todd's folks?" Hal asked.

"His dad, Dick, is head of the legal department. Todd says he's interested in going up to the valley, but doesn't want to leave yet. Todd's mom, Aunt Linda, says she'll go when Dick goes. They live on Forty-Nine East, so I'm not too worried about them yet."

"Have you ever been married?"

"I don't talk about that."

Sam turned away. It still hurt. She knew he was gone; Dondo said so. But Jerg was still here, and she couldn't erase that tiny trickle of doubt.

They reached the border between the human and Ambaak sectors. Seeing the gap between the roofs, Sam winced at the way the Ambaak sector slanted away and down to the southwest. They turned north into the hills to camp. That night, Hal kissed Sam on the cheek, and she did not feel repulsed by it.

*   *   *

The next day, she woke with the knowledge that this world and the nanobots that made up the Volen material had somehow joined to rid the place of those who refused to live with the natural world.

Sam shivered, but said nothing to Hal.

After following a tree-lined river, they found an Ambaak place. Rows of apartments, a group of buildings, and flowers everywhere. Sam asked for Liia, and the gal told her how to get to Liia's place. She also gave them dark strips when she saw them squinting into the sun. "We have plenty. We'll show you how to make them."

Sam thanked her, and they moved on, following the river west. This one had fewer bushes, smaller trees, and was narrower than theirs.

After they passed through a second settlement, where the people gave them food and water, they came to a small dell and decided to camp there, even though it was a couple hours until sundown.

Sam and Hal flopped down, too exhausted to move.

"One more day," Sam said.

These trees had long, narrow leaves. A stream trickled down from the hills to the river. Dark green moss lined the creek.

"Yep. I guess I didn't realize it was this far, this far."

"How are you doing without your hood?" Sam asked.

"Not bad. I'm getting used to all this space, and this wonderful air. I had no idea how bad it was getting inside."

"Yeah, if you're always inside, you don't know how much better it is outside."

"I wonder how long it's been since anyone's checked the air works." Hal picked up a leaf.

"Good question."

Sam savored the fresh air with flowery aromas, from three different kinds of blossoms around her. The trees whispered above her, and she heard the song of the river, the voices of the presence. Even the air felt softer on her arms and face. She wondered how she could get people to understand they needed to work with the world, not against it.

This is what she'd always longed for, but she couldn't stay there forever. She had a job to do.

*   *   *

World pulled back.

44

S AM AND HAL FINALLY REACHED LIIA'S SETTLEMENT. Sam asked for her, and a young man in blue directed her to one of the buildings.

When they arrived, Liia was working on a garment.

"Hello, Liia," Sam said as they approached her.

"Sam, you made it," Liia exclaimed as she turned around.

"Yes." Sam smiled. "This is Hal, he's a friend of Todd's. We walked from our settlement around above City."

"Walked? It must have taken days."

"Four, I think. We spent one night at home on the way. We had to go down to the roof of City to get across the river, so we went down the hatch to my apartment."

"Oh. Well, come on." She led the way out to a bench nearby.

"How are your people doing?" Sam asked.

"The same. Too many people won't come. Most of the top five levels are out or up into top level, but lower ones only move up when their clan home becomes unlivable, and then only up to the next available. How is your place doing?"

"Crumbling. Everything below Fifteen's a mess. What about Central?"

"Still nothing. They must know what's happening. They're not even taking calls. At least I can reach you on this." She waved her call device around.

Sam noticed the Ambaak roof looked patchy. "What's going on with your roof?"

"We're transplanting those plants to our new area. The little ship is a blessing."

"Good. Four days is much too long between us. We need some kind of faster transportation than on foot." Sam waved her hand around.

"True. I've been thinking about rail cars. I know they're going to go, but Giil and some others have pulled apart a few of the cars and studied them to see if we can make one of our own."

"What would you use for track?"

"That's another problem. Do you have any ideas?"

"Not off-hand, but I'll put it to my brothers."

Liia stood. "Meanwhile, come and eat. You, too, Hal."

Liia's people had set up an open dining area, with a roof and side curtains that could be pulled down in bad weather. They found Jone and the children. Sam noticed Betty was wearing her mother's locket.

"This is Sam, Brad's sister, and her friend Hal," Liia said. "Jone, Jim, and his sister Betty."

"Welcome," Jone said.

Jim stared at Sam.

Betty said, "You're so pretty."

Sam felt her face grow warm and said, "How do you like living out here?"

"It's real neat," Jim said. "I can run as far as I want."

"I like all the flowers," Betty added.

"It is so wonderful out here." Jone stacked dishes. "The youngsters are doing wonderfully. They've made friends with our children and are learning their lessons well."

"Lessons," Sam said. "They need to learn human history. How can we manage that?"

One more thing for me to think about. Growl.

"Crumbles. Yes, they do. I forget they're not ours." Liia looked at Sam. "You must be tired. I show you a place to rest."

Hal said, "Great. I've done all the walking I want to for a while."

Sam and Hal followed Liia to a shady place under a tree.

As they settled down, Sam said, "We need to connect more devices to this system, so I can talk to people in City when I'm not there, and in Starview."

"I know. I'll talk to the comm people."

*   *   *

Liia showed Sam around her new place. Rows of structures, with alternating doors and windows lined the hillsides.

"Our homes," Liia said.

On the flat land below stood two rows of buildings. She showed Sam a meeting place, the schoolhouse, a medical clinic, a large kitchen, and craft houses.

"Very nice," Sam said, after they toured the buildings. "I love this air out here. Ours inside was getting quite stale."

"Inside air never as good as outside. I always wish we could open our skylights to get some air in."

The two women sat on a bench under a tree near the river.

"Have your people always lived in clans like this?" Sam asked. "Are you all related?"

"More or less. On our home world, all the clans in a province get together for several days, and those who were ready pick mates. Here, all prospects go visit other clans, along streets. The couple chooses which clan to live with. They visit back and forth."

"That's not the way we do it. There was a time on our home world when the parents would arrange marriages. That's what we called 'matings'. But we get this deep emotional attachment to one another we call love, we marry and have children, and are family. Sometimes it's just an attraction. It's hard to tell the difference when we're young."

"Have you a mate?" Liia asked.

"No. Not now." Sam thought someday she might tell Liia about her marriage, but not yet.

"Sam, have you ever felt the world was trying to talk to you?"

"Yes. You, too?" Sam bounced in her seat.

"We have always tried to live with nature, but when so many people together, not easy. Have to provide food and shelter. But here, now we are out of that unpleasant building, we take only what we need. Ambworld guides us to trees and plants we can use."

"Do others in your clan feel this?" Sam asked.

"Some do."

"I seem to be the only one of the humans." Sam sat back.

"Did you not say once your mother came from other planet?"

"Yes. Oh, Liia, that must be it." Suddenly excited, Sam searched back in her memories. "I remember now. Mother used to tell us she lived in vast gardens, in little tent things where the sides could roll up in nice weather, which it was most of the time, and thick, soft moss on the floor." She stopped and thought. "Well, everyone thinks I look like her, so maybe I have more of her in me than I figured."

"Use it to help your people."

An older woman in red came up to them and asked Liia for help.

"Do you know where the *dati* seeds are?"

"Let's go look." Liia stood. "See you at late meal," she said to Sam as she left.

Sam sat and thought about their two different worlds.

*   *   *

That night, when Sam and Hal returned to their sleep area, Hal pulled her into a hug and kissed her. Places she thought were shut down forever, awoke.

Finally, he pushed her away. "Not here, not here."

Sam's body felt alive for the first time in years.

Was it really possible for me to have a relationship with a man?

She had a hard time getting to sleep. She liked Hal. He was comfortable to be around, yet she couldn't think of actually living with him.

*   *   *

In the morning, Sam woke before Hal and shivered, thinking of the night before. She felt an urge to kiss him, but dismissed it. The presence was there, as always.

At first meal, Liia asked Sam how long she wanted to stay.

"A few days, at least. We won't walk all the way back to Starview. I figure if we can find an open hatch at this end, we can catch a car to our place."

Jone and the children joined them.

"Jim," Sam asked, "How much do you know about your human history?"

He looked at her with a questioning expression. "Huh?"

"You did have school down there, didn't you?"

"Oh. Yeah."

"So what do you know?"

"Our people came here a long time ago in big spaceships, and then the Volen came and built City and gave us things."

"Good. That's a start. Would you like to come and see our place?"

Jim shrugged.

"I would like to," Liia said. "May I take you back in my ship?"

"Oh, would you? That'd be great."

"Yes," said Hal. "That would be a lot better than walking back."

Sam and Hal spent another day there, tutoring Jim, helping out with whatever needed to be done, and walking around the area.

*   *   *

The next morning, after chores, and Giil had brought up a load of people and their belongings, Sam and Hal piled into the little ship with Liia and took off.

As she approached Todd's port, she requested permission to land, adding that she was bringing two citizens of City. After verifying Sam's and Hal's identities through their comms, the port controller let her dock.

When they passed through the tube into the waiting room, Liia gasped. "How can you breathe in here?"

"I stay out as much as possible," Sam said.

The air was no worse than when she left a few days ago.

When they went down the stairs and into the street on Fifty, Liia looked around and said, "Oh my Amb, how can people live here?"

"They don't know anything else."

Sam led her down and around to her apartment. Hal waved and entered his place. In Sam's apartment, the emptiness overwhelmed her. The other men were at work, and Maxee was in Starview.

Liia examined the apartment. "At least you have skylights," she said. "This not too bad."

Sam showed her the other rooms and the hatch, which was open.

"Of course, this is one of the best places," Sam said. "Only our top level has skylights and hatches. In the middle levels, they have one bedroom, and the lowest levels are a single room and bath. The shop I had down on Twenty had one bedroom."

"Oh, my."

They went for a meal, of which Liia only ate a few bites and, after how much Sam had eaten the past few days, she didn't eat much more. Sam dumped the plates into a to-go bag. The men would eat it, and they couldn't afford to throw any food away.

"I like the way you feed your people better," Sam said. "We never know what we're going to get, and we're only allowed two meals a day because of the food shortage."

They returned to the apartment. Sam led Liia to her room, opened a drawer, and pulled out her little plant that Maxee had given her. It had six leaves now.

"It needs to be outside," Liia said.

"When I'm here, I keep it under the hatch, but when I'm gone, it sits in the drawer so it won't fall if the place moves. I'm planning to take it up the next time I go. The seeds you gave me are up there and sprouted."

Liia nodded.

Sam showed her the carved wooden figure the Ghind had given her, and the little purple pot from Maya. "These are tokens of friendship from those people."

"You do have a way with other people." She looked around. "Is that a screen?" she asked."

"Yes." Sam turned it on. "I won't have it much longer. The screen is Volen, and it keeps shutting down by itself, or goes to a different page."

"Oh, my. Wonderful, you have it to use all the time."

"I wouldn't know what to do without it. But I've got the most important things down on paper. Our screen guys are supposedly working on a non-Volen computer."

"Is possible you can get them to make one for us? We have two or three screens in each clan, for our local use, but they won't last long."

"I can ask."

"Thank you. I must go."

"Okay."

Sam grabbed her bag and they left, retracing their steps. Liia was gasping when we reached the port.

"This air," she said.

"I know. Thanks for the ride." Sam touched her shoulder.

"Glad to help. I admire your work. Keep going and do as much as you can. That's all we can do." Liia smiled at Sam.

"I will. Take care."

"You too." She trotted down the tube to her ship.

*   *   *

World found another being it could reach.

45

S AM RETURNED HOME AND CHECKED HER SCREEN. About two-thirds of the people they had talked to had responded. She dealt with messages and updated her paper forms. An emptiness surrounded her without Maxee around, and the presence gone.

She needed to tell someone about the presence, now that she knew others sensed it. Brad came home first, and she cornered him.

"Brad, I've got to tell you something I've been experiencing."

"What?" He sat her down on a couch.

"This world is alive. Both Liia and I have heard it." *Please believe me.*

"What are you talking about? You, level-headed Sam, hearing things?"

"Yes. I've changed in case you hadn't noticed. I'm out of my rut and feeling things around me." She pounded her fist. "This world is not just a rock; it's a living being. Apparently the Volen material has something in it that can bind to microbes in the soil."

"Sam, this is not you. You've never cared much about things outside your little circle of life." Brad crossed his legs.

"Well, I do now. I've learned all sorts of things after being ripped out of my rut. I wish I'd found out sooner, but not from my ex coming back. Why didn't you tell me about your experiences in Space Service?"

"I though you weren't interested."

"How could I know if I was interested if you didn't tell me?" Sam bounced in her seat.

"Sam, calm down." He put an arm around her and pulled her to him. "Tell me about this presence."

"I only feel it when I'm outside of City. Sometimes I get words. It doesn't want us to mess up this world. That's why the Volen material is disappearing faster than they said. I don't want to have to destroy any more of this place than we absolutely have to."

"Okay, okay. We'll do what we can."

Before Sam could say any more, Todd arrived.

"What's up?" he asked.

Sam told him.

"Nonsense. You're hearing things. I think this job is getting to you." Todd dropped into a chair.

Sam jumped up. "I am not. You'll see."

Brad pulled her back down. "Later."

Hal showed up and they went to eat. Sam and Hal told the others about their trip.

"I'm glad they're doing well over there," Brad said. "And you're right about teaching the children about their human heritage. I hadn't thought about that."

"Anything new with the governor?" Sam asked.

"He's disappeared." Todd waved a breadstick. "Arlene thinks he's hiding out in his basement. His house has three levels, you know."

"No, I didn't," Sam said. "So who's running the sector?"

"Arlene, of course. She's working on getting all non-essential employees out and up to the valley. There are groups going up every day, now." Todd took a bite of stew.

"Good. But will it be enough?"

"I don't know, Sam. We'll just have to keep working at it."

"You're awful quiet, Brad," Sam noted.

"Thinking. I checked the way up at the reservoir. Since the place slipped, we can't reach the walkway, but there are rungs in the cliff. I think we can climb up that way. Maybe at the top we can get around the reservoir."

"Rungs," Sam repeated.

"Yes. Flat black metal steps bolted into the cliff. They don't look Volen at all."

"How far down do the rungs go?" she asked. "Because City will keep slipping."

"Probably down to the bottom of Centrex," Hal said. "But it would help to a have a way out closer to the west end."

"I agree," Todd said. "But then, what do we do after City gets below the rungs?"

Sam remembered the baskets the Itza had used. "The Itza had baskets on ropes to bring things up to their homes. Could we do that, over the side of the cliff? To bring people and their bags up?"

"Great idea, Sam." Brad patted her shoulder. "Now, what can we use for baskets and where can we find ropes?"

*   *   *

Back at the apartment, Brad and Todd researched ropes and baskets, and Sam worked on her stats. Suddenly another big jolt hit, and the place dropped. Sam fell out of her chair and huddled on the floor.

"There goes Levels Fifteen through Eighteen," Todd yelled from his room.

Sam sat and shook. Panic enveloped her, and she made fast little sobbing sounds.

I need out. Now.

Brad staggered in and dropped down beside her. "All right, Sammie, I'm here."

She nestled into him and fought her way out of the panic. Todd joined them and sat in her chair.

"I'm afraid the place is starting to go. That's the first time two cube levels went at the same time."

"What are we going to do now?" Sam whispered.

"First, there's a bunch of rope in Level Forty-One in Centrex. I suggest we go get as much as we can carry tomorrow morning. Brad and I can get off, and we can take the ropes up the rungs. Any more slippage and we'll be below the ladder." Todd stood. "Any luck on baskets?"

"None of the basket makers I've found make any big enough," Brad said.

"Well, someone made Gloria's basket. Maybe one a little smaller, for children and bags of stuff," Sam replied.

"Okay, I'll keep checking. But ropes up first while we can." Brad gave me a squeeze.

They staggered out to the main room and dropped onto a couch.

"Everything's off again," Todd observed.

He rose and turned on the auxiliary power.

*   *   *

In the morning, the three of them and Hal went over to Centrex and down to Forty-One. They wound as much rope around themselves as they could and took the tube back up, one at a time.

At the bottom of the rungs, Brad said, "Sam, you go first."

Sam reached for the first rung, and he boosted her up.

One rung at a time, stop to breathe, boost, more rungs, finally the top.

She heaved herself over the top onto the ground above. The others followed. They sat next to the reservoir, panted, and stared into space. The silver roof appeared to be crumpled in the center. Todd handed around a water jug and they all partook. The walkway seemed to be undamaged.

They rested awhile and headed west until they reached a huge tree near the edge. They dumped their ropes, and Brad tied an end of one around the tree. He dropped the other end over the side. They all knelt and peered over.

Was the rope long enough? Sam couldn't tell.

"I think we need more," Brad said.

They pawed through the ropes and found a short piece, hauled up the rope, tied the short piece to the end, and dropped it back down.

"Okay, that's good." Brad stood up and stretched.

They gathered the rest of the ropes and continued along the top of the cliff, finding four more large trees near the edge. They tied ropes around all of them, which exhausted their supply of rope.

Back down, Brad and Todd went to work. Hal and Sam returned to her apartment.

"I'll be glad when we get out of here for good." Hal wandered around.

"Me, too." Sam looked for food and only found a crust of bread. "When do we get to eat again? I'm starving."

"Not 'til tonight. I'll go see what I have."

Sam turned on the screen. A message read:

If you are on or below Level Twenty, leave now and go east.
If you are on Twenty-One through Twenty-Five, prepare to
leave as soon as possible.

The notice repeated several times before her logon page appeared.

"Thank Oneness I'm not down there anymore," Sam said aloud.

She called Connie down on Twenty. "Have you seen the message about leaving now?" Sam asked.

"Yes. Do you think we should go? I haven't got a job in several days and I'm running out of credits. People are panicking, and I'm keeping my shop door locked. I'm afraid for my little girls."

"Yes. Pack up and get out of there as soon as you can. Take what you can carry, any food you have, and head east. You might want to go up one level, just to be safe. Once you get to the end, there will be people to direct you to a portal to the outdoors and up to the settlement. Take something to wear over your head if the space is too open for you. Find an older couple to walk with, if you can. And pass the word to everyone you see that it's time to leave,"

"Okay. Thanks."

Sam disconnected and sat back. *Who else can I call down there to warn and spread the word?*

Judy.

Sam called her, and Judy said she and her sons were packing up. Gloria had died peacefully in her sleep one night, but they had had some nice conversations. They would take Gloria's little treasures.

Better for Gloria this way, Sam thought. She couldn't imagine someone carrying the old woman all that way.

*　　　*　　　*

Hal returned with a handful of food bars. "I forgot I had these," he said, and gave Sam a couple.

They were condensed nutritional bars that one factory processed, to be used when regular food was scarce.

"Thanks."

Sam could not concentrate on anything. She tried a few different entertainments which failed to entertain her at all. The shows were boring and the puzzles uninteresting.

When Brad and Todd came home, they all went to the caff. They stuffed themselves with bread to make up for the meager stew.

Brad told them he had found a basket maker who was willing to make several big ones. "I told him we needed four big ones and four smaller ones. He'll bring them up when they are done."

"Good," Sam said. She wasn't looking forward to riding up a cliff in a basket.

*　　　*　　　*

World continued to pull down more Volen constructs.

46

A FEW DAYS LATER, Brad brought home a reddish, tightly woven basket big enough for Sam to sit in. Brad, Todd, and Sam went to the bottom of the nearest rope and tied on the basket. Brad knew what kind of knots to use. The men went up the rungs, and she climbed into the basket.

"Ready, Sam?" Brad called from above.

"Yes." *Please, Oneness, don't let the rope break.*

They hauled her up about halfway, then let her down.

At first, the ride wasn't bad; the swinging didn't bother her. But later, looking down, her stomach lurched, and her heart raced. She was glad when they let her down, slowly, except for a few jerks now and then.

Reaching bottom, Sam climbed out and took a deep breath. She waited for them at the rungs. They were breathing hard, also.

"How was it?" Brad asked.

"Not bad, until I looked down."

"We need to set up a pulley system. Even with three of us, it was hard work."

"Okay, you figure it out." *I don't need any more problems.* "And you need to recruit some hefty young men to operate it."

"Yeah. I'll work on that and getting more rope up there." Brad smiled at her.

The men went to get more rope, and Sam returned to the apartment.

She tried to imagine going all the way up. *We'll need more blindfolds.*

Sam tried to settle down and do some work, but something kept jiggling her chair. The place continually moved around, shifting sideways, up and down, jittering. Sam wanted out in the worst way.

How could the governor and his cronies ignore this?

One big jolt, and the room tilted toward the south, with the front door at the low end. After Sam caught her breath, she scrambled to the door and looked out into the street. Several other people came out of their homes.

"What's happening?" a thin woman with a red scarf asked.

"I thought it was supposed to be safe up here," an older man said.

"It's not safe anywhere in City anymore. Your best bet is to get out and go up to the settlement in the valley," Sam said.

"How?" a narrow man with a belly asked.

"There's two ways. One, go as far east as you can, and someone will show you the way. Two, go out your hatch and over to Centrex and climb the rungs in back of it. We are working on ropes hanging down the cliff with baskets to haul stuff up. Pass the word."

Sam held on to the doorway, as the place shook again.

Back inside, she thought, *We've got to find a way to broadcast to everyone.*

She called Arlene.

"Arlene, we need to broadcast to everyone to leave now. Go east or go to rungs in back of Centrex."

"Okay. There are only a few people left in Security. I'll get them to do it. I'm pretty much packed up and ready to go."

"Good. Thanks."

* * *

At late meal, Sam asked Hal, "So, what's going on in Centrex?"

"Most people from the lower levels are leaving or have already left," Brad interjected.

"Quite a few Councilors from lower levels have packed up and taken their families up," Hal said. "Others are getting their families ready. A few more jolts like this and there won't be enough left for a quorum, which means nothing can get done here anyway."

"What about the legal offices?" Sam asked Todd.

"We've shut down everything not vital, destroyed a lot of unnecessary paper records, let anyone who wanted to go, leave. Getting the few open cases on paper, plus all sorts of records. Dad and I will stay there as long as we can."

"The medical clinic. Do we have a team up there yet? I didn't see one last time I was up."

"Yes, most of the medical people went to Starview three or four days ago. I think there are small medical groups associated with the factories." Todd took a bite.

"The labs." Sam sipped from her mug.

"They're packing up as much as they can, waiting for the building to be completed," Brad said. "So many people have quit that Security dropped the don't-miss-time-or-you're-fired bit. We'll get there." He smiled at her.

The caff manager, in a spotted white apron, told them that lower caffs were closing and moving up to the valley, to make a joint kitchen. "We on Levels Forty-Eight through Fifty will stay open as long we can get food," the woman in the apron said.

"Good." Sam smiled.

Another night with little sleep.

* * *

World noticed that the beings on the outside did less damage than the Volen constructs.

47

T HE NEXT DAY, WHEN HAL CAME OVER for evening meal, he asked Sam if she'd like to go meet his mother and sister.

"Sure."

"Let's go in the morning."

"Okay." She looked forward to meeting Hal's family.

*   *   *

Sam and Hal took the Forty-Eight car through Centrex and no one stopped them.

"I guess Security doesn't have enough people left to bother with this," Sam said.

At his mother's place on Forty-Nine, Hal tapped on the door and went in.

"Hal," a woman with reddish-blonde hair exclaimed.

A slight girl with similar hair, who sat in a chair nearby, looked up. A plain chair stood next to her padded one.

Sam blinked. That chair had small wheels on the bottom of its legs.

"Hello, Mother, Jan. This is Samanda Lar, the lady who is in charge of moving everyone up to Starview."

"Welcome. I'm Evelyn, and this is Jan," the older woman said, laying down her needlework. She stood and hugged him. "You're looking wonderful. Isn't he, Jan?"

"Yes. Your skin is darker."

Hal went to Jan, pulled her up out of the chair, and gave her a brotherly hug. "How are you doing, sis?"

"I want to get out of here. Sometimes it's hard to breathe."

Sam wanted to pick her up and carry her out right then, but knew better than to interfere with a family. "Are the tubes out here still working?" she asked.

"Most of the time," Evelyn said.

"Maybe we could get Jan up to Fifty and over to our place." Sam looked around. "We have hatches that open to the sky, and we can get better air."

"Would you like that, Jan?" Hal asked.

Jan tilted her head to one side and stared at the wall.

"Do you have room in your place?" Evelyn asked.

"Oh, yes. I can put her in the room with the hatch. We leave it open all the time now."

"We?"

"My brothers and I live in one apartment, and Hal and his roommate in his. They both have three bedrooms." Sam smiled at Evelyn.

"Let me think. Jan?"

"Yes, Mother, I'd like to go. Only we can't get my chair on the tube platform, and I can't do stairs. If the tubes are even working." She sank back in her chair.

Sam sat on a couch, and Hal fetched her some water.

"How are you doing for food?" he asked his mother.

"We're managing. We still have a small stash." Evelyn sat and picked up her needlework.

Sam looked around. Pictures in bright colors of stitchery covered the pale-yellow walls and shelves. Many were of flowers or creatures.

"Do you sell these?"

"Only privately, now and then. Why?" Evelyn asked.

"This would be a good project for you and Jan in Starview. Most people up there would like to have a colorful piece in their homes."

Jan looked up. "You think so?" Her hands held a piece of fabric with blue stitches.

"I'm sure of it. You could also teach others how to do stitchery."

"How did you meet Hal?" Jan demanded. Her round face held large, dark eyes and a wide mouth.

"He knew my brother, Brad, and when we needed to move up, he found us an apartment next to his."

"Okay." A little smile crossed Jan's face.

"Can you stay over?" Evelyn asked.

"Do you have room for us?" Sam asked.

"We can manage. What about her things?"

"I can carry a lot, Mother, and Sam can carry some, too," Hal said.

Sam nodded. "What about food?"

"How could I not feed my son and his friend?"

"All right, Mother." To Sam, Hal said, "She has food stashed all over the place."

"Hal." Evelyn smiled.

"Roll me into my room," Jan demanded.

She had transferred into the little chair with wheels. Hal sighed, shrugged, and rolled Jan's chair into her room. The handmade chair, with little wheels on the four narrow legs, moved jerkily over the Volen pebbled floor.

"Go away," Jan said with a smile, to her brother. "I want to show Sam some things."

Pale pink walls set off her purple bedcover, and white shelves lined the room, holding her stitchery creations. Little three-drawer white chests sat in a row on a long table beside her bed.

"Those are all my threads and things." Jan pointed to the chests.

She showed Sam a small case with a photo of a man and a woman in clothes like the first colonists wore.

"This is my fortieth great grandmother and grandfather. Mother gave it to me on my twenty-first birthday last year."

"Wow," Sam said, impressed. "I haven't got anything older than two hundred years."

"This has also been handed down from the beginning."

She held out a globe inside a clear box that just fit in the palm of her hand. The globe's white bottom held a pile of white flakes, and green triangles dotted the blue sides and top.

"Watch." Jan turned it over. The flakes in the bottom drifted down to the blue area. She shook it, and the white stuff swirled. "It's called a snow globe."

"Snow," Sam repeated.

"Frozen rain, when it's cold enough for water to freeze."

"Oh." *I'll have to check that out. One more thing …*

Jan sat back on her bed. "We know all about you and moving up to the valley," she said. "But I thought you'd be big and bossy. I'm glad you're not."

"Thanks. Sometimes I have to be bossy, though, to get things done." Sam was beginning to like this young woman.

"It'll be nice to have Hal around. I miss him sometimes." Jan looked at Sam. "I think he's falling in love with you."

"No." Love was a word she only applied to brothers. But Hal did pop up at her side a lot.

"Don't you like him?"

"Yes, as a friend."

"He'd make a good husband."

"I'm sure." Sam twisted her fingers together.

Hal entered. "Time to go eat," he said.

Jan plopped into her chair, and he wheeled her out. Sam and Evelyn joined them, and they all went down to the caff.

This one had plenty of food. "They have their own farm down in the hills at the base of City along the sea," Evelyn told Sam.

For the first time in weeks, Sam was full.

*   *   *

Sam and Hal returned to their apartments, and she told Brad and Todd about Jan and her chair.

"How does it move?" Brad asked.

"It's like a regular table chair made of wood, with little wheels on the bottom of the legs," Sam said. "She said they can't get it on the tubes."

"In the first place, it needs bigger wheels and a way to fold it, so it can't be all wood. Let me see what I can come up with." Brad smiled at her.

Sam packed more belongings to take up and did paperwork.

The next day, Brad came home with a folding chair with larger wheels in back. "I found it in the bottom level storage. Or rather, Arlene's people found it and put it aside in case someone needed it."

"Wonderful," Sam said.

*   *   *

The next afternoon, after Brad got off work, the three of them took the chair over to Jan. Brad had no trouble carrying it on the tube.

In the apartment, Hal greeted his mother and sister. "Here, try this."

Hal took the chair from Brad and opened it up. "Brad found it. He's Sam's brother."

Jan nodded as Hal rolled the chair over to her. The seat and back were of a heavy fabric. Jan stood in her boots, turned around, and dropped into the new chair.

"I like this," she said. She put her hands back on the big wheels and moved the chair. "Oh, nice." Jan wheeled herself around the room, grinning.

"Are you ready to go now?" Hal asked.

"Yes. Sam, come help me pack." She wheeled herself into her room.

"That is quite wonderful," Evelyn said. "How did you ever think of it?"

"I saw one once on another world, when I was in the Space Service, and I thought we might have one tucked away somewhere, and we did."

"Sam, are you coming?" Jan yelled from her room.

"Coming," Sam said, heading down the hall.

In Jan's pink and purple room, Sam got her big bag out of the closet. The little chests and her creations almost filled the large carryall.

"Hal gets to carry that," Jan said.

They packed up her clothes and personals, and a little bag with her trinkets, that she could carry.

"Hal brought me those." There were several little figurines carved from different materials in different colors, a yellow duck with a bobbing head, and a multicolored ball.

"He must have got them from Spaceport," Sam said. "I have several little trinkets, too." Sam pulled Jan's big bag out to the other room, and Jan carried the others on her lap.

Her father, David, arrived, was introduced all around, and admired Jan's new chair. After they went for a meal, they talked for a while, then retired.

Sam slept with Jan in her big bed. Hal used his old room and Brad took the couch.

Sam heard Evelyn arguing with David after they went to bed. That brought back memories of Mother and Dad arguing, just before she left. She pushed them away and tried to sleep.

*　　*　　*

In the morning, Evelyn said she was going with Hal and Jan. She had packed up. David left for Centrex, wishing us well.

Sam folded Jan's blankets and stuffed them into her carryall. Brad took Jan's carryall, and Hal carried his mother's. Evelyn and Sam carried more bags.

At the nearest working down-tube, Hal helped Jan, in her boots, onto the platform, and held her on as she hung onto the pole strap. Evelyn and Sam followed on the next platform, with Brad on the last one with the chair.

They caught the Forty-Eight car across, up their tube, and put Jan in her chair. Hal helped her wheel it as the rest walked to Hal's apartment.

Jan rolled to the nearest comfortable chair and swiveled herself into it. She sighed. "These boots hurt," she said, taking them off. Her pantlegs hung over empty space.

"Maybe we can get you better ones when we get to Starview," Sam said, looking around.

Some of the pictures on the walls were definitely slanted. She couldn't wait to get out of there.

"This air is better." Jan took a deep breath. "Hey, did you know your floor slants?"

"Oh." That hadn't occurred to Sam. "Will you be all right with that?"

"No problem. It's not very much."

Evelyn collapsed on a couch. Sam sat beside her.

"As long as she's happy," Jan's mother said. "My poor baby."

*　　　*　　　*

The next day, Hal said, "I want to take Mother and Jan up as soon as possible."

"I'll take them up in my ship," Todd said. "You can come, too, Hal."

"Why didn't you do that before?" Hal asked.

"She only holds four, including the pilot, and I need to get her an annual checkup. I have taken up some things too large for anyone to carry."

"Where is it?"

"Not far. I'll take you up tomorrow."

*　　　*　　　*

World jiggled harder.

48

I N THE MORNING, Sam and Brad walked with them back to the tube. "Take care," Sam said. "I think you'll like up there."

"It's got to be better than our old place," Jan said. "Thanks again for the chair." Todd carried it this time.

"See you soon," Hal said to Sam as he settled Jan on the platform and put his arms around her.

"Bye," Sam said. She wondered when she would see him again.

On the way back, Brad said, "You and I can go as soon as we get the pulleys set up. Should be ready in a few days."

*   *   *

Two days later, Sam and Brad left for Starview with bags of their belongings. Sam and the bags went up in the baskets. Sam held her breath most of the way. Brad climbed the rungs. At the top, Sam and Brad turned and looked out over the remains of City.

Three rows of cube blocks jutted out from the cliff below. Beyond that was a jumbled mass of chunks of blocks, tubes, cars, conduits, and discarded belongings. Sam saw a few people struggling along on top of the heap, heading east, and wished she could help them.

"What a mess," Brad said. "I'll miss the paddle ball and bag toss at the rest areas."

"We can set up those games in Starview." Sam spoke absently.

That sense of loss Sam had felt after Mother left, and again when Dad died, returned as she stared out over the remains of City. It had been her home, her life, her haven. She wasn't sure exactly how she felt. But a new home, a new life awaited her in Starview.

"Let's go." Brad turned and headed for the walkway around the reservoir to the other side of the river.

That way was shorter, but steeper. Sam showed Brad where she had collected the purple fruits, and they picked a bunch more. When they turned eastward, Sam noticed that some of the leaves on a few trees were turning yellow.

As they approached the headland, a young woman who was scouting the river saw them, waved, and ran back to spread the news. Several people greeted them, led by Maxee.

"Sammie," she squealed, hugging Sam.

A gal with a pink sleeve on her tunic came up to Sam and asked, "How did you come that way?"

"There are hatches in the roof of the top level, and we can go up that side," Sam said, relieved to be back at her new home. "Where did you get that pink color?'

She looked down at her sleeve. "We found berries that we can't eat, but they make a nice dye."

"Great." Sam grinned.

"Come see," Maxee said, pulling Sam's hand.

Sam followed her to their house. The walls of the front room were streaked with swirls of pink.

"You did this?" It was beautiful.

"I paint walls. The no-good berries. Want another color."

"Wonderful." Sam sat on the bed and stared at her colorful walls. "How's Baby Max?" *It's so good to be home.*

Maxee pulled open her pouch and let her see in. A tiny pink creature wiggled in the depths. "Be a while before he come out."

"You have everything you need?"

"Most. Need lots food."

Sam lay down on the bed. "So what's been going on here?"

"Big caff now. Little one up here. Lots more people. I stay up here."

"Good."

Maxee twiddled her fingers and looked around. Finally, she said, not looking at Sam, "Sammie, world talk to me."

"So you hear it, too." Sam was not surprised.

Maxee nodded. "We take care of world, it take care of us."

"Very true. How can we tell all the others?"

"I do." She refused to say how.

"I told Brad, but he didn't believe me, even when I told him Liia heard it too. I never sensed the presence when I came up here with him. I guess it's just the three of us."

"We do," Maxee said, nodding her head.

They talked a bit, then Sam went out to see for herself. The caff on the mesa was average size, but the one down on the level was huge. She found the woman in charge, June.

"I've heard about you," she said. "All my workers are former caff owners, so everyone knows what to do."

"How are you on food?" Sam asked.

"Not enough. We need more food factories up here."

"We also need to figure out what we're going to eat when they are gone."

Sam left to find Evelyn and Jan. They had been assigned a cozy, one-room apartment near the large caff.

"How are you two doing?" Sam asked.

"Fine." Evelyn smiled. "I miss Dave, though. Wish he'd come up."

"I can breathe so much better here," Jan added.

"Good. Eventually, you will get a larger apartment, but so many people are showing up, a lot of them are still in tents. Glad you're here. I've got to go. See you around."

Sam continued her rounds and collected complaints. Most of them were about shortages. The few factories had been working around the clock, but they were running out of supplies. She delegated a few problems and decided she needed to call a meeting. There were so many people up there that she asked for delegations from the factories and departments, and one person from each neighborhood group. They could spread the word to the others.

Sam stood on a table at the rear wall. "I've been hearing a lot of complaints, so we need to figure out what to do about them. First, food: I know there's not enough. Most of the Volen foodstuff is gone. Food management is working on converting local plants so that we can eat them. We need a group to go upriver into the hills to search for other plants, fruits, and vegetables. Anyone who wants to volunteer, see me afterwards. Meanwhile, let us all be very careful of what we have and not waste any."

"Let's go back to City, there's food there," an older man called out.

"No there isn't. They have less than we do, and no options to get more." Sam looked around at everyone.

Her people. She shivered. *This was not what I had imagined in my office months ago. Where is the leisurely outdoor life I'd thought of then?*

"Second, the weather. Inside, the temperature was always the same. Out here in the real world, we have weather. We will just have to deal with it. It's getting cooler, because out here we have seasons. We are now in fall, going into winter, which is the cold season. The clothing people are working on ways to make warmer clothing and bed covers. Wear more layers of clothing if you can. They are getting groups together to go back to empty apartments in City to collect clothing left behind."

"How long is this cold going to last?" a young woman down front asked.

"We're not sure, but most likely one fourth of a year. You can make bigger beds and cuddle up." Sam thought of Hal and pushed the idea away.

"Now, rain. I know a lot of you didn't know about rain. It will occur every now and then. There may be a time of year when it rains a lot, another time when it hardly rains at all. We'll all have to learn together. For those of you in houses and apartments, next time it rains, check to see if there are any leaks in your roofs. There shouldn't be, but that doesn't mean there won't be. Make sure all your very special important belongings are in boxes or drawers, so they won't get wet if there is a leak. Report any leaks to construction so they can fix your roof."

Sam paused. Over half the people looked numb. She had always known this wasn't going to be easy.

"Someone asked me why we don't have screens down here. We don't, because screens are Volen and are going away. Our comms will go too. The comm department is working on getting important files onto a non-Volen system that we can use up here, when we get power set up."

"When's that?" someone yelled.

"Maintenance is working on solar panels, and Doug and his crew are working on a bigger water wheel in the river. Be patient and do what you can. We all need to do whatever we need to get this going right. I'm setting up a place at the inland end of the mesa to collect ideas or suggestions. If you think of something, tell whoever's there, and I will hear it and get back to you." Sam took a deep breath. "Anything else?"

"Is there any way to find out what's going on down in City?" an older woman with white hair asked.

Sam shook her head. "Only from the new people coming up. One more thing. Starview's new motto is this. 'Take care of the world around you and it will take care of you.'"

"How do we do that?" a man with big ears demanded.

"Don't damage the world any more than absolutely necessary. Don't waste the world's resources," Sam said. "If you do this, world will provide more food and other things we need."

"Nonsense," someone from the back yelled. "The planet is an inanimate object. It can't do anything."

"How do you know?" Sam shot back. "It has trees and other plants growing out of it. The seas move, the ground shakes, the river flows."

"This means it's alive?" Evelyn asked from the front row.

"It is. I sense its presence. So does Maxee, and Liia from Ambaak."

"Loony bin," someone muttered.

"I believe you, Sam." Evelyn stood. "Sometimes I think I have felt something."

Amid a chorus of nos, nonsense, and ridiculous, Glenda and a woman Sam didn't know rose. A few other followed. Brad got to his feet as did Hal. Many others followed.

A chant began. "Take care of world and it will take care of you."

Tears came to Sam's eyes. *But I never cry, not since after my ex left the first time.* After the people quieted, she said, "Now, let's go back to work and get this place rolling."

One of the clothing supervisors and three recent arrivals volunteered to go retrieve clothing. Sam decided to go back with them. She asked Maxee if she wanted to go back.

"No. This my home now. I take suggestions, talk to people."

"Okay." Sam nodded. *Maxee had her own life now and would be safe here.*

Most people who met Maxee had accepted her as one of the community — the children, especially. She helped at the school and had picked up a lot of information from the screen the last few months before she came up.

Sam and the clothing people went back the old way. They had to go down to the Twenty-Four portal to get in. Sam suggested that they gather as much as they could and stash the blankets and clothing just outside the portal. Then other people could come down and collect the clothes and blankets.

"That way we won't lose them if that portal goes."

*   *   *

Back home, it was just Brad and Sam. Todd was flying up lab equipment he could fit in his ship. Sam told Brad about her meeting.

"We need a means of communicating other than just trying to find the person we want to talk to. I want to take my calling device to the comm people and see if they can make more."

Brad agreed that it was a good idea. "Meanwhile, Arlene and I got the security people to let us broadcast one short message. Apparently, Security doesn't have many workers left. Here's the message. We broadcasted it last night, because I didn't know when you were coming back. It said:

"*Attention all citizens. City is dying, and you must leave now for Starview, our settlement in the hills. Bring what you can, all food and clothing and anything special, and go east if you are on east side. On west side, go north to the cliff. There are ways up from there. Top-five-level-people, stay as long as safe, so people without homes can go first.*"

"Oh, wow," Sam said. "I wonder how many will believe it and leave."

"I'm sure there'll be a lot of doubters, but we did the best we could. I don't know what else we could have done."

"I know." *Best was not good enough.* The pain consumed her.

*   *   *

In the morning, Sam and Brad went to the comm department. Sam insisted on seeing the boss, Harriet.

"I'm Samanda Lar and this is my brother, Brad. I have this device that Dondo gave me so I can communicate with the other sectors, but it doesn't work inside City or from Starview. We're not sure whether it's Volen or not, but we need to see if you can duplicate it and make more, with non-Volen material."

"Let me see it." Harriet turned the device in her hands and peered at it. "It doesn't appear to be Volen. May I take it apart?"

"Yes," Sam said. "Oh, first I need to make a call."

She called Liia and told her she would be without her device for a while. "I'll call you as soon as I get it back."

They followed Harriet to her lab and watched her take it apart. She laid the pieces out neatly and made many images with a special comm during the process. Sam recorded every action and item in her eidetic memory.

"I think this is doable," Harriet said. "I came across a case of old handhelds, I'll see if I can use them."

"Thank you. It would be an immense help." Sam took a deep breath.

"I can see that. I'll call you, Sam, when I get something ready for testing."

"Great, thanks so much." Sam heaved a sigh of relief.

Brad left for his job. Since Harriet's lab was on Level Forty-two, Sam went out from there, on the west side. She checked a few people along that street and met one woman who said Sam was lucky to find her there; she was only home for a short while.

"Are you getting ready to leave?"

"Yes, I've gone through my things and know what I'm going to take. Is it really better out there?"

"Oh yes," Sam assured her. "The air is much, much cleaner than in here. Don't wait too long."

Always one more person.

Sam continued on toward the apartment.

On her way, Sam had to intervene in a dispute between a woman who wanted to leave and her elderly husband who refused because he thought it was nonsense. Sam managed to get the woman to go with her. She was quite timid, and Sam had to work to get the woman to tell her anything. Sam sensed that she was glad to get away from her husband.

They soon ran into a group heading north, three middle-aged couples. One woman asked, "Are we going the right way?"

"I'll ask the questions," a squat man with her said.

"Yes," Sam said. "When you get to the end, turn right, look for an empty apartment and find the hatch in the ceiling of one of the bedrooms, go up through it and you will find a way up to the valley."

"May I go with you?" the timid woman asked.

"Her husband refused to go," Sam added.

"Idiots everywhere," the squat man said.

Sam left the timid woman with the group and went on her way.

Two blocks later, an anxious woman wanted Sam to tell her what she should take. After an hour, she still hadn't decided on everything, so Sam wished her luck and left.

I can't cope with this anymore.

Sam was beginning to understand why the governor went and hid. She wished she could.

When Brad came home, Sam told him about her adventures. He soothed her with a shoulder rub.

Finally, Sam asked, "Have you thought about cars and tracks yet?"

"Yeah. Some. Trouble is, the ones we have here are powered by electricity, which we don't have in the valley. Yet."

Sam had been thinking. "When we get the new devices here, so I can keep in touch with you, then I'll move up. Meanwhile, I'll stay here. Tell Harriet we need the call devices pronto."

"Okay." *Please make it real pronto.*

*   *   *

World brought rain to the river and valley.

49

E VERY DAY WHEN BRAD CAME HOME, Sam asked him if there was anything new. Harriet was having to redo something inside the old handheld phones, but she should have a few ready in a couple of days. Her people were packing up everything they could.

Hal came down from the cliff and ate with Sam and her brothers. He told them one of the younger Councilors had come up his rope.

"He said more and more Councilors were paying attention to what was going on. Several had told their assistants and clerks to go ahead and leave if they felt they needed to. Most of the councilors for levels Thirty and below were leaving or had already left."

Sam itched to get out of there and back to Starview.

The next day, Sam got a call from the screen department. They had a machine they wanted her to test, to see if she could transfer her files to it. She practically ran over to Centrex.

Gary met her and showed her the machine, a square box with a screen on the front and a keyboard below.

"It's powered by this crank," he said. "It has an adapter inside that moves the motor a thousand times faster than the crank."

Next to it sat a regular screen, connected to the other by a wire. Gary had Sam log on to that one and pull up her main files. After an hour or so, and much cussing from both of them, her files showed up on the new machine. She went into her files. The system seemed to be working, but very slowly.

"Why so slow?" Sam asked.

"Hand cranking can't go anywhere close to as fast as the electronic works." He showed her how to use the crank.

Gary carried it over to Sam's apartment. They had to rearrange her screen table to put the new machine on it. He showed her how to plug in the wire between the screens, and she logged on the box again. It worked.

"When it slows down, you need to crank it some more."

Sam played with her new toy all afternoon ... and spent a lot of time cranking.

Todd returned from Starview, and Sam showed him her new screen. "Gary said you would get the next one."

"Good. Cranking will give it power, but it's going to be a lot slower than the Volen one. But it'll do. Have to get Doug and his crew working on the power wheel."

When Brad came home, Sam showed him her new screen.

"Not bad." He lifted it to see how much it weighed. "Going to be fun getting these things up to the valley."

"Maybe Todd can fly it up."

Todd grunted.

*   *   *

Harriet called the next day. Sam and Brad went over to her lab. She gave Sam her device back and a new one to Brad.

"A lot of people are calling about bad screens," she said.

"I imagine so," Brad said. "Ours aren't that trustworthy."

"I tell them that's the Volen material dissolving, and there's nothing we can do about it," Harriet said. "Then I say, maybe it's time for you to leave. Half of them don't even know what we're talking about, so I have to have someone explain it. We're trying to plan when we can leave. I have everything I want here, and don't even go home anymore."

"Thanks, Harriet." Sam smiled at her.

* * *

Todd and Sam called a meeting one evening when Doug had come down. He got Arlene to come, and Hal, Brad and Ross, who were also working the ropes. Bill and Susan were there as well.

"Since our government is absent, I think it falls on us to create a new one for our new community. I nominate Sam as our new leader," Todd began.

"Why me?" she demanded. She had had more than enough of leading.

"Because you are our leader."

"Todd," Sam growled.

"For the rest, I suggest department heads that report to Sam or an assistant." Todd looked at Arlene.

"At least, she'll listen to me." Arlene swung her foot.

"I've started setting up Chiefs of Neighborhood up there, for each group of people who come up together. Not Councilors," Sam said.

"No. Possibly later, when we have more people," Arlene agreed.

Todd continued. "We'll keep the current heads for now. Dad and I will head Legal, and, as such, I will be department coordinator."

"Oh?" said Hal. "I would have thought that was more in my line."

"You can head government offices."

"Okay." He shrugged.

"Susan, you and Bill are officially in charge of resettlement. That means moving people and their belongings and getting them settled. Do whatever you need to do, and if there are any problems, contact Sam or me."

"That's what we've been doing all along," Susan said. "Nice to have it official. We've already arranged for monitors and for them to find more, for every fifth corner on every third level. We tell them to pair children and older or weak folk with a strong person to help carry their loads."

317

"Is this forever? Or are we going to have term limits?" Brad asked.

"We can decide that later. You or George will be head of labs. Ross, you will head the supplies and maintenance department. Get whoever you want to work with you. Just make sure they do work."

"Yes," Sam said. "Some of the newest people don't think they have to work. I tell them: no work, no food. We found a place where the river narrows when it turns north. Glenda has a crew up there looking into how to build a bridge there."

"Good," Todd said. "That would open up the other side of the valley."

Todd, Brad, Arlene, and Sam went to Centrex to inform the department heads of what they decided. Most of them accepted it. Security said their people were being used as guides, and none of them were below Eighteen.

Susan and Bill went back to their jobs, and Hal and Ross to their ropes. Sam, Brad, and Doug returned to Starview.

It was drizzling when they arrived and rained three days straight. Sam's roof had no leaks, but many others did. The river overflowed, and Sam watched the water come up to the bottom of the cliff. It flowed farther inland on either side of the mesa, and several places were flooded.

Sam sloshed around until her cloth shoes were soaked, then went barefoot.

We need waterproof footwear. Something else we'd have to figure out.

Nothing much got done, just some inside work on buildings, and whatever else people could do indoors. Maxee sat on the porch the first day, then stayed inside.

"Not nice out there," she said. "Too wet, too cold."

Everywhere Sam went, people were cold. People stayed indoors, wearing as many layers of clothing as they could. Those in tents or camping out huddled together and stayed in the caffs as long as they were allowed. Sam told June to let them stay as long as there was room.

"Okay, but they better scrape the mud off before they come in. We have to keep this place clean."

Sam nodded and left. She rounded up people to move the people camping out into buildings. When the residents complained, she told them they'll keep warmer with more people inside. The factory people and their families moved into their factories, and more into the other buildings.

Glenda told Sam someone had asked her about fire. The caffs and factories had fire starters. "We'd have to have something to hold the fire in, so the houses won't burn," she cautioned.

"True. How can we make more containers?"

"I'll think about it and ask others."

"Good." Sam sloshed off.

She went to Evelyn's apartment near the big caff.

"I feel so much better," Jan said. "The shoemaker is making me new boots. And I can look out my window."

"Yes, it is so much nicer here," Evelyn said. "I enjoyed being able to go outside and walk around in something other than a gray hall. Until the rain came."

Sam nodded. "I know. We need to come up with waterproof shoes. Jan, when the shoemaker brings your boots, ask him how we can do this, would you please?"

"So many new things to figure out up here," Evelyn picked up her needlework. "But still better than City."

"I know. I hate going back to City, but I can't leave for good until everyone's out."

Finally, the rain stopped, and the river receded.

Sam had people mark how far the river had come up, and Brad began making a map of the highwater line. Brad had told her to expect this, but she was still appalled. Only one row of apartments was flooded, but Louise told her that they were going to move the food factory farther back from the river.

*　　*　　*

A few days later, Brad said, "I need to go back to City. Do you want to come?"

Sam thought about it and decided she would.

They took the shorter route, along the rushing river to the cliffs. In several places, the river stretched wider than it had been before. At the reservoir, she saw that the waterfall was much larger, and the roar was deafening. Centrex tipped farther to the west.

Hal worked the first rope. He and some others had devised a pulley system, so they didn't have to work as hard.

"Hey, Sam," he said when he turned in our direction. "Brad."

"Hi, Hal. How's it going?" Sam smiled.

"Keeping busy. Also keeping an eye on Centrex. See how it's leaning?"

"Oh."

Uh oh. Everything loose must be piled in the southwest corners of the rooms.

Brad studied the pulley system. "Where did you find those round barrels?"

"In a storeroom on Forty-one. Public business only takes up about a half of that level. The rest is storage. I told Arlene to get people to go through all that stuff. Who knows what we may find."

"Is that the only storage in Centrex?"

"No. Every level has some. Most levels have been gone through. I guess no one thought of the bottom level, because the only people who go there are the people who work in the public offices."

Hal looked at Sam with his great brown eyes. Something inside her shivered.

"Okay, I'll keep in touch with Arlene."

Hal lowered them down the cliff and, at the bottom, Sam jumped out of the basket. While waiting for Brad to take his turn, she walked over toward Centrex. The waterfall poured down the side as well as the back of the structure.

When Brad came down and prepared to jump out, City jerked again. He dropped awkwardly and twisted his ankle.

Before Sam could say anything, he said, "I'm all right," took out his comm, and called Arlene.

"We heard you've got people going through the storage area on the bottom."

Pause. Sam watched him.

"Good. I'm calling because we need more rope out here. If anybody finds any, get it out here to Hal as soon as you can."

Pause. Brad stared into space.

"Okay, thanks." He put the comm away. "Let's go."

They returned to their place. Sam noticed that he was limping, but didn't say anything about it. He would just say he was fine. There was always the med kit in the apartment ... if he needed it.

Checking the news, Sam saw that caffs below Twenty and in the central area up to Twenty-Three had closed and moved up to higher levels. The Volen protein blocks were in short supply, but there was still plenty of flour to make bread. The new harvest from the fields between Noreg and Ghind was coming in. The Noreg farmed that area, and the Ghind the area of vegetables and fruit between them and the Felce.

Everything was closed and moved out of the southwest quadrant. Medical clinics continued to move up and northeast. Security had shut down the tubes below Forty, and only the Forty-four and Forty-eight east-west cars were running. They'd shut down all the north-south cars except the first six rows from the cliffs. A few people looted other people's places, not that there was much to find. When Security caught a looter, they set him to carrying belongings to the nearest exit to the east.

Sam felt like she should be out helping, but didn't know what she could do. She worked on transferring her files to the new machine. Todd had gotten a new, non-Volen computer and was doing the same thing.

After the evening meal, Sam checked her master list. Of the ones checked off as having received the information, only about half of them were marked as having gone up to the valley.

Where are they, she thought. *Why aren't they leaving?*

*   *   *

World surveyed other sectors.

50

S USAN CHECKED IN WITH SAM. They were getting people out, but didn't have enough guides who could lead them to the valley, so they were camping among the Noreg trees.

"That's something I can do. What's the best way to get there?"

"We're at the Twenty-Six portal."

"I'll be over tomorrow."

I should stay here and coordinate everything, but on the other hand, I do know the way. And I would be outside.

Hal arrived with an abandoned briefcase for Sam's growing pile of papers. Her Volen screen would shut itself down occasionally, and sometimes the web would disappear.

*   *   *

The place jittered almost all the time now, and people were getting used to it. Except Sam. She had a nasty feeling in her gut and every day it got worse. Evening meal was a half loaf of bread and a scrawny carrot.

"What's this?" Brad demanded.

"I'm sorry, this is all we have today. We should have more tomorrow. We're taking turns doing bread days, food is so short."

Again, Sam thought, *we've got to get people out of here.*

There were problems with the water. The water pumps were breaking down and, although Sam and her brothers usually only had a trickle, once in a while they'd get bursts and tried to save as much as possible.

*　　　*　　　*

Sam made her way over to Portal Twenty-Six in the morning. She passed through the portal between groups of people.

Susan met her. "You made it."

"I had to walk down fifteen flights of stairs. I need to sit for a minute." Sam paused to catch her breath.

"Come over here and we'll talk. Did you see the monitors along the way?"

"Yes. Moving people along, when there were people." Sam looked around at the masses of men, women, and children. "How are you feeding them?"

"Not as well as I'd like." Susan pursed her lips. "Most people brought some food, but they're running out of that. There are some caff people over there baking bread. They're using the natural trees here for fuel. It keeps us going."

Sam rose and left the coolness of the shade. The sun felt good on her back. "I'm ready. Show me my group."

"Up at the top. We keep moving them up."

Susan led her to the first group, three-quarters of the way up the slope: about fifteen or twenty persons, a gray mass huddled on the brown ground. Sam heard some whining and a few children crying.

Susan yelled and got the attention of most of them. "Samanda will take you to the valley," she announced. "She will leave as soon as you are ready. Who's in charge?"

A dark young man clad in the standard gray pants and tunic, a hood over his eyes, stepped up. "Kirk," he said, lifting his hood so he could see Sam.

324

"We need guides. Would you be willing to learn?" she asked.

"Uh." He looked around and pulled his hood down. "Do I have to decide now?"

"No," Sam said. "I'll show you the trail and landmarks, then you can decide when we get up there."

"Okay."

"Sam, I'm going to tell the other groups to follow you if they want to, so don't be surprised if you see more people behind you," Susan said.

"Fine," Sam replied.

Most of the people were wearing hoods.

Susan left, and Kirk's people packed up.

Sam set a slow pace. She didn't know how fit these people were, and they carried a lot more than she did. She called stops often, and they only made it to the top of the first hill by the end of the day. Sam heard a lot of complaining and, when they stopped for the night, one woman dropped her bag and said she wasn't going any farther.

"Is that our valley?" someone asked.

"No. We have to go across it and over the hill beyond. Take it easy and get a good night's rest." Sam doled out the food and water that Susan had given her.

*   *   *

Sam showed Kirk where the trail went through the brown grass and clumps of bushes and pointed out good places to stop. Three other young men approached her about being guides. The four of them accompanied her as she led on.

That day, the group only made it halfway up the next hill before they had to stop for the night. People straggled in for almost an hour after Sam made camp in a group of trees. She went around and checked on everyone. She found almost twice as many as her original group.

"How much farther?" a middle-aged man asked.

"When are we going to get back inside?" a young woman with long, straggly blond hair demanded.

"Where's the caff?" A voice from the crowd.

"Hold it," Sam said. "There are no caffs out here. You were all supposed to bring enough food for two days. Anyone who has enough to share needs to do it. Our new home is in the valley on the other side of that hill." She pointed uphill.

People mumbled and grumbled, sat in unhappy groups. Older children looked about curiously. Little ones huddled with soothing adults.

"It's the children," one large woman near the rear said. She carried an infant in a snuggie on her front and a toddler on her back, plus a large bag over her shoulder. "Not only mine, but all of them, especially the little ones. They simply can't keep up. Can we rest here for a day?"

"Maybe." Sam wanted to keep going, but she understood the woman's concerns. "Tell you what. Tomorrow morning, I, and whoever wants to come with me, will start off and go to the top of the hill. The rest of you can leave when you feel like it and go at your own pace. We'll camp up there tomorrow night. If you like, I'll carry that bag for you. I just have my back bag."

"That would be a big help. I'm Suli." She also had a small bag of supplies which she kept.

Sam took the bag off her shoulder and hoisted it onto her own. "No problem. You spread the word down here and I'll take care of it at the other end."

*   *   *

In the morning, half of the group followed Sam. At the first stop, by a bunch of sprawling bushes loaded with blue berries, she looked back down the hill. Most of the rest were moving up. When they reached the stop, some people dropped their bags and went back down to help the others. Several returned carrying small children.

The long berries puzzled her. Sam had never seen blue food. She tested the berries. The gadget showed them at the edge of the danger zone. She told everyone around her they were not safe to eat.

"Tell anyone else that comes here." She walked over to a large rock and squatted behind it.

It's going to take forever to get all these people up to the valley. And where are we going to put them?

When Sam returned, two half grown boys lay on the ground, moaning. A couple knelt beside them.

"What happened?" Sam asked, fear tightening around her.

The woman looked up. "They ate some berries. We warned them not to eat them, but you know how boys are. Terrence and I are medics. I'm Zilla."

"Will they be okay?"

"We got them to vomit most of the stuff out. How dangerous were the berries?"

Sam sat beside to her. "They were just at the edge of the danger zone."

She nodded. "Then they will probably survive. We gave them the rest of our water. We'll just have to wait and see. I suggest you put up a big sign to warn the next group."

"Right." *One more thing ...*

One boy stopped moaning, and Sam gasped.

Zilla checked him. "Good. He's asleep. You'll have to find someone to carry them."

Sam looked at her. "Zilla, who is in charge of the medical department?"

She rolled her eyes. "'Doctor' Tam Owens is supposed to be, but he took off awhile back. Terrance and I are overseeing what we can. Why?"

"I need to know who's in charge. Since I've been elected leader, I hereby pronounce you and Terrance to be the joint heads of the medical department." Sam grinned.

Zilla sighed and smiled wide. "Thank you. Will we have our own building there?"

"Yes. When we get there, I'll introduce you to Glenda who's running the place. Her husband is in charge of construction, and you can get with them on what you want in your building."

"Wonderful. Thank you, Sam."

Sam nodded.

One more thing taken care of.

327

But she still felt like the weight of the world was on her shoulders. Sam heaved herself to her feet and started looking for strong men to carry the boys and something to make a sign with.

The first was easy. The boys' parents had arrived, and the fathers said they would carry their sons. One hefted his boy over his shoulder and the other followed suit and started on up the hill.

No one had anything that could be used for signs, so Sam pulled out an extra tunic and her laser. After lasing the words DANGER, POISON, DO NOT EAT into the back, she stuck it on the bushes, pulling branches through the sleeves, so it wouldn't blow away. The nasty things had thorns and left her hands a mass of scratches.

"Okay, people, let's go." Sam put on her pack and picked up Suli's bag. Seeing that most of the others were on their feet, she started off.

The higher section was steeper than the low part. She stopped every half hour to take a breather.

At midafternoon, Sam reached the top, dropped her bags, and collapsed to the ground. The two fathers laid their sons near her. Both boys were sound asleep.

Zilla sat beside her. "Sleep will do them good. All their vitals are normal, as far as we can tell." Her mate dropped down next to her. "They'll make it," he added.

More people arrived and collapsed around them.

It took most of the day for everyone to reach the top. The quiet of exhaustion enveloped the group. Empty and breathless, Sam was ready to rest, too. Susan had marked everyone off on her list, so she didn't have to do that. The presence ...

Sam gathered herself and called for attention. "Okay, folks, there is our valley. It's all downhill from here, and we'll be there tomorrow. Do not eat any fruit you see here until I test it and tell you it's okay. Two boys tried the berries at the stop below and became very sick. We don't want that to happen to anyone else."

Kirk, beside her, nodded. He took off his hood and spoke over the crowd murmurs. "Hear the lady. She's in charge, she knows what she's doing."

*　　*　　*

Most of the people, even with their hoods on, stayed among the trees on the way down. When Sam's group left the forest, people from Starview met them. Sam knew that Glenda had told everyone to keep an eye out for newcomers. The greeters took children's bags and walked with them. The rest of them followed along the bottom of the forest until they came to an open area between the forest and the apartments. One of the greeters told Sam this is where Glenda wanted them.

Sam announced, "Here is where you will stay. Sanitary facilities are over there. Let me know if you need food, I'll have people bring you some. Just rest here for now. Tomorrow we'll start planning your new lives."

After everyone settled down, Sam talked to the four fellows who were interested in becoming guides. Kirk and two others agreed to do so.

"We'll stay here tomorrow," Sam told them. "Then we'll go back the next day,"

*   *   *

World jiggled.

51

T HE NEXT DAY, Sam had too many problems to deal with, not
including the rain, and was unable to leave. Few of the new
people wanted to do any work; they just wanted their new homes.
Even though Sam explained to them they would have to help build
their apartments, that didn't do any good.

She went to talk to Glenda. "These new people aren't interested
in building their new homes," Sam said. "I think you and Gus need
to set up a group of about three people to go to the new groups and
set up work crews. Tell them: no work, no food. If you have any
other ideas, go for it. And we will need more sanitary facilities."

"Okay. I don't suppose any of these new people are supervisor
types."

"Maybe one or two. There'll be more coming every day now."

"Wonderful." Glenda rolled her eyes. "We'll do what we have
to do."

Sam nodded and left. She checked with the caffs. Few of the
new people brought any food, and they had to cut rations.

One good thing happened that lifted her spirits. A group of people from one of the food factories returned from scouting upstream with bags full of nuts. George tested one and found it good, containing lots of protein and other nutrients they needed. Louise immediately sent another group of her people with larger bags.

Sam heard continuing complaints about the cold. Glenda again suggested fire.

"If we can come up with kind of nonflammable containers to keep the fire in," Sam said. "We don't want our houses to burn down."

Sam checked her house and felt drafts.

"Are you warm enough?" she asked Maxee.

"Yes. More fur." She did look fluffier.

"I'm sorry I haven't had much time to spend with you." Sam patted her. "How is baby Max?"

Maxee showed her. He was almost as long as Sam's little finger and had tiny wiggling limbs.

"Ooh," Sam breathed. "Are you getting enough nutrients?"

Maxee nodded and sat down. Sam patted her shoulder as she left with a smile.

Sam found Glenda in the meeting room. "Have you noticed any drafts in your buildings?"

"Yes," she said.

"Do we have anything we can put in the cracks to keep the buildings warmer? It's going to get even colder."

"I put mud from the bottom of my water bucket in a hole in my wall," a young woman next to us said.

"Did it work?" Sam asked.

"Seemed to."

Sam thought for a moment. "Okay, let people know, in the afternoon, after they've used their water or put it in another container, they are to take their buckets down to the river and fill them with mud, then fill in cracks. Then, in the morning, wash out what's left in their buckets and get their water for the day."

"Good idea, Sam," Glenda said.

"I'm going to go do mine right now." Sam ran to her house, grabbed her bucket, and ran down to the river.

When Sam returned with her bucket of mud, Maxee asked, "What is?"

"To seal the cracks in the walls to keep the wind out."

Sam dug out a probe stick and poked the mud in everywhere she felt a draft. That night, the place felt noticeably less cold.

*   *   *

Sam, Kirk, and two other young men set off back to City. They were able to go a lot faster, since they didn't have to carry much. The sun was a pale ghost of itself, and the north wind blew right through them. They had to keep moving rapidly to keep warm.

In the afternoon, they passed a group going up led by one of Judy's sons. She was with him, and she and Sam exchanged greetings.

"It's so good to breathe again," Judy said, grinning.

"I know. Enjoy the new place. I'll find you when I get back."

At the first night's camp, Sam asked the men how they were doing.

"Good," Kirk said. "This place gives me so much energy." He was no longer wearing his hood.

The other two nodded.

They passed two more groups the next day. On the way down the hill, people grabbed at them, demanding to know what was going on, why were they being dragged out of City, where was food and water.

"I haven't had anything all day," one woman screamed.

"We'll get you something," Sam said, and marched on.

The lower groups clamored more loudly, and Sam tried to ignore them. There was nothing she could do right then to help them.

Back at the portal, Sam checked in. "What a mess."

"I know. We're doing the best we can." Susan grimaced.

Sam nodded. "I know you are.

"We've dropped some more," Susan told her. "We're having to use the next portal down, which is the last usable one. Hal told me they can't use the ropes anymore because Fifty is too low now, so everyone's coming over here."

"Oh, bugs." Sam knew it was going to happen, but ... "Okay, these three are ready to be guides. I see you've got groups all the way up the hill."

"We have to, to make room for the newcomers. At least most of them have their own food. A few caffs have also brought food — mainly bread."

"Good. I need to call Brad."

Sam went into the portal. The City entrance was blocked by a wall.

"Hi Brad. I'm at portal Twenty-Six."

"Sam. Good to hear from you. How's things out there?"

"Masses of people all over this side of the Noreg sector. I'm going to lead two more groups up, then come back in and get the last of my stuff."

"Okay. It's a mess in here. Everything in Centrex is shut down except Security and Arlene's office. She insists on staying. Even Hal can't convince her to leave. He and Ross are back down here and going around looking for strays."

"When are you guys going?"

"When you go the last time."

"Okay, see you soon."

Outside, Sam found a quiet place to sit and think. She knew what Brad hadn't said: the place wasn't going to last much longer. She wasn't looking forward to another long trek to Starview, but she dreaded going back into City. The City she knew was gone.

*   *   *

World brought the cold.

52

S AM AND SUSAN SELECTED A GROUP, and Sam started out slowly, with lots of rest stops and much complaining from the people. Too many of them had not grasped the enormity of the situation. Sam had to explain several times that the only food available was what they brought with them. There would be more when they arrived at the valley.

Two men volunteered to learn to be guides. They helped Sam calm people down and get them moving. It took three days to get to Starview, and another two to get people settled. Sam was immensely relieved when she could take a break and relax with Maxee at her house.

Later, when Sam sat down with Glenda to go over what was happening in Starview, Glenda told Sam the mud chinking was working.

"I've got people going around trying to set up work crews. A lot don't want to work, they expected to have homes ready for them. We keep telling them if they want food, they have to work.

A few tried to eat native plants and got sick. Even the ones who agreed to work have to be trained."

"Right," Sam said. It was what she'd expected. "And that takes time. How's the food situation?"

"Not good. There's plenty of grain for bread, but we're coming to the end of the vegetable harvest. George is finding more and more local plants we can use, with preparation, but with all these new people coming in, it's not enough. It's going to be a long winter."

"I know." Sam shivered.

They discussed a few other matters, then Sam left to find June at the large caff.

"Do what you can," Sam told her. "We'll survive somehow."

"I know." June sighed. "We're starting another large caff down the valley." She pointed east.

"Good. We'll need it."

Sam trotted off to meet a group coming in. After welcoming them and showing them where to settle, she told them about the work requirements

"If you don't want to work, you can continue to sleep out in the cold and find your own food or go back to the remains of City," she said.

A few did. Sam never saw them again.

More groups came in, led by Kirk and his friends. Sam assigned one person in each group to be in charge. They would report to her or someone she chose. The throngs lined the valley to the east. Kirk and a few others went back with Sam. They passed more people every day.

At the portal, Sam called Brad again. "It's a huge mess up there," she told him.

"It feels like we're creeping down a very slow tube," he said. "Do you have to go again?"

"Yes, I promised Susan I would." They chatted a little and disconnected.

As Sam left the portal, she bumped into Bill.

"Sorry," he said, holding her up. "Sam! What are you doing here?"

"Guide duty. You?"

"We're down to stragglers, so I decided to go."

"I'm going back in a couple days. Come with me."

Susan joined them on a makeshift bench under a tree. They ate together and had a pleasant visit. Susan told him that she would go with the last bunch.

Sam's last trip was no easier than the first. Most everyone was anxious, if not scared. This group had a half dozen complainers who never seemed to stop, and still a few who didn't believe there was a problem. Now, throngs of people lined the valley along the base of the forest. More new apartment buildings had sprung up along the center of the valley.

The next day, Sam set up a communications network among the various groups, leading up to area leaders who reported to department heads or Arlene.

That night, she had nightmares of City collapsing and not being able to find anyone, so she left the next day.

She passed several groups and wondered where Glenda's people were going to put them. There were still a lot of people outside the portals, and more trickling out. Besides Susan, she found Brad there.

"I wanted to see how things were down here," he said. "And I didn't want you coming back by yourself."

Sam rolled her eyes at him and said, "Glad to see you."

Portal Twenty-Two was half blocked, but people were squeezing through. Brad decided to camp out there and go in the morning. Sam couldn't sleep; the ground kept moving, a slight rocking motion.

Finally, she dozed.

*   *   *

World shook down more Volen structures.

53

A FTER A MEAGER MEAL IN THE MORNING, Sam and Brad squeezed into the portal and on through. In the dimness, Sam started for the stairs.

"No," Brad said, catching her arm. "Look."

He pointed his lightstick toward the down stairs. A pale, gloppy mess splotched the steps and lower walls.

"Stay here."

He went down a step and waved his lightstick around.

"No, Brad." Sam's heart clenched.

Brad cussed and hopped back up.

"What?"

"Let's go." He trotted down the street.

Sam followed, feeling the darkness closing in.

Brad stopped at the next intersection and peered down the stairs. More gloppiness. They trotted on.

Sam thought she heard something and stopped. A faint voice called out, "Help."

"Brad, stop," she called, as she approached the door the voice came from. It was locked.

"What are you doing?"

"Someone's in there."

Sam fished out her laser, blasted the lock, and put the laser away. Inside, in the dimness, she saw a man on a bed against the wall in a corner and went to him. Brad followed her inside.

"Help," the man said.

"What ..." Sam began, then saw his arm up against the wall, his hand covered in the pale goop. "Oh, my Oneness."

Brad swore. "That's the Volen material growing back together again."

Sam gave the man a drink of her water.

"Thanks. Can you get me out of here?"

Brad poked at it with his knife. "Can't cut it. The only way I see is to cut your hand off.

"No." He jerked at his hand.

Sam shuddered, but saw what Brad meant, and she had a laser.

"It's that or lie here until the stuff covers you and kills you."

The man closed his eyes.

"I can do it with my laser. It'll seal the stump, so it won't bleed a lot." Sam shivered.

Can I do this? Yes, I can, I must. I can't leave him here to die.

"Okay," he groaned.

"By the way, what's your name?"

"Curtis Brown."

"Okay, Curtis. Brad, you hold him." Sam fished a small bottle out of her bag. "Here, drink this. It will help with the pain."

He drank it.

Sam took the laser from her pocket and set it to narrowest beam.

Brad sat on the bed, with his legs over Curtis's thighs, his back with a blanket over his shoulders against the wall, and grasped Curtis' arm.

"Here," he said, and moved his hands down a little.

Sam put her hand over his, laid the laser next to Curtis's arm, and took a deep breath. Turned it on and pushed the beam through as fast as it would go. She felt like the beam was shuddering through her own body.

Curtis screamed and rolled away from the wall. Brad followed, yanking the blanket off. Sam and Brad held him for a few minutes until he passed out.

Brad examined his stump. It oozed a little. Sam found a clean cloth and they bound it.

"We have to get him out," Sam said, staring at the wall where the goop oozed with a splash of blood.

Curtis was a small man and Brad slung him over his shoulder. Sam picked up some of his things and dumped them in a bag. They carried him and his possessions back to the portal. Sam eased through with the bag and between them, slid him out and laid him on the ground. Sam called Susan, and she came down.

"We'll take care of him," she said.

"Thanks." *One more thing off my shoulders. How many more will load them up again?"*

Sam sat down fast and huddled into a shaking ball. Brad sank down beside her and held her close.

I will never forget that scream, ever.

After a while, Brad said, "We need to get moving."

"Okay." She sighed.

He helped Sam to her feet, and they climbed back through the portal. Sam was still shaking and clung to him. This time, they went up the first flight, then west on that street. It was so dim she could barely see to step around the discarded belongings all over the place. They collected a few blankets they came across.

Sam and Brad couldn't go as fast as they wanted, because it was hard to breathe. Sam tried to ignore the stale odors that attempted to gag her.

Just keep moving, Sam.

At the next stairway, they went up, and up three more. The smell wasn't as bad here, so they took a break in an empty room. Most people had left their doors open. They found a pair of thin blankets and tied them around their shoulders like capes.

From there, they headed west. Sam hoped Brad was keeping track, it was too dim to read the signs. They found an open caff, scrounged around, and found a couple packets of protein that had slipped down behind a large box. The emptiness and silence of the place gave Sam the shivers.

Onward and upward they trudged. Neither of them had anything to say. They held hands. Sam, at least, needed the contact. At one place, they came to an open room with a young girl sitting on the bed, staring at a puzzle block in her hand. There were few images on the gray walls, but the place looked neat as far as Sam could tell.

Sam stopped. "Hello. Are you alone?"

"My mother's in there." She indicated the bathroom. "She won't answer me." Her voice shook.

Sam entered and tapped on the bathroom door. "Hello?"

No answer.

She opened the door. A woman lay curled on the floor.

"Brad, come here."

He came, knelt beside her, and felt her neck. "She's dead. For a while. I think."

They left the little room and closed the door.

"What's your name?" Sam asked the girl. She appeared to be about ten or eleven.

"Annie." She stared at me with large eyes and white face. "What ..."

"Your mother is dead. You need to come with us," Sam said gently.

"I'm afraid," she said, and began to quiver.

Sam sat beside her and put her arm around the girl. "You'll be safe with us. I'm Samanda Lar, and he's my brother, Brad. We are going up to our place on Fifty and then up to the new community in Starview."

"Oh. Outside?"

"Yes. Pack up what you want to take and can carry, including warm clothes and blankets."

"Momma."

"There's nothing we can do for her. I'll say a little prayer, if you wish."

She nodded.

"Oneness, please bring this woman into your allness, take care of her, and be with her daughter. Thank you." Sam gave Annie a squeeze. "You can call me Aunt Sam, if you want."

Tears ran down Annie's face as she rose and pulled out a back bag from the closet. Sam talked about Starview as Annie put clothes, a doll, and other items in her bag. She picked up an image of four people, clutched it to her chest, and broke into sobs. Sam held the girl as Sam's heart broke. For the first time, she understood what it was to have a child, and how her mother had felt when she left Sam and Brad.

After a while, Annie quieted down, tucked the photo in her bag, and the three of them left.

A little later, Brad stopped at an open apartment. "I think this is Todd's old place."

He went in. Sam was about to drop. They shared out the last of their food and slept there, Sam and Annie on the bed; Brad on the long seat.

* * *

In the morning, the three of them climbed up to Centrex, where Brad checked the up-tube.

"No, the tube's dead. Come on."

He headed for the stairway. They went out the Forty-Eight exit and Brad started down the street.

"Where are you going?" Sam asked.

"To check the caffs," Brad said without stopping.

Sam and Annie followed. The first caff was closed, as was the one on Forty-Nine. At Fifty, they found a basket with two loaves of bread.

Brad picked them up. "Can't leave them to spoil."

"Hello there."

Sam and Brad turned. A group of people approached from the west. A tall middle-aged man, a short, dark haired woman clutching him, with three adolescent children, stopped in front of Sam's group. Fear and hunger filled their faces.

"Hello," Sam said. "Where have you come from?"

The woman waved her hand back toward the west. "Do you know where we can get some food?" She eyed the bread in Brad's hand.

Brad stepped back, clutching the bread to his chest.

"Yes. Come with us, it's not far. I'm Sam, this is Brad, and Annie."

"Thank you. I'm Toni."

Sam led them to her apartment. Inside, one of the boys reached for the bread.

"Hold on," Brad said, moving toward the back of the room.

"Sit down, all of you," Toni said, doing so.

Brad returned with the bread sliced into fourths of loaves and passed them out. Toni and the girl gobbled theirs down, and the boys inhaled theirs. Annie nibbled at her piece, but held it away from the others. Brad brought small cups of water from our meager supply for the family and Annie.

The man wiped his lips. "Thank you. I'm Charles, and this is Shelly, Alex and Tim."

"We're triplets," Shelly said. "Thanks for finding us. This is a nice place."

The boys nodded.

"Wow," Sam said. "I have another brother, Todd, who lives here and should be home soon. If we're lucky, he'll bring more food." She looked around at the packed bags, got to her feet, and showed the newcomers the bathroom. "No hogging the bathroom," she added.

Toni asked if she could lie down.

Sam showed her Brad's bed under the open hatch. "Fresh air," she said. "Lovely."

Sam went to her room. Her screen box was gone, packed up, she supposed. She gathered what was left and returned to the main room. Charles slept leaning back in his chair, and Brad was showing the youngsters his multitool knife. Shelly sat next to Annie. Sam hoped they could become good friends.

Presently, Todd came home with Arlene and her bags, and a bag of bread, protein packets, and a bag of spinach. The family refused to touch the greens.

"We have no way to cook them," Toni said.

The rest of them shared the spinach raw.

Sam greeted Arlene and introduced everyone.

"Quite a crowd you got here," Todd said. "Hal and Ross should be down shortly. They put together a long rope and a series of pulleys. There's a group of guys still up there, and they'll stay up there."

Sam, Todd, and Arlene sat at the table and set out some of the food. Brad and the others took theirs back to the couch.

Sam told Todd and Arlene about the groups going to Starview and their trip up inside City. "We found Annie alone with her dead mother and brought her along, so be kind to her. She seems to be getting along with Shelly."

"That's good. We gals need to stick together." Arlene grinned.

Toni came out, was introduced, and had some food.

"We'll go east in the morning," Todd said. "There was a landslide from the Noreg land and I think we can get up that."

Sam let Arlene and Annie have her bed and slept on one of the couches. Brad took the other couch, and Toni and Shelly slept in his bed. Charles had Todd's, Todd slept in a chair, and the boys on the floor. City kept creeping down. Sam felt like she was sleeping in a slow down-tube.

Sleep from exhaustion held her for about five hours, when a jolt awakened her and, from then on, her mind roiled.

The skylights were still dark when she heard, "Sam?" in a low voice.

"Brad?" Sam whispered, sitting up. She heard him shuffle over to her.

The whole place jerked.

Sam reached for Brad and he grasped her arm. "We should go soon."

"I'm ready."

"You two awake?" Todd asked.

"Yes," Sam said. "Are you ready to go? I can't sleep anymore." She turned the lights up. Not much visibility even with them on.

"The backup power is going." Todd said. "Sam, you go get the gals, I'll get Charles and the boys up."

Sam went back to the bathroom, then into her room and brought up the light a little.

Arlene stirred.

"Time to get up and get going," Sam said softly.

"Okay," Arlene said. She rose and dressed. "Annie?" She touched the girl's shoulder. Arlene looked at Sam. "You go on, I'll get her up."

Sam roused Toni and Shelly. They all gathered in the main room, and Brad left to get Hal and Ross.

After they ate some bread and collected their bags, Sam said, "Toilet time. We will be outside on the roof with no place to go, so make sure you're empty."

After that, Charles turned toward the front door.

"No, this way. I don't think we can get past Centrex in the street." Sam said.

"Yes, we can," Todd put in. "We'll go to the next street, down, and go around Centrex at the bottom. Then up to Fifty until we find an open place and go up their hatch."

Sam thought a moment. "Okay, that sounds good. They do all have hatches over there, right."

"Yes." Todd led the way to the door.

They trudged out and down the street.

Another home just a memory now. I hope my new place can be as nice.

Sam fought down terror as the fear that they wouldn't make it out overwhelmed her.

And how many other Annies were sitting alone in their rooms?

*   *   *

World considered a plague, but some of the beings were helpful.

54

WHEN THE GROUP REACHED the bottom of Centrex, they found they had to go down two more levels, on the stairways, and another block south, to get around the gaps between Centrex and the other buildings. The tops of the building on the south side of the road were halfway down the side of those on the north side. Todd led the others, walking single file as close to the north side buildings as they could.

After Sam and her companions climbed the stairs up the east side to Forty, they found a nearby open apartment and piled in for a rest break. The place had a large bag of bread, so the group had something to eat. All of them ignored the fact that the toilet didn't flush; they weren't staying long.

Since the tubes were no longer working, they began the long trek up to Fifty. Every level they had to stop and rest. Every level they rested longer, but no one complained.

Finally, they reached Fifty, turned right, and trudged into the first open apartment they came to. It was like Sam's, pale green. Sam found a seat. Toni led Annie into a bedroom.

Susan plopped down beside Sam. "And we're not even outside yet."

Sam nodded. The place shifted around them. Tiny motions, sideways, back and forth, up and down, but rarely stopping. Charles dropped into a seat and the boys sat on the floor. Shelly, beside Susan, slumped over, head hanging between her legs, hands on floor. Arlene curled up in another large chair.

Hal and Ross followed them in and dropped on the floor in a corner. Hal hung his arm over Ross's shoulder. Sam thought they looked like more than just friends, but had too many other things on her mind to deal with it.

Finally, Todd and Brad arrived and found places to sit.

"Okay, people," Todd said after a while. "Has anyone looked for food in here?"

"Yes," Arlene said. She waved a bag she held. "Here."

She passed out bread to everyone and food bars to the children, saving a couple for the sleepers. Brad found a large container of water and meted it out.

The group sat and dozed, until the place shook.

Todd got up. "Time to move on."

They all climbed to their feet, roused Toni and Annie, and gave them food. They trudged east along the street. Todd told the boys go into every open apartment to look for food. They stopped for the night in a blue-green place. The occupants had left a large cache of food, and a food heater that actually worked, so they had a feast.

*   *   *

After midday meal the next day, when Sam and her group were gathering their bags, a strong shaking threw them around, accompanied by a great roaring cacophony of growling sounds. Sam covered her ears and huddled under a table where she'd been thrown. Finally, it registered on her that the place had not dropped.

When things settled down, Sam sat up. The others stirred. Todd pulled himself up onto a couch. She saw blood on his arm and winced.

"Hey, people," he croaked. "Sam?"

"I'm here. Only bruised, I think."

"Brad?" Todd looked around.

"Over here. Someone get these bags off me."

Todd continued the roll call. There were no serious injuries. Toni attended to their cuts and scrapes.

They left and proceeded as quickly as they could. Todd had the boys look for open hatches. Alex found one, and they all crowded into the little room. Sam went first, crawled east and sat, facing south. She gasped at the view. The once flat silver roof existed only as a border along the east and north sides, surrounding a gray mass of scattered block cubes, tubes, and wires as far as she could see. She couldn't see Centrex at all. Automatically she grabbed her bag that someone pushed up through the hatch and scooted along.

One of the boys appeared, followed by the other, and a procession of bags. The boys put them to the west side and passed them out to their owners as they came through. Sam pulled herself up and started walking along the edge along the cliff. In some places, rocks and dirt had fallen, and she had to walk around it on the roof.

"Hey, Sam," Brad called.

Sam turned and looked back. He waved from the rear of the line. Everyone was out. Todd trotted alongside them on the roof. When he reached her, he moved in front with her.

"We'll just keep moving until we find an open hatch or get there." Todd pointed to a mass of brown some distance ahead of them. "That's the landslide."

"How do we get up it?"

"Climb." He turned and moved on.

They moved as fast as they could.

Just before midday, Sam heard a moan, and stopped. Something pink waved a block away to the south. She started toward it.

"Sam, where are you going?" Brad yelled.

"There's someone out here," she called.

"Sam, we don't have time." Todd added, "Hal, keep going with the others."

Sam reached the pink scarf and scrabbled around the hand that held it. She heaved a large block out of the way and heard a woman call "Help" in a faint voice.

"I'm coming," Sam said, pulling half a chair away. Two more heaves and she uncovered an arm. A face stared up at her — a once pretty face with dark hair.

"Help me," she pleaded.

Sam gave her some water.

Thanks. I'm Emily. Are you Samanda?"

"Yes. Hang on, we'll get you out."

Todd arrived with Brad. The three of them soon uncovered her. A couch had covered most of the woman's body without crushing it. One foot was twisted badly and, when she sat up, she grabbed her back.

The place shook, and Sam fell on top of her.

"Sorry."

After Sam pulled herself up, the men carefully lifted Emily to her feet. She hung on to Brad as he and Todd helped her back to the roof. Sam followed, placing her feet carefully in case anything shifted underneath them. They made their way to the others who had stopped not far ahead.

The group ate a bit, and Brad held Emily. She had a cut on her lower leg, beginning to scab over. Toni bandaged that, and her scraped arms. Todd bound up her foot as best he could.

"I don't like it out here," Shelly said, huddling into herself. "When are we going home?"

"City's gone," Sam said. "We're going to our new home." She hoped, trying to keep herself from falling apart.

"We'll make it," Toni assured them, one arm around Shelly and the other around Charles.

He had been very quiet, but kept a sharp eye on the boys, who were exchanging looks.

"I know this is rough," Arlene said, "but hang in there."

Annie curled into Arlene's arms, who smiled wanly. Sam nestled into Brad's arms, and Todd sat nearby.

"I wonder how Liia's doing," Brad said,

"Oh." Sam dug out her comm device and called her.

"We're settling in," Liia told her. "Still bringing up people. We are all right."

Sam told her where they were and called Mantz. "I believe people have accepted this life. We will continue."

Joba said much the same thing. The new Elder would allow the tribes in Starview to decide where they wanted to settle.

Maya related the exodus of her people upward. They had found a place of caves in the higher hills, along with small creatures they could eat.

"This will do."

Sam still could not reach Hive. They would have to survive on their own.

*   *   *

World paused and pondered.

55

THE AREA SHUDDERED, and part of the roof behind them caved in.

Todd jumped up. "Time to go."

He and Brad helped Emily up, and Brad half-carried her. Charles and one of the boys half-carried Toni, one of her arms around each, and the group moved out. They proceeded as far and as fast as they could, with several rest stops, until sundown. The sky glowed red through the dust rising from the remains of City.

There'd been no more big falls, but they were all, except maybe the boys, in a state of terror. Annie cried off and on, holding onto Arlene's hand.

That poor child, Sam thought. *But we can't do much right now. Our first priority is to get off this roof before it collapses.*

As the sun dropped behind them, Sam saw something brown covering the way ahead.

"Here's the landslide," Todd said. "Let's camp here and go up in the morning."

Sam looked around. She thought she saw something moving to the south.

"Looks like a couple of people coming this way," Brad said.

They made camp and shared out what food was left. The family huddled together around Toni, while Arlene held Annie. Sam sat between Brad and Todd, while Hal and Ross held hands. No one said anything. The only sound Sam heard was Annie whimpering. Damp dirt odor mingled with an assortment of smells from the debris of City.

Sam watched the two people approach. Whoever they were, she had to help them. They must have come up a hatch.

The larger one collapsed, and the other sat beside him. Sam rose, walked over to them, and her jaw dropped when she saw her ex.

"Eugene Waller," Sam said, anger battling with pity, "What are you doing here?"

"Find you," he gasped. His face was red. "My beloved Samanda." He reached up a hand.

Sam closed her eyes.

Not now.

But she could not ignore the man. She took his damp hand. He squeezed hers, smiled, and died. Something also died in Sam's heart. She dropped his hand and turned to the other man.

Jerg, of course. He held his face in his hands. His world was gone, too. All the anger she'd had for him dropped away. He was just someone else who needed her help.

"Jerg," Sam said.

He looked up.

"Come with us to Starview. There's nothing left for anyone here."

He looked at the dead man. "What about him?"

"You can leave him here or bury him in the dirt over there. We're camped here. You may join us, if you want."

He shook his head.

Stunned and saddened, Sam went back to the camp and told the others.

We could have had a good life if he hadn't gone wrong. How on City did he, they, get back here? At least, this time I saw him die.

That night, Sam could not sleep. The landslide looked like a mountain. Even here in the corner, she could feel City moving, and she could hear Annie crying for her mother. Her heart ached for the child, but the only thing they could do was get to Starview and set up a house for Arlene and Annie. Arlene had volunteered to take Annie in as her granddaughter.

$$*\qquad*\qquad*$$

In the morning, Brad and Todd studied the slope before them. Sam thought it appeared very steep.

How are we going to get all of us and our bags up there?

"I think over here is the best," Brad said, pointing to a less slanted section.

Sam looked around. Jerg still sat with the dead man. She went to him. "We are going up that way." She pointed. "If you want to bury him, you can do so over there. If not, come with us."

He sighed, rose, and plucked a small item out of the dead man's pocket. "He wanted you to have this." He held it out to her.

Sam took the dark blue box and turned it over in her hands. Curiously, she opened it. On a bed of white lay the red jewel made of strands of ruby she'd seen in Waller's black box long ago.

So he had noticed me staring at it.

"Are you coming, Sam?" Brad yelled.

Sam slapped the lid on and dropped the box in her bag as she turned. "I'm coming." To Jerg, "Are you?"

"Yes."

Sam took one last look at the man who changed her life and returned to the group. They charged up the hill, but soon bogged down. Unlike the other hillsides, this one mostly consisted of loose dirt, with occasional hard spots. Most of them had to stop and drop their bags every few minutes.

They struggled up the slope, dragging their bags behind them. Toni dropped first. Charles helped her up and took her bag. Then Arlene went down, Annie beside her. Brad kept Emily on her feet, but stopped, dropping his bag. They were about halfway up.

"Boys, take these bags up to that ledge up there and come back." Charles gave them Toni's and Arlene's bags.

The boys churned upward. The youngsters hadn't needed their hoods after the first morning.

Sam sat down beside the two women. "Once we get to the top here, there'll be other people to help us, and with food," Sam said.

"I know we don't have any choice," Arlene remarked, "but this is not my idea of fun."

"At least we can breathe out here," Toni said. "I can't believe how much better it is outside."

"It was getting pretty bad in there."

Sam picked up a fistful of dirt and let it trickle through her fingers. A small purple stone remained. She brushed it off and put it in her little bag. Maxee would like it.

"Come on, let's get going," Todd called.

The men were almost up to the ledge. The women hauled themselves to their feet and slogged onward. Charles helped Toni.

The sun hung low in the west when they reached the top, after several rest periods.

Sam lay there panting, listening to the others gasp and pant. She shivered; she'd lost her blanket-cape somewhere.

"We made it," Brad said, lying next to her.

Mumbles from the others. Sam thought she heard Susan's voice.

The ground beneath her shook.

"No," Sam whispered and reached for Brad.

The ground beneath her moved. She began to slide down. Tossed this way and that, falling, Sam found herself wrapped in soil and plants, in darkness. Yells and screams surrounded her. She was afraid to open her mouth, afraid to get a mouthful of dirt.

The shaking went on and on, rolling her around and downward.

When the hill finally stopped moving, Sam's face was buried in dirt, a weight pushing her down. The weight rolled off and someone began scrabbling at her head.

"Sammie," he cried, and turned her head so she could breathe.

Sam coughed up a ton of dirt, spitting it out. "Brad," she choked.

"I'm here." He offered her his water pouch.

Sam drank and spat out mud. "What happened?" She heard yells, smelled dust, but her eyes wouldn't focus.

"More of the hill came down." He paused, holding her, and yelled, "Arlene, Todd, Hal."

"Here," Arlene grunted nearby.

Other people cried out or moaned.

"Stay here," Brad said, and moved away.

Sam dug herself out with her right hand and sat up. Her left arm didn't work too well. When she tried to use it to move herself around, she yelped with pain.

"Sam," Arlene croaked, crawling over to her, followed by Annie, who collapsed in a heap.

"Arlene." *That's two. That poor child is going to need a lot of loving.*

They hugged. "Oww. Be careful, I think my arm's broken."

"Oh, dear." Arlene sat up. "We'll have to get that fixed."

Sam heard voices and turned her head. People were pushing their way out of the piles of dirt, while Brad and Todd dug away up above. More people were coming down from the east and farther south.

A sickening feeling crept over her. Her world was crumbling around her, literally. She was injured and couldn't see how she could get out of there. The top of the hill was a mile away. Her arm hurt, and her mouth still tasted of dirt. Sam didn't know if everyone else was okay — or even if they'd all survived. And she was totally exhausted. Just sitting up had taken all of what strength she had left. And she had to pee.

Sam managed to shift her clothes around so she could do it there, but every movement was agony.

Please, Oneness, help us. Oneness, every being, thing and place that ever was, is and will be, in all the universes.

Brad returned with Shelly and looked at Annie, who was unconscious.

"Brad," Sam whispered, but he didn't hear her.

He examined the girl. "No obvious wounds, and her heart and breathing sound okay." He laid her out flat and wiped off her face.

Shelly sat next to Annie and held her hand.

Hal appeared, biting his lip.

"I found Ross but couldn't save him." He turned away.

"No," Sam moaned. "What about Charles and his family?"

"Here they come," Arlene said.

Charles and one of the boys carried Toni, the other carried a couple of bags. "Have you seen Shelly?" he asked.

"I'm here, Dad," Shelly said. "I rolled into a ball with Annie when the hill started moving."

"Thank Oneness," Toni gasped. "My leg or something is broken, I think."

Charles laid her down beside Annie, and Shelly leaned against her mother's good side.

"What do we do now?" Charles asked.

"Wait for those people," Brad said, pointing.

Sam looked around. A group inched down the slope, pulling a Noreg walkway behind it.

Why?, her numbed brain asked.

Sam shivered. Darkness crept over them. Or was it her?

∗   ∗   ∗

World relaxed and touched the one being.

56

S AM CAME TO LYING ON A WIDE BOARD. The sun shone on the side
of her face. Blue sky. The presence was with her, in her. Sam
breathed in. Her mouth felt clean. Someone propped her up and
gave her water. Brad.

"Sammie. Thank goodness," he said.

"At least I got a good night's sleep," Sam murmured. She tried
to sit up.

Brad held her down.

"The others?"

"Todd's okay, except for bruises and small cuts. Hal, too. He's
still upset over Ross. Charles and the children are good, Annie's
come around and seems to be okay. Emily and Toni are in bad
shape. Broken bones and something inside. You rest. There's a
group here; they'll carry you up to Starview."

"I can walk."

"No, you can't. You have a broken leg, too."

"What?!" Then Sam felt the pain.

"Sam, you're awake," someone said.

"Susan. What are you doing here?"

"I said I'd stay 'til the last group went." She knelt beside Sam and held her hand. "We saw you come up over the cliff, and then the cliff disappeared. I was scared stiff. I knew it was your group."

"Yes," Sam said, holding onto Susan's hand for dear life.

Still in a daze, her thoughts in a scrambled mess, Sam needed something physical to hang onto to stay in the here and now. She fixed on her house, and Maxee. She would be there in a few days. Maybe she wouldn't be able to go anywhere, but she would be in her house with Maxee. Sam wondered how she was doing, but felt no worry. She was sure her sister would be fine.

Brad had his arm around her other shoulder. Her arm was wrapped up. "I'm here."

"Wonderful," Sam murmured. "I'm here, too."

"Thank Oneness," Susan said. "I sent some people down to see if they could find any of your bags. When they return, we'll leave. I've lined up some strong young men to carry you, Emily, and Toni. Our medic thinks they'll be okay once we get them to Starview and proper treatment."

Sam's stomach growled. "Is there any food?"

"I have someone checking everyone to see if they have any. I think some are hoarding some for themselves." Susan grimaced.

Sam nodded. *That made sense. Idiots.*

"Susan called Louise, and she's sending a group with food to meet us. They left yesterday, so maybe we'll meet them tonight." Brad smiled at Sam.

Sam nodded and dozed, feeling the presence, and displeasure.

"Big problems in Starview," she heard Susan say. "A big windstorm blew down a lot of apartments. Everything on the mesa is okay. The factories and caffs lost some outer walls but are still operating."

"Oh, shit," Brad said.

TOO MANY PEOPLE, Sam understood from the presence.

"We can't just let our people die," she whispered.

MOVE. SPACE WEST, NORTH.

"We will do what we must to survive, no matter what you do." Sam took a breath. "This our home now and we will defend it. But we will not harm it."

The presence oozed away, leaving her with a sense of peace.

Sam sighed. *More work for the weary. How much more can I take?*

"Yes," she murmured.

*   *   *

Later, they started up the hill. Sam's mind was a little clearer now. All she wanted was to get home to her little house and Maxee. Sam was facing downhill and saw the mess of the remains of City.

Dad's ashes are in there somewhere. And my past.

She closed her eyes and pictured Maxee.

Brad walked between the stretchers carrying Sam and Emily, while Hal trudged on Sam's other side. Sam sensed the attraction between her twin and Emily as they held hands and was pleased.

Brad needs someone to partner with — someone more than just a sister.

At the top, the young men set the stretchers down and everyone sat.

Todd came over and sat beside Sam. "How are you doing?"

"Okay. Did you hear what Susan said about the storm?"

"Yes. There's plenty of room above City. It will take some work, though. I also heard construction is building a bridge across the river up north."

"Good. We can move people over there."

"We can. You need to rest and get well. Glenda's running Starview now." Todd paused. "If you want Hal, I won't get in your way." He rose and strode off.

Sam watched him walk away. *Oh, Todd. You'll always be my brother. He needed someone, too, but who? Arlene? She was too much older. He hadn't shown much interest in Susan. Well, that was his problem.*

Hal came back and sat beside her. Sam reached out for his hand. He gripped it fiercely.

"How well did you know him?" she asked.

"We grew up together."

"It's not easy, losing someone you care about. My dad ..."

"You don't know," he turned to her, jerking her good arm. "He was my lover. I'll never get over it. Why did he have to go like that?" He burst into sobs.

Sam let go of his hand and pulled him to her. She wept, too. Now she understood. She could never let a man touch her. But maybe with Hal ...

*   *   *

They camped in the little valley that night. Hal stayed by Sam's side. She told him about her marriage and the aftermath.

"I see. You've had your pain, too." He touched her face. "Maybe we were meant for each other, should be together, together." He closed his eyes for a moment. "I feel something for you I've never felt for another woman. Maybe something in me is changing, is changing. I've researched sexuality, it's not just either, or, either, or."

Sam didn't know what to say. She found herself caring for him, wanting to be with him always. Her past was gone, sealed. Her new future — her new life — awaited her in Starview.

Sam reached up with her good arm and touched his cheek.

*   *   *

World will always watch.

EPILOGUE

S AM SAT ON HER PORCH with her leg propped up on a stool, Maxee by her side. Maxee wore the purple stone in an embroidered holder on a braided string that Jan had made for her. The two had become fast friends.

Across the river, people were building round structures, while several worked in a crop field. The spring breeze ruffled Sam's hair and Maxee's fur. Pale gray Baby Max crawled in and out of his mother's pouch as she kept a hand on him.

"Oh, there you are," Hal said, stepping out onto the porch and touching Sam's hair. "Upper City is moving right along."

"Hi, Hal. Isn't it beautiful out here?" Sam smiled at him.

He sat beside them. "Everyone's so happy to be outside after that long winter. Crops are sprouting, and a group who hiked up into the higher hills found some new kind of fruit that tested good."

"Wonderful," Sam said. "Did you hear? Emily and Brad are expecting a baby. And Todd needs a mate. I hope he finds one soon." Sam smiled.

"No, really? Good for them." He touched her hand. "And you, you're happy here? You don't mind not having children, do you?"

"Very happy. I have you, and this world, that's enough."

ABOUT THE AUTHOR

Lorna Hopkins Keith was born in Hollywood, California, earned a B.A. in Mathematics, and has been writing since her teens. Fascinated by both numbers and words, she is also a musician, photographer, and puzzler.

Lorna has self-published a science fiction trilogy, attended many science fiction conventions and writing workshops, and has read science fiction most of her life.

She grew up in California, lived in Colorado, and moved to Florida with her physical therapist husband, where they live by a lake with a chatty calico cat.